AROUND EMILY, SCREAMING ECHOED...

...horrifying and deep, screaming like she never heard before. She coughed the water out of her lungs and breathed, and then she turned around, reaching for the dock as she did.

The air was filled with black smoke and an awful rancid burning smell. She could recognize part of the smell—hair burning—but the rest was something she had never encountered before.

The inky blackness poured off the dock and across the lake, engulfing her. She grabbed the ancient wood, then saw through the slats what was burning.

It was Daddy.

She screamed for him, but he didn't seem to hear her. He was slapping himself and dancing on the top of the dock, trying to put out the fire, which seemed to come from his chest and burn upwards....

— *FantasyLife*

ALSO BY KRISTINE KATHRYN RUSCH

The Devil's Churn

Facade

Familiarity

"Unnatural Disaster"

"Shadow Side"

THE FEY SAGA

Destiny: A Story of The Fey

The Sacrifice: The First Book of The Fey

The Changeling: The Second Book of The Fey

The Rival: The Third Book of The Fey

The Resistance: The Fourth Book of The Fey

Victory: The Fifth Book of The Fey

The Black Queen: The Sixth Book of The Fey

The Black King: The Seventh Book of The Fey

FANTASYLIFE AND OTHER STORIES

AUTHOR PREFERRED EDITION

KRISTINE KATHRYN RUSCH

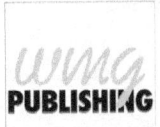
PUBLISHING

CONTENTS

Introduction   ix

The Women of Whale Rock   1
Strange Creatures   35
The Light in Whale Cove   69
FantasyLife   105

INTRODUCTION

Ever since 2009, I have written a weekly nonfiction blog on my website, kriswrites.com. Most of those weekly posts discussed the changes in the publishing industry. The Kindle disrupted the industry in 2009, which was already suffering from some serious mismanagement and corporate consolidation in the late 1990s.

From the creative point of view, the biggest change in the industry is that our projects are our own again. In the past, we would start a series or write under a particular name, and those projects would be subject to the whims of traditional publishing. Sometimes the whims made sense; often they didn't.

The novel that provides the anchor for this volume of stories is a victim of several whims. In 2001, John Ordover, then a major editor at Pocket Books, wanted to start a fantasy imprint there that would get a lot of mainstream attention. He was going to publish the books he bought in hardcover and give them the kind of push that would get books on *The New York Times* bestseller list.

It's hard to remember back to those pre-9/11 days. Harry Potter had only been around for four years, and a lot of people in the industry thought the novels not only poorly written, but a blip that would disappear soon, rather than seeing the phenomenon they would become—for adults as well as kids.

Fantasy was not really in vogue, especially among the gatekeepers in the publishing industry. They didn't want to put a lot of money into the genre at all, which is laughable by 2018 standards.

So John's idea was cutting edge.

He wanted a novel from me to start the line. I pitched a project based on the Oregon Coast setting that I had written a few short stories about. John read the stories, liked them, and wanted something like them "but bigger." I came up with the novel that would become *FantasyLife*, along with a follow-up novel.

I got a fat two-book contract, and turned the book in early, then went on to other projects, planning to get to book two in six months or so.

A few months later, John talked to me. Pocket Books had gone through some changes at the corporate level, and John's fledgling imprint got tossed into the trash without publishing a single novel.

Mine was the only one turned in and it was published—in the terms of the industry—dead. Meaning that it had no promotion at all. Worse, they had to use stock art on the cover (no cover artist) and it was published as a mass market paperback.

John turned in his resignation either just before or just after the book got published. (The details are foggy in my ancient memory.) Before he left, he did me a favor: he canceled the second book in the contract. I got to keep every dime I was paid (usually when a book is canceled, you have to repay the advance on that book), but I didn't have to write a second book that would be published dead.

So *FantasyLife* hung out there by itself, filled with promise, but not really fulfilled. There were other issues as well. Pocket Books screwed up the title. It's *FantasyLife* (one word) not *Fantasy Life* (two words). When you read the book, you'll understand the difference.

There were some other changes as well, which I have since fixed.

Fantasy Life (the book from Pocket) gave me other grief as well. I couldn't get Pocket to take the book out of print. Their edition, with all its errors, still exists in an ancient print-on-demand file, which they sell as a $26 trade paperback. For years, they sold the ebook edition for $20. I checked as I wrote this: it's now $15.99.

I found their mismanagement so discouraging that, as I finished other projects, I didn't really want to revisit the other books that I had planned in this world. If I wrote those books, I would end up boosting the Pocket Books edition, which is a bad deal for my fans because it forced them to buy an expensive inferior version of the book.

So I diligently worked over the years, getting my license back. I still can't get that stupid edition out of print, but I own the rights to omnibus editions and to other forms of the novel. I have licensed the audio rights and other rights, but I never found the time to put together an omnibus edition of the stories covered in the book and the novel itself.

Finally, Allyson Longueira of WMG Publishing scheduled *Fantasy-Life* into a promotion she was running, and that got me to take the time to put my author's preferred edition together. You now see the book with the right title and proper language usage.

Because this is an omnibus, it features the three short stories that precede the novel. You'll see Hamilton Denne change over time, meet Dan Retsler (who has moved on to other climes by the time this novel starts), and see one of the selkie problems mentioned in the novel.

I think your reading experience will be a lot richer once you've read the short stories and then read the novel.

I've written other pieces set in Seavy County, but no others set in Anchor Bay. I found my notes for the next book, and my brain is now toying with some of the things I left behind.

It's amazing to me how many stopped-up tributaries writing careers used to have in the bad old days of traditional-only publishing. I used to spend a lot of time apologizing for the fact that some corporate decision broke one of my series or destroyed one of my pen names.

Now, I spend a bit more time apologizing for my lack of time. Yes, there will be more stories in Anchor Bay. But if you want something to tide you over, take a look at my Seavy County stories and novels. There are a lot of them, all set in the same milieu as *FantasyLife*.

I do hope you enjoy this book. It was fun to revisit it as I restored pieces that had been excised for all the wrong reasons.

And if you happen to read this on a windy, rainy night, make sure that no water leaks into your house. You have no idea what might slip in with it....

—Kristine Kathryn Rusch
Las Vegas, NV
August 26, 2018

THE WOMEN OF
WHALE ROCK

THE WOMEN OF WHALE ROCK

The gulls swarmed over the Sandcastle Hotel. Whipping and diving and cawing to their fellows, they looked like something out of Daphne Du Maurier's "The Birds," a novelette more sinister and terrifying than anything Hitchcock ever produced.

Charles watched from his deck. The morning breeze was harsh and smelled of salt. He still wore his silk pajamas. Rain the night before had left the wood damp and cold. His ancient tattered slippers, the ones Grace had given him before she died, were getting wet.

Grace and gulls. He closed his eyes, knowing what the night would bring. Then he shook off the thought, hoping, this time, he would have the resolve to let it end.

Charles opened his eyes and rested his hands on the damp rail. The swarming had grown worse. Nearly a hundred birds flocked to that tiny section of beach.

There was no way he would go down there.

At least, not alone.

He sighed, went inside, and called Dan Retsler.

Dan Retsler was scanning the *Oregonian* as he stood near the window of the police department. The window overlooked Highway 101, the main thoroughfare down the Oregon Coast. Every morning, Retsler scanned the newspaper and the street simultaneously. In the summer, he would be the primary witness to petty thefts, tourists running red lights, and the occasional fender bender.

His police department had a staff of three, not counting the dispatcher. He put two officers on at night. During the day, he and a lone officer could handle the problems with the help of the dispatcher. The dispatcher, one Miss Lucy Wexel, had been with the department since Retsler was a teenage hoodlum at Taft High School. He doubted she was any different when she was hired than she was now. She chewed gum, talked tough, and believed her work safeguarded the mean streets of Whale Rock for yet another day.

The phone rang and she answered. Then she stabbed the hold button with a stubby finger, and paused to take a draw from her cigarette before facing him. Smoke curled around her face, making her look like someone's kindly grandmother instead of the hardest woman he had ever known.

"Charles Bishop," she said, and from her tone Retsler knew what the call was about.

He wound around the gunmetal desks to the small cubicle he called an office. Then he grabbed the receiver on the ancient black phone, and punched line one.

"Gulls?" he asked.

"Got another report, huh?" Bishop sounded vaguely relieved, as if a burden were being lifted from him.

"No," Retsler said. "Lucky guess."

He rubbed his nose with his thumb and forefinger, trying to ease a building headache. He knew the drill: first the gulls, then the body pecked beyond recognition, and finally the county coroner, who would claim death by drowning and deny everything else.

"Where should I meet you?" Bishop asked.

"At the turnout," Retsler said. He'd long ago stopped demanding that Bishop stay home. Bishop would do as he pleased. For some reason, he always chose to join Retsler in shooing the gulls away.

And then holding watch over the ruined mass of flesh until the coroner arrived to lie to them again.

The first one showed up just after Bishop arrived in town. He had called Retsler and begun their tradition. A young woman, somewhere between sixteen and twenty-six (judging by the age and condition of her remaining internal organs), washed up on the beach. The gulls swarmed. The tourists were terrified, and someone started a rumor that she had jumped from the Sandcastle's roof, desolate about a love affair gone bad.

Only no one knew her, and no one was reported missing.

Definitely not a suicide, the coroner, Hamilton Denne, had said as he knelt gingerly beside the body, getting his expensive gray slacks covered with sand. But he couldn't rule out death by drowning. He couldn't confirm it either since her lungs were missing, her chest cavity ravaged, and her face gone.

He could say for certain that she had died, and that she had spent a long time in the water.

He would say nothing more. Not even when Retsler asked about her dental records. Her lower jaw remained intact, and some of her teeth had fillings. Not enough to identify her, but enough to cause Bishop consternation. He was a newly retired dentist, and he said, with a single glance, that no one used that odd mixture of iron and silver fillings anymore. No one had since the thirties.

A week later, a second body turned up. A boy, between ten and eighteen, dead against the seawall.

Then the stories emerged, stories about why the Sandcastle had closed in the early seventies. Guests reported strangers in their rooms, a strange briny smell in the hallway, and frightening attacks in the middle of the night. Soon the hotel stood empty, even in the busy summer. The owners tried to sell the hotel, failed, and closed the doors. Lucy heard that they had discovered another body inside the day they boarded it up, but no one had any record of it.

And so the curse of the Sandcastle began.

But locals did not discuss it, except for Retsler and Bishop. Retsler because he had to deal with the bodies, and Bishop because of guilt.

Because of his wife.

❀

Charles stood in the gravel turnout near the beach access. He wore his waterproof jacket, and a pair of knitted gloves, the last pair Grace had made for him. The other gloves were in his bedroom closet, frayed reminders of her and the lack of her. He had his back to the path, hands shoved in his pockets, the wind off the ocean whipping his remaining hair into his face. The traffic on 101 was Saturday heavy, but so far no one had stopped to see what was drawing the gulls.

They were still diving for the body. Their caws sounded like screams up close, a woman's scream, desperate and alone.

He shivered in spite of himself.

At last, Retsler's blue sedan pulled into the turnout, spraying gravel like shotgun pellets. Dan Retsler was forty, but drove as if he were eighteen and immortal. Charles often wondered how Retsler managed to pick up speeders without feeling like a hypocrite.

Retsler got out, wearing his green cop's rain slicker and waders. In his right hand, he clutched the bullhorn. In his left, a rifle. He handed Charles the bullhorn, then dug in the car a moment longer, emerging with a bag of popcorn big enough to feed a family of five.

"Where's Eddie?" Charles asked.

"The Billows. He knows what to do."

They all did. They had done it often enough.

Charles hefted the bullhorn, turned it on its side, made sure the speaker was off, and turned the control onto "siren." Retsler loaded his rifle, but kept the safety on. The bag of popcorn leaned against his leg like a small child.

"Ready?" he asked.

Charles nodded. They turned together, and stared at the gulls, circling and crying, white perfection against an azure sky. The ocean smelled strongly of brine, but the wind had died.

Retsler led the way across the narrow footpath and down the concrete steps. The previous night's storm had churned up the beach, leaving piles of sea-blackened driftwood and gifts of garbage from the sea bottom. The tide was out, but the sand was still wet, attesting to the power of the storm. Sea-foam dried in a reflective green pattern across the flat part of the beach.

No one walked here except summer people. Locals avoided this stretch of beach, making excuses about the rocks, the driftwood, the soft sand. Sometimes Charles walked down the steps, sitting on the bottom one, and staring at the remains of Whale Rock, the one that gave the town its name. It no longer looked like a whale as it had at the turn of the century; now it looked like a parking lot in the middle of the sea. Even the strength of rock succumbed to the power of the ocean.

The gulls formed a sea of their own near the Sandcastle's deteriorating wall. The sight was formidable, not frightening, something none of the stories about birds—not even Du Maurier's classic—managed to capture. Charles stood on a flat rock protruding from the sand and clutched the bullhorn. Retsler stood beside him, popcorn in one hand, rifle in the other.

"Here goes nothing," Charles said. He picked up the bullhorn and flicked it on. The siren wailed like amplified feedback. He cringed, wishing he had remembered earplugs. Retsler hadn't moved. He stared intently at the gulls.

They took a few hesitant steps, then the first flew into the sky, followed by another, then another until the entire flock was airborne. They soared, their screeches hidden by the bullhorn's wail.

This was where Eddie came in. He was supposed to toss bread from the Billows' deck. Sometimes he caught the birds' attention; sometimes he didn't.

This time he did. They flew in ever widening circles north, crying their protest at the siren, and communicating the message to other gulls about food ahead. They left this isolated section of beach torn up and covered with droppings, feathers, bits of food.

And the body, one leg bent as if the person were just resting on its back, watching the clouds.

Neither Charles nor Retsler left the rock. They had done that too early once, and he still had nightmares about it.

Of all the creatures on God's earth, birds seemed to be the only ones without souls.

Finally the last gull disappeared behind the bluff that hid the Billows. Charles shut off the bullhorn. The sound stopped, but his ears ached, and would, probably, until the following day. But if things ran true to form, he wouldn't notice.

He shuddered, wished, just once, that this would all end.

Then Retsler inclined his head toward the body, and Charles nodded.

Together they stepped off the rock and headed down the beach.

Retsler clutched the bag tightly. The rifle was heavy in his right hand. He hoped he wouldn't have to use either. The last time had convinced him that the gulls weren't afraid of the gun, and the time before that he discovered that a single bag of popcorn barely gave him time enough to escape. The extra large bag might give them a few extra seconds, which they would need. Bishop didn't run well any more. Retsler always worried about bringing him to the beach.

But if they didn't go together, Bishop might have come alone, a risk that Retsler just couldn't take.

The fetid odor of decaying flesh mixed with the scent of salt. This one had been out here longer than the others. Odd that the gulls would prey on it now.

He led the way across the rocks and onto the soft sand. The body was shoved against the sea wall like all the others, one leg bent in a V, arms out flung above the head. Retsler knew without looking that the eyes would be gone. The gulls always took those first, some kind of avian delicacy, followed by the tongue if they could get it, and then they would peck their way into the stomach. He had seen it more than once, not just here, but on bodies washed up all over the beach.

Retsler followed the three-pronged bird prints to the corpse's side. He set down the popcorn, reached in his pocket for the Vicks, and smeared some inside his nose. Without looking, he handed the bottle over his shoulder to Bishop. No one needed to smell this, not even for a moment.

Bishop took the bottle but stayed back. Retsler crouched near the body, tried to see what it had been through the mess the gulls had made.

Male, older judging by the strands of gray mixed with the wet curls on top of the head, corpse white and bloated. It had been in the water a long, long time. Maybe it wasn't one of the bodies that came to this beach. Maybe it was a true death by drowning, not some mystery killing offshore.

Then he saw what he hoped he wouldn't; the remains of a vest with a gold watch still tucked inside, pants with buttons, not zippers, and on the bent leg, garters to hold up the socks. Old man clothing pre-1950.

He glanced at Bishop who pointed at the open mouth. Tobacco-stained teeth, cracked, crooked, and broken. No modern dentist would allow such a travesty.

Bishop set down the bullhorn. "I'll call the coroner," he said.

That night, they got drunk. Bishop tried to beg off, but Retsler, afraid he'd go home and brood, convinced him to brood in public. They went to the False Colors, a local bar that had once started as a tourist attraction. But the pirate theme seemed more foreboding than touristy, and tourists usually spent an uncomfortable hour before sliding their way out the door. Retsler usually liked the black and white skull and crossbones hanging over the door, the uneven wooden floor, the skulls lining the fireplace mantel, the sound of sea chanties sung with unusual heartiness through the stereo speakers.

Usually. On this night it seemed a bit much.

But Lucy had picked the place. She was drinking whiskey and smoking a cigar, her unpainted chair tilted back against the stones in the fireplace. Eddie was nursing his third beer, and Bishop was downing gin and tonics as if he actually liked the stuff. Retsler had just bummed one of Lucy's cigars when the coroner walked in.

Hamilton Denne never set foot in a bar. He occasionally frequented establishments where fine liquor was served. He lived in Glen Ellyn Cove, a gated community for Whale Rock's considerable wealthy population. The Cove had a five-star restaurant near its gate, a private club upstairs, and an atmosphere as snooty as Denne's name. Most of Denne's neighbors had no idea what he did for a living. If they asked, he always told them that he was a medical examiner. He worked hard to keep his name out of the papers, easy to do since the coroner's position in Seavy County was an appointed, not an elected, position. If it was necessary to mention the coroner at all, the paper usually did it by title, not by name. No sense in offending the Dennes of Glen Ellyn Cove.

Denne ordered a Glenlivet and was tersely informed he would get Chivas or the bar scotch or no scotch at all. He settled for the Chivas, and carried it to the table himself.

Retsler said nothing. He was on his second local stout and his judgment was impaired, but not that impaired. Eddie peered over his longneck as if he didn't believe what he saw. Bishop slid his gin and tonic toward the center of the table, unfinished. Lucy set her chair down on all four legs, leaned forward, and said, "Want a cigar, Your Highness?"

"No thanks," Denne said, and pulled out a silver cigarette case engraved with his initials, no doubt a gift from his obscenely wealthy wife. Being the coroner, Retsler believed, was Denne's secret rebellion against that elegant woman whose bank account had bought Denne all the good things in life. Denne removed a cigarette, tapped the end, then twirled it in his long, clean fingers.

He looked at all of them as if he saw what their breathalyzer results would be. Then he put the cigarette in his mouth, lit it with a matching silver lighter, and took a long drag. "I wasn't here," he said, smoke billowing out with each word. "Not now, not ever. You ever claim I was or breathe a word about what I'm about to say, I'll deny it. Is that clear?"

Lucy tilted her chair back. Bishop stared blearily at the table.

Eddie lifted his longneck in mock toast, then cradled it against his chest.

"I'm sure no one would believe us anyway," Retsler said.

"I'm sure you're right." Denne took another drag, the gesture curiously defiant, like a teenage boy smoking in front of his parents. "Some coroners aren't very thorough, you know."

Retsler knew. He and Denne had come on at the same time and had to clean up similar messes. They had commiserated about it more than once over lunch—in North County, away from Denne's snobby friends.

"But for those who are, the human cadaver is a wealth of information."

"So you going to dick with us or tell us what you found?" Eddie said.

Retsler shushed him. He knew Denne. Denne would talk in his own time.

"Take, for instance, someone who drowned. Easy call, from the general condition of the body to water in the lungs. Most coroners would leave it there. Some would do a routine check for other fluids, and some would test the water in the lungs."

Bishop had picked up his drink. He clutched it in one hand, knuckles white.

"If the water's salt, possible accidental death by drowning. But if the water's fresh—"

"He had his lungs?" Retsler asked.

"Regrettably no," Denne said. "And if he had, it wouldn't have mattered. The fish had gotten to him before the gulls."

"So he'd been there a long time?" Bishop asked.

Denne didn't answer. He took a sip of the scotch, winced, and pushed the glass aside. "In 1936, a yacht went down near the Rock."

"The *Lady June*," Lucy said. "Quite a scandal."

Retsler peered at her, doing a slow calculation in his head. She had been six at the time. It was hard to imagine her as a six-year-old.

"Right," Denne said. "You know about it?"

"They don't," Lucy said.

Denne nodded, resumed as if he hadn't been interrupted at all.

"It had been a clear night. She'd gone out of the bay with a complement of fifty, all there to celebrate the engagement of June Brooks to Lester Dyston. June, the darling daughter of J. William Brooks of the Portland Brookses—"

"The lumber baron's family," Lucy added helpfully.

"—was eighteen and quite a catch. Dyston was a Midwestern transplant who held some sort of managerial position at Brooks Lumber. Thirty of Portland's best families were invited to the celebration. Many declined because the party was being held in Whale Rock in May, and most weren't ready to open their beach houses just yet."

"Lucky most of them did, too," Lucy said, "or it would have been Portland's version of the *Titanic.*"

This time, Denne glared at her. She shrugged, stuck the cigar back in her mouth, and crossed her arms, as if she thought he'd get the story all wrong.

"The ship went down in the middle of a storm. Only Dyston survived. He claimed he was carried to shore by mermaids." Denne glanced at Lucy who didn't even blink.

"And people believed him?" Eddie said.

Denne smiled. "Maybe not about the mermaids. But he was young, he was strong, and he was a good swimmer. Whale Rock isn't so very far away when the tide is out."

"So what does this have to with our bodies?" Bishop asked.

"A couple of things." Denne stubbed out his half-finished cigarette, grabbed his glass, and downed the scotch like water. The taste apparently didn't matter to him any more. "First, the Sandcastle was built from the old Brooks mansion. Second, neither the yacht nor the bodies were ever recovered, and third, we have in the cooler, the body of J. William himself."

Retsler felt a lightness in his stomach that had nothing to do with the beer. "You're sure?"

"As sure as I'll ever be," Denne said. "This one came complete with identification. The watch was engraved, so was his wedding ring."

"That's not enough," Retsler said.

"You're right. J. William's habits were legendary, from his love of a good cigar to his adoration of spicy food. He nearly lost his right leg in World War One, and from then on, that leg was shorter than the other. His ulcer operation made medical history at the time."

"You studied a lot about this man," Retsler said.

"I had cause." Denne let the words hang, but Retsler knew why. The bodies had been bothering Denne too, only he had some idea where they had come from. He had been waiting for definitive proof. And apparently he had found it.

"What convinced you this was Brooks?" Bishop asked.

"The leg might have done it," Denne said. "But it was the ulcer scar. The surgeon stitched the stomach closed, then stitched the skin incision separately. He removed the external stitches not the internal ones. That was bad enough, but I could have chalked it up to carelessness. No. But that wasn't it. It was the stitches themselves. No one uses wire for sutures these days. No one has for a long, long time."

"You're saying all the bodies came from that ship?" Bishop asked.

Denne nodded.

"So what, they all return on the anniversary of the sinking?" Eddie asked.

"Nothing as romantic as all that," Denne said. "The storm last night stirred the ocean. That ship must have gone down deep, some place cold enough to keep bodies from decaying, to keep clothing intact."

"And the ocean spits them back up, in the same place?" Eddie asked. "I don't think so."

"Oh, I do," Denne said. "A certain kind of tide must bring them out of that place. Something that happens during storms, maybe, or the storms' interaction with what's left of the Rock. Every now and then the conditions are right, and the sea returns a body."

"I suppose you believe in mermaids too," Bishop said. His words were slightly slurred, his tone odd, almost hopeful.

Denne shook his head. "I agree with the local police chief. Dyston sabotaged the yacht, killing everyone on board except himself."

"How would the chief know that?" Retsler asked.

"Because the lifeboat made it to shore, rope cut, boat empty. Because all the lifesavers made it too, also empty. Because a passing fishing boat saw the boy jump over the side while the party was in full swing. It looked to them like the yacht was in trouble but no one seemed to be noticing."

"Little vague, I think," Retsler said.

"No more vague than mermaids," Denne said.

"You've been holding out on me," Retsler said.

"Maybe." Denne stood, and put a twenty on the table. "Or maybe I made this up to justify my presence in this sleazy little bar. Goodnight all."

He shoved his hands in his pockets and picked his way carefully around the wooden tables. None of the other patrons even seemed to notice him.

"He couldn't have made it all up," Eddie said, looking at Lucy. "You knew about it."

Lucy nodded. "My mom kept all the clippings."

"So why'd he kill them?" Eddie asked.

"Because he was a drifter," she said. "Because he was marrying June for her money."

"Seems to me you don't kill the golden goose," Retsler said.

"You do when Daddy reveals your secrets at what should have been your night of triumph, when he humiliates you in front of what must have seemed like the whole world."

Retsler shook his head. "Sounds to me more like June had cause to kill Dyston."

Lucy grinned. "Don't look at me. I'm just telling you what the papers said. Me, I've always believed in the mermaids."

"They're not saints either," Bishop said, and passed out.

Charles woke up in his own bed, cold and fully clothed. His mouth tasted of cotton, and his head ached. He had gotten drunk, and he had vowed not to. The sound of running water in the master bath made him sit up, hand to head, trying not to moan. At first he thought the toilet was running, but the sound was too bathtub-like, too full.

Someone else was in the house. Visions of Darryl Hannah in *Splash*, himself as an aging Tom Hanks, made him realize that he was watching too many videos, substituting books and movies for human companionship.

His life had enough drama.

Of course someone else was in the house. Someone had brought him home.

Besides, it couldn't be mermaids. They rarely came into his house. He only knew of them doing so once. The night Grace died.

Still, as he stumbled to the bathroom, he couldn't shake the image of them as he last saw them, looking not lanky and graceful, not the semi-naked beauties of Disney animation or with the erotic suggestiveness of Yeats. Instead they reminded him of ancient figureheads carved by inexpert sailors, women with eyes that were flat, features rough-hewn, hair plastered to misshapen heads. Their land legs had feet as big as flippers. The mermaids walked as if they were in pain—Hans Christian Andersen had gotten that much right—but that could have been as easily caused by the huge feet as "daggers through the flesh."

So when he entered the bathroom, he was startled to find it empty. The tub was dry, and the toilet wasn't running at all. Not even the faucet in the sink was dripping. But he hadn't dreamed the sound. It continued in the plumbing like a garrulous ghost.

He went down the stairs to the guest bathroom and found it empty too. The kitchen was as spotless as he had left it, and the washer was off. No water running anywhere in the house.

Then he looked outside. Down the hill from him, the sea glowed with its strange luminosity. A few clouds blew across the moon, but there was no rain.

No water anywhere.

Except in his imagination.

With the mermaids.

Not even Dan Retsler had enough guts to go to the Sandcastle at night. But after he dropped off Bishop—fireman-carried him, actually, upstairs and into bed—he stopped at the bottom of Bishop's hill and stared at the hotel.

The moon was full and the ocean shone, as it always did at night, as if someone had lit it up from underneath. The natural light, combined with the street lights, made the west side of Highway 101 as bright as dawn, when the shadows were just receding from the land, replaced by the whitewash of early morning.

The Sandcastle didn't look like a mansion. But it didn't look like a hotel, either. It was three stories high, rectangular, and had doors every ten feet that faced the highway. The balconies were made of metal, which were beginning to look red from rust. The rest of the building was a bright peeling blue. Someone had added fake turrets on either side—if he hadn't known better, he would have guessed they were cardboard—and the word "Sandcastle" was painted across one of them in white gothic script.

What kind of man would build a mansion like that? What kind of heirs would sell it? Beachfront property was rare on the Oregon Coast, rare and expensive, while the rest of the land was cheap. He couldn't imagine what that land would have gone for in 1936, or why, despite the bodies, it still hadn't sold in 1997.

The turrets, he imagined, were an addition, as were the balconies and the doors, added in the tourist-boom of the 1950s. He couldn't, for the life of him, see the original shape of the building, how all the pieces had once fit together into an elegant whole.

He wasn't certain why that was important, but he would wager Denne had an idea. Denne, with his stories about tides and deep cold and bodies remaining preserved for sixty years. Denne, who clearly believed none of it.

Laughter broke his reverie. Women's laughter. Three women surrounded his car. Tall women, with straw-like hair, and the ugliest faces he had ever seen. They had bulging eyes, naturally pursed lips and nearly flat noses. *Fish women*, he thought, and shuddered. He'd had too much to drink. They leaned on his hood, peered into his windshield and laughed at him. Their gray-green eyes were the color of the sea on stormy mornings, their skin the same sallow bloodless white of the corpses he'd found on the beach.

"Hey!" he shouted. "Hey, get away from the car!"

But they didn't. They moved closer, like people peering into a fish tank. He slapped at the windshield, and when they still didn't move, he punched the horn, quick and loud.

The women jumped away, startled. The one on the hood rolled off, unable to catch herself. Her friends disappeared in front of the car, then reappeared in his headlights clutching her and staring at him as if he were more than a curiosity, as if he were a threat.

He tapped the horn one more time, and they backed away from the front of the car. He turned north on 101, hands shaking, mouth dry. It wasn't until he had reached the movie theater a mile away that the realization hit him.

The women hadn't just been ugly.

They had also been naked.

Charles woke after a restless night's sleep, filled with dreams of running water and bloated, decaying bodies. His head pounded, and his stomach churned. The sour taste of gin and tonics coated his tongue.

He sat up, one hand to his head, wondering why he'd let Retsler talk him into going to the False Colors. He knew better than to drink. When he drank, he forgot, and when he forgot...

He threw the covers back and stood up, startled at the sudden chill on his legs. His silk pajama bottoms were missing. His upper thighs were coated with sand, and a strand of seaweed was wrapped around his left knee. He got out of bed quickly, his heart pounding. Maybe he and Retsler had gone down to the beach after they left the bar. Maybe he had put on his pajama top and had forgotten his bottoms. Maybe, but not likely.

The house smelled of brine.

And he thought of Grace, feeling that same sickly stab of guilt he always felt when he thought of her. She had remained trim into her mid-fifties. Silver hair capping her well shaped head. Every morning she went down to the beach, the entire beach, legends be damned.

Every morning.

Including the last.

He closed his eyes, and tilted his head back, restraining an anguish so deep he had no words for it. He should have known. He should have known yesterday when the body appeared on the beach. He should have known he would awaken like this.

He had known, and he had ignored it, preferring the company of friends to the silence of the house. Knowing that only drink would get rid of the images in his mind.

Maybe he had allowed himself to get drunk. Because he didn't have the willpower to say no.

"I'm sorry, Grace," he whispered. "Sorry for everything."

But sorry would never ever be enough.

"Okay," Lucy said. "This is what I got."

She dumped two notebooks with black construction paper and cardboard covers on Retsler's desk. The smell of stale cigar smoke and mildew rose from them. He pushed his copy of the *Oregonian* aside. No newspaper this morning, no surveying the street. These deaths were bothering him, Denne's comments bothering him even more.

And the three women from the night before, they too had haunted him during his pitifully short sleep. He had awakened annoyed, his body aching, as though he had been interrupted in the middle of an erotic dream. Only he hadn't found the women attractive, nor the dream in the least way sexual.

"Dan," Lucy said. "You gonna look or should I take these away?"

Her voice snapped him out of his reverie. He wasn't a teenager any more. He really needed a full night's sleep.

"No," he said. "No, I'm going to look." He smiled at her, and took the notebooks. He was wrong about the material on the covers. It wasn't a cardboard and construction paper combination but something that felt like both of them and neither at the same time. The scrapbooks were bound with a thick gold string.

"Well, don't rip nothing," Lucy said. She picked up his newspaper and went back to her desk.

He opened the first notebook carefully. The front page of the local weekly, the *News Guard*, from 1936 flapped at him. The paper was brittle and was held in place by tape so yellow it nearly looked brown. Beneath the page, in small black script, someone had written: *Accident at Whale Rock.*

At first, he didn't read the articles. He merely scanned them, thumbing his way through the entire notebook. When he reached the end, he realized that this was more than a curiosity to Lucy. She had been six when the accident happened. Someone else had kept the notebooks and passed them on to Lucy in later years.

He almost asked her whose notebooks they had been. Almost. He wasn't ready to hear. He needed to study the clippings first.

The first notebook held only clippings from the *News Guard*. The second notebook held clippings from papers as diverse as the *Oregonian* and *The New York Times*. The death of J. William and his friends sent a ripple through the national financial community, a ripple that became evident almost immediately. J. William was an old-time fiscal conservative, with ties all over the Northwest. He had fought the bids for dams on the Columbia. He had fought the arrival of federal money into Oregon. He had lost the battles twice, but during the spring of 1936, he was working against Roosevelt, against the New Dealers, and against the flow of federal money. If he hadn't died, if he hadn't lost, the Pacific Northwest would have looked completely different. No public funds would have supported the Bonneville Power Administration. No defense contracts would have flowed to Seattle.

The money would have stayed with J. William Brooks and his friends.

The national papers called the destruction of the yacht murder. And some papers claimed that Lester Dyston was part of a larger conspiracy. The conspiracy of the New Dealers to rid themselves of the conservative Northwest factions, the friends of J. William Brooks.

The papers claimed the trial, its mockery of justice, and its result proved the conspiracy, but nothing was ever done about it.

None of those facts made it to the *News Guard*. The local paper focused solely on the issue of mermaids.

Charles took a long hot shower. Steam rose around him as he washed off the sand. He had hidden the seaweed in toilet paper and flushed it, never wanting to look at it again.

Then, when he was done, he wrapped himself in a big fluffy towel and stepped out of the stall, pausing for a moment at the tiny bathroom window with its view of the sea.

The morning ocean was multicolored: the front section a steely blue, the middle a solid gray, and the section near the horizon golden where the sun broke through the clouds. Gulls sat on the roof of the Sandcastle as they always did, but none dove, none circled, none flocked.

He swallowed and leaned his head against the cool glass, cursing the day he had bought the house. The day after he and Grace had moved in, they had showered together, then stood before this window, marveling at their luck. That afternoon, they had walked to the beach and he had found a bottle with a half torn label that read Château Lafite Rothschild 1924, covered with seaweed and still chilled from its days in the ocean. Pulling it out of the sand had reminded him, even then, of that scene in *Notorious* where Ingrid Bergman and Cary Grant watch as Claude Rains poured uranium dust from a wine bottle. Grace had wanted to leave the bottle, but Charles had not. He had taken it, thanked the ocean for her gift, and brought it to the house. They had wine with their fresh halibut dinner that night. Grace had taken one sip and declared the wine vinegar, but he believed her palate was off. It was, quite simply, the best wine he had ever tasted, and he drank the entire bottle himself.

That night, after Grace fell asleep, he had wandered drunkenly down to the beach. He had later told her he had blundered into the surf, and she had scolded him for his carelessness, made him promise to never do so again, afraid he would die from exposure or drowning or his own drunken stupidity.

But he had lied to her. He had not touched the water. His memory, his dreams, were of a song as fine as the wine, the ocean singing, he had thought, and he had followed that sound to the Sandcastle, to the beach. The Sandcastle had been lit from the inside, and he followed the lights through the open doorway into a polished oak hallway and a magnificent staircase covered with a red carpet. A mirror covered the wall on the first landing, and he saw himself as he thought of himself, a slim middling handsome man in his early twenties, looking young and bewildered in the soft light. He wore a tuxedo of a type he had never had in real life, complete with spats, tails, and a top hat. The outfit gave him a dignity he had never had before.

The music carried him upstairs into the open door of a darkened bedroom. As he stepped inside, a woman with cool hands touched his face, removed his hat, and he thought, started to undress him, until he realized that the hands below belonged to another woman. The second woman unbuttoned his fly and took him in her mouth. Her lips and tongue were cool and refreshing, and he was instantly more aroused than he had ever been in his life.

The first woman undressed him, not allowing him to participate, and when he was naked, she guided him to the bed. The second woman continued her fellatio, and as they eased him onto a velvet spread, he felt the presence of a third woman.

He was getting hard remembering. He groaned and pulled away from the window, hand on the wall to steady himself. His memory of that night was of mouths all over him, cool mouths, caressing him like rain. And when he came—and he did come, in powerful pulsing spasms, more powerful than anything he had experienced before—it felt as if his essence were flowing outward and joining a vast ocean of sensation, like a river flowing into the sea.

The next morning he had awakened in his own bed, covered with seaweed and sand and tiny bite marks that looked like the circles left by octopus suckers.

He knew that the circle marks would be on him this morning, but he hadn't looked. He couldn't face it, just like he couldn't face any memory of the experience the night before. He had touched the women only once, and had felt hair like straw and skin like scales. From that moment on, he had let them do to him whatever they wanted, allowing his hands to be held captive while they marked him with their mouths. The experience was never as erotic as the first time. The first time he had thought it all a drunken dream and later when he realized it was real and he was being unfaithful to Grace, his mind rebelled and his body was unable to stop.

Then, after Grace died, he had stopped drinking, and the women had stopped visiting. Except for last night. Except for last night, and a handful of sloppy self-pitying nights when the loneliness was so bad, that a touch, any touch, even their touch was preferable to none.

His penis throbbed. He glanced down at it, poking out from the towel. Red circles flared against the hardened skin. Red circles the size of a dime.

His stomach spasmed and he swallowed, barely able to keep the contents down. He grabbed himself and began masturbating, letting the memory of the night return, knowing that this was the only way to rid himself of it, and of the self-loathing that came with it, the self-loathing that grew worse each time.

Each time Grace's killers summoned him, and he went, valuing the ecstasy they gave him more than life itself.

Retsler rested his chin on his hands, staring at the two-page spread from the *News Guard* in December of 1937. Dyston's trial had been held in Newport, and it had drawn people from all over the world. The grainy, poorly reproduced photographs made the tiny courthouse look as if it were under siege: a Simpsonesque circus long before O.J. Simpson was even born.

The paper dutifully reported the case, until the day Dyston testified. And then the paper had reprinted the testimony, using ellipses and editorial comments in brackets as it cut out sections it deemed unworthy for a family newspaper.

Retsler couldn't believe what he was reading. If it hadn't been on the same yellowing newsprint, if the same brittle tape weren't holding the pages in place, he would have thought Lucy was playing a trick on him. Even then he wasn't entirely sure.

"Luce!" he shouted.

She set down her cigar and stood with a dignity foreign to her. She had been listening to the pages turn, waiting for just this moment. And somehow that thought unnerved him.

She came inside his office and closed the door. They were the only two in the building. Closing the door seemed unnecessary.

"He testified about the mermaids?" he asked, his tone deliberately ironic.

"You're reading the transcript," she said. Her expression was guarded, her voice flat. She used this tone with dumb tourists —"tourons," she called them. Tourist-morons.

"Tuxedos? A gift of wine from the sea? Destroying his one true love? He was delusional."

"He was telling the truth," she said.

"He was nuts. He should never have been allowed to testify," Retsler said. He closed the notebook. "No wonder the national press was so angry that he was acquitted. He should have at least been institutionalized. I don't know how a jury could have let him off."

"They were a jury of his peers," she said softly.

She was serious, more serious than he'd ever seen her. She believed this too, although he didn't know why. A small shiver ran down his back, raising goose bumps on his flesh. And for an instant, those naked women flashed through his mind, their mouths pressed against his windshield. Their tongues had a suction cup on the tip, leaving small dime-shaped impressions on the glass.

"That's nonsense," he said, as much to her as to himself.

She took the notebooks and hugged them to her chest. She studied him, the reserve gone. "Have you taken any gifts from the sea?" she asked.

"Only the bodies," he said.

"Those aren't gifts," she said. "They're warnings."

"Of what?"

She shook her head, more serious than he had ever seen her. "I wish I knew."

❀

After his second shower of the day and a meager meal of tea and dry toast, Charles made his way down the rickety steps into his wine cellar. He wasn't feeling well: dizzy, hungover, and angry at himself for being weak yet again. He couldn't believe that Grace would forgive him if she knew—his sins had gone long past forgiveness. All he could hope for now was that death was truly an oblivion, and not that all-knowing, all-seeing place some religions made it out to be.

A cobweb brushed against his face as he stepped onto the thin carpet. The cellar was cooler than the rest of the house and smelled faintly damp, the effects of living on the coast. Bottles of wine shone in the light from a single bulb. He and Grace had built up this collection, and he hadn't touched it since she died.

But he still knew where the bottle was. He had kept it, a compulsion he had, like all the others since he'd come here. Compulsions he hadn't tried to deny.

He didn't know why he was trying now. Perhaps there truly was, as some people said, a last straw. And perhaps it was tiny, a small thing immeasurable by real world standards.

Perhaps.

Or perhaps he had been planning this since the first time he knew the women were real, and he had finally gained enough courage.

Or perhaps he finally realized he had nothing to lose.

He rounded the corner, and grabbed the bottle from its bin. The bottle was made of thick glass. The torn label was still there—funny that neither he nor Grace had commented on that, considering how long they had thought the bottle had been in the water—and the bottle felt full, even though he knew he had polished it off on his own. He had saved it as a memento, thinking somehow that the bottle alone would be worth money, not knowing, instead, it would cost him his soul.

He clutched the bottle to his chest and headed out of the wine cellar. He would grab his coat and go to the beach.

To the Sandcastle.

Alone.

The Glen Ellyn Lodge stood atop a cliff face overlooking the ocean. Behind the lodge was one of the most spectacular private golf courses in the nation, and beside the fairways stood the homes of Whale Rock's rich.

Retsler hated going there. He thought the fact that it was a gated community appropriate to its attitudes, its snob appeal, its closed-mindedness.

But he parked in the lot reserved for guests and went inside the seventy-year-old structure, knowing he would find Denne in its dining room, surrounded by Whale Rock's elite, and staring down at the ocean.

The lodge was decorated like an English country manor, in dark wood, with hunting greens and browns on the carpet and upholstery. A fire burned in the stone fireplace, and from the dining room came the sound of soft voices and the clink of glasses. The maître d', a man Retsler had gone to high school with, raised a single eyebrow.

"Business," Retsler said, and slipped by. He turned the corner and stepped into what he considered to be the most spectacular room on the Oregon Coast.

The greens and browns continued in here, but they were nearly invisible compared to the view. The architect had let the ocean speak for itself. The walls were made of paneled glass, with only the water and the sky visible on all three sides. It felt as if a person were outside, without the wind and the chill and the hint of spray rising from the surf below.

Denne sat alone in a corner table, cigarette in one hand, glasses on the end of his nose, peering at the *Wall Street Journal*. Retsler crossed the room, ignoring the other patrons who surreptitiously watched him, and sat across from Denne.

"You knew about the mermaids, didn't you?" Retsler asked.

Denne folded his paper, removed his glasses and set the cigarette in a cut glass ashtray. "Hello, Dan," he said as if Retsler hadn't spoken. "Would you like a cocktail? Or perhaps a bit of lunch?"

"Mermaids," Retsler said. He was exhausted and not in the mood to be civil.

"Of course I knew about them," Denne said. "I told you about them when I told you about the *Lady June*." He had lowered his voice and leaned forward as he spoke.

"You knew about Dyston's testimony? About the idea that mythical creatures trashed the entire yacht in order to have him to themselves, to get rid of the competition?"

"I find it amazing the man was not committed," Denne said. He picked up his cigarette. "Now, if you're not going to have lunch, then let me get back to my paper."

Retsler put his hand on the paper, pushing it flat. "Lucy says other locals have seen the mermaids."

"You're local. Have you?" Denne asked.

The three women surrounding his car rose in his mind. He swallowed.

Denne's small, superior smile faded. His face drained of color. "Have you?" he whispered.

"I saw three strange women last night. I had just poured Charles home. They were at the base of the hill."

"On land."

Retsler nodded.

"And did you hear anything odd or unusual?"

"No," Retsler said.

Denne let out a small sigh.

"You believe Dyston's story, don't you?"

Denne gazed out the window. The sea crashed and boomed against the rocks below, the sound loud over the hushed voices around them. "My father talked of them," he said softly. "After my mother died. He killed himself, you know."

"No, I didn't know."

Denne's smile was small, tight. "It wasn't a surprise. He drank too much, blamed himself for her death. He sent me away, made me promise never to come back."

"But you did."

"Of course."

"And you believe in the mermaids?"

Denne took a deep breath, and met Retsler's gaze. "I don't go to the beach alone. Neither does my wife. And on nights when the moon is full, I sleep with the windows closed, with earplugs in both ears, and the stereo on."

Retsler frowned. "Because of mermaids?"

"Because of the mermaids," he said.

In the daylight, the Sandcastle looked like a gothic ruin. Its blue paint was peeling, and the fake facades were crumbling. Vandals had broken through the plywood over the windows, revealing the wide staircase from Charles' dream/vision. The carpet was rotted, the mirrors smashed, and the stairs rotted through. He shivered just looking at it.

Charles clutched the bottle to his chest, and made his way to the hotel's beach access. High tides had broken the stone steps, and the metal rail added decades ago had rusted through. He went down the steps gingerly, one hand on the stone wall for balance.

The sea was loud here, louder than anywhere else on the coast. He remembered remarking on that to Grace the night they had come down, the night they had found the bottle. He had noticed it again when he found her body almost a year later.

He knew why they had taken her. Just the night before he had spoken to them, told them he had someone else, someone he loved, and that he wanted them to leave him alone. He had left, thinking he was safe. The next morning, the gulls had circled, and he had found Grace's body, lying in a tidal pool near the edge of the Sandcastle Hotel. Denne had ruled it accidental, death by drowning, and there was nothing to prove otherwise.

Nothing except Charles' feeling, nothing except the mermaids' sense of triumph each time they encircled him and made him theirs.

The wind was cool and damp. It carried small grains of sand that pelted him as he stepped out of the protection of the stairwell. This section of beach was completely deserted. Not even a gull sat at the water's edge. The sand was thin, revealing the thick black lava rock beneath. Only the ocean seemed alive, booming and cascading along the rocks with more energy than he had ever had.

He used to think of the ocean as a vast desert. It always made him marvel at the ancient sailors' ability to navigate such a broad and empty expanse. He had wondered, early in his enchantment, how the mermaids did the same. He doubted they used stars, and he wondered about the consistency of the ocean bottom. It wasn't until he realized that the bodies turned up on shore the very day the mermaids would summon him that he knew what happened.

The mermaids lived near the Sandcastle, and when they wanted his attention, they used the bodies as a calling card.

There was no calling card today. Only him, the ocean, and the broad expanse of sky. He scrambled onto the rocks, his feet slipping on the wet sand. The bottle grew heavy in his arms. He had to get close to the water. He was not as strong as he used to be. With his right hand, he grabbed the bottle by its neck, and picked a spot farther out, a spot where the ocean was almost black, and threw with all his strength.

The bottle spun in the air, its green sides catching the light, winking at him. He wished, at this moment, that he could see in black and white. This part of his life needed to be like a *noir* film, all darkness and shadows, with the light shimmering high and out of reach.

Then the bottle hit the water and disappeared into the darkness. He waited a moment, to see if it would surface, and it did not. A relief so profound it was almost sexual ran through him. He let out a sigh, turned and scrabbled along the rocks.

The ocean boomed behind him, and a thin wave, nearly gone, wrapped itself around his shoes. Hands gripped him from behind, scaly hands, clawlike hands, and hair coarse as straw blew across his face. Now he knew why he'd been thinking of death all day, why he had made this choice at this moment.

He had never had enough courage to do things on his own. He had always needed help.

He turned, and for the first time ever, returned the mermaids' embrace.

As Retsler drove back to Whale Rock, he couldn't shake a feeling of unease. Denne's words kept circling through his mind. Mermaids and fear. Too many people taking such a preposterous thing so seriously.

He needed to talk to Bishop, to see why he had mentioned them the night before.

But as Retsler crested the rise near the Sandcastle, he saw gulls. Hundreds of them, swarming, filling the blue-gray sky. The Sandcastle was nearly blanketed with them, and with all the falling feathers, the neighborhood looked as if it were buried in snow.

He picked up the radio. "Luce," he said. "Any call from Bishop?"

"No," she said. "Should there have been?"

"We have gulls at the Sandcastle. Send Eddie down, would you?"

"And the coroner?" she asked.

He took a deep breath. "I'll let you know."

He clipped the receiver back onto the radio, and drove into the turnout. His blue Taurus slid on the gravel before stopping. He had been driving too fast. As usual.

He got out, heart pounding. He wasn't used to being alone on this stretch of highway. The gulls were thick. He wasn't sure he'd be able to get down to the beach without Eddie's help.

Retsler reached into the back seat and removed his bullhorn. He hadn't brought the rifle. All he had was his service revolver. He promised himself he wouldn't get too close.

He walked along the narrow footpath and down the stairs. The gulls covered the beach like a blanket—too many for him to approach. But he didn't need to. The corpse was leaning against the rock retaining wall, body intact except for the missing eyes. A single gull stood on the corpse's wet hair, but the others kept their distance, as if showing Retsler the kill.

The kill.

His friend.

Charles Bishop. Clearly and irrevocably dead.

Retsler felt bile rise in his throat, and he swallowed, keeping control as best he could. He had taken Bishop home the night before, he knew he had. Besides, Bishop was dressed differently.

Bishop had come down here, alone, for no apparent reason at all.

Retsler backed away, never taking his gaze off the birds. One false move and they would swarm him too.

It wasn't until he reached the narrow footpath that he started to run.

That night, Lucy forced him to go to the False Colors. She was afraid he would go home and brood. He didn't know how brooding in public was any different from brooding alone, so he went along. He sat in a dark corner of the bar, listening to Lucy chatter about the day's silliest events. Eddie nursed a longneck and listened as well.

It felt as if they had lost one of their own.

Retsler couldn't get Bishop's body from his mind, the mocking position it had been left in. Just as his wife's had been.

And the last thing Bishop said before he passed out at this very bar the night before. He was talking about mermaids. He'd sounded wistful. As if he knew.

"Dan?" Lucy's voice was soft, as if she'd been trying to reach him more than once. "We can talk about Charles if you like."

He didn't like. He took a sip from the local stout and shook his head. There was nothing he could do. He'd stood beside Denne during the autopsy, saw all the evidence. Bishop had drowned. Just like his wife had. Denne ruled it accidental death, but he said he could have ruled suicide just as easily.

There was nothing Retsler could do, and that galled him even more.

He drained his third pint of stout and stood, a bit more unsteadily than he had thought he would.

"Dan?" Lucy asked.

"Going home," he said.

"I'll drive you."

He shook his head. She'd had more to drink than he had. "I'll walk."

He grabbed his windbreaker and swung it over his shoulders, then went out the bar's back door. The night was clear, the stars dabbed across the heavens like spots of white in black velvet canvas. The cool salty air refreshed him just enough, and he followed the footpath down to the beach.

The False Colors was nearly four miles away from the Sandcastle, and his home was between them both. He'd walked the beach home numerous times without a twinge. But this time, when he reached the deep brown sand farthest from the ocean, his heart did a double-flip.

The salty freshness had changed. There was another smell here, a bitter, biting scent that he associated with death. His stomach flipped again and he winced. Tonight he would have to find another way home.

He turned, and his boot hit something hard in the sand. He peered down, expecting a rock, and seeing instead a bottle filled with liquid.

"Damn tourists," he said, and swept it up, realizing as his fingers touched it that the bottle was old and still damp from the sea. Its label was torn in half, and in the light from the beach front hotels he could just parse out some French words, and a date: 1924.

Wine, old and expensive. He grinned. He would give it to Denne. Denne liked expensive things.

Retsler tucked the bottle under his arm, and had already reached the footpath, when the hair on the back of his neck stood on end. He removed the bottle once more, and looked at it, heart pounding.

An expensive bottle of wine. Bottled before 1936. When the *Lady June* went down. This was another gift from the sea. A benign one, perhaps, but still a gift from a tragedy best laid to rest.

Besides, how did a wet bottle appear in dry sand? Tourists, he thought again.

Or mermaids.

And what if they did exist? What if, after he took their gift, he could hear their song? And what if it lured him, like it had lured Dyston? He had no girlfriend to drown. But he had friends. So many friends.

God, he was drunk. He would never have believed these thoughts sober. He staggered back down the path until he reached the sand. He slogged through it, reaching the water's edge. A black spot the size of a child's wading pool proved a perfect target. He raised the bottle and threw it into the darkness.

The bottle landed in the inky spot with a splash. Concentric circles flared outward. A cool breeze touched him, and for a moment he felt suddenly sober. Too sober. Then the surface of the water smoothed, and his mouth went dry.

A woman rose out of the darkness. She had bulging eyes and a flat nose. Her long wet hair flowed along her neck and shoulders like seaweed. She clutched the bottle against her large breasts.

All the light from the area seemed focused on her. Her white skin seemed even whiter against the dark backdrop of the sky and sea.

When she saw him, she smiled. The smile was benign, almost questioning. She held out the bottle, as if he hadn't understood the invitation.

He shook his head. He had seen the results of gifts from the sea and he wanted no part of it. But he was so aroused his body hurt. How did that happen? He thought she was the ugliest woman he had ever seen.

"No," he said. "No. Thank you, but no."

Her smile faded. She sank beneath the water as if she had never been. With her went his arousal, and in place of it, he felt a vague unease in the pit of his stomach.

A wind whipped up. Waves the size of trees formed at the inky spot and headed toward shore. He backed away, never taking his gaze from the ocean, until his feet hit the footpath. Then he started to run.

Gulls dive-bombed him, cawing as they swooped near his face. He covered his eyes, and bowed his head, peering through his fingers as he negotiated the path. Things brushed his hair, and droppings fell all over him. He let one hand fall to his side, slid the other arm across his eyes, and reached for his service revolver. He grabbed it and shot skyward, the bang startlingly loud.

The cawing stopped. The rustle of wings disappeared. He sat abruptly and watched as fifty gulls flew heavenward, their white feathers the color of stars. He had never seen a gull at night before. A chill ran down his spine, and he remembered some movie he had seen as a kid, a Hitchcock movie about birds going out of control, attacking for no reason. It had terrified him, that movie, because those birds seemed like real birds, their behavior as cold and inexplicable as the sea.

The gulls were gone. He was alone, covered in bird droppings and feathers, and feeling shaky.

He had refused. He had refused the gift from the sea. And the birds, the woman, they had been angry at him, but they hadn't hurt him.

They hadn't touched him.

He had survived the curse, something Dyston hadn't been able to do. Something, Retsler suspected, his friend Bishop hadn't been able to do either.

"God, Bishop," he whispered, "if you'd only talked about it."

But Retsler wouldn't have believed Bishop if Bishop had told him. Retsler wouldn't have believed unless confronted with it himself.

Mermaids did hunt along the beach.

And they were as natural as birds, plucking eyeballs from the dead.

STRANGE CREATURES

STRANGE CREATURES

Dan Retsler sat on the hull of a half-submerged boat, the mud thick around his thigh-high fishing waders. In his right hand, he held an industrial quality flashlight; in his left, a pocket knife. He was filthy and wet and exhausted. Night was coming and there was still hours of work to do, buildings to search, items to move. He had managed to send the warning out early enough to evacuate most of the homes along the river, but the destruction was still heart-rending, the loss almost unimaginable.

The trailers were the worst. The water had knocked them about like Tonka toys, ripping them in half, crushing them, scattering them all over the low-lying valley as if they weighed little more than matchsticks.

They were worth about that much now.

He ran a hand through his hair, feeling the thick silt that seemed to have become a part of him. The foul stench of the mud might never come out of his nostrils.

The river looked so tame now, a narrow trickle through the valley. He had seen the Dee flood before: once after a particularly wet December, and during the 1996 February storms, dubbed The Storm of the Century by commentators who felt it was pretty safe to apply that label when the century was nearly done. But he had never seen anything like this, so sudden, so furious, and so severe.

The Dee was a tidal river which opened into Hoover Bay just south of Whale Rock. High tides and too much rain often caused the Dee to flood her banks, but the floods were low and fairly predictable. Until 1996, no water had ever touched the trailer park, dubbed Hoover Village by some wag, and until that morning, had never touched the highway winding its way along the valley and into the Coastal Mountain Range.

The sun was going down, turning the sky a brilliant orange and red, with shades of deep blue where the clouds appeared. The Pacific reflected the colors. Retsler stared at it, knowing that any other day, he would have stopped, appreciated the beautiful sunset, and called someone else's attention to it.

A hand touched his shoulder. He looked up, saw the coroner, Hamilton Denne, standing beside him. Denne had a streak of river mud on the left side of his face, and his blond hair was spiked with dirt. His silk suit had splotches and water marks, and his Gucci loafers were ruined.

Denne's wife would probably have a fit—she came from one of Oregon's richest families, and despised the fact that Denne still insisted on doing his job even though they didn't need the money. If anyone asked her what Denne did, she would tell them he was a doctor, or if they pushed, a pathologist. She never admitted to the fact that he worked best with corpses. He was able to keep the secret because the coroner's position was an appointed one in Seavy County, and no one ever printed his name in the papers.

In his left hand, Denne balanced a clean McDonald's bag and a cardboard tray with two Styrofoam cups of coffee. He nodded toward the sunset. "This looks like the best seat in the house. Mind if I share it? I'll pay my way with food."

Retsler didn't reply. Any other time, he would have bantered back, said something about bribing a public official, or teased Denne about whether or not he could have afforded the food. But Retsler didn't feel like banter. He didn't feel like company either, although he didn't say so.

Denne handed him the coffee tray, then sat beside him. Retsler took out a cup and wrapped his hand around it, letting the warmth sink through him.

"Didn't know what you liked, so I got everything," Denne said. "Whopper, Fish something or other, Biggie Fry—"

"Whopper's from Burger King," Retsler said.

"Well, you know me," Denne said. "It was my first time at a drive-through window. The wonders of technology."

Retsler was too exhausted to smile. He knew it wasn't Denne's first time in a fast-food joint, since he'd dragged Denne to them countless times. Denne always protested, and then ate like a thirteen-year-old at a basketball game.

Denne was holding the bag open. Retsler reached inside, and pulled out a Big Mac and fries. The smell of grease and sugar made his stomach cramp, but he knew he had to eat. He pulled the wrapper back and took a bite, tasting lettuce, pickles, onions, and cheese long before he got to the meat.

With the lining of his silk suit, Denne wiped mud off the boat's aluminum hull. Then he set the bag down, and rooted inside of it, pulling out a Filet-O-Fish. Denne had a penchant for the things, which Retsler always found odd, considering they lived in a place where they could get the freshest fish in the world.

"At the Club," Denne said, peeling the wrapper from his fish sandwich. He was referring to the Club at Glen Ellyn Cove, Whale Rock's gated community. "They have old maps of this coastline, some dating from the turn of the century. The last century."

Half of Retsler's Big Mac was gone. He was hungrier than he thought. He took a sip of coffee, waiting for Denne to finish. It was always easier to ignore Denne when the man was talking.

"Up until 1925 or so, this river wasn't the Dee at all. It was the Devil's River."

That didn't surprise Retsler. The Devil, in his opinion, had once dwelt on the Oregon Coast, eventually leaving behind his Punchbowl, his Churn, and oddly, his Elbow.

"When folks decided they wanted to bring tourism into Whale Rock, they shortened the name of the river." Denne took a bite of the sandwich and talked while he chewed. "Know why it was called the Devil's River?"

"Sea monster?" Retsler said. The food must have helped him feel slightly better. He answered Denne this time.

"No," Denne said. "That's Lincoln City. Devils Lake."

Retsler wadded up the sandwich wrapper, and shoved it in the bag. He sipped his coffee. It was black and burned. He drank it anyway.

"They called it Devil's River," Denne said, "because it flooded unexpectedly fourteen times between 1899 and 1919. On clear nights, they said, the river would rise and fill the valley until this place looked like a lake."

In the distance, cars swooshed across the Dee River bridge, oblivious to the destruction hundreds of feet below them. The sun was gone now, leaving traces of orange against the night sky.

"You're saying this is not my fault," Retsler said.

"Acts of God happen," Denne said.

Retsler drained the Styrofoam cup. "You don't believe that."

"Of course I do."

Retsler turned to him. "Hamilton, you and I've seen some strange things in Whale Rock."

Denne's eyes were hidden by the growing darkness. "It was a freak storm."

"You've never lied to me before, Hamilton. Don't start now." Retsler stood, grabbed his flashlight, and flicked it on. The beam made the mud glisten. "Thanks for the comfort food."

Denne had his elbows on his knees, his right hand holding the coffee cup by the lip. "Dan," he said. "You didn't start this thing."

Retsler paused, wondering why that didn't make him feel better. Then he said, "And I didn't end it, either."

It began a few days earlier, on the first day of the new year. Retsler answered the call about a suspicious smell on the beach.

The woman who had obviously made the call sat in the loose sand near the concrete cinder blocks lining the beach access. Her black hair flowed down her back. The constant ocean breeze stirred a few strands, but she didn't seem to notice. Her legs were spread in front of her, her toes buried in the sand. She wore a light jacket despite the day's chill. Retsler had a sense that she had been crying, but she wasn't now. Instead, she was staring out to sea, as if the frothy brown surface—filled with dirt from the rainstorms of the last few days— held the answers to questions he hadn't even heard yet.

Retsler stood on the concrete slab above the beach access and watched her for a moment. She didn't seem to know she was being observed. Cool mist pelted his face. The moisture felt good. He hadn't gotten much sleep last night: fifteen drunk and disorderlies; dozens of drunk driving stops; illegal fireworks on the beach. By the time he had turned in, about four a.m., he was praying that the Y2K bug would hit on Christmas so that no one could travel to the coast for New Year's Eve. Vain hope, he knew, but it was the only one he had.

He walked down the sand-covered ramp. Driftwood littered the beach, a testament to the rough surf of the last month. The air stank of charred wood and something else, something he didn't want to think about.

When he reached her, he crouched. "Maria Selvado?"

She raised luminous brown eyes to his. Her eyes were so dark they seemed to have no pupils. The whites were stunningly clear. There was moisture on her lower lashes, but he couldn't tell if it was from the mist or from tears. "Yes?"

"I'm Dan Retsler. I'm the chief of police here in Whale Rock." As if that meant something. He ran a department of ten, double what they'd had two years ago. Whale Rock was big enough to keep them busy, but not big enough to pay the salaries of more officers.

"Thanks for coming. I didn't know who to call."

Probably Fish and Game, he thought. Or the State Department of Natural Resources. Half a dozen agencies probably had jurisdiction over this one.

"Where?"

She waved a hand toward the surf. "That one."

He followed her gaze. The remains of a bonfire, piled high on a dune. He swallowed hard, thankful that he hadn't partied the night before, and stood.

The stench was intermittent, whenever the breeze happened to blow in his direction. Otherwise, he smelled only the salty ocean freshness and knew it could lull him into thinking nothing was wrong.

He slogged through deep sand as he walked up the dune, then crossed to a driftwood log the color of long abandoned houses. On the other side of the log was a pile of charred wood half covered in sand, and about two dozen beer cans, scattered in a semi-circle. The odor was strong here, and mixed with the smell of Budweiser and old vomit.

The carcass lay half in the fire, flesh burned and bubbled, but still recognizable by shape: a seal pup, skinned. Bile rose in his throat and he swallowed it down, reminding himself that he had seen worse and not too long ago: the cats in the bag by the river, the dog the vet said had been tortured for days, the horse, still alive, and half crazed by knife wounds all along its flank.

Retsler had read the studies, been to schools, knew the psychiatric lingo. Serial killers started like this—usually as teenagers, practicing on bigger or more difficult targets, needing a greater thrill each time to duplicate that same sick feeling of pleasure.

Seal pups. Jesus.

He looked away, stared at the ocean just as the woman had been doing. The sun peeked through a break in the clouds, falling on the whitecaps, adding a golden hue to the ocean's brown and blue surface. He reached into his pocket and pulled out his cell phone, flipping it open and hitting his speed dial.

After two rings, he got an answer. "Hamilton," he said, "sorry to disturb your holiday, but I've got something I need you to see."

The woman chose to wait beside him. When he told her he could take her statement, if she wanted, and then she could go, she shook her head. She seemed to think her actions warranted an explanation because, after a few moments, she told him that she worked at the

Hatfield Marine Science Center in Newport. Her specialty was seals.

Denne saved him from answering. Retsler heard the rumble of Denne's rusted Ford truck, the one he'd bought in November against his wife's wishes, because he was tired, he said, of showing up at crime scenes in his silver Mercedes. Not that there were that many murders in Seavy County, which was Denne's jurisdiction. But Denne had an eye for detail and a knowledge of the obscure that made him useful to all the police departments in the county. For a job that was supposed to be part-time, a job that should have taken very little of his precious social time, it seemed to be a major preoccupation for him, one that was growing more and more of late.

The door slammed and Denne made his way down the beach. Retsler led him to the carcass, and watched as Denne's face went white.

"This is how someone chose to ring in the New Year?" he asked.

Retsler stuck his hands in the back pockets of his jeans. "I want you to treat this like a human murder scene. And then we'll—"

"Compare it to that dog, I know." Denne glanced at the ocean, then at the bonfire. "They wanted us to find this. It's above the high-water line."

"Or maybe they were just careless," Retsler said. "That's a lot of beer."

"Looks like it was some party," Denne said. "I'll bet there're one or two people who aren't happy about how it ended."

"Thought of that," Retsler said.

"You know you'll have to call the State. These pups are protected. Hell, you could get slapped with a gigantic fine if you move a live one. I have no idea what happens if you kill one."

"It's the same thing," Retsler said. Tourists came across seal pups alone on the beach all the time, then picked "the poor things" up and hauled them to a vet, thinking they were orphans. The act of kindness always doomed the pup, whose mother had left it on the beach on purpose and would have been back for it. Very few pups were ever safely returned to the wild; most died after being separated from the mother.

"It's not quite the same," Denne said, and went to work.

After he'd collected the beer cans and all the other evidence he could find, Retsler offered to drive Maria Selvado back to Newport, but she refused. She said she was staying in Whale Rock for her work. She had told him, as if it were more a threat than a promise, that she would drop in his office on Monday to find out how his work was progressing.

He had left Denne to the mess, and had driven back to the station. It was in the center of downtown, with a display window that overlooked Highway 101. The station had once been prime retail space, but Retsler's predecessor had demanded, and received, the building because, he said, most crimes were committed just outside its doors.

That was true enough. On most days, the police log was something Jay Leno might read as a joke: two people pulled over for running red lights; *Slow Children* sign vandalized (for the eighth time) on South Jetty Road; lost puppy found before Safeway store, identified, and returned to owner.

It was the other days that were difficult: the spur-of-the-moment kidnapping outside the local Dairy Queen; the gang war, featuring rival gangs imported from Portland, on the Fourth of July; the drownings, search-and-rescue operations, all caused by the stupid things tourists did on the beach. If someone asked him how hard his job could get, those were the things he mentioned. He never brought up Whale Rock's secret side.

Denne was familiar with it, and Retsler's dispatch, Lucy Wexel, was a firm believer that there was some sort of vortex here that brought out the magic in the world. Retsler's introduction had come two years ago when intact and seemingly recently deceased bodies appeared on the beach, all from the same sixty-year-old shipwreck. Then there were the three so-called women who seduced people to their deaths in the sea; Retsler had seen them, and narrowly escaped. Denne called them mermaids, but they weren't. They were sirens, perhaps, or sea hags, and they were something Retsler never ever talked about.

Eddie was working dispatch today, with Retsler on call. New Year's Eve was always a nightmare, but New Year's Day was usually as quiet as a church—people were either too hung-over or too tired to get out of the house. Even though the sun was peeking through the clouds, the beach was empty, something Retsler was grateful for.

Eddie was sitting with his feet on Lucy's desk, a *Car and Driver* magazine on his lap, and three Hershey's candy wrappers littering the floor around him. When Retsler entered, Eddie sat up, and immediately started cleaning.

"Sorry, boss. Didn't expect you."

Retsler waved a hand. "You're fine."

"Figure out what died on the beach?" Eddie, of course, had taken Selvado's call.

"Seal pup. Skinned and burned."

"Je-Zus." Eddie whistled, then shook his head. He'd seen a lot of the strange things around Whale Rock as well, but they never ceased to surprise him either. "What the hell would anyone do that for?"

"Kicks, it looks like." He took one of Eddie's candy bars. "Mind?"

Eddie shook his head.

"Do me a favor. Look through the files, see if you can find more animal killings, anything that predates that spate of them we had last year."

"You got it."

"And do a location map for me too, would you?"

"Sure." Eddie actually looked relieved. He was usually patrolling because he liked to be busy. He wasn't suited for dispatch.

Retsler went through the open door into his tiny office. He didn't pull the blinds on the glass windows—another feature left over from the retail days—but he sat hard at his desk. Incident reports from the night before littered the left corner. He stared at them for a moment, as if they were the enemy, then he frowned.

He might find something in them as well.

He slid them over to the center of his desk, and began to scan. He had to sign off on them anyway—a departmental policy as old as

Whale Rock and one he saw no need to change—and he may as well do so now while he was waiting for Denne. Retsler had a few incident reports of his own to file from the night before, as well as the one this afternoon, but he wasn't ready to put anything down on paper.

Fifteen reports later, almost all of them drunk and disorderlies, almost all of them depressing in their sameness, Retsler stood and stretched his cramping hand.

"Hey!" Eddie said from the front. "Got something weird."

Retsler left his desk and walked to the dispatch area. Eddie had files scattered around him—both of them would pay dearly for that when Lucy came in on Monday morning—and at the center of it all, a map of Whale Rock. There were multicolored dots all over the village. Retsler had forgotten how good Eddie was at details. Usually he didn't have to focus on them when he was on the street.

"I used red for this year," Eddie said. "I mean, last year. You know, '98. Green's for '97, and blue's for '96. I put the seal pup in last year's because the poor thing probably died before sundown."

"How do you figure?" Retsler asked.

"It takes a lot of work to skin an animal, don't care how good you are at it. It's harder if you can't see too good."

"They had a bonfire."

"And found a seal pup at night? I don't think so."

He had a good point. Retsler made a mental note of it. He leaned over the map and saw, while there were a few dots all over the city, the biggest concentration of them was around Hoover Bay.

"That's odd," Retsler said.

"That's what I thought," Eddie said, pointing to them. "And they're mostly from the last year or so. The rest're what you'd expect, and if I'd had time, I'd've marked 'em by month too. Outside the bay, most of the animals died between May and September."

"Tourists."

"Sicko, psycho kids, probably brought to the beach because there's nothing for them to tear up, or so the parents think."

That was one of the things Retsler hated the most about summer, the teenagers who invaded from other towns. After they saw the single movie playing at the Bijou, shopped at all the stores, and found out that the casino just outside of town really did enforce its 18 and above rule, they turned to vandalism or small acts of terror to take up their time.

"What about the others?" Retsler asked.

"Late '96, spaced about a month apart. Been escalating since October. That dog you found tied to the river piling was only two weeks ago, and the cats a week before that."

"You forgot the horse," Retsler said.

"Horse?"

"You know, Draytons' new mare, the one they'd bought their daughter for Christmas."

"Oh, yeah," Eddie said, and grimaced in distaste. "It's not down here as a killing."

"It should have been," Retsler said. "The vet had to put her down." The little girl had been heartbroken, and convinced, somehow, that it was her fault. The parents had promised her a new horse, but she had refused, saying she couldn't be sure it would be safe. The parents had looked at Retsler then, perhaps wanting him to reassure her, but he said nothing. He wasn't sure the family would be safe on hillside retreat, with its two-mile long road and 360-degree view of the ocean and the river. He'd thought the horse incident particularly cruel and had thought perhaps it had been directed at the Draytons.

Now he wasn't so sure. They lived awfully close to Hoover Bay, and a horse wasn't a dog or a seal pup. Horses had an amazing amount of strength.

Had the horse been the killer's attempt to ratchet up the pleasure, only to be thwarted? Maybe that's why the killer went after something like a seal pup, something so helpless and vulnerable and cute that it would be easy to kill.

A shiver ran through Retsler. He didn't like what was loose in his little town.

Denne showed up three hours later. He was wearing a Harvard sweatshirt over a pair of chinos. His deck shoes were mottled and ruined, and he wore no socks. Retsler had seen the outfit before. It was the one Denne kept at his office and used only when something at a crime scene made him leave his regular clothes behind.

Denne's blond hair was ruffled and his mouth a thin line. He pulled open the door, nodded to Eddie, and then came into Retsler's office without knocking.

Retsler had just finished going through the reports. Nothing from the area of the beach where they had found the seal pup. He would have expected something to come from the nearby hotels, perhaps, someone seeing the skinning of the pup or getting upset by the conduct of the beer drinkers. He was surprised no one had complained about the smell until that afternoon.

Denne sat in the chair before Retsler's desk. Even though he was wearing his grubbiest clothes, Denne's pants still had a crease, and even his sweatshirt looked pressed.

"If you can call two a pattern," Denne said without preamble, "we've got one."

"Looks like a different MO to me," Retsler said. He'd had all afternoon to think about it. "Dog tortured to death, left on a stake beneath the Dee River Bridge. Pup's skinned and burned on the beach. All those beer cans. I'm thinking a bunch of drunk kids got carried away—"

"Whoever skinned that pup was an expert," Denne said. "The flesh was clean in the unburned areas. And the pup bled. It was alive, at least for part of it. But that isn't the clincher."

Retsler folded his hands over the report. He hadn't wanted to hear that the pup was alive. He hated some of the things this profession made him think about.

"The clincher is the knife itself. It's one of those thin serrated knives, made especially for that sort of work. Around here, folks usually use knives like that on deer or elk. It's got a slight nick in the blade. It leaves an identifiable mark. The dog and the pup had it. If I'd thought to keep those cats, I bet they'd have had it too."

Retsler sighed. Apparently Denne took that for disappointment because he added, "If I were dealing with human deaths here, I could make a case for a serial killer based on the knife evidence alone."

"What else have you got?"

"Some fibers. A pretty good print, in blood, on the body itself."

"Good," Retsler said. "That's a start. With that, and the cans, we might be able to find something."

"Hope so." Denne stood, then paused as if he had a thought. "There's one more thing. It may be nothing, or it might be everything."

"What?" Retsler asked.

"Did you find the pelt?"

Retsler shook his head. "I assumed it got burned."

"No. There was no fur in the fire at all, and they were too far from the water line for it to have been swept away with the tide."

"I'd better get someone to comb the beach, then," Retsler said.

"Yeah," Denne said. "But I don't think you'll find anything."

Retsler met his gaze. "You think our friend is selling the pelts?"

"Probably not. I have a hunch we're dealing with someone young here."

Retsler felt himself go cold. "Trophy hunter."

Denne nodded. "I suspected it with the dog, and I bet, if I looked at your report on the cats, I could find something too."

"The horse's mane," Retsler murmured.

"Hmm?"

"Nothing," Retsler said.

"If you don't find that pelt," Denne said, "I'd bet every dime I've got that our killer still has it."

"Should make it easier to convict someone."

"On what? Animal cruelty?" Denne said. "Seems minor for this kind of offense."

Retsler agreed, but felt the day's frustration fill him. "What am I supposed to charge him with? Prospective serial killing?"

"Wish you could," Denne said.

"We'll get the state involved," Retsler said. "Maybe they'll have ideas."

"They'll think we're a small town with too much time on our hands."

"Maybe they would have with the dog or the horse," Retsler said.

"But we're dealing with a seal pup. That makes these TV news reporters sit up and beg."

"Think twice before you invite those vultures here," Denne said. "They'll mess up the entire case."

"I'll wait," Retsler said, "until I have something that'll stick."

Denne nodded. "I'll give you all the help I can."

Retsler smiled. "You've already given me plenty."

The weekend wasn't as calm as Retsler would have liked. Two major traffic accidents on 101 backed traffic for hours, and caused several more citations. A suspicious fire downtown in one of Whale Rocks failing seasonal businesses had Retsler calling in a state arson team. A Saturday night bar fight got out of control and spilled into the street, forcing Retsler to call his entire team to help quell the violence. He wasn't able to think about seal pups and animal mutilations until he arrived at work at eight a.m. Monday morning, sleep-deprived, bruised, and more thankful than he cared to admit that all the tourists had finally gone home.

Lucy was already at her desk, an unlit cigar in her mouth. She had curly gray hair and a military manner that her grandmotherly face somehow softened. Retsler had known her since he was a boy, and sometimes she still made him feel like that boy. He really didn't want to cross her.

She had two tall cups from Java Joes on her desk. As he passed, she handed him one. He turned to her in surprise. She had made it clear, when he became chief, that she didn't do windows or coffee.

"What's this for?"

"I figure you haven't gotten no rest since New Year's Eve. Caffeine won't cure it, but it'll cover it up."

He grinned at her. "You're a lifesaver, Lucy."

She frowned. "Don't go ruining my reputation."

"I won't tell a soul."

"Good," she said. Then she leaned back in her chair. "You got a woman in your office."

He glanced over, surprised he had missed it. Maria Selvado was sitting primly in the chair in front of his desk, a vinyl purse clutched to her white sweater. Her coat hung over the back of the chair, and she wore what appeared to be a very cheap pair of boots beneath her faded jeans.

"How long's she been here?"

"Half hour or so. I told her you don't normally come in until ten."

"Lucy!"

Lucy chuckled. "Well, I figured if you got in any earlier than ten, she'd think you were good at your job."

"I am good at my job."

"Just goes to show," Lucy said. Then she raised an eyebrow at him. "And if you let that Eddie dig in my files again, so help me God, I'll pour that coffee down your back."

"Yes, ma'am."

This time it was Retsler who chuckled as he headed to his office. Maria Selvado turned her face toward him. She looked even more exotic in the artificial light. "Chief," she said in greeting.

"Dan," he corrected.

She nodded. He sat behind his desk. She leaned forward, still clutching that purse. "I came for an update."

"I can't tell you much," he said. "We know that the pup's death is part of a pattern, and we are working on that angle. We have some leads—"

"A pattern?" she murmured.

He stopped, frowning. She seemed disturbed by his words. "Yes. There have been other animals killed in the same area—"

"But not other pups."

"Not that we know of."

She let out a small breath. The news seemed to relieve her. "But you have nothing on the killer."

"Not yet."

She raised those liquid eyes to his, and he thought he saw accusation in them. He parted his hands defensively, and then shook his head a little. He didn't have to defend himself to anyone.

But he did say, because he felt she needed to know, "We don't have much of a lab facility here. We've sent several items to the State Crime Lab. We should hear later today."

She bit her lower lip. "You'll keep me informed."

"If I know where I can find you."

"I'm at the Sandcastle."

He shuddered. He couldn't help it. Someone bought the land a year ago, and in that time tore down the old hotel. The new one had the look of the old—once one of the Coast's premiere resorts—and people from all over the world had flocked to it in the last few days of the summer. But he had memories of the Sandcastle, memories of finding intact bodies before it, memories of unusual goings-on that dated to his boyhood—talk of ghosts and kelpies and strange creatures that emerged from the sea.

She looked amused. His reaction must have been visible. "They've remodeled," she said. "It's quite nice."

"I have no doubt."

She smiled and stood, her movements fluid and graceful. "Thank you for cooperating with me, Chief."

"You're welcome," he said, and waited for her to leave before he shut his office door.

That night, Lucy chose the dinner spot and, as always, she picked the False Colors. It was a pirate-themed bar just off 101, but more locals went there than tourists. The sea chanties, played low, the fireplace that burned real wood, the ropes and life rings that came from real ships played to the out-of-towners, but most people who came to the coast brought their families. The skull and crossbones that decorated most corners, the human skulls on the mantel, the tales of death and murder framed on the walls were not the best atmosphere for children. So tourists usually came once and left, allowing the locals to enjoy the excellent food and the even better bar.

Retsler ordered his usual, a cutely named fish and chips entree that came with a large salad and a double order of bread. He got a

Rogue Ale with that, and planned to get a huge dessert, thinking that the combination might allow him to go home and go to sleep at nine p.m.

Lucy had the fisherman's platter, a meal three times the size of Retsler's, and he knew by the end of the evening, she would have eaten all of it. After a few minutes, Eddie joined them.

He was still in uniform, and as he sat down, June the waitress scurried over. "You know Jeff don't like it when you guys come in your blues," she said in a half whisper.

"What's he going to do, call the cops?" Lucy asked and then smiled, a grandmother with fangs.

"It's just he doesn't think the presence of police adds to the atmosphere."

"He's afraid the real pirates will stop patronizing the place," Lucy said and chuckled.

"It's okay," Eddie said. "I won't do it again. It's just I had to talk to Dan and I didn't have time to change."

"Tell Jeff it's January 4th and the tourists went home, not that they're going to be in here anyway," Dan said. "And tell him he can chase his regulars away if he wants, but this is the slow season and it probably wouldn't be wise."

June bobbed her head. "It wasn't from me, you know. It's just that Jeff—"

"Is delusional." Lucy picked up a crab leg and broke it in half. "We know."

June flushed. "You want something, Eddie?"

"Burger and fries and a diet."

June left and Eddie leaned forward. "I've got a couple of things on that seal pup killing," he said softly, even though there were no other patrons within hearing range. "Okay to tell you here?"

Sometimes Retsler frowned on discussing work at the False Colors. But that was usually in the summer, when the place was packed with first-timers who really didn't need tales of car crashes and children crushed by driftwood logs as an accompaniment to their meals.

Retsler picked up a fry. "Let's hear it."

Any news would be good news. Retsler expected a visit the next morning from Maria Selvado, and he hadn't heard from the crime lab yet. He supposed he could give her some information from Denne's autopsy of the pup, but even someone as involved as Selvado probably didn't want to hear about knife serrations and the fact that the pup had been skinned alive.

Retsler winced at the memory.

"You okay?" Eddie asked.

Retsler nodded. Then the main door opened, and Denne walked in. Retsler looked up. Denne's wife had expressly forbidden him from coming here. She had discovered, through small-town gossip probably, that twice before he had shown up here to discuss a case, and had demanded that he not disgrace the family by showing his face in the False Colors again.

Yet there he was, in a charcoal-colored silk suit with a sterling silver pocket watch attached to a fob on the outside. His blond hair had been slicked back, and his aesthetic face looked almost haunted.

"She's pushing him too hard," Lucy murmured. "He's drifting over to the other side."

Retsler started, then considered the evidence: the truck, the clothes Denne had worn home on New Years, and now the appearance at the False Colors. Denne was abandoning his gated community for the peasants who ran this small town.

Eddie sighed. "You want to hear this or not?"

"Let's wait for Hamilton," Retsler said as he waved. Denne smiled —he never quite grinned—and walked down the worn stairs into the main dining area. As he did, he stopped June and ordered, then took the only empty chair at the table.

"Eddie," Retsler said, "was about to tell us news on our seal pup."

"Really?" Denne removed his suit coat and hung it on the back of the chair.

Then he rolled up the sleeves of his white button-down shirt, revealing muscular forearms. With his left hand, he loosened his tie, and pulled it off. The entire group was watching him with astonishment. Retsler could feel his own mouth open in surprise.

Denne raised his eyebrows. "Don't let me stop you, Eddie."

"Um, yeah." Eddie shot Denne a slightly perplexed look, then said, "I been having conversations all day, casual ones, you know."

Retsler did know. One of the strengths of Whale Rock was its citizens' willingness to discuss anything if approached properly by someone they knew. A glance at the ocean, a mention of the dead pup, and a softly worded query about something related often got a glut of information.

"And I didn't get nothing on anyone selling pelts."

"I called fifteen different departments," Lucy said as she stabbed a scallop with her fork, "and no one in the entire State of Oregon has heard of anyone poaching seals."

"I asked her to. Hope you don't mind, boss," Eddie said.

A year ago, Eddie never would have taken that kind of initiative. "I gave you the legwork of the investigation," Retsler said. "You can divide it up how you want."

June brought a longneck for Eddie and an Alaskan Amber for Denne. Retsler looked at him in surprise, but Denne didn't seem to notice. Lucy did, however, and winked.

"Then what did you need to tell me?" Retsler asked when June left.

"You remember when they tore down the Sandcastle to make way for the new version?"

"A mistake if there ever was one," Denne said. "You do realize the hotel is on the beach."

They all looked at him. Building on the beaches—on the sand— was against the law in Oregon.

"How'd that happen?" Retsler said.

"You know the Planning Commission." Denne took a sip of the amber and looked like a man who had just had the most sublime experience of his life.

"It's a state law," Lucy said.

Denne raised his eyebrows. "The Sandcastle Hotel predates the law. The Commission claimed they couldn't do anything because it grandfathers in."

"How much did Roman Taylor pay them?" Retsler asked.

"Pay them? Kickbacks, in our small town? Impossible." Denne leaned back. "Just a sidebar. Didn't mean to derail you, Eddie."

Eddie grunted, and took a sip out of his longneck. "Anyway," he said, "when they were bulldozing the Sandcastle, they found an open area underneath it. There was all kinds of junk under there, old watches, gold coins, shiny stuff. Some of it wasn't worth much, but some of it was worth a lot, and Taylor said he got it, because he bought the property. Nobody fought him about it and nobody tried to trace it."

"And, not surprisingly, nobody thought to call us," Retsler said.

Eddie nodded, meeting his gaze. "Ain't it amazing how some things just don't make it to our attention until we can't do nothing about them."

"So what do the shiny things have to do with this investigation?" Lucy asked.

"Well, in there was a pile of fur, all sleek and shiny. Turns out it was seal pelts—about twenty of them. Just beautiful things. I guess Taylor's the kind of guy who hangs deer heads on the walls and he was really excited about them pelts. He took them home."

Retsler whistled. "This was what? Last January?"

"Yep," Eddie said. "And that's not all. Various folks have come up asking for them seal pelts, even though the only people who knew about them were the digging crew and Taylor. Taylor won't talk to anybody about them."

"Curiouser and curiouser," Lucy said.

June set down Eddie's hamburger, and placed a double cheese-burger—an item the False Colors proudly called its Gut Blaster—in front of Denne. Retsler couldn't resist.

"Your wife isn't going to be too happy when you come home smelling of hot sauce, jalapeños, and onions."

Denne shrugged. "The woman's got to learn to calm down."

This time, Eddie was the one who raised his eyebrows. He picked up the catsup and proceeded to pour it all over his food. "I got one more thing to tell you about them pelts," he said. "The latest person who's come to inquire about them is Maria Selvado. She's been after Taylor since the first of December, and she's got the Marine Science

Center behind her. Guess they're doing some sort of seal study or something, and the pelts would be really useful. They're even offering to pay him. But he won't meet with her. She says she's not leaving until he does."

"Our Miss Selvado gets around," Lucy said.

"Yeah," Eddie said. "She even went up to his house on the Dee. Got real mad when she saw how he's displaying the pelts. Guess he's got them in one of those wall-sized glass cases beside his fireplace. He came to the door and she was yelling something about pins ruining the fur, or something. Anyway, he threw her off the porch, damn near landed her in the river. She hasn't been up there since."

"But there was a break-in," Retsler said.

"Thwarted break-in," Lucy said. "The alarm kicked on with the sirens and all the lights, remember?"

"And tiny footprints, woman-sized, in the mud beside the window on the fireplace side of the house. Passionate woman," Retsler said.

"Mystery woman," Denne said. "She called me, asking if she could have the pup's body when I was through with it, said she wanted it for the Science Center. I offered to drive it over there for her —I mean, who wants a corpse in your car if you can help it?—and she turned me down. That made me suspicious, so I called the Science Center."

"And they'd never heard of her," Lucy said, her eyes sparkling as they always did when the story started getting juicy.

"Oh, they'd heard of her all right. But she hadn't worked for them for six months. Seems that she broke into the Oregon Coast Aquarium last summer, and was going to liberate the seals. Security stopped her before she made it to the outdoor pen, but the Aquarium offered not to press charges—which would have embarrassed the Science Center—if she promised to leave Newport. She did."

"And came here?" Retsler asked. "That seems odd to me. We're not that far from Newport."

Denne nodded. "The Science Center is none too happy that she's still representing herself as part of their staff. Not that she was ever staff-staff anyway. She was one of the student projects, interns or whatever, that they get coming through. But they still don't want their name connected to hers."

"And they have no interest in the seal pelts?" Retsler asked.

"None," Denne said.

Lucy nodded. "Selkies," she said.

All three of them turned to her. She grinned and shrugged. "Come on," she said. "We have no secrets between us. We are talking Whale Rock, aren't we?"

"Silkies?" Eddie asked.

"Selkies," Retsler said. He'd been boning up on his sea-faring lore since the last strange encounter. "They look like seals in the sea, but when they come on shore and shed their skin, they look human."

"Oh, God," Eddie said.

"But don't they usually come looking for love?" Denne asked. "Aren't they supposed to mate with human women, leave them pregnant, and return to the sea?"

"You've been reading too many Celtic stories," Lucy said. "That may have been true hundreds of years ago. But I think selkies are more sophisticated than that."

"Sophisticated?" Denne placed his chin on the palm of his hand and looked at her. "Do you mean they're sending their children ashore in search of a better education?"

"You may mock me, young man, but think about it. What better way to find out about the things that threaten your people than to study those things?"

Retsler was silent. A lot threatened the seal population, which had been thinning in recent years. Some blamed oil spills farther up the coast, others blamed changes in commercial fishing laws, and still others blamed things like tourists taking pups off the beaches. Whatever the cause, there were fewer seals in the last few years than there had been in a long time.

"That seal pup," Denne said, "was 100 percent seal. There was nothing magical about it."

"The myths say that the smaller seals—like the common seal—belong entirely to the animal world, but the larger seals, like the gray, the great, and the crested, can be selkie folk." Lucy pushed her plate aside. "How else do you explain the clean, unrotted pelts, found among all that shiny stuff, as Eddie calls it. It was a nest, a place to hide wealth that enabled them to trade in Whale Rock."

Retsler put aside the remains of his fish and chips. "So?" he asked. "We have a bunch of selkies in human form walking around Whale Rock?"

"Or in the sea without their pelts. It's probably hazardous to their health." Lucy shook her head. "A year's a long time."

"What does this have to do with our dead pup?" Denne asked.

"Maybe nothing," Lucy said, "but selkies do have a kinship with seals. They're probably not happy about this."

"You think Maria Selvado is a selkie?" Retsler asked.

"I didn't say that." Lucy sniffed loudly. Of course she hadn't said that. She had implied it, like she often did, and Retsler could ignore her at his own peril.

"Selkies," Denne mused. "I thought selkies were dangerous."

"Only if you're a man in lust," Retsler said.

"No," Lucy said. "They are dangerous, if you kill one."

"What?" Eddie asked, setting down the longneck. "All the other selkies toss their pelts at you?"

"No," Lucy said. "If you kill one, don't get its blood in the ocean."

"Or?" Denne asked.

"Or a storm'll come up the likes of which you've never seen."

Retsler sighed. "Do you actually believe that, Lucy?"

She met his gaze. There was no twinkle in her gray eyes. "I've seen a lot of things, Dan. I don't disbelieve anything."

"But you don't actually believe it."

"Let me put it this way," Lucy said. "That myth is not one I'd want to test."

"The language is plain, Retsler." Roman Taylor was a large man, made to seem even larger by the low ceilings in the second story of his riverside home. He hunched over a rough-hewn log table, made to match the rough edges on the outer walls. The inner walls were smooth and painted white. It was on one of those that a huge case with the pelts gleamed in the morning sunshine. "I bought the Sandcastle Hotel and all its contents. The pelts and the treasures in that room around them were inside the Sandcastle. No one disputes that."

Retsler stared at the deed before him. Apparently he stared too long because Taylor shifted from one foot to another.

The language was clear. Taylor did own the pelts and there was nothing Retsler could do about it.

"Maybe you should show this to the city attorney," Taylor said. "Then maybe people'll leave me alone."

"They'll leave you alone now," Retsler said. "Sorry to bother you."

Taylor nodded once at the apology. Then he glanced at the case. "That woman's crazy, you know. If I could find a way to get her out of my hotel I would. If you could think of something, I'd be forever in your debt."

"Has she broken any laws, Mr. Taylor?"

"I'd be the first to scream if she did." He walked over to the case. "She says the seals that had these pelts are still alive, and they need them. Isn't that nuts? You can't skin an animal like this and have the animal live."

"Can I see one?" Retsler asked.

Taylor opened the case. The glass swung open, and the scent of fur and an animal musk filled the room. "Come here."

Retsler obliged. The pelts glistened as if they were still wet, but there was a dullness that was starting to appear around their edges.

Taylor picked up a corner of the nearest fur. "See that?" he asked. "Best work I've ever seen. Not a trace of flesh, no knife marks. Just the fur. Isn't it beautiful?"

Beautiful wasn't a word that Retsler would have used, but he nodded anyway.

"Hey, Dad!"

Both men turned. A teenage boy stood in the stairwell, face flushing when he saw Retsler.

"Didn't know you had company," the boy said.

"The chief's just leaving."

The boy grunted. He stood perfectly still as if movement weren't allowed. "Why're you showing him the pelts?"

Something in the question made Retsler look at the boy. The boy's eyes were bright, almost too bright. And cold. So cold that Retsler felt a chill run through him.

"He'd heard about them, that's all," Taylor said.

"Dad thinks those pelts are the real thing," the boy said, his chin raised in something of a challenge.

Retsler became completely still. "You don't?"

"I think they're fake. I think he should get them checked."

"Why?" Retsler asked.

"Because I don't care how good you are, you can't remove a pelt making a single cut."

"Hmm," Retsler said. "Have you tried?"

"He hunts with me sometimes," Taylor said too fast. "Don't you, Michael?"

"We've never hunted together in our lives. My father never pays attention to me." The boy tilted his head, eyeing Retsler speculatively. "You ever spend New Year's Eve on the beach, chief?"

Retsler didn't answer. Taylor's face flushed.

"It's amazing what people'll burn—"

"Michael!" Taylor said.

The boy grinned and shrugged, as if he had just been making conversation. "Nice seeing you. *Chief.*"

And then he walked down the stairs. Retsler's entire body had turned numb. He had expected a teenager, but not one that would challenge him. Although he had heard stories about Michael Taylor for the last year. A teacher at the high school had asked how to deal with a boy who seemed to love violence. A female student filed a complaint, only to withdraw it a day later.

Retsler debated for a moment whether or not he should follow, whether or not he should search the boy's room, and then decided the boy wouldn't issue a challenge like that if he expected to get caught. Better to take it slow, build a case the right way. Maybe Retsler could even talk to Taylor, convince him to send the boy to a hospital where he could get help.

"Sorry about that," Taylor was saying. "He's at that age when no adult is worth his time."

Retsler stared at him. Taylor's flush deepened. "You know we found a skinned pup on the beach New Year's Day."

"No," Taylor said. "I hadn't. It's amazing what people will do."

"Isn't it?" Retsler asked. He looked at the case again. "How many of these did you find?"

"Twenty," Taylor said. "And that's how many are there."

Retsler silently counted to himself. Twenty. If the other pelt was here, it was somewhere else. "Maybe I should take a peek at your son's room."

"Not without a warrant," Taylor said.

Retsler nodded. It played out just as he expected. He shrugged, like the boy had, then he thanked Taylor for his time, and left the house.

The river was low here, sixty feet down the bank, and sparkling in the bright sunshine. Taylor had bought the land and built the house the year before he had bought the Sandcastle. Lucy said that Taylor had spent that year getting on the good side of the Planning Commission. Lucy would know.

The pelts were disturbing, the boy more so. But Taylor had a legal right to the pelts, and Retsler would have to work hard to make anything more than a misdemeanor stick on the boy. Taylor had more money than God, which meant that he could afford the biggest lawyers in the country.

Retsler was suddenly walking into the big leagues, and he wasn't even sure he wanted to play the game.

The State Crime Lab could find no match on the fingerprints, nor did they have anything to say about the requests from Whale Rock. They apologized profusely, but perfunctorily, and probably, when they got off the phone, chuckled at the things that passed for important in small towns.

Retsler didn't care. He had other things to check. Lucy had called

Seavy County Deeds and Records, and had found the date of Taylor's home purchase. It was one month before the animal mutilations started near Hoover Bay. Now she was checking with the local police department in Taylor's previous home in San Jose, hoping to find another pattern.

It wasn't much, but it was a start. He also had a call in to an old friend at the FBI who might have a few ideas on how to proceed in a case as delicate, and insubstantial, as this one. Animal deaths and mutilations were bad enough, but, truth be told, they weren't what Retsler was really worried about. What worried him the most were the coldness of that boy's eyes, and the possibility—make that the probability—of what the boy would become.

Retsler had all that on his mind as he drove to the Sandcastle. He wasn't sure why he wanted to see Maria Selvado, but he knew he probably should.

Her room was on the top floor of the Sandcastle Hotel. Like all of the rooms, it had double glass doors on the ocean side that opened onto an extra-long balcony. When she led Retsler onto it, it made him feel as if he were standing over the water. He supposed, in high tide, that he would be. The balconies hung over the concrete breaker that protected the hotel from high surf—another illegal measure grandfathered in by the Planning Commission. Retsler had hated the look from the ground, but he had to admit that, from the balconies themselves, the view was spectacular.

Selvado had let him in, no questions asked. That she had been in her room on such a beautiful afternoon, neither of them mentioned. The room itself was spectacular. The door opened into a hallway which led to a large bathroom, passed a king-sized bedroom, and opened into a well-apportioned sitting room filled with antiques and facing a marble fireplace. The ubiquitous television was hidden in a wall unit that still looked suspiciously out of place. It was also covered with dust.

The ocean breeze had a trace of mist. Selvado raised her face to it as if it gave her life. She was obviously waiting for him to speak.

He cleared his throat. "I spoke to Roman Taylor today about the pelts."

She turned, stunned.

"He showed me the deed. They're clearly his."

"They have nothing to do with him," she said fiercely. "They don't belong to him."

"By law they do."

She bit her lip and turned away. "The law is wrong."

"The law is what we have, Ms. Selvado. It may not be right all the time, it may not make things easy, but it's what we have."

She shook her head. "It's not enough."

He knew that. He leaned on the balcony railing, and dangled his arms over the edge. This next part he did partly because he knew he had made her angry, and he agreed with Taylor: she had to leave Whale Rock. She was too unpredictable. Retsler was afraid she would try to break into Taylor's house again. If she got near that teenage boy, her own life might be in danger.

"I've also learned that you're presenting yourself as an employee of the Marine Science Center, and asking for privileges due to your position."

"I am—"

"You were," he said. "I found out about the dismissal. You're bordering on fraud, Ms. Selvado. I'll look at your actions as a simple misunderstanding right now, but any more of it, and I'll have to inform the Newport police."

She whirled toward him, her liquid eyes full of fire. There was a power to her, like the sea the day before a storm. "You wouldn't."

"I have to, Ms. Selvado."

"Taylor put you up to this."

"No." Retsler sighed. He would give her this next because he had to give her something, and then he would ask her to leave. "I'm dealing with Taylor in my own fashion. I'm trying to make a case against his son. I'm pretty sure the boy is the one who slaughtered that pup."

"Pretty sure?"

He held out his hands. "Meaning I'm convinced the boy's the one we want. I simply have to prove it. So if you'll leave me to my work, maybe I'll be able to help you."

"Bargain the boy's freedom for the pelts?"

"No," Retsler said. "I think the boy's too dangerous for that."

"Then what?"

"I'm not sure yet," he said, and felt the emptiness of his promise. "But I'll do the best I can."

"By asking me to leave town?" she asked.

"It's a start," he said.

"For you perhaps." Then she paused. The ocean was a deep clear blue. The sunshine this early in January was unusual, and welcome. She stared at it as if it gave her an idea. "And maybe for me as well."

The next morning brought a spate of strange calls: boats all over the coastline and up the river had been damaged, not badly enough to ruin them, but enough to prevent anyone from going on the ocean that day. At a dock near Hoover Village, one old fisherman claimed he saw a group of seals nudging a hole in the hull of his boat, then moving to his neighbor's boat at the next mooring. Retsler had to call his entire staff in to meet the workload of examining each and every boat, and Lucy had the volunteer firemen help as well.

Retsler was so busy, he missed what later turned out to be the most important calls of the day.

Hotel patrons of the Sandcastle lit up the emergency lines with a gruesome tale: a dark-haired woman, bleeding from both arms, dove off her balcony into the sea.

When Retsler finally got the page, he knew at once who had died. Maria Selvado. And he had felt a chill. He went over to the Sandcastle, and demanded to be let into her room.

The door was locked from the inside. A bloody knife sat on the back of the toilet. The bathroom floor was covered with blood. The trail led to the balcony. There was only one set of footprints— women's size six, flat footed (no arch) with webs between the toes. They ended at the railing, although there were bloody handprints on the iron, and another splotch of blood on the top of the concrete breaker.

The body below was gone, taken by the rising tide, returned to the sea.

On the fireplace mantel was a note addressed to Retsler. It said, simply: *When the laws of man fail, we rely on the laws of God.* And it was signed with an M.

The storm came an hour later, at high tide. Intense and furious, it concentrated on Hoover Bay, the Dee River, and Whale Rock. The rest of the coast had delicious sun and a perfect January day. In Whale Rock, sustained winds of 100 miles per hour ripped the roof off a gas station, tore down several signs, and knocked out power to half the town. Waves crossed the concrete breaker and smashed into the Sandcastle Hotel, destroying it as if it were made of paper.

Retsler had ordered an emergency evacuation of all low-lying areas, even though the National Weather Service swore that the satellite pictures showed no storm system in the vicinity. He had the radio and TV stations broadcast warnings, ordering everyone to high ground, to places that could survive winds, to places of safety. And because he was trusted, the town listened.

Someone later said that the storm would have caused a lot more destruction if it weren't for Retsler's clear thinking. Later they would call him a hero because he had saved hundreds of lives. That only two were lost in a freak storm, the governor would say, was miraculous. But Retsler knew better. He knew, the moment he saw the blood, how he had failed.

Denne stood, a shadow in the growing darkness. He picked up the McDonald's bag and shoved his Styrofoam cup into it. Then he walked around the boat to Retsler.

"You've ruined those clothes," Retsler said, avoiding, knowing that he was avoiding. He shut off his flashlight, listening to the calm ocean in the distance, the gurgle of the river behind him. In the darkness, the cloying stink of the mud was almost overpowering. "The wife'll be mad."

"The wife isn't entitled to an opinion anymore," Denne said. "New Year's resolution."

"You can't stop a woman from having an opinion."

"You can when you move out." Denne turned on his own flashlight. The beam illuminated the mud before them, and the footprints that led up to the Taylor's log house. He put a hand on Retsler's back. "You can't avoid this forever, Danny."

"I'm no sure I want to see this in the dark."

"It won't be any better in the light."

Denne led the way down the path that, twenty-four hours before, had been covered with greenery and winter flowers. He mounted the stairs to the main level.

The windows were gone, the door off its hinges. The water damage was so severe that the rough-hewn logs looked as if they'd been polished smooth.

Denne ducked inside. He shone a light toward the fireplace. It took a moment for Retsler's eyes to adjust. The light was reflecting off the glass on the case. He stepped away from the beam and peered inside.

Roman Taylor had been crammed into the square space, his arms and legs held in place by some wickedly tight knots. It didn't take a degree in forensic medicine to know that the man had been alive when he had been tied down. The water mark was two inches below the ceiling, and there was mud in the bottom of the case.

Mercifully, Denne moved the light. Retsler didn't use his.

"I'll photograph all of this tomorrow," Denne said.

"There's no need," Retsler said. "He drowned."

Denne looked sharply at him.

Retsler shrugged. "Who am I going to charge?"

"You might want to wait until you see the rest." Denne led him down the stairs into the daylight basement. In the corner, someone had stuck a log into the floor. It looked like one of the mooring posts that littered the river. On it, Taylor's son Michael—or what was left of him—stared balefully at them.

Retsler swallowed hard to keep down the bile. He recognized the position—recognized everything, in fact, right down to the expression on Michael's face.

The dog. That was how they had found the dog.

Denne raised his flashlight beam. It caught on a knife stuck into the pole. The knife was serrated and used for gutting animals. The handle was ivory, and engraved on it, was this: *Michael Taylor. Happy 13th Birthday. Love, Dad.*

"Is it our knife?" Retsler asked.

"No doubt about it," Denne said.

Retsler closed his eyes. He would have had the proof he needed after all. Damn him for talking to Selvado. Damn him and his worries about a conviction. Damn him, and the lack of respect he had for his own abilities.

"Of course," Denne said slowly, "any good lawyer could make hash of a case based on one single knife."

"Really?" Retsler asked.

"I think so," Denne said. He took one more glance at the body. "And I don't think I was alone in that belief."

"Millions of dollars in damage," Retsler said. "Lives ruined. Two deaths. Because of me and my mouth."

"You didn't start this," Denne said.

"But I should have ended it," Retsler said. He sighed and sloshed his way back to the stairs. "Next time, I trust Lucy."

"Next time?" Denne asked, following him. "Let's hope to God there is no next time."

But there would be, Retsler knew. As long as Whale Rock was here, as long as strange things happened, there would be another clash between the humans and the strange creatures that lived in the sea. He only hoped that the next time, he would try some cooperation, maybe learn how to bend the laws of man, so that no one had to rely on the laws of God.

THE LIGHT IN WHALE COVE

THE LIGHT IN WHALE COVE

Dan Retsler ripped the packing tape from the tape gun and tossed the thing aside. Useless. Completely useless. He was better off using fingers and teeth to put tape on his boxes. The tape gun jammed and twisted every time he tried to use it.

He sealed the box on his desk, got his finger wrapped in tape, and finally reached across the box to grab the scissors. He managed to cut himself free, then he cursed and tossed the tape in the same direction as the tape gun.

Outside his office, in the front reception area, Lucy swiveled her seat so that she could look at him through the glass window. The police station had once been a retail store and still looked like it. The only office had a large window so that the retail manager could keep an eye on the stock. The last thing Retsler, Whale Rock's police chief for another three weeks, wanted was his staff laughing at his attempts to pack. He stepped over a pile of boxes, walked to the window, and pulled the blinds closed.

Then he sank onto the pile, hearing the cardboard groan beneath his weight. He hated packing almost as much as he hated moving. But he had been excited about the new job and still was, despite the pain-in-the-ass transition.

He was going to be police chief in a Montana town not much bigger than Whale Rock. Only his new police station had a view of the Bitterroot Mountains, not Highway 101, and the police logs were filled with nothing more severe than shoplifting. It would be a relief to go to a place where the dispatcher hadn't known him since he was in diapers, where the only people who came to town were the occasional hunter instead of hordes of tourists determined to see the Pacific Ocean, and where there were no supernatural occurrences.

Retsler sighed and scanned his office. Maybe he didn't need all this junk. Maybe he'd just leave it for his successor. Jaclyn Tadero was an extremely capable woman who had been hired over his protests. The female city council members had accused him of sexism, but he hadn't opposed Tadero because she was a woman.

He had opposed her because she had never lived in a small town. She had never worked on a small force. She didn't understand the politics or the dynamics, and no matter what the city council said, it was politics and dynamics that made this job work, not experience with high-powered murder investigations.

Outside, the dispatch rang and Lucy answered. He could hear her voice but not what she was saying. Still he strained to catch a word or two. Old habits die hard.

When the murmur of her voice stopped, he stood. He didn't want Lucy to catch him moping. He walked over to the corner to pick up the tape gun. He was trying to shove the tape roll back on it as Lucy pushed open his door.

She had looked the same since he was a little boy, her curly gray hair worn in a short cap over her grandmotherly face. Despite her all-American cuteness, she was ex-military and tough, with a voice so deep that it growled.

"Where's Jaclyn?" she asked.

Retsler shrugged. "Eddie was going to take her to the outlying areas, but that was hours ago. I have no idea where they are now. Why?"

"We just got a call. We got a dead body at the lighthouse."

Retsler set down his tape gun. "I'll take it."

"She needs to go."

He glared at Lucy. "I still have three weeks on the payroll. No matter what anyone says, I haven't lost my abilities to do the job."

"I wasn't questioning your abilities. You just need to take her with you."

This was why he had to leave. Technically Lucy worked for him, but it never turned out that way. She still had an adult's authority over him, as if he were a child instead a middle-aged man.

"Why do I need to take her along?" Retsler asked.

"Because she has to learn this part of her job now."

"What part?" he asked.

Lucy raised her eyebrows. "You don't know?"

"Obviously not," he said, straining to keep his frustration under control.

"Whale Cove Lighthouse is haunted."

The first winter storm of the season was blowing in. Retsler's car was old and heavy, but not up to the gale force winds cutting across the highway. Rain came down in horizontal sheets and his windshield wipers, set on high, barely cleared the water enough for him to see. It was midday but the sky was black.

He hadn't seen a storm like this since the Dee flooded eleven months ago. He had hoped to be gone before the storm season hit, but he had promised to stay and train Tadero, and she hadn't been able to leave the Chicago force until the middle of November. She had driven across the country alone and arrived here on Thanksgiving.

The car slid sideways on the road, and he twisted the wheel to return to his lane. He slowed down. He hadn't been paying enough attention. There was at least three inches of water on the road. At the speed he'd been going, he was probably hydroplaning.

He wondered what Tadero thought of the storm. She had said nothing could be worse than a Chicago cold snap, but she'd never experienced a winter on the Oregon Coast. Winters here usually drove people back to where they had come from, vowing they would never return.

The road dipped. Waves crested over the guardrail, covering his windshield with spray. He slowed down even more. With the spray, the darkness, and the driving rain, he couldn't even see the headland, jutting out into the Pacific. Usually, Evergreen Cliff was the most prominent feature of this part of the coast, and the old lighthouse on top of it looked like a beacon, even though its beacon had been dark for nearly half a century.

On a day like this, the light would actually be a blessing.

With some difficulty—surprising considering he'd grown up here —he found the road that led to the lighthouse. The road had been rebuilt during the summer so that the construction crews would have no trouble getting their heavy vehicles onto Evergreen Cliff.

The lighthouse, which was on the National Register of Historic Places, was being put back into service. After the dedication ceremony on December 15th, its light would once again steer ships safely into Whale Rock's harbor.

Apparently it had taken a lot of internal work to get the light-house functioning again. And the work wasn't done yet. There was some talk among council members that the light wouldn't be ready for the ceremony, which was only two short weeks away.

Lighthouse Road was even more treacherous than the highway had been. The new asphalt was black and almost impossible to see. He hugged the cliffside as he drove, trying to stay as far away from the guardrail on his left as possible.

It was with great relief that he finally reached the Visitor's Center on the south side of the hill. But the Center was dark and obviously empty. A van was parked behind the dumpster, obviously in employee parking. A decrepit one-ton pickup, covered with rust and missing its back fender, was parked haphazardly near the path.

Apparently, the coroner, Hamilton Denne, had already arrived.

Retsler pulled up next to the pickup and got out of his car, yanking his dark green rain slicker hood over his head. The rain pelted him, big thick drops made lethal by the wind. His slicker flapped around him and his face was raw within seconds.

He glanced at the path, which wound around the mountainside, and shook his head slightly. He knew the state had paved the path and put a stone railing along the side, but it still didn't look safe, especially in this weather. But he couldn't turn back now, not after snapping at Lucy and telling her he could still do his job.

The asphalt path looked like wet tar. He stepped on it, clutching the railing attached to the stone side, his hand slipping on the cold metal surface. The wind howled around him, and the surf exploded against the rocks below. The path shook beneath him.

The first storm of the season and he had to be on a headland, heading toward the lighthouse. He'd rather be walking through a Montana blizzard right now than be this close to the sea.

Over the whistle of the wind, he thought he heard a voice and a car door. He turned, saw Eddie's police car parked near his and dark shapes at the head of the path. An arm waved at him, probably asking him to wait, but he turned away.

Jaclyn Tadero could learn her business the same way he learned his—through experience. He wasn't going to coddle her. He didn't want her to get used to him. He was leaving no matter how she felt about storms or the Oregon Coast or haunted lighthouses.

Damn that Lucy, putting that idea in his head.

He rounded the corner and saw the lighthouse ahead. It was an old building—one of the oldest on the Central Coast. It had been a working lighthouse until the 1920s, when the state finally shut it down. They'd let it rot for years, then the feds declared it an historical site and someone got the bright idea of making the lighthouse a working lighthouse once again.

He made his way up the stone steps to the lighthouse proper, noting a newly built ramp on the side. As if someone in a wheelchair was going to come to this desolate place. But regulations were regulations were regulations and the Lighthouse Board had been assiduous in following them.

He ran the last few steps to the main door, and pushed it open, resisting the urge to shake himself off like a dog. Water dripping off his slicker might destroy the potential crime scene. He pulled off the slicker and set it near Denne's, on a metal chair near the door.

Denne's shoes were also there—loafers, their shine still evident despite the mud and water beading on the leather surface.

Retsler removed his own shoes, a battered pair of tennies, and set them beside Denne's. Then Retsler wiped his hands on his thighs and headed inside.

The base of the lighthouse was wide. Windows facing the sea let in some light, although not enough on a gray day like this one. The entry had flyers and brochures, as well as the standard tourist information. Two tables and a chair were pushed off to the side, as well as a small booth with a phone and emergency equipment.

Farther inside were the stairs, reinforced metal now, but curving like they had been in the original plans, disappearing toward the lighthouse's narrow top.

Voices echoed down them, speaking softly, the words indistinguishable thanks to the overlap of the echo. It almost sounded as if dozens of people were whispering all at once.

A shiver ran down Retsler's back and he concentrated on the one voice he recognized—Denne's. Retsler went to the base of the stairs and looked up. They curved all the way to the top, but the state had built several landings so that the tourists who visited this place could rest. The light was at the very top on a level all its own. He couldn't see that, only the white painted metal protecting it.

An arm hung off one of the landings. Shadows indicated Denne's presence and possibly that of one other person.

Then the door blew open and a woman stepped in. Jaclyn Tadero, slight, muscular, her hair plastered to her face. Her raincoat was soaked through, as were her jeans and tennis shoes. Her dark eyes met his, daring him to comment.

He looked away.

Eddie staggered in, his rain slicker almost an obscene yellow. He had to push hard to get the door to close, and when it did, he leaned against it.

"Why can't people die on sunny days?" he said.

Tadero glared at him, but Retsler nodded. The levity was necessary, especially given the tension inherent in the situation.

"Where's the body?" Her voice was a rich soprano. It would have been beautiful if it weren't for her accent. Hers was a thick Chicago accent, a mixture of Norwegian consonants and Polish vowels, flat and almost nasal.

It grated on Retsler as much as her glare had.

"Don't know," he said, working at nonchalance. "Just got here myself."

She started forward and he held out a hand to stop her.

"You'll drip on the crime scene."

She cursed and stopped moving. "What do you suggest? I'm soaked."

"Give me a minute," he said. "Let's see how far down the scene extends."

"I thought your crime scene unit was already here. They probably have everything they need."

"The crime scene unit," he said as patiently as he could, "is composed of you, me, Eddie, and the coroner who is upstairs now. We don't have enough people on the force to do all that fancy work."

He had explained that to her during her interview and he had thought she understood. But apparently she hadn't.

"I thought we had use of the state's criminologists."

"We do," he said, "if we request them in time. We have no idea what we're facing here, so I haven't requested anyone. Have you?"

That last was more sarcastic than he wanted it to be. She frowned at him and turned away, wiping at her face with the back of her hand. Eddie was pulling off his rain slicker. He was dry underneath.

Retsler didn't wait for them. He mounted the metal stairs, examining each one before he put his foot down, so that he didn't contaminate more than necessary.

"I hope to God that's you, Dan." Denne's voice, stronger this time, floated down to him.

"It's me," Retsler said. "Have you done the stairs?"

"No," Denne said. "I just got here a few minutes ago."

Retsler sighed softly and continued to curve up the circular staircase. As he got closer to Denne's voice, he saw more of the arm, pale and limp, hanging over the edge as if it were reaching for something below.

"You alone?" Retsler asked.

"Clay Emory is with me. He was here when it happened." Denne sounded as unflappable as usual. The man could view anything and remain unshaken. Even last year, during the worst disaster Retsler ever experienced, Denne remained calm.

Retsler rounded the last corner in the stairway before reaching the landing. Emory sat on the next set of stairs going up, his elbows resting on his thighs. He was a big man who had lived in the area all of his life. He wore a Coast Electrics cap over his balding head, and light brown work coveralls, stained with grease. His face, normally tan from the western sun, was unnaturally pale.

He didn't even acknowledge Retsler's arrival. Instead, he stared at the body on the landing as if he could will it away.

Retsler looked at the body too. It belonged to a woman. Her face was turned away from him. She had long brown hair, which trailed through the diamond-shaped metal pattern that made up the landing. Her arm was extended, just as he had noticed from below. The rest of her body was twisted away from the arm, curled in a partial fetal position.

He couldn't immediately tell what killed her.

Denne was crouched by her head, his back to Emory, his camera on the step near his left hand. His bag was open against the wall. He looked dapper as always, even though he had been trying to dress down since he separated from his wife. His sweatshirt, with its Harvard logo, looked pressed, and the white collar of a shirt stuck out from beneath it. His jeans were damp from the storm, but they too looked pressed. Even his bare feet looked manicured.

Retsler's were merely cold.

He stepped on the edge of the landing, not willing to go farther—at least not yet. "What'd you find?"

Denne gave Retsler a quick unreadable glance, then looked down. "I'd say she tripped and fell down the stairs."

After all these years, Retsler was familiar with Denne's way of making a point. "Except?"

With a slight movement of his right hand, Denne beckoned Retsler forward. He nodded toward the face.

Retsler caught his breath. It was Pippa Gage. Her features were slack in death, but there were long black markings on each cheek, as if someone had taken a charcoal pencil and drawn lines across her face.

"What's that?" Retsler asked as he crouched beside Denne.

Denne pointed to her clothes. They too were stained with black.

"So what is it?" Retsler asked.

Denne shrugged and was about to answer when someone else spoke.

"I don't think you should be discussing this in front of the witness."

Retsler didn't have to look up to recognize that voice. Jaclyn Tadero had finally made it up the stairs. Still, when he did look up, he made certain his expression was cool. This was his investigation. She was just here to learn.

He would remind her of that when they returned to the station.

She was standing on the top step, hanging tightly to the railing with her left hand. She had pulled her hair away from her face and tucked it into the back of her shirt so that the strands wouldn't drip on the crime scene. She too had removed her shoes. Her mascara had run, making her look like a tired raccoon.

Denne was the one who answered her. "We don't have much of a choice. Even if we asked Clay to go upstairs or down, he'd still hear everything. In case you hadn't noticed, this place has a hell of an echo."

"You know this man?" Her voice was harsh.

Retsler gave her a small smile. "This is a small town, Jaclyn. You'll have to get used to that."

She glared at him. She knew that he had opposed her hire, and she knew he had opposed it because he thought she couldn't handle small town life.

"Clay Emory," Retsler said, "meet Whale Rock's new police chief as of the first of the year. This is Jaclyn Tadero."

Emory raised his head and touched the bill of his cap, then refocused his attention on Gage.

"He been like that the whole time?" Retsler asked Denne quietly.

Denne nodded.

"You about done here?"

"Yeah." Denne reached for his camera. "I have the scene photos to shoot, and then I'll be ready to take her to the morgue."

"Your crew is going to have to be very careful," Tadero said. "That storm will wash away a lot of evidence if you don't have the bag sealed right."

Denne's eyes narrowed as he studied her. He didn't seem to like her much either. He watched her as he shouted, "Eddie! You think you can get the bag and gurney from my truck all by yourself?"

Retsler suppressed a smile. Tadero was certainly getting her education this afternoon.

"Not in this wind, Hamilton," Eddie said. "It's going to take at least two of us. And we might be better off without the gurney. A shoulder carry might work better."

Denne tested the body's arm. Rigor hadn't set in yet. "Okay. I'll do a few things before you get to that. If you don't mind bringing the bag."

"If I'd thought of it, I'd've brought it with me," Eddie said. "I don't relish going out there again."

Retsler thought of the steep edge and the slick asphalt. None of them were safe in this kind of storm.

"Go with him," he said to Tadero.

"You heard him," she said. "He can do this."

"I know. But I don't want any of us alone on this headland."

"Why?" she asked. "What do you think happened?"

She was thinking about the body. She had no idea how dangerous these storms were, how the coast killed dozens of tourists every year because they weren't cautious enough when they faced Mother Nature's wrath.

"I think the storm's too severe for anyone to be alone," he said.

She glanced at the window. The wind wasn't even audible. He could feel her reluctance. She was ready to do the hands-on police work. Hell, she'd had five times as much experience with dead bodies as he'd had. He might actually have let her do the work if it weren't for Lucy's comment about the lighthouse being haunted.

He'd ignored comments like that from Lucy twice in the past. The first time it might have gotten a friend killed. The second time, it had cost two people their lives and destroyed most of the trailers along the Dee.

"How long will this storm last?" Tadero asked.

"A day, maybe two. Why?"

She shrugged. "I thought maybe we could wait it out, but it doesn't sound like we can."

"No, we can't," Retsler said.

"Then make sure you get all the evidence you can while you're here." She said that last to Denne, as if he had never worked a crime scene before, and then thumped down the stairs.

Denne rolled his eyes. "Remind me to sit on more committees."

"Wouldn't have made any difference," Retsler said. "Then there would have been two of us who disapproved. Not a majority by a long shot."

Denne nodded and continued his work. Retsler turned his attention to the corpse of an old friend.

What had she been doing here? Pippa Gage had hated heights. The views out of these windows would have paralyzed her. Even if she could have ignored those, the open banisters would have made it impossible for her to miss the distance to the floor below.

He wished dead faces registered their last emotions, like they did in detective novels. He wanted to know how Pippa had been feeling when she died. Or maybe he didn't. Pippa had been a gentle soul who didn't deserve to die in fear.

Retsler looked up at Clay Emory. Emory was still staring at her body, his expression so full of regret that Retsler could almost feel it himself.

"Clay," he said, "you want to tell me what happened?"

Emory didn't move.

"Clay," Denne said.

Then Emory raised his head, like a man who had just come out of a very deep sleep.

"The chief asked you a question."

"Sorry." Emory's voice was deep and slow. Raspier than usual, as if he had a cold or as if he had been talking a lot.

Retsler wasn't going to get anything out of him up here, not with Pippa's body so close. "Come on downstairs. You can tell me what you saw."

Emory's head shook just slightly. Retsler couldn't tell if he didn't want to talk or if he were already answering an unspoken question.

"Come on," Denne said softly. "I'll help you around."

Emory reached behind himself for the banister, hand shaking. He pulled himself up, looking back down on Pippa. This time his head shake was noticeable. "She really is dead, isn't she?"

Retsler realized what he'd heard as hoarseness was actually with-held tears. "Yes," he said.

Denne shot Retsler an uncomfortable glance, then walked over to Emory. Denne extended his gloved hand.

"Come on, Clay," he said. "Let's get you downstairs."

Emory gripped Denne's hand the way a child would grip a parent's. He let Denne lead him around the body, and then, when they reached Retsler, Emory finally moved on his own.

His eyes were swimming with tears. "You know, it's so weird. One minute you're talking to somebody. You can feel them. You know they're there. Then the next minute—"

His voice broke.

Denne still stood behind him, blocking him from the body. Retsler stepped aside so that Emory could start down the stairs. Emory grabbed the banister and started down, his knuckles white against the metal. Retsler followed and Denne returned to the crime scene to finish the small details he had left.

The light at the base of the stairs seemed dimmer. It took a moment for Retsler to realize that was because the storm was directly overhead. The natural light which came in through the windows above was fading. The artificial light had a greenish gray quality to it, like institution lighting—the kind found in big city police stations and the waiting rooms of prisons.

His coat still dripped near the door, his shoes getting soaked beneath it. There were footprints near the exit, probably from Eddie and Tadero.

Retsler grabbed one of the old wooden captain's chairs leaning against the wall and set it in the small alcove behind the stairs. He helped Emory into that chair, then grabbed another for himself.

"What happened up there, Clay?" he asked.

Emory tilted his head back as if he could make the tears recede into his eyes. He sighed, then swiped at his face with the back of his hand.

"I was working," he said after a moment. "Finishing the light. They've all updated everything. It's computerized now. Inside a casing, ready to go. Won't need anyone to babysit it any more. Kinda strange, huh?"

Retsler made a sympathetic sound, but didn't say anything more. Clay Emory was not a talkative man under the best of circumstances. Interrupting him now could possibly stop him permanently.

"We were gonna test it before it got dark because no one's supposed to see the light before the grand opening on the 15th. But we had to make sure it worked. The storm was rolling in and Pippa wanted me to hurry. She was afraid when the clouds hit, the entire county would see the light shining off the waves."

Retsler nodded, waiting. He still found it surprising that Pippa was here.

"Pippa, she didn't like the idea of being in the lighthouse when the storm hit." Emory's voice broke again and he brought his head forward, wiping at his eyes some more. "Ah, shit, Dan. I can't do this. I—"

"Take your time," Retsler said.

"But she wouldn't've been here if I hadn't asked her to come. I thought maybe she and me—we were—" Emory stopped all by himself, put his face in his hands, his shoulders shuddering.

Retsler watched him, coming to the realization all on his own. They were having an affair. Amazing how much he knew about this town and yet how little.

He put his hand on Emory's back, felt shudders run through the man. "Just tell me what happened."

"You're not gonna tell Paula, are you?" Paula was Emory's wife.

"Not if I don't have to," Retsler said. "But she might wonder what Pippa was doing here. Everyone knew she was afraid of heights."

"I did that." Emory sat up. He was calm now, as if he'd reached a different state. "I told her she could get past the fears if she just confronted them. We'd been working on it. The stairs first, then places like the path to the lighthouse. She was going to help me finish the light, and then as a reward for staying so high, we were going to…"

His voice trailed off, but the implication was clear.

"Something got in the way?" Retsler asked.

Emory nodded. "Damn light."

"What happened with the light?"

Emory looked at him, eyes flat. "You wouldn't believe me if I told you."

A shiver ran through Retsler. Maybe he wouldn't have five years ago. But he believed most things now. That was one reason he had to leave Whale Rock.

"Try me," Retsler said.

Emory lowered his head and stared at his callused hands. He spoke slowly, measuring his words. "We turned on the light, and for a moment, it was glorious. It worked right. It turned like it was supposed to. It made that little electric hum which meant everything was working properly…"

He brought his hands to his face. Retsler didn't move. He figured he had only one chance at this.

"Then—things—swarmed toward us from the ocean. I saw them coming, under the clouds. Pippa, she said the air had gotten sharp, charged, like it did before a lightning strike. She begged me to turn the light off, and just as I did, the door banged open—"

A bang echoed through the lighthouse, and Retsler jumped. Emory rose out of his chair, his hands before him, as if he were protecting himself.

Retsler turned. It was just Eddie and Tadero, coming back with the bag. They struggled with the door in the wind, pushing it shut. They set the bag on the floor near Retsler's shoes, then pulled off their wet coats. The bag wasn't as wet as they were; someone must have covered it.

"This is normal weather?" Tadero asked, wringing out her hair.

"Welcome to winter," Eddie said.

Retsler watched them, arms crossed. Tadero glanced his way, saw that he was talking with Emory, and her lips thinned. Emory was still standing, his hands before him like a shield.

Eddie called up the stairs, "You ready for the bag, Hamilton?"

"Ready as I can be," Denne said.

"C'mon," Eddie said to Tadero. They hurried past Retsler and started up the stairs.

"It's all right," Retsler said softly, hoping that Emory would take his cue and lower his voice as well. "What happened next?"

"I—I don't know."

"What do you mean?" Retsler asked.

"The door banged open, and Pippa laughed, you know, nervous, like people do. She said it must have been the wind, and she went down to close it. I told her not to, but she really wanted to go down those stairs, away from being so high, if you know what I mean."

Retsler did. Being startled had probably made Pippa's fear of heights worse.

"She started down the stairs, and then she screamed and then…" Emory shook his head.

"And then?" Retsler prompted.

"There was this big crash." Emory was whispering now. "I went down the stairs and I found her. There was nothing I could do. I finally sat on the steps and got my phone out of my pocket and I called—"

His voice broke and the tears swam in his eyes again. "How am I gonna tell Paula. And everybody. What am I going to say?"

Retsler hated this part of his job. "I don't know, Clay."

There was clanging above them as Denne bagged the body. Emory closed his eyes, as if that would shut out the sound.

"Come on, Clay," Retsler said. "Let me drive you home."

"I need my van."

"You can come back for it. You're not in any shape to drive."

Emory nodded. Retsler glanced at the stairs. He was surprised to find Tadero looking at him.

"You're not going to let him go, are you?" she asked.

Retsler decided he wasn't even going to dignify her question with an answer. "Meet me at the False Colors. Make sure Eddie and Hamilton come."

"This is not the time to go to a bar."

"Jaclyn," he said, "you're not in Chicago any more. For the next few weeks, you're doing things my way or you're not participating at all. Is that clear?"

"Unfortunately," she said, and watched, disapproval evident, as he led Emory to the door.

It was clear from the moment Tadero entered the False Colors that she had never been inside the restaurant before. Retsler leaned back in his wooden captain's chair and watched her. She ran her hands over the rope banister, and looked up at the skulls above the bar.

The sea chantey on the sound system was something about death and rum. Tadero stopped in front of the black and white photographs of wrecked ships lining the walls, made a face, and then looked for Retsler.

He was sitting at their usual table, Lucy studying the menu beside him. Eddie had already arrived, saying that Denne would come as soon as he finished preparing the body.

Tadero had changed out of her wet clothes into a cable knit sweater and a pair of tight jeans. Her hair was down, curving around her face, softening the angles. From this distance she looked younger than she was, younger and less sure of herself.

For the first time, Retsler wondered why a career detective on the promotion path decided to leave Chicago. He hadn't really thought about how unusual it was before.

She finally saw them and came down the worn wooden steps, walking past the huge fireplace as if it didn't exist. Retsler was amazed. Both he and Eddie had stopped to warm their hands before coming to the table.

"Charming place," Tadero said as she slipped into an empty chair.

"Tourists hate it." Lucy pulled a cigar from her pocket. "So we feel safe here."

Tadero shot her a strange glance. Lucy put the cigar in her mouth and Eddie lit it for her.

"Is this the smoking section?" Tadero asked pointedly.

"It is now," Lucy said.

June, the waitress, handed Tadero a menu, then, behind Tadero's back, raised her eyes in question. Retsler gave her a half smile. "Junie, meet our new police chief as of January."

Tadero looked up in surprise, obviously not used to conversing with waitresses. They gave each other an uncomfortable hello, and then Tadero studied the menu, clearly dismissing June.

"All right, Lucy," Retsler said. "I don't want to wait for Hamilton. Tell me now so I know what the hell I'm dealing with."

"You really should know the history of Whale Rock by now," Lucy said.

"I'm trying to put it out of my mind," Retsler said.

"So he has more room for the history of Buttfuck, Montana," Eddie said, holding his longneck between his index and middle fingers.

Retsler didn't even try to correct him. Eddie knew the name of Retsler's new town, and still insisted on his crude version. Eddie had made it clear from the very beginning that he was opposed to Retsler's move.

Tadero set her menu down. "What are we talking about?"

"The lighthouse." Lucy puffed her cigar. It had a foul odor. Retsler made a mental note to buy her an expensive box before he left.

"Why would its history be important?" Tadero asked.

"You didn't tell her, did you?" Lucy said.

Retsler shrugged. "Not my place."

Lucy set the cigar on the ashtray shaped like a skull and crossbones. "It is your place. You have to give her the tools to work around here."

"Tools?" Tadero said.

"She'll learn fast enough." Retsler smiled at June, who had returned with his shrimp cocktail. June set the appetizer down, took the other orders, and then left. She knew better than to hang around when the entire police department showed up to talk shop.

"The lighthouse," Lucy said, "is one of the oldest structures on this part of the coast. There've been problems from the beginning."

"What has this to do with Pippa Gage?" Tadero asked.

"You probably shouldn't have told her to come here," Eddie said to Retsler, then took a swig of his beer.

"She has to learn sometime," Retsler said. "May as well be now."

"Learn what?"

Denne had arrived. He too had changed clothes. He was wearing pressed jeans with a corduroy jacket over a buttoned down shirt. As he passed the bar, he stopped to order a drink.

"The first lighthouse keeper," Lucy said as if she hadn't been interrupted, "started a fire his first winter there. It burned the stairs and the interior pretty badly. He died, of course—at least everyone assumes it was him. The body was unrecognizable. His wife saw the flames and smoke pouring out of the lighthouse, but she couldn't do anything. In those days, they were too far away from anywhere."

"So it has a bad history," Tadero said.

"Just listen," Retsler said, even though he doubted she would.

Lucy took a shrimp off Retsler's plate. "About 1890, a group of spiritualists settled Whale Rock. They were told by one of their ghostly guides that this place had a special power."

"No shit," Eddie said.

"They held séances, and mapped out Whale Rock. They used the lighthouse as their base, since no one else would work there, not after that hideous death. They rebuilt the stairs and the light, and kept the ships safe out at sea."

"Spiritualists?" Retsler asked. "I thought that was an East Coast phenomenon."

"Technically, it was," Lucy said. "But there were some all over the country."

"And remember," Denne said as he sat down, "Astoria was named after John Jacob Astor. He sent a lot of people here to look after his interests. In those days, there was a strong Eastern contingent on this coast."

"You know this story?" Retsler asked, but without surprise. Denne seemed to know the entire history of the coast.

"Having only heard that last part, I'm not sure," Denne said. "But I have heard that the lighthouse is haunted. At the closed door meetings about the reopenings, there was a lot of discussion about that."

"Excuse me," Tadero said. "People believe in that crap?"

Everyone at the table stared at her. Retsler remembered what such disbelief felt like, but dispassionately, the way he remembered what it felt like to learn his multiplication tables. But with all the group had been through—the January storm sparked by a curse placed on the town by a selkie, a curse Retsler could have prevented; the mermaids that still haunted the beaches; the seventy-year-old bodies that the sea still regurgitated from time to time—they had little tolerance for someone who didn't believe.

At that moment, June brought their meals. She set the plates down as if they weren't hot at all.

"Come on," Tadero said, breaking the code that no one spoke about business before June. "You're not telling me you think ghosts killed her."

"You guys talking about Pippa?" June asked.

News traveled fast in a small town. Only Tadero seemed surprised that June knew about the death.

"After what happened to those hippies, I'm amazed anyone's allowed in the lighthouse. I've thought they were crazy to reopen it. I was with the committee that wanted to tear the whole thing down and start from scratch."

"Hippies?" Retsler looked at Lucy.

"You should remember that, Dan. You were living here then."

"I was a little boy. My mother sheltered me from all bad things," he said. "Unless this was somewhat recent?"

"No," June said. "1970-something. Pretty ugly. I don't remember the details, just that people couldn't believe no one warned them."

"Warned them about what?" Eddie asked. He was too young to remember anything that happened in 1970-something.

"Not to have a séance up there," June said. At that moment, a bell dinged in the back and she left.

"You people are crazy," Tadero said.

"Certifiable," Denne said agreeably, and Retsler got a sense of how the man had survived in that awful marriage for so long.

"You expect me to believe that a woman died because of ghosts?" Tadero asked.

"No," Denne said. "We expect you to believe she died because she fell down a flight of stairs."

"Because she was pushed," Tadero said. "And what about those marks on her face?"

"What did they look like?" Retsler couldn't resist asking her. He slid the shrimp plate to Lucy and then started in on his crab-stuffed halibut.

"Scorch—" Tadero cut herself off and, to Retsler's surprise, she flushed.

"Go ahead," Eddie said. "It's okay to say scorch marks."

"But that's not possible," Tadero said.

"Wasn't it Sherlock Holmes who said when you eliminate the possible, that leaves only the impossible?" Denne asked.

"Right," Tadero said, taking a bite from her salmon burger. "We should base this entire investigation on our belief in ghosts and the advice of a fictional character."

"We're so refreshingly small town, aren't we?" Lucy asked, without a smile on her face. "You can look down your nose so easily at us because we don't have the benefit of your big city education. Did you ever think that maybe we know Whale Rock better than you do?"

"Did you ever think that crime scene analysis should be about science, not superstition?" Tadero asked.

"The first rule of any investigation," Denne said with an edge in his voice, "is to examine the evidence without preconceptions. You're assuming that a crime has been committed."

Retsler's halibut was sweet and fresh. He was content to eat it and let the others argue with Tadero for a change.

"The man was alone with her in the lighthouse. They were having an affair, if what Eddie tells me is true. They fight, he gets rough, pushes her, and that's the end of it," Tadero said. "Open and shut."

"Except for the fact that you have no evidence of that," Denne said.

"I haven't looked through the evidence yet," Tadero said. "First rule of investigation: the eyewitness should be your first suspect."

"If there's something to suspect," Denne said.

"She's young and she's dead, isn't she?" Tadero said. "That's a suspicious death."

Retsler finished the halibut and started on his plank potatoes. He glanced around the restaurant. No one sat close enough to hear the conversation.

"Okay," Denne said. "Let's pretend we like your theory. How'd she get the—what did you call them?—scorch marks?"

"You tell me," Tadero said. "You're the coroner."

"It's your theory," Denne said.

"Well, I can tell you that they weren't caused by a ghostly presence," Tadero said.

"You're sure?" Lucy asked.

"Positive," Tadero said.

"You want to lay some money down on that?" Lucy asked.

Retsler set his fork down. Eddie gave him a small secret grin. Lucy never made a bet she wasn't certain of winning.

Tadero looked at Lucy. "You've got a bet."

"How much?" Lucy asked.

"How much can you afford to lose?"

Lucy grinned. "A lot more than you can."

"I can't believe I'm going to bet on this," Tadero said, almost to herself.

"Neither can I," Retsler said.

She glared at him. "Fifty bucks."

Eddie whistled. Lucy said, "You want to make that a hundred?"

Tadero frowned. "No. I'll have enough trouble taking your money as it is."

"Have you thought about how you're going to prove this?" Denne asked her.

"I'm going to solve this crime using science," Tadero said. "Then there won't be any more talk about ghosts on my watch."

Lucy laughed. "I love it when they're young and idealistic," she said and picked up her cigar.

After Tadero left, Denne ordered a second Alaskan Amber. "She's going to be a problem," he said.

"Nonsense." Lucy had put out her cigar. "Dan didn't believe for years and he grew up here. He's done all right."

Retsler said nothing. Now that he believed that there were supernatural things that gathered in Whale Rock, he was leaving. His lack of belief, his unwillingness to look at the supernatural—even after he learned of its existence—had caused him to make some of the bigger mistakes of his career.

He waved off June's offer of dessert, ordered a cup of decaf, and leaned back in his chair. The room had a chill.

"So," he said to Lucy, "give me the short version of the lighthouse's history."

She sighed. "Near as anyone can figure, the lighthouse itself acts as a type of lightning rod. It draws spirits to it, but only when the light is on."

Retsler felt the threads of disbelief again. "Why when the light is on? Why not all the time?"

"The theory is that it brings souls out of the darkness. They think they're heading toward the light—you know that death light?—when instead, they're coming for the lighthouse."

"So they're angry when they get here?" Retsler asked.

Lucy shook her head. "They're just lost and confused. The only angry ghost is the lighthouse keeper. He apparently attacks, but in panic, one of the hippies said. Like he was still surrounded by flame and smoke and trying to escape."

"What about those hippies?" Retsler asked.

"They held a séance up there, long after the lighthouse had closed."

"So the light wasn't working?"

"They brought one of their own," Lucy said. "It was a big old oil lamp, like the kind they thought the lighthouse keeper would have used."

Retsler felt his stomach clench. "Then what? A fire?"

"The survivors claimed there was a fire," Lucy said. "They claimed the entire lighthouse was going up in smoke and flames, only there was no evidence of it. Everything was normal inside when investigators came."

"Except…" Eddie intoned in a deep radio announcer voice.

"Except the hippies who died were burned to death."

Retsler wrapped his hands around his mug. The ceramic was hot against his palms.

"The survivors say they tried to call the spirits of the dead from the area. They claimed they saw a lot of lost and sad sailors, and a few other folk they didn't recognize. It was the lighthouse keeper who chased the others away."

"The guy who burned to death."

"Right," Lucy said. "He gave them a warning, which they didn't listen too, and scorched one boy's face. He didn't go back, that boy. The others did, determined to put the lighthouse keeper's soul to rest."

"And they all died?"

"All but two girls who made it out. They were treated for severe smoke inhalation."

Retsler frowned. "Surely someone thought that was odd."

"Well," Lucy waved, caught June's attention, and mimed drinking a beer. "They might have if it weren't for a few things."

"Like what?" Retsler asked.

June brought Lucy a Rogue Ale.

"Like," Lucy said, "the hippies were all tourists, and they had some drugs stashed in their van."

"LSD?" Retsler asked.

"Who knows?" Lucy said.

"Pot mostly." Denne spoke for the first time since Lucy started reciting the story. "And the girls' systems were clean. I had the toxicology tests in my office for the longest time."

"This one interests you?" Retsler asked.

"This one scares me," Denne said. "We're reopening that lighthouse."

Retsler set his chair down on all four of its legs. How had he missed this argument? Probably because he had been spending all spring and summer finding a way out of Whale Rock. Probably because he felt any part of Whale Rock's future had nothing to do with him.

"So, doc," he said to Denne, "what's your professional opinion? Was Pippa pushed down those stairs?"

"It's kind of hard to tell without a witness, unless there's two large handprints outlined squarely in her back." Denne set his amber down. "I haven't done the autopsy yet, but I do know that she died of a broken neck. So her injury is consistent with a fall down the stairs."

"Bruising? Any sign of a fight?" Retsler asked.

"Just what you'd expect from a fall," Denne said.

"I went to school with Clay Emory," Eddie said. He was still nursing the same longneck he'd started with, hours ago. "There's no way he would hurt anyone."

"He was having an affair with her," Retsler said. "And that was news to me. People can surprise you."

"Not Clay. She wasn't his first and she won't be his last. Paula's a —" Eddie lowered his voice so that no one around them would overhear "—Grade A Number One bitch."

"Eddie," Denne said.

"It's true. She's a real ball-buster, and Clay's had trouble keeping it in his pants since high school."

"But you don't think he killed Pippa."

"Hell, man, have you ever seen Clay in a fight?" Eddie asked.

Retsler shook his head.

"That's my point. He wouldn't hit anyone, not even when we were doing a boxing unit in school. If someone got violent around him, he'd hide his face in his hands and cringe. If someone starts yelling, he leaves the room. I've even seen him take spiders outside instead of smashing them. This is not a man who gets angry and pushes someone down a flight of stairs."

Eddie directed this last toward Denne, as if it were Denne's fault that the accusation was even being made.

"All I said was that the bruises and the neck injury were consistent with a fall," Denne said. "I didn't say he pushed her."

"I hear a 'but' in that sentence," Retsler said.

"I haven't done the official tests yet," Denne said, "but I did some preliminary work. The streaks on Pippa's face are consistent with streaks a person gets when they're in a lot of smoke."

"What does that mean?" Retsler said.

"Think about it," Denne said. "Someone's lit a fire so close to your face that you're feeling the heat. What do you do?"

"Try to put it out," Lucy said.

"And she was panicked because of her fear of heights," Denne said. "She probably waved it away, or pushed it away, and tumbled forward."

Retsler downed the last of his decaf. "Interesting theory, but what are the odds that Clay Emory knows the lighthouse's history?"

"And went to all that trouble to make it look like ghosts killed Pippa?" Lucy asked, her voice rising incredulously.

Retsler shrugged. "He was alone with her all afternoon. He had time."

Denne shook his head. "There was no ash residue, no smell of sulfur, no signs of fire anywhere in that lighthouse. I checked. Besides, the time of death is consistent with Clay's story. The body was still warm when I arrived. You remember, Dan. Rigor hadn't even really started yet."

Retsler did remember the arm hanging limply over the landing. "What about Paula? Anyway she could have been there?"

Eddie shook his head. "She had a shift at Safeway this afternoon. A lot of people saw her."

"We can't just close this one up," Retsler said. "Tadero won't let it ride."

"You can't prove the existence of ghosts," Denne said.

"Why not?" Retsler asked. "All it takes is a scientific method."

"And an open mind." Denne sipped his amber. "She's missing the second part."

"I missed it once too," Retsler said.

"What are you going to do?" Lucy asked.

Retsler smiled at her. "Rely on you," he said.

Storm clouds gathered on the horizon, black against a gray sky. The line between the clouds and the ocean was blurred—it was pouring not three miles away.

Retsler stood in front of the lighthouse, the wind tugging at his coat. It had gotten cooler in the last few minutes and he could smell rain in the air.

"I got a call from the state crime lab this morning." Denne was standing beside him, hands clasped behind his back, staring up at the lighthouse as if he'd never seen it before. "They wanted to know why someone they'd never heard of had requested an autopsy on a case I hadn't even listed as a suspicious death."

"Tadero?" Retsler asked.

Denne nodded. His hair blew across his face, and he pushed at the strands as if they annoyed him.

"Are you sending the body?"

"She has no authority yet," Denne said.

"What did you tell them?"

"That she's new and hungry and won't be chief until January." A strand of hair caught on the edge of his mouth. He didn't seem to notice. "They understood. They're turning down the request."

Lucy came up beside them, a large bag over her shoulder. She looked small and frail in the wind. "Where's Eddie?"

"Getting Emory," Retsler said.

"Do you really think we should do this?" Denne asked. "They did all sorts of cleansings once the reopening was approved."

"Of the lighthouse." Lucy was standing in the same position Denne had been in, her head tilted back, staring at the top of the massive building before them. "Anyone with a brain can tell the problem comes when the light is lit."

The clouds were swirling in the distance, and the chill had gotten deeper. Retsler pulled his coat tighter.

"Besides," Lucy said, "this place is going to be a spirit magnet for the rest of its days."

"So what are we doing here?" Denne asked.

"That's what I'd like to know." Tadero had come up behind Retsler. Even though he had been expecting her, he jumped.

"You're observing."

"Like hell. You guys are messing with a crime scene."

Retsler smiled. "We're the police, Jaclyn. We're allowed."

At that moment, Eddie and Emory crested the hill. Eddie had one hand on Emory's back, as if propelling him forward.

"What is this?" Tadero asked.

"He's going to show us what he was doing when Pippa died," Retsler said.

"He already gave a statement," Tadero said.

"I still fail to see what we can do that the others haven't," Denne said, referring not to Emory, but the other cleansings.

"The way I see it," Lucy said, "the light will be automated. There will rarely be anyone here when it comes on."

"What are we talking about?" Tadero asked. No one answered her.

"The lighthouse will be open to the public on summer days, but for safety reasons will close anytime the light has to go on. So we're only concerned with a few interactions and only one that could possibly be dangerous."

She didn't have to say which one. Retsler and Denne both knew she was referring to the lighthouse keeper.

"So are we making the same mistake those hippies made?" Denne asked.

"Goodness, no. We're not holding a séance. No one here is that reckless, are we?" Lucy looked at Tadero as if this had all been her idea.

"You people are really and truly crazy," Tadero said.

At that moment, Eddie and Emory reached them. Emory's face was ashen. He looked at Tadero, and Retsler thought he saw fear in Emory's eyes.

"What's she doing here, Dan? You gonna charge me with something?"

So Emory had heard about Tadero's theory of Pippa's death.

"No, Clay," Retsler said. "And even if I did, any good lawyer would throw this afternoon's proceedings out of court."

Tadero sighed and shook her head.

"So what're we doing here?"

"You're going to turn the light on for us."

Emory shook his head. "I quit, didn't you hear? I don't want to go inside this place ever again."

"I know," Retsler said.

"I don't got permission to turn on the light," Emory said. "This is state property. I could get in trouble."

"We have permission," Retsler said.

"To have me do it?"

"They wanted a certified electrician here. The work's not completely done, Clay. We need to be safe."

Emory continued shaking his head. He was backing away. Eddie caught his arm. "I told you what happened. You can't—"

"It's all right," Retsler said. "It'll take ten minutes."

Emory blinked hard. "You don't know what you're risking."

"I think we do, Clay," Lucy said. "Come on."

He looked at her and all the strength seemed to leave him. Apparently Clay Emory, like the rest of Whale Rock, trusted Lucy.

Eddie led Emory inside, followed by Denne and Lucy. As Retsler headed for the door, Tadero kept pace with him.

"Very melodramatic," she said. "Is this show for me?"

"Actually, the others didn't want you here," Retsler said, stating only part of the objection his crew had to the afternoon's proceedings. "Consider your presence to be professional courtesy."

She raised her eyebrows, but followed him inside.

Weak sunlight came through the thick glass windows and the skylight, reflecting off the newly painted white walls. The light made the interior of the lighthouse a completely different place than it had been during the storm.

Emory and Eddie were already past the landing where Pippa's body had been found. The sound of footsteps on metal stairs echoed in the small space.

Retsler followed. Through the windows on the landing, he could see the clouds, black in the distance. They had gotten a lot closer.

When he and Tadero reached the top, the others were already gathered around the light. Emory stood to one side, near the control box.

"They haven't got it automated yet," he said. "That won't happen until the day after the dedication ceremony."

Lucy had reached inside her bag. She held it against her, one hand inside, the other clutching the bag tightly. The lines on her face seemed deeper than they ever had, and she had lost all of her grandmother-cute.

Denne had slipped his hands into his back pockets and was staring out at the storm clouds. Eddie was standing beside Emory as if he didn't trust him to go through with this. Tadero had stopped beside Retsler. He could feel the tension in her body.

"I—I don't think this is smart, Dan," Emory said again.

"Let's just do it," Retsler said. "The way you did the day Pippa died. Keep the timing the same."

Emory took a deep breath and hit a switch. The light, in the center of the round room, hummed. The bulbs lit up and then the light began to rotate, just like it was supposed to. Retsler could feel the vibration through the floor.

The air did feel charged. He glanced at Tadero and saw that strands of her hair had risen as if they were covered with static electricity.

"Dan," Denne said. There was an urgency in his voice.

Retsler followed Denne's gaze and so did Tadero. Shapes had formed over the ocean, small wisps, like fog, all of them scuttling forward. Retsler turned. He saw more wisps coming up the beach from the south.

"What is that?" Tadero asked.

Then the lighthouse door banged open.

"Oh, Jesus," Emory said. He fumbled with the box, punching the switch trying to shut it off.

"One of us should go down the stairs," Lucy said. She had dropped her bag and was now holding a small vial in her left hand.

"I'll go," Retsler said. "You want me to take that?"

"No." Lucy came up beside him. She held the vial before her as if it were a shield.

Tadero's eyes were wide. "What the hell is this?"

"Don't know yet," Retsler said, but he smelled smoke. Tadero did too—he could tell from the way her nostrils moved.

"Oh, for god's sake," she said, rolling her eyes. "Let's scare the new recruit."

She started down the stairs without them.

"Jaclyn!" Denne called, but she didn't stop.

Retsler hurried down after Tadero, Lucy beside him.

Flames had formed on the landing. As Tadero got close, the flames rose up in the shape of a man. He reached toward her, fire blazing off his fingers.

"What the…?" Tadero stopped.

"Back off," Lucy said, but Retsler didn't know if she was talking to Tadero or the fiery shape.

Black smoke filled the air around them. In the space of a few seconds, it got so thick that Retsler could barely see.

"Shut off the damn light!" Denne yelled from upstairs. Eddie cursed.

"I can't get close, Dan," Lucy said.

Tadero backed up the stairs, fumbling for her gun.

Retsler grabbed the vial from Lucy. His eyes stung and he was coughing. "What do I do?"

"Dump it on the flames," she said.

He pulled the cork. The burning man was coming after Tadero, the only light in the smoke.

Retsler tossed the contents at the wall of fire.

"We're helping! We're helping! We're putting you out!" Lucy called.

The liquid hit the flames and they rose up, sparking. Tadero let out a small cry and crouched, protecting her face. Then the flames sucked inward, and the smoke vanished. All that was left was a man in severe black clothing, wearing muttonchop whiskers and a confused expression.

"Rest now," Lucy said. "You're free. Go home."

He looked upward and his body lost definition, becoming fog. It floated through the ceiling and disappeared through the roof.

"Shut off the damn light!" Denne yelled again.

"Move," Eddie said, and Retsler heard clanging. There was a loud click and then the humming stopped.

The door banged again. Closed, Retsler guessed, and somehow that relieved him. The feeling of electricity had left the air.

Retsler handed the vial back to Lucy. "What the hell was in here?"

"Holy water," she said.

Retsler started in surprise. "You knew that would work?"

"No," she said and smiled. Her face was streaked with soot. He supposed his was too. "I hoped it would, though."

Retsler shook his head. He hated to think what would have happened if the holy water hadn't worked. The spirit might have vanished anyway, as it had when Emory shut off the light the first time. Or it might have stayed.

He shuddered. He heard the sound of footsteps on the stairs behind him, but didn't turn, knowing it was Denne, Eddie, and Emory.

Tadero was sitting on the stairs. She was covered in black, and clutching her gun. Retsler climbed down to her.

"What the hell was that?" she asked, her voice shaking.

"What Pippa Gage saw before she fell down the stairs."

"I'm supposed to believe that?"

Retsler shrugged. "Believe what you want."

Tadero looked at him. Her eyes were wide, her confidence gone. She seemed as shaken as a rookie at her first arrest.

Retsler took pity on her. He sat down beside her. "You never asked me why I was getting out of here."

"Because the lighthouse is haunted?" The usual bravado was not in her voice.

"Because this isn't the first strange and hard-to-believe thing I've seen in Whale Rock," he said. "Believe it or not, I used to be more skeptical than you are."

"You're leaving because you're afraid of ghosts?" she asked.

Retsler shook his head. "Because I don't handle them well. Because they disturb me on a level that makes me ineffective at my job."

"You don't seem ineffective," she said, and he realized that was the first time she had complimented him.

"Yet," he said.

She nodded, holstered her gun and looked out the window. The storm clouds had gotten closer, and the waves were large and tipped with white.

"Like ten-year-old crack dealers with guns," she said.

"What?" Retsler asked.

"You never asked me why I gave up a career-track position in Chicago to come here," she said.

"Ten-year-old crack addicts?" he asked.

"With guns," she said. "They disturb me on a level that made me ineffective at my job."

Retsler wasn't sure he knew what to say to that. He'd never seen a crack addict, let alone a ten-year-old brandishing a weapon. "So you'd rather face ghosts?"

She looked at her hands, smudged with black from the smoke. "I'd rather believe this was a prank that you all pulled, but Pippa Gage is dead. To believe this is a prank, I have to believe that you took her death lightly, and I see no evidence of that."

"You called the state crime lab," Denne said, and Retsler heard suppressed fury in his tones.

Tadero nodded. "I was going to prove to you that science was better than superstition."

"But?" Lucy asked.

"My eyes sting from smoke that's not here," Tadero said.

"What are you going to do about the lighthouse?" Emory asked Retsler. "You can't let it open."

Retsler sighed and stood. "It'll be all right, Clay."

"But—"

"But nothing. We got rid of the hostile spirit."

"That won't stop more from coming," Emory said.

"The lighthouse will be empty when the light's on," Retsler said.

"Except if some poor electrician has to fix it." Emory's voice was shaking.

Eddie put his hand on Emory's shoulder. Denne shoved his hands in his pocket, ruining the lines of his pants. He looked more uncomfortable than Retsler had ever seen him.

"I'll talk to some people," Denne said, "and see what we can do."

"You know better," Emory said. "They should have stopped this thing from the beginning, but they didn't. And now Pippa's dead. More people are going to die here, Dan, you know that."

Retsler did know that, but it wasn't his problem any more. It was Tadero's.

He reached a hand down to help her up. She took it reluctantly.

"Still willing to stay?" he asked her softly.

"Still planning to leave?" she asked with a touch of the old toughness.

He gazed at the storm clouds which were hovering just off-shore. The storm made him less nervous that the last one had. He was, apparently, coming to terms with the past—and that meant he was ready to move on.

He had needed the experience in the lighthouse to prove to himself that no matter what came his way, he could handle it. He might not be able to solve it, any more than Tadero could stop kids from getting crack or guns, but he could survive whatever was thrown at him.

"Dan?" Denne asked, as if he were waiting for Retsler to respond. "Still plan to leave?"

"Yeah," Retsler said softly, feeling relief for the first time in nearly a year. "Now that I know my successor is up to the job."

FANTASYLIFE

For Dean Wesley Smith,
with love.
Now you get to say I told you so.

ACKNOWLEDGMENTS

I owe a great deal of gratitude to a lot of people on this project. Thanks go first and foremost to John Ordover, for pushing me and for tolerating the mystical writer's talk. Thanks also to Dean, who held me up the whole way. And a great deal of thanks to John Helfers, Larry Segriff, and Martin H. Greenberg, who got me to write the first stories set in Seavy County.

PART I

THE FIRST DEATH

JULY 2002

ONE

Madison, Wisconsin

On the hottest day of the year, Emily Buckingham—who, until two months before had been known as Emily Walters—took her bike out of the garage, filled two bottles of water, stuck them in the bottle cages, and dusted off her bike helmet. If she got caught, she would say she was just out for a ride, and she got lost.

Her mom might not believe that, but there'd be no proof. And proof, Emily knew from watching too many cop show reruns while Mommy was teaching summer school, was all that mattered. Mommy could guess all she wanted, but she'd never really know the truth.

Sonia, this week's babysitter, had the radio on really loud in the kitchen. Emily could hear it on the porch of the old house the university rented cheap to needy professors. Emily hated the house. It'd been built by some famous Frank guy who seemed to like sloping windows and lots of stone and sixties crap that Mommy said was expensive but ugly.

Emily thought the whole house was ugly, even the living room that was supposed to be the centerpiece. The house was so ancient that it didn't have air-conditioning, and regular air didn't flow right, so the porch was the only comfortable place in this heat spell.

At lunch—which Emily had to make because Sonia was too wrapped up in some phone conversation with a guy named Jimmy, who promised her he'd help with her green cards and her Visa and had somehow gone back on that promise—the guy on the radio news announced it was ninety-nine degrees with ninety-five-percent humidity, and it was only going to get hotter. He recommended everybody hunker down and stay cool and drink a lot of fluids, which made Emily remember the water bottles, because she would have forgotten otherwise.

After she finished her peanut butter sandwich, she told Sonia she was going outside, but she didn't say where. Sonia waved at her, probably thinking more about the Visa than about Emily. One thing about Emily, her mom always said, she was a good kid.

And this time, being a good kid was going to work in Emily's favor.

When she went out into the heat, she almost changed her mind. It felt hotter than ninety-nine degrees with ninety-five-percent humidity. It always felt hotter in this crummy neighborhood so far away from the lake.

Here the houses were crammed together like kids on a bus, and the trees, even though they gave shade, made everything seem even more crowded. The streets were hilly, and Camp Randall Stadium was nearby, which Mommy said would be a really big pain in the fall.

Emily didn't want to be here in the fall. She didn't want to be here now, but she didn't have a lot of choice. Mommy let Daddy have the big house on Lake Mendota in the divorce, kinda like a consolation prize, Mommy said, although having a house didn't seem like a real consolation to Emily for losing the whole family.

Mommy changed her last name and said Emily had to do the same thing, which Emily hadn't liked but hadn't known how to argue. The lawyer lady, who had lots of big teeth and even bigger hair and wore too much perfume, had put a hand on Emily's shoulder and said, *Trust me, honey, it's for the best.*

But it wasn't for the best.

People didn't lose their daddies because "his personality has changed, sweetheart" and because some judge thought that was a big deal. It wasn't a big deal. Daddy was still Daddy. He just couldn't be home as much and when he was home, he couldn't spend as much time with her and Mommy.

Then Daddy said that thing no one would say what it was and everything went bad and he got to keep all his family money that somehow paid for the house and Mommy got to keep her job and Emily got to keep her clothes and her books and her toys and nothing else, not even her daddy.

And no one asked her what she wanted, not then, and not now. They just figured she'd live with it, because they were.

They figured her wrong.

But then, they always figured her wrong. Emily might have been a good girl, but that was mostly because she was interested in good girl things. She thought kids who broke the rules at school were stupid because school was interesting and a whole lot better than staying at home by yourself all summer, watching reruns on TV and Jerry Springer and this really bad soap opera in Spanish that her other babysitter, Inez, liked. Emily was learning Spanish from the show and from Inez, whose English wasn't too good, but that wasn't like sitting in class.

Nothing was.

This fall, Emily'd have to go to a whole new school because they lived in this crummy neighborhood now, where there weren't a lot of kids and where what kids who lived here were pretty stuck up. Emily had been alone all summer, and reading when she wasn't watching TV, and thinking a lot about Daddy being alone all summer.

So she came up with the plan.

She had to pick the right day because it would take a long time to ride from Camp Randall to Shorewood. She'd have to stay away from University Avenue because when it merged with Campus Drive it got lots of lanes and stoplights and people not caring who they hit when they went too fast around corners.

Emily figured Old Middleton Road was her best bet, and one afternoon, she had to get Inez to drive it for her so that she could see it. That worked kinda, although Inez kept telling Mommy that Emily was being weird, wanting to see her old house and everything, even though the house was on the opposite side of University from Old Middleton Road.

Inez wasn't dumb, which was why Emily had to pick a Sonia day to take the bike.

There weren't going to be a lot more Sonia days because Mommy didn't like the mess she left the house in, so on days without Inez, Emily might have to do something lame like day care on campus. The University of Wisconsin sponsored day care for kids all summer long, but the kids who were usually there were little kids, not ten-year-olds. Ten-year-olds were supposed to be at camp or summer school or on vacation, not trying to read while some baby screamed his lungs out.

Emily was going to ask Daddy if he could take her on non-Inez days, even if the judge didn't like it. Daddy could afford somebody to come in and watch both of them to make sure nothing bad happened, although Emily wasn't sure what that bad stuff was that could happen around Daddy.

Of course, she hadn't seen him a lot since his personality changed, but in court, his lawyer said he'd be better if he took drugs. Mommy said the problem was there was no guarantee he'd take the drugs, but Emily thought there was no guarantee that he wouldn't either.

So when she called this morning and listened to the phone ring, her stomach twisting so much she wasn't sure her breakfast bar would stay down, and heard Daddy's familiar deep voice saying, "Hello? Hello? Is anyone there?", she just knew he was taking the drugs and he'd be fine, he'd be the daddy who told her stories and rode her around on his shoulder and taught her how to ride this very bike.

It took all of Emily's patience to get through lunch, which would be the last time Sonia would notice where she was. Even so, Emily was real quiet when she took out the bike, and she was real responsible too, because even though it was hot, she strapped her helmet on first thing.

She coasted down the hill to the intersection, where she took a right. She knew if she kept going west, she'd hit Old Middleton, and from there it was pretty much a straight shot to Whitney Way. Somewhere near there—she hadn't scoped this part out—she'd have to cross at the lights, and ride for a treacherous block or two on University.

Then she'd go into her old neighborhood and maybe ride around it a bit because she hadn't done that since last summer, which was a really long time ago. When she got to her old house, which Daddy had built just before she was born on his family's property near Lake Mendota, she'd go around to the back to the cabana, lock her bike inside, and put on her swimming suit.

It would be an easy visit, her and Daddy, not talking a lot (unless he wanted to), and just enjoying being together, because, after all, he had to miss her as much as she missed him.

Because that last day in the court, where she had to go talk to the judge all by herself, and the judge asked her weird questions about Daddy, none of which seemed to make any sense, and then asked her who she'd rather live with, Mommy or Daddy, and Emily said both, on that day, Daddy had put his arms around her, and told her she was just great and everything would be fine, she would see, and he never meant any of that bad stuff anyway, that was just the illness talking.

And she couldn't ask what he meant about the bad stuff and being sick because Mommy's lawyer with the big teeth and the big hair whisked her away, and made her sit outside with some guy in a uniform while they waited for the judge to ask some more questions to both Mommy and Daddy.

Good thing Emily brought a book.

But then, she always brought a book. She even had one in the bike pack Mommy had given her for her birthday. A book and her swimming suit and a towel and a candy bar and an apple in case she got hungry and Daddy didn't have any kid food.

So Emily rode and followed the plan, even though it was really hot and her T-shirt stuck to her back, and icky sweat ran down her neck from her helmet. She drank most of the water by the time she got to Whitney Way and stared at all the cars zooming from one place to the next, making that whooshing sound as they went by.

And part of her, the good girl part, understood why her Mommy and Daddy never wanted her to ride on this side of University Avenue, why when she lived in her old house she had to stay in the neighborhood, and ride the windy streets that usually ended in a dead end.

She almost turned around, with all the cars and being by herself and no one knowing who she was, and what if one hit her? Who would tell Mommy? And then Emily decided she just had to be real careful. It was up to her to be vigilant, Mommy always said, because other people rarely were.

Emily didn't know how long she waited at the light on Whitney Way so that she could merge with the traffic on University, but when she finally got enough guts to go, she rode really fast. Her bike wobbled under her legs, and she was afraid it would slip sideways like it did sometimes on gravel, but she was as careful as she could be, and vigilant too, even though some of the cars passed so close they almost touched her, and the wind from them going by made her bike wobble all the more.

She peddled just a little ways on University, but it was enough, with the guard rail on one side and the trees not giving any shade and the cars on the other, whooshing like they had no idea there was a kid nearby struggling to stay on a bike.

Then she saw a familiar street, all narrow near the little bridge, and she turned on it, even though that street wasn't part of the plan. She coasted down the incline toward the cross streets and looked at houses she hadn't seen for almost a year.

Real houses. They were mostly big, like houses were supposed to be, and people who lived there had real cars like SUVs. They had yards and flowers and trees all their own and the other houses weren't all crammed next to them so that you could hear the neighbors shouting at each other, even if it was in Indonesian.

Emily was kinda relieved that everything looked as familiar as it did. At one point on the ride when she was beginning to wonder if she rode right past Old Middleton and hadn't even noticed, she also got scared thinking she might not recognize anything when she got to her old neighborhood.

But everything looked the same, right down to the cars, and it didn't take her long at all to find her old house.

It was still at the bottom of an incline, which Daddy used to complain about in the spring because the snow would melt and the water would run down the driveway and mix with the rain and flood the garage. He used to say it was the only flaw in the design and Mommy would laugh because they couldn't move the garage anywhere better without losing their view of the lake.

Emily took the old bike path around the side of the garage where no one could see her. Everything had grown up weedy and tall, even the dandelions, whose fluff floated in the humid air.

Some things had changed—Mommy would never have let the garden grow over like this, and she would have made Daddy or someone (even Emily, maybe) mow the lawn.

The house didn't look as good as she remembered either. The more she compared it to the Frank house, the bigger this house got, kind of like her mind made it grow. If she'd thought about it, really thought about it, she would have known it wasn't that big—what rooms would fill all that extra space?—but she hadn't thought about it.

All she'd thought about was the garden, with its roses and peony shrubs and bleeding hearts, and all those other plants whose names she didn't know but grew taller than she was, with big green leaves that reached for the sky. The garden was like a fence, even more so now that it was overgrown, but in her memory, in her imagination, the garden was what separated her house from all the neighbors.

In reality, the yard was so big, no neighbor house was even nearby. Emily had to squint through the trees to see the nearest house, a big red thing that had a pitched roof and a covered porch.

Her daddy's house seemed smaller than that. The second story was narrower and the windows weren't as big, and the porch was smaller than the one in the back of the Frank house. In fact, her daddy's house didn't look a lot bigger than the Frank house, although it was prettier with its light blue paint and the big modern windows and its stained glass front door.

Weeds covered the bike path, scratching her as she made her way around the house. Mosquitoes lived here too, and didn't seem to know they weren't supposed to be out in this heat. She slapped more than one, had to flick a spider off her arm, and swallowed a mouthful of gnats, which were swarming in front of a big black tree.

The bike's wheels click-click-clicked, which sounded loud now that she wasn't riding it and listening to the whoosh of cars. She wondered if her daddy could hear her moving through the underbrush and if he worried that some bogeyman was coming to get him, even though it wasn't dark.

Her old daddy, the one with the personality she knew, he wouldn't have been afraid of the bogeyman, but she wasn't so sure about this new daddy, the one the judge said didn't have the right to see Emily anymore.

What could a daddy do that was so bad that his daughter had to be punished too?

When she reached the little dip in the path, the one that used to be a fork until the Dixsens sold the next-door house and the new people didn't have kids so no one found out about the path, she let the bike tip over really slow so that she wouldn't knock the chain off.

Then she bent down, opened the pack, and got out her suit, along with the towel and the book just in case Daddy wasn't there after all. She wrapped the suit and the book in the towel, and tucked it under her arm. She walked the rest of the way, her breath catching in her throat.

The air was really still. There wasn't even a bird singing, although in her memory, birds always sang here. She stepped into the yard before she realized she'd lost the path; the tall grass confused her, made her think she was still in the no-man's-land by the garage.

The garage was almost lost in weeds, the door shut and locked, and one of the windows on the back side had a small round hole in it, the grass cracked in a circle all around it.

Emily's mouth was dry, and she wished she'd brought one of her bottles too, even though there wasn't much water left. She hadn't realized how thirsty she would be.

Her footsteps, knocking down the grass, were the only sound she heard. The air took on a familiar marshy scent, the smell she always associated with the lake in the summer.

As she got closer to the patio, she saw that the cabana had been taken down—all that was left was concrete where the floor used to be.

A shiver went through her even though she wasn't cold, and she glanced toward the lake to see if Daddy had at least put out the dock.

He had, and he was sitting on it, cross-legged, staring at the sailboats that looked pure white against the hazy sky. The lake itself was blue-gray, the air so full of water that the sunlight filtering through it almost looked like sun coming through fog.

Emily had never seen her daddy sit so still. It was almost like he was like those prayer guys she'd seen in Union South one day while she was waiting for her mommy.

Emily set her towel on the patio stones—which were cracked and weeds had grown through them, and no one had bothered to put out the big glass table with the umbrella and the cushioned green chairs with the white legs, even though it was the middle of the summer.

She glanced real quick at the patio doors, trying to see inside the house, but it was too dark. She couldn't even see if anyone moved around inside, like maybe Daddy had gotten a new housekeeper or something.

Mommy said to the lawyer lady that toward the end it wasn't good to sneak up on Daddy, so Emily made as much noise as she could coming down the hard path. She swished the grass and coughed and cleared her throat.

When she got to the edge of the dock, she jumped on it, so it bounced just like it always had, and the water rippled around it, and her heart lifted. No matter how much changed, this—this, at least, stayed the same.

Her daddy turned, real slow, like he was at the end of one of those ripples she caused. His hair was too long and it wasn't black anymore. It had lots of gray in it. And he had lines on his face that she'd never seen before. He was kinda thin and the polo shirt he wore, one of his favorites, seemed like it was made for someone else.

But he smiled when he realized it was her, and that was Daddy, that big goofy grin that covered most of the lower part of his face.

Emily grinned back and waved and said, "I missed you, Daddy," even though she'd promised herself, promised, promised, promised she wouldn't say anything like that because she didn't want him to feel bad.

He got up and held out his arms and she ran to him, hitting him so hard that she felt his body rock as she wrapped her arms around him.

"Em," he said, and his voice sounded a little funny, like it used to when he had a cold or when he talked too much to his classes.

His hand ran along her short hair. She'd forgot Mommy did that at the beginning of the summer, made Emily cut her hair so that she'd be cool and no one would have to worry about the tangles like they did in past years. Daddy hated short hair, he always said so, that his girls should look like girls.

"You're so tall." He grabbed her shoulders and pushed her back, just a little, so that he could see her face, and she was glad that he didn't say anything about her hair at all.

"Mommy didn't want me to come, but I had to see you, Daddy, so I rode all the way here, and I'm hot and I thought maybe on hot afternoons I could come and we could swim and pretend everything was okay."

Daddy's gray eyes seemed a little glassy, like Mommy's did when she had just woke up.

"Yes," he said, although Emily wasn't sure what he was agreeing with. "Yes, of course."

He crouched, touched the chopped part of her hair again, and smiled at her. Only this wasn't the goofy grin at all, and Emily's heart started to pound.

"Yes," he said again, "it makes sense that you would come now with the drought and the heat and the dying lake."

His hands slid down her arm. They were cold. His fingers dug into her skin.

"Daddy?" she asked, her heart pounding harder now. Was this what they meant about him being different? That he didn't make any sense and his smile had gone all funny and his fingers, which never ever hurt her before, were going to leave bruises in her skin?

"We'll solve it together, Emmie A.," he said, using his old nickname for her. It sounded funny, like a stranger talking with Daddy's voice. "Come on."

He let go of her shoulders and held out his hand like he used to do when they crossed the street, back when she was a little girl.

She stared at him for a minute. He seemed so funny with those glassy eyes and that flat smile and the gray hair. But the lines on his face made him look even sadder, and she had missed him, and maybe, just maybe, she'd been listening to Mommy too much.

It was time for Emily to make up her own mind.

She took his hand. He smiled at her, the soft Daddy smile that he used to use when she did something exactly right, and then they walked, together, to the end of the dock. The wood bobbed beneath their feet, and there were holes in the middle where there had once been boards. Nothing was like it used to be. Not the dock, not the yard, not Daddy.

Not even Emily.

She tried not to sigh. When they reached the edge of the dock, Daddy turned to her. "Are you ready to go in?"

She grinned. "I'll get my suit. I brought it."

"You won't need a suit," he said, and picked her up.

His eyes were wild now, and her heart was beating so hard it hurt. Emily struggled but Daddy didn't seem to notice.

Instead, he bent over and shoved her into the water. It was wet and hot on the thin upper layer, and then she hit a pocket of cold because he had shoved her so very deep.

There was water in her nose and she was coughing, the sound muffled by the water, and she tried not to get water in her lungs, but she was failing. Water was running down the back of her throat, and she was choking.

Daddy was holding her shoulders, pressing them down, playing too rough like he did last summer when he first scared Mommy, and he couldn't tell Emily was in trouble.

She thrashed and struggled and grabbed his wrists with her hands, trying to let him know that she couldn't breathe. Black spots danced in front of her eyes. Her chest burned, and she coughed again, this time sucking in a big mouthful of water.

She was dying, really dying, and Daddy wouldn't let her go.

TWO

Anchor Bay, Oregon

Gabriel Schelling crouched beside the body on the beach. The tide was out, and the sand should have been dry, but it was the texture of concrete, damp and smooth. The air stank of dead fish.

A crowd of tourists huddled near the cliffs that formed the southern end of the bay. He had asked the tourists to go away, but that was like asking the ocean to get rid of its salt. Tourists never did what you wanted them to, and they never ever left—especially when there was a body involved.

The tourist who had called the sheriff's office had reported finding a woman who appeared to be long dead. But as Gabriel looked over the body, he realized that, although the creature before him was female, it wasn't a woman.

Fortunately the face was pressed against the sand, and the tourist, like anyone who stumbled on something awful, didn't look too closely. This so-called woman had bulging eyes, almost no nose, and lips that were permanently pursed.

She also had chalk-white skin that was covered with a layer of nearly translucent scales.

Gabriel's father had called these creatures Fish Women, but the residents of the southern part of Seavy County called them mermaids. Gabriel didn't think either description was exactly right.

He also had never seen a dead one before, and he doubted that anyone else had either. For all he knew, these creatures lived forever in their strange home deep in the sea, even though there was talk that they were amphibians, and that they often walked the land.

Gabriel grabbed his radio, and pressed the talk button. "Athena, where's Hamilton?"

Athena Buckingham had been the North County dispatcher for the Seavy County Sheriff's office ever since Gabriel was a boy. She was efficient and tough, and someone who still put the fear of God into Gabriel even though he was, technically, her boss.

"He left the moment I contacted him." Athena's voice, operatic in person, seemed tailored for the radio. "He should be there at any moment."

Depending on traffic and accidents along the way. Getting from one part of Seavy County in the summer was a nightmare, which was why the sheriff's office had finally split into three districts.

Only one road, Highway 101, ran all the way down the Oregon Coast. In Seavy County, particularly in the northern part, the highway was often the only north-south road for miles. The Coastal Mountain Range was wider here, placing tall mountains on the east side of the highway. With the ocean on the left, there wasn't a lot of room for roads, houses, or anything else.

And the traffic in the summer got worse every year. July was peak tourist season and roads that were built for hundreds of cars had to cope with thousands. Usually if Gabriel saw a body, it was on the highway, inside a demolished car that had tried to pass in a no-passing zone. If he had a dollar for every one of those accidents he had seen in the seven years he had served as North Seavy County's sheriff, he would be able to retire already.

Gabriel said, "Tell him to get his butt here as fast as he can. He's going to like this one."

"He's going to like this one?" Athena repeated. "What does that mean?"

Gabriel let go of the radio and reattached it to his belt. He knew better than to answer that question on the public bands. But he also knew that Athena would repeat his words to the coroner, Hamilton Denne.

And Denne, who had a great scientific and historical interest in what he had once dubbed the FantasyLife of Seavy County, would love this one. He would find out everything he possibly could about this creature, and then some.

Gabriel thought he saw movement out of the corner of his eye. He looked over at the tourists. At least two families waited by the black rocks, as well as a single man standing off to the side. Two women wearing wet suits and holding their surfboards watched as if they were waiting for the right wave.

Gabriel studied the tourists out of reflex. If this were a dead human body before him, he would be thinking about suspects. Seavy County had at most two or three murders a year, but there were a lot of accidental deaths. And in accidental deaths, especially ones around the ocean, murder always had to be ruled out.

The family on the left had the same avid look on their faces as the surfers did. The children, a boy and a girl both nearing puberty, were beginning to lose interest. They were casting longing gazes at the ocean.

But the parents seemed riveted. Gabriel would guess that they were Southern Californians just by their clothing. The shirts were tasteful, although short-sleeved, and their shorts were khaki, but completely inappropriate. Even though the sun was out, making the sky a brilliant blue, the temperature down here hadn't gone higher than sixty-five. In areas the wind could reach, the temperature went down at least ten degrees.

No wonder the children wanted to move. They were probably cold.

The wind didn't get to this part of the beach because of the cliff that the tourists were leaning against. The cliff, which extended for at least two miles, curved against the beach, forming a natural barrier to anything that came from the south.

The cliff was black and large. On the tip, the cliff rose even farther up, forming a shape that people had once compared to a goblet, giving the entire southern tip of Anchor Bay its name—the Devil's Goblet.

A friend of Gabriel's often joked that the Devil used to live on the Oregon Coast, and when he left, he abandoned a lot of things. Lincoln City had Devil's Lake, and farther south tourists could find the Devil's Punchbowl, his Churn, and his Elbow.

Hamilton Denne had told Gabriel that Dee River in Whale Rock used to be called the Devil's River, and there were other sites in Seavy County either still named for the Devil or renamed away from the original devilish names.

At some point, Gabriel thought he would do a travel article on the Devil and the Oregon Coast, but he had a hunch his usual publishers, both Oregon-based tourist magazines, wouldn't take it.

The other family seemed even more intense than the first. These people, parents and three children, knew how to dress for the coast, and they looked vaguely familiar. Gabriel wondered if they were weekenders—people who owned a second home here, and often thought they belonged.

Anchor Bay's 600 year-round residents never believed that week-enders belonged, and many of the locals thought the tourists should stay away. Often, at the end of a long summer, Gabriel was one of them.

But the person who caught Gabriel's attention the most was the single man standing next to the surfers. The man was tall and thin, and had straggly gray hair. He seemed very nervous.

"Hey, Gabriel." Hamilton Denne stood on the beach access steps. He was holding his kit in one hand and a body bag in the other. "What've we got?"

"Come see for yourself, Hamilton," Gabriel said.

Denne stepped off the concrete steps, and started across the dry sand. He was the strangest person Gabriel knew in an area filled with misfits, ex-hippies, and people who simply didn't fit anywhere else. Denne's family had lived on the Oregon Coast forever, and somehow became one of the state's most influential families.

Denne's marriage to the daughter of the Portland's wealthiest families added to that. Hooking up their oldest daughter with a Denne was like having a member of the Bush family marry one of Bill Gates's daughters, only on an Oregon scale.

But about four years ago, Denne quietly divorced his wife. Since then, he seemed lighter, happier, and increasingly more ghoulish.

He didn't look ghoulish though. Denne still had an East Coast Prep School air to him. Some of that was his collection of Harvard sweatshirts, updated every year, and some of that was the fact that Gabriel had yet to see him in jeans. Even Denne's grungiest pants had a crease down the center.

This afternoon, he was wearing a brand new pair of Nikes, and the sleeves of his sweatshirt were rolled up, revealing surprisingly muscular arms. Denne's blond hair needed a trim, and his angular face actually looked a bit haggard.

"This doesn't look good," Denne said as he got closer.

That was precisely what Gabriel had thought when he first crossed the sand. "You have to see it from this angle."

Denne set the kit and the body bag down, then crossed over to Gabriel, careful not to step on anything that could be evidence. Gabriel appreciated Denne's caution. The two murders they had worked together resulted in convictions because of Denne's meticulousness.

Gabriel held his breath as Denne crouched. Denne loved anything unusual, and collected most everything that had to do with Seavy County lore.

Denne peered at the body and then, to Gabriel's surprise, lost all color in his face.

"Is this what I think it is?" Denne asked.

"What do you think it is?" Gabriel asked, knowing better than to put his assumptions on Denne.

"A mermaid." Denne breathed the word, as if he didn't want anyone to overhear him.

"I never technically think of them as mermaids." Gabriel swept his hand toward the legs, bent at the knees, and the long flipper-like feet. "No tail."

"That's true." Denne spoke like someone crouched over the body of a friend. "My father used to call them sirens, even though that's not accurate either. In Greek mythology, sirens never went into the water. They sang from the coastlines."

Gabriel studied him. "You okay, Hamilton?"

Denne shook his head slightly. Then he leaned even closer, careful not to touch the body. "Definitely dead. See? There's a bluish tint to the lips and nostrils that can't be natural, and there's some kind of substance in the gills."

"Nostrils and gills?" Gabriel asked.

"I'm pretty sure she's not the only one built like that," Denne said. "Real mermaids of the fairy-tale type would have to have them too, and so would water nymphs."

Gabriel grinned. This was one of the many things he loved about Seavy County. He knew of no other place in the world where he could have this kind of conversation.

"How about in the real world?" he asked.

Denne's smile was half-hearted and dismissive. "I don't specialize in the real world," he said.

That wasn't exactly true either, but Gabriel wasn't going to argue. He shifted a little, his legs growing tired from crouching.

Denne peered at the body like a little boy examining his first dead bird.

"Look at this." He pointed at a space in the thin, strawlike hair. "No ears. Not even a place for them."

Gabriel did look. The skull was perfectly rounded along the side, the skin—with no obvious scales—stretched taut.

"I expect you'll find a lot of differences," he said.

Denne gave him a look of surprise. "God, I hadn't even thought of that. I was just going to look for what killed her. But this is something, isn't it?"

"*Alien Autopsy*," Gabriel said, talking about a video they had both seen and laughed over. "Think of all the tourists we'll get on this beach now."

If anything, Denne grew paler. "I'm not letting this information out," he said. "The last thing we need is the *National Enquirer* here, making us all look like hicks."

Gabriel smiled. Now that reaction was pure Denne. He would rather avoid controversy and public notoriety than claim the discovery of the century.

"What do we do with it?" Gabriel asked.

"We'll treat this like any other body we find on the beach," Denne said. "Full crime scene investigation. Those people over there think this is human, right?"

He nodded toward the tourists.

"Yeah," Gabriel said. "They didn't give it a good look."

"Perfect," Denne said. "Then that's what we tell the *Anchor Weekly News*. A body on the beach, suspicious death."

Gabriel gave him a sideways glance. Denne hadn't moved from his crouch, his hands hovering over but not touching the body.

"You want to use county money to investigate this," Gabriel said.

"Damn straight," Denne said. "If everyone thinks we might have a murder, no one'll argue the state crime lab budget. They have better equipment than I do."

"I thought you didn't want outsiders to know about this," Gabriel said.

"They're not going to examine her," Denne said. "They're going to look at the stuff around her, just like they would for any other crime scene."

Gabriel nodded. Sometimes he liked how Denne thought.

"All right," Gabriel said. "Let's get to work."

THREE

Madison, Wisconsin

Lyssa Buckingham first heard the sirens when she stepped off the bus at the corner of University and Linden, but she didn't think much of them. Sirens had become a fact of her life since she moved so close to the University Hospitals and Clinic. Sirens, and bells from the First Congregational Church just a block away, and in the fall, there would be shouts from Camp Randall Stadium during the Badger football games.

Inconveniences that she didn't mind, just like she normally didn't mind taking the bus. On this day, though, it was a different matter. The bus's air-conditioning had been out, and since she left her office at five like the rest of Madison, the bus was crowded. She'd had to stand for the full two miles, swaying in the intense heat, and, as she had gotten off, the bus nearly drowned her in hot, smelly diesel exhaust.

Lyssa adjusted her book bag so that it fell across her back. Her purse was heavy enough by itself, but the bag—filled with the research materials she had finally gotten from a rare books website, made the purse seem like it weighed nothing.

In her right hand, she carried her briefcase, filled with this week's papers from the course she had specially designed for the summer session: *Women and the Vote, 1868 to 1922.* She got to talk about all her favorite female pioneers, from Susan B. Anthony to Victoria Wood-hull to Sojourner Truth. And she made the students understand that voting wasn't just a right; it was a privilege, one many of them hadn't had a hundred years before.

Lyssa wasn't enjoying the class as much as she usually did, partly because of the heat, and partly because she was still tying up the last few details from the divorce.

Emily still didn't understand what had happened, and Lyssa didn't want to explain it to her. In fact, Lyssa was perfectly willing to play the bad guy in the entire situation.

No little girl needed to know that her father thought she was a demon when he was off his medication. No little girl needed to know that her father had carried her sleeping form to the shore of Lake Mendota one hot summer evening and would have drowned her, if Lyssa hadn't awakened with a sense that something was about to go terribly wrong.

Lyssa had had the same sense all day, but she hadn't known why. She suspected it was the heat. Heat made her uneasy and restless. She had never really learned how to cope with it. She had grown up on the Oregon Coast, where the temperatures usually hovered between forty-five and seventy-five degrees year round. And Oregon, like so many western states, had very little humidity.

The sheer amount of moisture in the air in a Wisconsin summer was enough to make anyone ill at ease.

But it wasn't just the heat and humidity; it was also the memories they raised. Her ex-husband, Reginald, had always been a little crazy in the heat. He studied it, as if it were something that had been sent from the heavens to attack him personally.

Before Reginald had been diagnosed, indeed, before the symptoms had shown up, a psychologist had diagnosed his obsession with heat, global warming, and the coming end of the world as guilt.

Reginald was the prodigal son of the Walters family, the only Walters who didn't work for Walters Petroleum. He had tried to work for the family business, wanting to make the company environmentally responsible, but that went against the Walters way.

Reginald lived off his portion of the family trust, but he pretended he had nothing to do with them. If people asked him, back in the days when he was lucid, who he was and what he did, he told them he was a classics professor, which was true.

He also saw it as another failure in a life filled with failures.

Lyssa never did. She thought Reginald brilliant, creative, and interesting—at least, she had when they met at the University of Texas in Austin. She had also seen him as courageous, going against the family in their home state, often showing up at protests in the oil drilling fields and getting his picture on the front pages of the *Houston Chronicle* and the *Dallas Morning News*.

Lyssa never had that kind of courage. She had run away from her family as quickly as she could, and never tried to fight them on their home turf.

She walked the three short blocks to the house the UW had provided her for this semester. It was a Frank Lloyd Wright design, donated by an alumnus in his will. Eventually the university planned to turn the house into a museum, but until then, the UW got its use out of the place by renting it at minimal price to visiting professors.

Lyssa wasn't visiting, but the house had been empty, and she had been promised its use for another year. After that, she would have enough money in her savings account—provided there wasn't another financial emergency—to put a down payment on a house, or at least a first and last on a moderately comfortable duplex.

The divorce had left her broke and frightened and more than a little guilty. Wives promised to stick by their husbands through thick and thin, and she had fully expected to do that.

But Reginald's schizophrenia—which appeared full strength in the middle of May a year before—had made being traditional impossible. The psychiatrists never believed Lyssa that Reginald had shown no symptoms before. Being schizophrenic, the doctors claimed, didn't develop over time like Alzheimer's or diabetes. It usually manifested long before someone's thirty-fifth birthday.

The doctors claimed that Reginald's schizophrenia had to have existed before, and that Lyssa had done him a disservice by taking him off his medications.

The doctors also claimed Lyssa's negligence hurt Emily. For a while, until Lyssa hired the best lawyer in the area, it looked like the State of Wisconsin was going to remove Emily from the Walters household for good.

Lyssa had managed to shield Emily from all of that, somehow, and Emily didn't remember most of the bad stuff, since Reginald had been aware enough to stay away when the paranoia and hallucinations started.

But some magazine journalist got wind of Reginald's illness. The journalist was already doing a piece for *The Atlantic* on the link between the Dupont family's business and the mental illness that ran in that family. With the advent of Reginald's bizarre schizophrenia, and mental illness in other wealthy families whose initial source of wealth had to do with chemicals or petroleum, the journalist felt he had a wider story.

The Walters heard about the story before Lyssa did, and they swooped in to take care of Reginald. He got flown to their doctors, taken to their clinics, and forced to live in their ways. He couldn't really defend himself against the family any longer.

And the family decided to make Lyssa the villain, claiming that she had ignored his illness until it got extreme. That was when the need for the divorce became crystal clear.

After that, she knew that in order to keep her daughter out of the custody of the state or the Walters grandparents, who had never visited Emily, not once, and had never acknowledged her with a Christmas or birthday card, let alone a gift, Lyssa would have to get out of the marriage quickly.

She managed to, while the Walters family focused on quashing the negative publicity raised by Reginald's illness. Reginald managed to come back for the custody hearings, since he wanted joint custody, but Lyssa couldn't agree to that, not with the Walters doctors claiming that Reginald wasn't schizophrenic at all, just "exhausted," and refusing to give him proper treatment. Without the treatment, he might try to kill Emily again.

The Walters family stayed out of that battle. For the first time, Lyssa was pleased that they refused to acknowledge her as their daughter-in-law, and Emily as their granddaughter. It made the final fight that much easier. She doubted she would have been able to win otherwise against the Walters fortune.

Lyssa pushed the damp hair off her forehead. Her hair was black and heavy, and she had kept it long until the beginning of this summer. She couldn't face more heat and humidity with long hair trailing down her back. She had cropped her hair short, and Emily's too, making them both look a bit like Gainsborough's painting of the *Blue Boy*—young and somewhat surprised at the way things had gone.

Lyssa didn't feel young anymore. She knew, when she turned thirty, that her future would be different, but she hadn't realized how different. The past four years had aged her.

She suspected it would only get worse.

As she approached the house, she realized the garage door was open. She sighed. She had asked Emily time and again to close that door. Madison was a relatively safe town, but now that they lived near Camp Randall Stadium, they would be subject to game-day pranks and other student mischief.

Even though football season wouldn't officially start for another month and a half, Lyssa wanted the safety habits engrained early. She didn't want Emily to be anywhere near drunken students and football fans on game weekends.

In fact, if Lyssa had more money, she would have left town for the two days of festivities around each home game.

Living here was very different than living in the house she and Reginald had built near Lake Mendota. She had loved that house and she missed it, but she hadn't fought for it.

She had hoped that she would inherit it when Reginald moved back in with his family, but once the press crisis was over and the stories quashed, the Walters let Reginald come home. Lyssa had seen him once, the day the divorce was final. He had looked stable, although she suspected that was his attorney's doing, but too thin. He claimed to be back on his medication, and he seemed calm enough.

But there was something odd about Reginald now, something that hadn't been obvious before.

Lyssa, who had never been around mentally ill people before her husband got sick, wasn't sure if the oddness was a manifestation of his illness or something else. And even though she had never mentioned this to anyone, it was the something else that frightened her.

She mounted the old-fashioned stone steps that led to the house's ugly orange front door. For all of Wright's talk about wanting his homes to blend into their environment, he had fallen in love with the kinds of 1960s colors that were only part of the environment in the fall, if then. No wonder the alumnus rented out the home. If it were Lyssa's, she would sell it to some Wright fanatic, and buy herself some place livable.

As she stepped inside, she wished for air-conditioning. The interior seemed hotter than the exterior. She closed curtains before she left and set fans in strategic places throughout the house, but they never seemed to keep the rooms cool.

She sighed, set her book bag on the sharp flagstone stairway, and called for Emily. Her daughter was probably outside, where it was a half-degree cooler because of the breeze. Lyssa mounted the step, walked past the open living room, and turned left into the kitchen.

The phone sat on the counter, beside the dirty lunch dishes. She felt a thread of irritation. Sophia always spent her afternoons on the phone. She never did the work that Lyssa had hired her for.

If only Inez were available all of the time. Inez found ways to entertain Emily and keep the house clean. Sophia just took care of herself and let Emily run amok.

Fortunately, Emily wasn't the amok-running type.

Lyssa opened the refrigerator, and reveled in the blast of cool air that hit her. She took out a can of lemonade, and rubbed the cold metal against her forehead. A heat headache had started to form there.

"Sophia?" she called half-heartedly. She would probably find Sophia in the back bedroom, the one that Lyssa had converted into a den, with the television and the computer. The room was small enough that she could keep an eye on Emily when she surfed various websites, and still pretend to be watching television.

Lyssa popped the can open and took a long sip. The lemonade was too sweet, but the sugar would help her headache and perk her up just enough to find the strength to make some kind of evening meal.

She tried not to think of the elaborate grill that she and Reginald had splurged on the summer Emily was born. Lyssa had loved that thing, and she had loved using it on the back patio on hot summer nights.

She had never understood the rest of the country's preoccupation with grilling food—which was never a big thing in Oregon—until she moved east, and discovered that most kitchens were too hot to use in the summer, even with the air-conditioning on.

"Sophia?" Lyssa said as she wandered down the hall. The television wasn't on, which surprised her. Both Inez and Sophia seemed to love daytime television.

Lyssa would have objected if it weren't for the fact that Emily was picking up Spanish from Inez's soap operas. Sometimes people learned things in spite of themselves.

Lyssa reached past Emily's room to get to the den. Emily's bed was made and her clothes were folded in the laundry basket—a small miracle that didn't seem like one Sophia could have gotten her to perform. The book Emily had been reading, *Little Women*, which she had discovered on her own, was gone from the nightstand.

Lyssa smiled. Emily was probably sitting on the porch, engrossed in the adventures of Jo, Beth, and Marmee.

The house seemed quiet enough for that. If Emily was reading, it seemed odd that Sophia wasn't inside, talking on the phone, listening to the radio, or watching television. Maybe they had walked to Randall Street. But it seemed too hot to do that as well. Sophia rarely showed that kind of initiative.

Lyssa peered into the den. The television was off, and so was the computer. No one sat on the dingy second-hand couch she'd found at a nearby yard sale. The book Emily planned to read next, *Little Men*, still rested on the edge of the oak bookshelf, where Emily kept all of her to-read pile.

No Sophia, no Emily, and now Lyssa was getting nervous.

A movement caught her eye. She looked through the window into the backyard. Sophia was running from bush to bush, and she was shaking them frantically.

Lyssa had never seen Sophia be that active. Her loose cotton dress was covered with sweat, and her blond hair was falling out of its bun.

That wasn't good. That wasn't good at all.

Lyssa started for the window to shout out of it, to find out what was going on, and then changed her mind. Her neighbors at the lake house always learned her business, and it became a nightmare—one, she suspected, which led to the press finding out about Reginald. This time, she wanted to keep her problems to herself.

She ran through the house and out the back door. The screen banged shut.

Sophia stopped near the overgrown rose bush as if she had been caught robbing a bank. She turned slowly, hands up, as if to show she had nothing in them.

"Mrs. Walters," she said, her voice shaking.

Lyssa froze at the top of the porch steps. Sophia hadn't called her "Mrs. Walters" since the divorce was final in May. Sophia had been very careful to learn Lyssa's new last name—actually her old last name, her maiden name—and to use it whenever she could.

This slip, and the fact that Sophia didn't seem to notice she made it, alarmed Lyssa as much as Sophia's behavior had.

"I do not know what happened," Sophia said. "One minute, she was here. The next, I do not know. She does not come when I yell."

Lyssa was having trouble taking a breath. Her worst nightmares coming true: Emily had been abducted, just like those poor girls on TV a few years ago. Children disappearing right out of their yard.

The air seemed still. Next to her, a bee buzzed its way across the pioneer roses that grew below the porch. The heat seemed worse than it had all day, and for a moment, Lyssa thought she was going to faint.

Then she remembered to take a breath. She could handle

anything. She had learned that with Reginald. She just had to remember it.

Reginald. A shiver ran through her despite the heat. He had stayed away from Emily so far—Lyssa wasn't even sure he knew where they lived—but things could change. And Reginald might have had a serious mental illness, but he was always bright. Too bright.

Lyssa made herself walk down the steps. "When did you see her last?"

Sophia looked away. It was an obvious pretext so that she wouldn't have to look in Lyssa's eyes. "I do not know. I believe after lunch."

After lunch was hours ago, if Emily ate at her usual twelve. Anything could happen in the space of hours.

Lyssa wanted to scream at Sophia, but she knew that screaming would do no good. It took all of Lyssa's self-control to ask the next question.

"When after lunch exactly? It's important."

This time, Sophia did look at her. Sophia's big blue eyes were filled with tears.

"Ah, Mrs. Walters, I do not know, truly. She had the lunch, she went outside and I saw her on the yard. I was on the phone, you know, because there is problems with my green card, and I have to take care of that, and Emily has been so good, you know? I did not think she would be in any trouble back here. I really did not."

So Sophia was thinking the same thing, that someone had taken Emily. Lyssa forced down the panic in her brain. She made herself take rigid control of her emotions. All that mattered now was logic. Calm, rational logic was the only thing that would bring her daughter back.

And the first logical step was to assume that nothing was wrong. After all, Emily was getting older, and she hated being alone in this part of town. She might have taken a walk, out of shouting range. If she was wearing her watch, she would be back by six because that was dinnertime, and she knew better than to miss dinner.

But Lyssa could not wait around to see if Emily was going to come home. Lyssa had to check other possibilities first.

"Could Emily be at someone's house?" Lyssa asked Sophia.

"I do not know who the someone could be, Mrs. Walters. There is no little kids here."

Yes, said the sneaky panicked part of Lyssa's brain, *but there might be sex offenders. The studies said there were at least two in every square mile. Maybe one of them—*

Lyssa forced herself to step onto the lawn. The grass was dry and crackly from the summer heat. There were no really good kid parks nearby, but there was the stadium, which was a big explorable place.

Only Emily hated exploring alone, and she rarely disobeyed rules. In that, she was about as different from Lyssa as a child could get. Lyssa, at that age, had disobeyed every rule ever written.

"Have you seen her talking to any adults?" Lyssa asked, trying to make the statement sound casual.

"Mrs. Walters," Sophia said. "I know better than that. You never know what these grown-ups will do these days. I would tell you and I would stop her. No. No, of course not."

But they had already established that Sophia didn't watch Emily as closely as she could. Hell, Lyssa didn't watch her as closely as she could. She trusted her daughter, expected a lot from her daughter, and was often relieved at the degree of self-entertainment that Emily could achieve.

Lyssa let out a small sigh. She walked over to Sophia, who looked distraught, and put an arm on her shoulder. "Did she get any phone messages? Was she on the computer today?"

"No." Sophia shook her head for emphasis. "You said no computer when you are not home. I make sure of that. And the phone, well, I was...."

Then she looked at Lyssa, understanding dawning.

"You think Mr. Walters took her. Oh, and I am so panicked, I have been forgetting to call you Ms. Buckingham now. I'm so sorry."

"The name's minor," Lyssa said, scanning the lawn. "But I am worried about Mr. Walters. Did he call?"

Has he been calling? Has he been visiting? Have you been telling me everything you know, Sophia, or have you been lying to me about more than your immigrant status?

Lyssa didn't say any of those things, although she wanted to. The anger bubbled beneath the surface, ready to come out. This woman had lost Lyssa's daughter. She hadn't been paying attention, and Emily vanished.

Lyssa knew she should have fired Sophia weeks ago, but she hadn't had the heart. She put Sophia first instead of Emily, thinking, as she had too much lately, that Emily could take care of herself.

"No, ma'am." A tear trickled out of Sophia's left eye. She wiped at it angrily. "I would tell you if he called. You told me to let you know immediately if he even smile at Emily. You said call you at work, and I have not, because I have not seen him since, you know, last year. He scares me, ma'am. I would not let him near her. He is dangerous, that one. He can kill—."

Sophia put a hand to her mouth, stopping the sound.

"He could kill her, I know." Lyssa was surprised at how calm she sounded. "That's why I divorced him, and why I'm trying to find work somewhere else. So let me ask you again. Have you seen him or anyone you knew from the lake house?"

"No, ma'am."

Lyssa wasn't sure if that was good news or not. If Reginald had taken Emily, Lyssa would at least know what to do. She would call the police and her lawyer, and make sure her baby was all right.

But this was not as easy to figure out.

"All right," she said after a moment. "You have been yelling for her."

"Yes, ma'am. It has been almost an hour now."

Lyssa nodded. "Then she's not within hearing distance."

Lyssa ran a hand through her cropped hair, felt the sweat beaded beneath the hairline. It was hot. Had her baby gone somewhere and passed out from the heat?

"Go to the neighbors," Lyssa said, still trying to sound calm. She needed Sophia, and she needed Sophia thinking, not reacting. "See if they have seen Emily at any point today. Maybe we can figure out where she is."

"Yes, ma'am." Sophia scurried toward the alley. The nearest neighbor was right across the gravel.

Lyssa watched Sophia pick her way past the rose bushes. Lyssa wasn't sure what she would do. Shouting obviously wasn't going to help. Then she glanced at the garage.

The door was up, like it had been when she got home. But the Volkswagen Beetle she had bought with Reginald was still parked inside. Lyssa rarely drove it, partly because of the memories, and partly because she wanted to save money. Parking near the University was outrageous, and so were gas prices. Since she lived so close, she could take the bus or walk.

She was halfway to the garage before she realized she had made it her destination. The door shouldn't have been open. Sophia might not have noticed that. Sophia wasn't here as often as Inez was, and didn't know the way the household ran. Even if Sophia had known, she might have thought that Lyssa had left the garage door open that morning.

But Lyssa hadn't. She hadn't touched the car in days.

She stepped onto the narrow driveway. The garage predated the Frank Lloyd Wright creation that she lived in. The garage was old and made of white Mississippi river brick, which indicated—at least to Lyssa—that a beautiful home done in a fin de siècle style had been torn down to make way for Wright's uncomfortable ranch house.

The garage barely held a single modern car—in that, she was lucky to have wrested the Bug from Reginald (*What'm I gonna do?* he asked her plaintively. *Drive it with all my medication? Take it. Take it before my mind changes.*). Some possessions from previous renters hung on the walls—or maybe from the original owners; a pair of wooden snow-shoes with rotting leather laces, a hat that looked like it had once belonged to a fisherman, cross-country skis from the 1970s, and many other things.

Lyssa mentally inventoried them, and saw that nothing was missing.

She stepped inside the garage. It was cooler than the outdoors or than the house, and it smelled musty. The dry odor had a tinge of mold to it, which always made her think of the coast and the strange house in which she had grown up.

And then she thought of her mother, and her stomach clenched. Her mother would know where Emily was. If this turned out to be a real emergency, not something she made up in her head, Lyssa would have to call her mother.

It was the only sensible thing to do.

The car was cool and covered with a thin layer of dust. Lyssa used it even less than she thought she had. On one side of the dust layer, there were scrape marks, and the print of a child-sized hand.

Lyssa's breath caught. She peered under the car, thinking maybe something had happened to Emily. But she wasn't there. She wasn't anywhere in the garage.

But Lyssa did see one thing in the dirt covering the concrete floor. Tire tracks. Narrow tire tracks.

She glanced at the bike rack, hidden in the corner near the garage door. Her bicycle remained on the upper part of the rack, which was all she had looked at.

The lower part, where Emily kept her bike, was empty.

Bike-riding? On an afternoon like this? Where would Emily go that would keep her away from the house for so long?

Then Inez's voice from a few days ago rose in Lyssa's head.

Mrs. Buckingham, we need to watch our Emily. She is sick of the home, hmm? She needs little friends to keep her busy. She misses the lake. This afternoon, she tells me to take turns to go somewhere special. We get to the Whitney Way, and I know then what she is doing. She wants to see her old house. I tell her she cannot, and she says all she wants to do is swim in the lake. I say no. I say, next time, I take her to the city pool if that is okay. She will like the pool, maybe make new friends. All right?

Lyssa braced herself on the side of the car. A hot afternoon. The lake would seem inviting on a hot afternoon, and what would a child do? Wrap her swimming suit in a towel and ride to the lake.

Lyssa bolted out of the garage and into the house. She hurried to Emily's room. Emily's book was gone. Lyssa should have known what that meant right away. It meant that Emily had gone somewhere. She never traveled without a book.

The bedroom seemed even emptier than it had before. Lyssa went to Emily's dresser. The swimming suit was gone, along with her goggles.

Lyssa checked the other drawers and the closet to make sure it wasn't in them, but she knew, even as she looked, that the suit wouldn't be there.

It wouldn't be anywhere. It would be with Emily, on her bike, on her way to the only place where she knew to swim.

Her father's house.

Beside the lake.

FOUR

Madison, Wisconsin

Emily heard sirens. They were faint, but present, like the buzzing of the bees along the shoreline.

She sat on the edge of the dock, her knees against her chest. Her hair dripped down her back and her wet clothes clung to her skin. She was shivering, freezing cold, even though the air around her felt hotter than ever. She had her back to the lake.

If she kept her back to the lake, she didn't have to see Daddy floating out there, his hair burned and mostly gone, his face like a Halloween gross-out mask of a scary person's face.

She didn't mean it. She didn't mean any of it.

Only she couldn't breathe, and Daddy's hands pushed her deeper into the cold water, and all she could think about was how her lungs burned, they burned, and she pushed the burning away—

And Daddy's hands let go. She clawed her way up through the murky water, hearing a strange sound as she did. Something that was outside the water, so loud that she heard it even before her head broke the surface.

She burst from the water with a splash and a great gasp of much-needed air. Water streamed down her face and into her eyes, and she caught some of it in her mouth, choking her.

Around her, screaming echoed, horrifying and deep, screaming like she never heard before. She coughed the water out of her lungs and breathed, and then she turned around, reaching for the dock as she did.

The air was filled with black smoke and an awful rancid burning smell. She could recognize part of the smell—hair burning—but the rest was something she had never encountered before.

The inky blackness poured off the dock and across the lake, engulfing her. She grabbed the ancient wood, then saw through the slats what was burning.

It was Daddy.

She screamed for him, but he didn't seem to hear her. He was slapping himself and dancing on the top of the dock, trying to put out the fire, which seemed to come from his chest and burn upwards.

He had to get into the water. He had taught her that a long time ago. Get into the water, get into the water, get into the water, water puts out flames.

But he didn't and he wouldn't stop so that she could help him. She pulled herself onto the dock. When he saw her, he screamed louder, as if he was afraid of her, and he started running toward the dry grass.

If he did that, everything would burn up. The grass, the house, the neighborhood.

Emily wasn't going to catch him. She wished there was a barrier between him and the grass, so the worst wouldn't happen. But there wasn't. He was going to burn up the whole world—and the sad part was he could stop it if he just jumped into the water.

Then he tripped, and fell backwards, almost as if he had slammed into something. He lay sprawled on the dock, the fire still burning his clothes, and starting to catch the dry wood.

Emily reached him. His eyes were open, his face a hideous mask of black crustiness over red swelling. She could feel the heat rising off him, burning her like her lungs had.

"Daddy," she said. "Daddy, please, get in the water."

He wasn't screaming anymore. His eyes were open and they were staring at her, but they weren't understanding her. She couldn't see Daddy in them.

But that couldn't stop her. His clothes were still burning, only now the fire was moving down his arms and his stomach. She slid her arms under his back, wincing at the heat—it was burning her too—and rolled him over, once, twice, until he splashed into the lake.

Water rose in a funnel around her, like a giant whirlpool, rising, rising, rising but never touching her. The water spilled onto the dock, putting out the small fires that had started on it, and then dripped back into the lake where it belonged.

Daddy was floating on his stomach. That wasn't good.

Emily jumped in beside him, and rolled him over. His eyes were still open, his face almost gone, and his chest—

She could see his bones.

She screamed and shoved him away from her. He moved like a boat heading toward rapids, faster, and faster, as if the water took him where it wanted him to go.

Emily didn't reach for him anymore. She couldn't. She knew it would do no good.

Instead, she climbed out of the water, sat on the dock, and turned her back to the lake. She was too smart to think that if she couldn't see him everything would be all right.

It wasn't going to be all right. The sirens told her that. They were getting closer and closer, as if they were coming for her.

And why wouldn't they?

She had shoved him into the water, and he had been unconscious, and he couldn't hold his breath then like she had been able to do. He drowned, and she had drowned him, even though she had been trying to help him.

He had set himself on fire, but she had killed him.

She rested her chin on her knees and stared at the house where she used to live with her mommy and her daddy, back when they had been the perfect family.

Everything was gone now. Everything was ruined.

And it was all her fault.

FIVE

The Village of Anchor Bay, Oregon

Cassandra Buckingham held the boy's grubby hand in her own. With his other hand, the boy rubbed his nose. He was ten, reedy and wind-blown from being on the beach. His brown hair curled beneath his ears and he had dark brown eyes, alive with warmth.

His mother looked on fondly, her cheeks reddened by the wind. She didn't look anything like her son. She seemed too young to have a ten-year-old, and too buxom—she had probably never been reedy in her life. But her blue eyes were kind and she seemed polite, even though she was as sand-covered as her child.

For the thousandth time, Cassie wished the sign on the window outside read *Fortune Teller*, not *Palm Reader*. She should have thought the entire game through before she had set up her little shop.

She had tried to set up shops before, and had failed, usually because she had to borrow money from her mother. This time, she saved from last summer's waitressing job, and decided to do this on her own.

Fifty-four was too old to be borrowing money from your mother.

It was also too old to waitress, as her knees were telling her. She was still as thin as she had been when she was twenty, but she was getting tired of winding her long black hair on top of her head, and sticking her hands in burning hot water to scrub the dishes when the busboy failed to show.

Initially, she had gotten the waitressing job to prove to her mother that she could survive on her own. Twenty years into the work, and Cassie was still trying to prove herself.

She traced the lines on the boy's hand, even though she didn't have to. Her talents didn't lie in palms. She had psychic powers that one police department had described as scary, back in her younger days when she thought she could use her powers for the common good.

When the boy walked in the room, she had known that he was the one who wanted the reading. She also got his background—the fact that he had lived in or near Anchor Bay his whole life, and that he was here on the beach this afternoon because his aunt, uncle, and cousins were in town, and they wanted to see the touristy sites.

The boy, his mother, and Cassie sat at the table in the center of the room. This table was covered with scarves as well as lit candles and a fake crystal ball she had picked up at a store in Seavy Village. The rest of the room was decorated with some plush chairs (for the waiting customers), smaller tables with scarves (because customers expected that), and some magical doodads she had picked up all over the coast.

The reading would be fairly simple. Cassie didn't want to tell the boy's secrets in front of his mother—the woman didn't need to know that her son had manipulated her to get inside this building.

But talking about other things would be difficult as well, given the boy's very nature. He was sweet. He had a gentle goodness that went deeper than Cassie had ever seen. He was about a year away from middle school, where he'd learn to hide that goodness so that the other boys wouldn't call him names. But he would use it.

Cassie's trick was to talk to him about his nature without calling attention to his own gift. The last thing she wanted to do was stifle it by embarrassing him or shaming him or putting it into his mother's head that the poor little boy always had to take the "right" way out of every circumstance.

"Well?" the mother asked, and she sounded a little nervous, as if Cassie's silence had frightened her. The mother's tone frightened Cassie a little. She didn't want to have a true believer here. That would cause the boy even more problems.

Cassie gave the mother a warm smile. "It'll take just a moment."

Then she traced the lines on the boy's palm, what she could see of them through the sand and accumulated dirt. That had been another flaw in her plan—being this close to the beach always meant she had to deal with sand and dirty children. Next year, if she decided to do this again, she would find a different location, one that—

Funnels, funnels, funnels of water mixed with flames and screams and— sirens, a lot of sirens, from every direction, more and more sirens—she couldn't hear because of the sirens pounding, pounding, pounding...and then she got the sense of someone else, two someones—Lyssa, overwhelmed, terrified, lost—and someone else—Emily? She's so big now, and so powerful—

Cassie opened her eyes. The mother was staring at her, her face pale. The sirens were real. They were outside, blaring down Highway 101, the sounds of summer on the Oregon Coast. Some tourist probably got himself in trouble—

"What was that?" the mother asked.

Oh, damn. Cassie hoped she hadn't spoken out loud. She did that sometimes when she got nailed by an outside vision. Her heart was pounding, and she loosened her grip on the poor little boy's hand. Sweet thing that he was, he hadn't said a word.

Cassie made herself smile. "It was a flash," she said. "Your son here is a wonderful child. He has a strong sense of ethics. You won't ever have to worry about him."

"That was your flash?" the woman asked, as if she couldn't believe it.

"Yes," Cassie lied. "I saw pieces of his future. Once he gets beyond the usual pains of adolescence—"

Usual for someone a shade too kind, without a ruthless edge—

151

"—he'll go on to do some very good things for the people around him."

That was more than she intended to say, but she had no time for subtle language. The mother and her son would have to work out the expectations side of this.

Cassie gave a few more platitudes, a review of the boy's history as she had seen it—and she watched the mother pale even further as it all turned out to be correct—and then she closed the boy's hand and gently set it on the table.

He looked at her for the first time, and she realized that he wasn't afraid of her. If anything, he seemed a bit in awe.

"That's it?" the mother said.

Cassandra nodded. The sirens had grown quite loud, and she was getting a serious headache. She had to make a phone call before the post-vision migraine hit.

"Wow," the mother said. "That's amazing for ten dollars. What do you do for forty-five?"

Cassie made herself smile again. "Usually a bit more, but I rarely get a flash, like I did with your son. I had to share it."

"Without charging us for it?" The mother seemed stunned.

"He is a special child," Cassie said without lying. More people should have children as nice as this one.

The mother stood, and slipped her hand into the pocket of her jeans. She took out some crumpled bills and pried one out of the mess. She peered at it for a moment, then set it beside the crystal ball.

"Thanks ever so much," she said, and took her son's hand. They headed out of the shop.

Cassie rested one hand on the table. She had to pull herself together, pull her defenses back in place. They felt as if they had shattered.

Through the gauze-covered window, she saw the mother put an arm around her son. The boy grinned up at her, and Cassie got the sense that he was very pleased with the afternoon.

She staggered to the door, flipped the lock, and put out the "Closed" sign. Then she wandered into the small back room where she kept her microwave, her mugs, and her teas, as well as the herbal remedies she mixed herself for ailments caused by what her mother called her powers.

Cassie took a small headache draft, hoping it wasn't too late. She might have to go home, take some real medicine, and climb into bed.

But first she had things to do.

She picked up the phone and called the sheriff's dispatch. Athena Buckingham answered with a curt, "Sheriff's Office."

"Mother?" Cassie said. "Dial home. Find out if we have a message from Lyssa."

"Lyssa? Why would she call?"

"I got a flash. Something's wrong with Emily. Something horrible."

"I'm on it," Athena said and hung up.

Cassie hung up too, then grabbed herself a glass of water. The headache was receding just a little. She sank into a chair, and dialed Lyssa's home number in Wisconsin from memory.

The phone rang and rang, but the ringing sounded off. And then, just as Cassie was about to hang up, an automated voice said, *The number you have reached has been disconnected. If you have dialed this number in error, please hang up and try again.*

Cassie shut off her phone. She hadn't reached the number in error. There was no reason for Lyssa to shut off her phone. But then, they hadn't talked in nearly a year.

Lyssa hated having Cassie in her life. Mostly it was because of the psychic connection. Lyssa had felt like she had no privacy as a child. Even after she learned how to block most of Cassie's mental probes, she still wanted nothing to do with her mother.

It had gotten worse a year ago, or perhaps Lyssa had become blunt for the first time in her life.

I know you can raise a barrier against me and my emotions, Mother. Please do it. I don't want you to call every time I cut my finger.

There was more to that request than cut fingers and prying mothers. Something was going drastically wrong with Lyssa's life, and she didn't want Cassie to know about it.

Cassie had made the mistake of flying out to see Lyssa when Emily was born. Lyssa hadn't told her that she was pregnant, so all Cassie had felt was the sudden extreme pain. She had booked a flight, and arrived at the University Hospitals and Clinics in Madison just as the baby did.

Instead of joy at the birth, Lyssa had felt angry and violated, as if the experience she had was tainted somehow by Cassie's presence.

Cassie had tried to ignore that, for Emily was a little miracle. Not just the ten fingers and toes and the perfect little face, but the shape of her face, the deep brown of her hair and eyes proved to Cassie that her husband, Daray, lived on in the granddaughter he would never ever meet.

It was because of Emily that Lyssa kept Cassie in her life. Or, more precisely, because of Emily's paternal grandparents. The Walters wanted to deny that they were related in any way to Lyssa.

Lyssa had always thought it was because on the social scale, she was a nobody, and Cassie had never disabused her of that notion. But the truth of it was that with the Walters unavailable, Daray dead, and Lyssa an only child, Emily's only extended family became her maternal grandmother, Cassie, and her great-grandmother Athena. And because of Lyssa's refusal to return to Anchor Bay, their visits were limited to trips to Wisconsin or family vacations in specific spots.

Always, those trips were without Athena.

Can't leave Anchor Bay without a Buckingham, she would say. And even though Cassie wanted to disagree, she couldn't.

Athena was right.

Cassie tried dialing again, assuming that she might have scrambled the numbers because of her headache. She hadn't. She got the same message—the phone had been disconnected. And recently enough for that message to remain. Phone companies, any more, changed messages like that after three months.

What was going on?

Cassie felt like she was going to betray her daughter if she brought the barrier down—she had promised after all—but that flash had been so strong, so filled with terror.

Cassie held the phone, willing it to ring. And, to her surprise, it did.

She answered, a bit tentatively.

"No message," Athena said without a preamble. "What kind of flash?"

Cassie tried to explain, but as always, words failed her. Then she told her mother that the phone had been disconnected.

"I can find them," Cassie said, "but it means breaking my promise to Lyssa. In an emergency, I'm thinking that maybe that's okay."

"It won't be to Lys," Athena said. "Let me try first. If the phone's disconnected, then maybe she has a new number. I can find that through the office."

"What if it's worse than that, Mom? What if—?"

"Cassandra, phones are disconnected for two reasons: non-payment and moving. Since she's married to a Walters, I'm going to assume that payment wasn't the issue. So they've moved."

"From their dream house?"

Athena sighed, and Cassie got a whisper of something else, a sadness perhaps. But Cassie didn't pursue it. When Cassie was a baby, Athena had gotten a protection spell against Cassie's mental abilities. The spell had long since worn away, but not before Cassie was old enough to understand what it was and why it existed.

Cassie had honored her mother's privacy ever since.

"Cass, you've gotta start reading the gossip rags. You learn things."

Cassandra felt cold. She brushed her hair out of her face. "Like what?"

"Rumors that might be true."

"Don't play with me, Mom. I don't know if we have the time."

Athena shuffled in her chair. It made a familiar squeaking sound, and Cassie could picture her, back straight, her aristocratic features in their primmest position. If someone walked into the sheriff's office at that moment, Athena's expression would scare them away.

"Cass, there were rumors about a year ago that Reginald Walters was mentally ill. He was at some funny farm in Austin, getting his brain rewired."

Cassie gripped the phone tightly. She almost corrected her mother —funny farm, brain rewired, they weren't things people said in polite company. And then she realized that she was objecting, as she always did, to her mother's words when it was the content that disturbed her.

"Do you think that's true?" Cassie asked, her voice almost a whisper. But she could answer the question herself. Even though she had raised a barrier to Lyssa's emotions and because of Lyssa's request, Emily's too, Cassie could still feel a vague sense of them, almost like the background hum of the ocean.

She had the feeling if that hum went away, they would be gone— killed in a car accident or taken from her by the violence that seemed so much a part of American life.

So far the hum had remained. But it had changed in the last year. It had become sadder, angrier, and frightened. Very very frightened. Cassie had used all the restraint she had to keep her own curiosity at bay, figuring if things got bad enough, Lyssa would call.

But maybe Cassie was wrong about that. She always tried to take the best view of her relationship with her daughter.

Lyssa had always had a strong sense of independence, that was all.

Surely, she would come home if she needed to. She was stubborn, but not stupid.

Right?

"Yes, Cass, I think that's true," Athena said. "I did some digging at slow times at work, and I found a lot of things that supported the rumor."

Cassie twisted a strand of her black hair around her forefinger, a habit she hadn't indulged in since she was a girl.

"Why wouldn't she have called?" Cassie heard the plaintive note in her voice and wished it weren't there. But her mother already knew how isolated Cassie felt. It was the story of her entire life. "If they were having problems that serious, we could have helped. Even if she didn't want any magical assistance, she would need help with Emily, right? She would call us for that, surely."

"Cassie."

All it took was that single word, filled with compassion. Cassie blinked, her eyes burning, and tugged on her hair, freeing it from her finger.

"Sometimes you need family, Mom, no matter what your disagreement with them is." Cassie knew this one from personal experience.

"You forget," Athena said, her voice gentle. "Lyssa always wanted to be normal. Bringing us in would just reinforce how abnormal she really is."

Cassie bit her lower lip, tasted blood, and made herself stop. "Find her, Mom. Maybe you should just tell her that you saw those gossip rags and you were wondering if the stories were true."

"Cass, that would work with someone who isn't familiar with your talents, but Lyssa knows them better than anyone. She'll know you had a flash and that you sent me to find out what's going on."

Cassie was gripping the phone so hard her fingers hurt. It took all of her strength to keep from losing her rigid control on her emotions. She and Athena had had one version of this discussion every year of Lyssa's life.

Athena never got between the two of them, not even when she could have done some good.

"Mom." Cassie made sure her voice was even and calm, even though she wasn't feeling that way. "The flash—it was really scary. Lots of violence and horrible things. Please. Help me."

"I'll see what turns up with the department's connections," Athena said. "I'm not going to promise anything else."

Fine, Cassie wanted to say. *Then I'll just do it myself.* But she held that impulse in reserve. If Athena didn't find anything, Cassie would break her promise to Lyssa.

After all, a woman could only be pushed so far.

"Thanks, Mom," Cassie said, and hung up before she really spoke her mind. Then she set the phone back in its cradle, got up, and walked to the main room.

She picked up the crystal ball, wondering if it really worked. There was so much magic in the world, so much she didn't know about it, and she had studied it every day of her life.

If only she could see a half a year into the future. Or a half a day into the future.

Or if she could have perfect vision instead of these flashes.

What she needed to know was so very simple.

She needed to know if her daughter and her granddaughter were all right.

SIX

Whale Rock, Oregon

The False Colors smelled like fish. The odor hit Gabriel as he pulled open the heavy oak door, and he almost turned around and headed back into the parking lot.

It would be a day or two before he could eat fish again. That dead creature had smelled fishy, and the scent lingered on him, even though he hadn't so much as touched her. He wondered how Hamilton Denne would smell after he finished the autopsy, and then decided not to think about it.

Denne had asked Gabriel to meet him for dinner in the False Colors, a restaurant in the town of Whale Cove. The coroner's office was in Whale Cove, even though Seavy Village was the county seat. The fact that the coroner worked out of Whale Cove just showed how much pull Denne really had.

Denne lived in a gated community just south of Whale Cove, and had argued, apparently, that Whale Cove was a lot more convenient for his office than Seavy Village. It wasn't just because he lived in Whale Cove; it was also because Whale Cove was more or less in the center of the county. Whenever Denne had to report to a suspicious death scene, he would have less driving time if he was coming from Whale Cove.

Gabriel figured that driving time was the least of Denne's worries. Mostly, Gabriel believed, Denne just wanted the privacy of an office that was difficult to get to. State officials often visited Seavy Village; they rarely made it all the way to Whale Cove.

Denne's office was filled with marvelous toys and equipment no Oregon county, no matter how wealthy, could afford. Denne had set the place up as his own private laboratory, and he protected it as vigilantly as any mad scientist. Gabriel could count on one hand the number of times he had been allowed inside the place.

But Gabriel was used to Denne, and so, when Denne left the beach and proposed they meet at the False Colors, Gabriel had agreed. He now knew better than to argue that they had to get together in the coroner's office. Denne would show him pictures and maybe, if Gabriel played his cards right, Denne would let him see the interesting parts of the body itself.

If Gabriel could handle that fish smell.

He exhaled through his nostrils and stepped inside the False Colors, willing the fish smell away. It seemed to have faded just in the moment of his pause. Now the air smelled of frying foods, garlic, and beer.

Those were the scents he associated with the False Colors anyway. The restaurant served some of the best food on the Oregon Coast, but only the locals knew that. Tourists wandered in and, in local parlance, ran away screaming.

The décor wasn't that bad, and the incidents of screaming never really happened, but it was true that tourists usually only visited the False Colors once. That was because the restaurant's pirate theme had been seriously overdone. The black-and-white skull-and-cross-bones over the door would have been fine by itself, but combined with the skulls over the fireplace, the sea chanteys with lyrics about death and mayhem blaring from the speakers, and the wooden furniture so rustic that a diner occasionally got splinters, the place seemed forbidding in summer sunshine. Add the rain and windstorms of the winter, and the False Colors seemed like a setting in a Hitchcock movie.

Gabriel tolerated the False Colors. He came here often with Denne, and sometimes with Seavy County politicians. No one worried about outsiders listening into the local conversations. When no tourists came to the place, the owner turned the sea chanteys off and put on some nice jazz (which would be replaced mid-note if an outsider walked in), and the atmosphere became almost pleasant.

A waitress Gabriel had never seen before led him to a booth near the fireplace. Because it was the height of summer and the sun hadn't yet set, no fire burned. Still, the faint scent of woodsmoke lingered.

Gabriel had just ordered a Rogue Ale when Denne walked in. He had changed clothes—now wearing a button-down shirt, open at the collar, and a pair of khaki pants that looked neatly pressed—and his hair was wet.

So the smell had gotten to him too. Gabriel smiled and made himself look at the menu. Lots of little pirates, with scarred faces and greasy hair, decorated the pages. He looked at the specials card, which no one had time to dress up, and made his decision.

"Figured I'd get here first," Denne said as he slipped into his chair.

Gabriel closed the menu. "Nope. I didn't have a lot to do. I canvassed, but I didn't find any witnesses, at least to the death. No one saw the body wash ashore either, although it had been lying there all morning before someone realized it looked human."

Denne set his menu aside. "She. She looked human."

Gabriel put his menu on top of Denne's. "She's not human, is she?"

"No," he said, "but she is female, and damn close to human, close enough that I feel odd calling her 'it'."

"You think there was an intelligence there."

"I know there was." Denne picked up his water glass and took a sip. Then he leaned back in his chair and looked over his shoulder.

The waitress who had seated Gabriel held up a hand. "Just a minute, sir," she said to Denne.

"Is June here?" he asked.

"She'll be here soon, sir."

"Sir." Denne set his chair back down on all four legs. "Crap. She's new."

"That's all right, isn't it?" Gabriel asked, not sure how it mattered.

"Always have to educate the new ones," Denne said.

The waitress came over and, as Denne ordered, Gabriel began to understand why someone new irritated him. His order wasn't on the menu, and it was complicated, and every time she told him that his request wasn't possible, sir, he told her to check in the kitchen.

When Denne finished and Gabriel had ordered, and the waitress had gone back to the kitchen, Gabriel said, "You know, you could have just told her you were a regular and you'd done this before."

Denne grinned, which made him look like a cherubic prep school student. "There's no sport in that."

Gabriel shook his head. "I'm never going to understand you."

"And now you sound like my ex-wife." Denne finished his glass of water and set it at the edge of the table, so that the waitress couldn't miss it when she returned.

Another waiter came by and dropped off Gabriel's pale ale, along with Denne's scotch.

"So you didn't get anything from the canvass?" Denne asked as the waiter left.

Gabriel wrapped his hand around the glass of ale. The liquid was slightly cool, nearly room temperature, the way they served beer in England. He liked it that way; the warmer the beer, the more flavor it had.

"I didn't say that I didn't get anything," Gabriel said. "No one saw her wash up, is all. What killed her?"

Denne shrugged. "I'm taking it slow, but I'm thinking that she suffocated. Her gills were filled with that gooey substance we saw. I haven't gotten to her lungs yet, but I suspect they'll be filled with it too. Then again, I'm just guessing. I've never autopsied one of these creatures. I have no idea if the goo is a natural substance or not."

"I thought you said the physiology was similar to ours."

"The physiology of an ape is similar to ours, too," Denne said, "but there are enough differences that I wouldn't trust myself to know exactly what killed one—if whatever it was was subtle."

"And this was subtle?" Gabriel asked.

"I was hoping for a bullet through the abdomen, or spear hole in the back, or a smashed skull, something that would tell me unequivocally what killed this thing. But I didn't find anything like that. For all I know, she died of old age."

"Like a whale washing ashore," Gabriel said.

Denne shook his head. "This is mysterious in a whole different way. When whales beach, they're usually alive. We just can't get them back out to sea. I've always thought it's like animals in the wild. The old ones somehow know they're going to die, and they leave the pride or whatever and go off on their own, so that they don't jeopardize the herd."

"A herd is not a pride," Gabriel said, a smile playing at his lips. He loved the chance to correct Denne the expert. Gabriel took a sip of the ale, savored the taste of slightly sweet hops, and swallowed.

"You know what I mean," Denne said. "I think the whales are beaching themselves so that they'll die here—like a suicidal man will dive into the ocean. I always had the sense that beached whales get very annoyed with humans who try to save them."

"You don't think she did that, though," Gabriel said.

"I found no sand in her mouth, and nothing to indicate that she was alive when she reached the beach. Judging from her position in the sand, she came in with the tide."

"But didn't go out with it?"

Denne sipped his scotch, winced, and set it down. He had a constant battle going with the False Colors to get them to buy the higher end scotches.

"I have a hunch the water moved her around. She wasn't in the best of shape, and if she were human, I would say she'd been in the water for a while. But she isn't, and I don't know if that rubbery feel to her skin is natural or not. None of my usual cues work in this case. I'm not even sure the smell is one of decay or her usual odor."

Gabriel's stomach turned and he set his ale down. "Thanks for that reminder."

Denne smiled. "You didn't have to spend all afternoon with her.

You should have been there when I opened the body cavity. You could practically see the odor molecules."

Gabriel held up his hands. "I'm crying uncle. In fact, uncle half this conversation ago."

"You're not normally squeamish, Gabe."

"I don't normally find a fish woman on my beach, either."

"All right. We'll stop focusing on her for a moment." Denne pushed his scotch glass away. "If you didn't get time of death, what did you get?"

"Something interesting," Gabriel said. "Most of the tourists had no idea that the body wasn't human. A few said they thought it was a weird-looking fish. But that nervous guy, the one by the cliffs?"

"I really wasn't paying attention to the crowd," Denne said.

The waitress brought Gabriel's meal. He had ordered the Gut-Buster burger—a thick, well-done hamburger patty, with three different kinds of cheese, guacamole, bacon, and salsa—along with a side of french fries and coleslaw.

"Planning to live forever, are you?" Denne asked with some amusement. Usually Gabriel ordered healthier foods.

"I can't handle anything fishy right now," Gabriel said. "Especially after that last description."

Neither, apparently, could Denne. The waitress set grilled chicken, rice, and a side of tomatoes down in front of him. The meal looked lovely, even though it wasn't on the regular menu.

"So," Denne said. "Tell me about the nervous guy."

"He'd seen her before," Gabriel said.

"Her?"

"Or creatures like her." Gabriel took a bite from his burger. Juice ran down his chin, and the guacamole spurted out the back side of the bun, plopping on his plate.

He was coping with his meal and not watching Denne's reaction. When Gabriel finally looked up, he realized that Denne's face had turned pale again.

"What do you know?" Gabriel asked.

"Nothing about your man." Denne had set his fork down.

"No, but you know something about our fish woman."

"I know a lot about our fish woman," Denne said, "but you didn't want to have that conversation during dinner."

"Hamilton," Gabriel said. "Stop playing with me."

Denne's fingers found his scotch glass. They rubbed its sides as if he could absorb the liquid through his skin. "Just tell me what this guy said."

Gabriel took another bite of his burger before reluctantly setting it down. It would take him a while to pick it back up again. The sandwich was falling apart.

"He waited until I got through with everyone else," Gabriel said. "Then he made sure no one was listening. He asked me if I had ever seen creatures like that before."

"Had you?" Denne asked the question sharply. He seemed more intense than usual.

"No," Gabriel said. "But I'd heard about them, mostly from some old-timers."

And he accepted them, because he'd seen stranger things than fish women on this stretch of Oregon beach. He had grown up here, and had had terrifying experiences as a child. When he'd started traveling as an adult, he realized that nothing would compare to the experiences he'd had in Anchor Bay. Finally, he came home, and started the slow process of accepting the supernatural as part of life.

"What did they tell you?" Denne asked.

"What the old-timers told me isn't important," Gabriel said. "What the guy told me was weird."

"Does the guy have a name?" Denne asked.

"Yeah." Gabriel shrugged. "I have it written down somewhere."

Denne picked up his fork and pushed the rice around. It seemed like his appetite was gone. "So he saw her."

"And two others. They attacked his car one night."

"Attacked?"

"His word. I got the sense he was covering something up. He said that was the beginning, and they've harassed him ever since. He said he was happy to see one dead."

Denne pushed the rice so that it lined the edges of his plate. "I trust you asked him what he meant by 'harassed.'"

"He said they came into his house at night, and then he blushed. I thought that part was weird. He said that they left seaweed trails and sand, and sometimes they left sucker marks on the outside of the windows."

"Sucker marks?" Denne said.

"She didn't have suckers?" Gabriel said.

"Not like an octopus." Denne frowned. "I don't recall seeing anything like that at all."

"You're telling me he's making all this up?"

"No," Denne said. "I'm not saying anything of the sort. I haven't finished examining that body. I just did a cursory, looking for cause of death. I'm going to have to do much more, obviously."

"You believe him then, even though you didn't find anything to make the marks?" Gabriel didn't understand what Denne was getting at.

"Just keep going," Denne said.

"He said that these women were driving him crazy. He couldn't sleep because they sang so loudly, and if he did sleep, he'd wake up on the beach, and they'd be there. He said he hoped her death meant he was done with them for good now."

Denne nodded. He knew more than he was letting on.

Gabriel picked up his burger. A slice of bacon fell off the side and into the pile of guacamole. The bun squished between his fingers, and he took a bite before everything slid off.

Denne still hadn't eaten any of his meal.

Gabriel finished the burger in four quick bites, knowing he would probably regret that later. Then he wiped off his fingers.

"Tell me what I should think of this guy," Gabriel said. "His story sure made you quiet."

"What do you think of him?" Denne asked as if he were a shrink, unwilling to express his own opinion for fear it would taint Gabriel's.

"I don't know what to think of his story," Gabriel said, "but his emotions are consistent with someone who's being harassed. He's nervous and confused and angry, and he's pleased that she's dead. I would expect all of that."

"But?" Denne asked.

Gabriel gave him a sideways look. Denne was always too perceptive.

"But," Gabriel said, "he's hiding something."

"He's hiding a lot of somethings," Denne said. "Have you ever heard of *The Lady June*?"

"The Oregon Coast's answer to the *Titanic*." Gabriel picked up a french fry. "What does that have to do with fish women?"

"A lot, actually." Denne pushed his plate aside and picked up his scotch. He took a sip, then looked at the glass as if he were contemplating something in the liquid. "But *The Lady June* really isn't anything like the *Titanic*. We don't have icebergs, and she didn't run aground."

Maritime disasters didn't interest Gabriel. He sometimes had to deal with their aftermath—he'd called the coast guard more times than he cared to think about to help disabled yachts in the surf—but he had no real interest in ships and sailing. Which was, he knew, rather odd for someone who had grown up on the ocean.

"Fish women got her?" he asked, trying to lighten the conversation a little.

"She went down in the middle of a storm. Pretty common for the Oregon Coast."

Gabriel nodded. He ate another fry, and watched Denne play with his alcohol glass. Gabriel had never seen Denne so reflective, and it bothered him.

"Pretty common, except that there were lots of famous people on the yacht, right?" Gabriel asked, mostly to get Denne to continue.

"Not as many as there could have been," Denne said. "Only thirty of Oregon's best families got touched by that disaster."

"Only thirty" was disingenuous. Oregon was a small state—and had been even smaller in the 1930s when *The Lady June* went down. Thirty families had probably been a significant portion of the "important"—i.e. wealthy—families in Oregon at that time.

"I don't understand how *The Lady June* relates," Gabriel said.

"Long story short," Denne said. "There was only one survivor that night. A man by the name of Henry Dyston. He claimed he was brought ashore by mermaids."

"Our fish women?"

Denne nodded.

"Did anyone believe him?"

"The locals did," Denne said. "But the press made a fool of him, not that he cared."

"Why would they rescue only one man?" Gabriel asked.

"Well, that's where local history comes in." Denne set the scotch glass down. He ran his finger along the rim, as if he couldn't quite let go. "These creatures are like the sirens of Greek mythology—"

"Not really," Gabriel said. He hated it when people had a superficial understanding of mythology and literature. "The sirens lived on an island and never went into the water. They lured sailors to their death by singing a haunting song. The sailors crashed their ships against the rocks surrounding the island, never noticing the danger because they were charmed."

Denne stopped moving his finger along the rim of the glass. "I had no idea you were a classical scholar."

Gabriel shrugged. "I've been to Greece. I have an appreciation for the places where legends begin."

Denne didn't say anything. For a moment, Gabriel thought he wasn't going to go on. Then he picked up his fork, scooped up some rice, and ate some.

Gabriel let him eat. Denne had always been strange, but Gabriel had never seen him behave quite like this.

After he ate a few bites, Denne pushed his plate away. He picked up his napkin, and wiped his mouth. Gabriel thought he was going to leave, but instead, Denne pushed his chair away from the table.

"The fish women," he said quietly, "have a song like the sirens did. It lures men, charms them, makes them do things that they wouldn't normally do."

Gabriel nodded. He decided not to interrupt again.

"Most of us can't hear it. The women issue an invitation, and the man must take it. I've heard that it's a simple thing, usually something found in the sand. One man…" and here Denne paused, as if he were remembering. Then he shook his head. "A man I knew said that he found a bottle of wine, an expensive old one, on the beach.

He shared it with his wife, and shortly thereafter, heard the mermaids."

"The wife too?"

Denne reached for his scotch. "She died not long after that. An accident on the beach—at least, that was what it looked like to me. The husband seemed guilty and Dan Retsler—remember him?"

Gabriel did. Retsler had been police chief of Whale Cove for a number of years. He left after the freak New Year's storm of 2000. Something had broken in him, something Denne once hinted had to do with the strange supernatural activity of Seavy County.

"Well, Retsler had me do a full autopsy to see if I could find anything suspicious." Denne paused, staring into his scotch glass. "I didn't—at least at the time. Although she did have sucker marks on her arms and neck. At the time, I thought they were something sexual."

"You don't any longer?" Gabriel asked.

"Sucker marks are a theme with these fish women," Denne said. "I had no idea then, although I should have."

"Why should you have an idea?" Gabriel asked.

Denne gave a small half-smile and didn't answer the question. Instead, he said, "My friend knew a lot about these women. He could hear their song. It made him crazy. He'd wake up on the beach—naked. I think he was convinced they killed his wife."

Gabriel frowned.

Denne swirled the scotch in the glass. "They killed him, I know that much. But I could never decide if it was suicide. All of the men these fish women killed—it's like they have an addiction, and they don't know any other way to cure it except to let it take them."

"All?" Gabriel asked. "How many have there been?"

"I don't know," Denne said. "A dozen. A hundred. Most of them don't talk."

"So how do you know there's been more than one?"

"I know of three," Denne said. "Henry Dyston, my friend."

Denne paused, swirled the scotch again, then downed it in a single gulp.

"And you?" Gabriel couldn't resist the question.

"Close." Denne set the glass down. "My father."

Gabriel's heart started pounding as hard as if he had been running. "I thought your father drowned."

"That's the official story," Denne said.

"And the unofficial story?" Gabriel asked.

"The night he died, he came into my room." Denne's fingers played with the table edge. He wouldn't look at Gabriel. "He gave me some earmuffs, and a copy of Dyston's testimony at his trial, where he was defending himself from charges that he sank *The Lady June* and murdered all those people. My father told me to read the testimony, reminded me that Dyston was acquitted by a jury of his peers—which at the time was an all-male jury gathered from Seavy County—and he begged me to wear the muffs whenever I slept."

"Did you?"

Denne's lips moved in that small smile again. "I still do."

Gabriel frowned. He'd heard the mermaids were dangerous. He had just never heard how. Had he missed warnings somewhere?

"Then my father told me to leave Whale Cove as soon as I got old enough to travel."

"But you didn't," Gabriel said.

"Oh, I did." This time Denne did look up. His blue-gray eyes were sad. "College, med school, internship, and residency. Between them all, I managed to stay away for ten years."

"Why did you come back?" Gabriel asked.

"Why did you?" Denne asked.

It was Gabriel's turn to look down. Denne knew the answer; he had to. It was probably the same for both of them.

At some point, the lure of the ocean—this ocean, the dark Pacific —was too strong. No matter where Gabriel went—the Atlantic seacoast, the Aegean, the Caribbean, the warm Pacific off the tropical islands—it didn't matter. He wanted the rugged coastline and violent waters of his youth.

All of the beaches had a hint of magic to them, but none of them had hold of his heart like this one did. It was as if the Oregon Coast were a woman he loved with more passion than any other woman of his acquaintance. He compared everyone he met to her, and found them all lacking.

Finally, he had given up and come home.

"Point taken," Gabriel said.

Denne looked at him then. "My father also made me swear one thing. He made me swear I would never take a gift from the sea."

"Like a bottle of wine," Gabriel said.

"A bottle of wine, a seashell, seaweed—anything."

"Couldn't our fish woman be considered a gift from the sea?" Gabriel asked.

Denne's head jerked back as if he had been struck. "If so, she's not mine," he said. "You're the one who had her taken away from the beach."

But he didn't sound convinced. After all, he had been excited about the find, as if it was something extra special for him.

"Maybe if you give her back when you're done," Gabriel said.

Denne shook his head. "I don't think this is what my father meant. I think her appearance there is something unusual. I think it's wrong somehow, something gone awry."

"But you don't know," Gabriel said.

"I don't think any of us can know," Denne said, "unless it happens again."

SEVEN

Madison, Wisconsin

More sirens.

Lyssa drove the Bug through the rush hour traffic traveling west on University Avenue. Everyone was leaving the city, heading home—to Middleton and the cookie-cutter west end suburbs. Lyssa had made this drive countless times, and usually she was oblivious to everything but the pattern of the traffic and the comfortingly familiar voices of the *All Things Considered* news crew on the radio.

This time, she had the radio off, and the traffic patterns felt unfamiliar. Her shoulders ached from holding them rigidly, her hands clenched the steering wheel so tightly that her fingers hurt.

The sirens only made things worse. They echoed in the distance and seemed to be moving away from her. No one else on the road even seemed to hear them.

Perhaps they didn't. Perhaps they all had their radios on and the sirens were so faint that the music—the rap, hip-hop, rock, and country—covered it all.

But she could only hear the blood rushing in her ears, the pounding of her heart, and the nervous rapidity of her breathing.

Something was wrong. She had felt it all day. But that feeling, that something-wrong feeling had been so much a part of her life since the beginning of Reginald's illness, she had taken it for granted. It became part of the everyday patter, like highway noise or the hum of a refrigerator. Things heard but not heard.

She probably would notice more if the feeling vanished. She had lived with it so long.

Her turn finally came, abruptly, just like it always had. The roads to the lake were hidden by trees and weeds, making the right side of University Avenue seem like an untended forest instead of the barrier between one of Madison's nicest neighborhoods and the main thoroughfare.

The drive felt both familiar and unfamiliar. She had lived here so long—ten years, all of Emily's life—that each dip in the road felt like a homecoming. But new cars were parked at some of the houses, and Mrs. Nelanic had planted sunflowers to line her borders this year instead of an ornamental grass.

Each difference seemed like a neon sign that the changes in the neighborhood were as permanent as the changes in her life.

Finally, Lyssa turned onto her old street. The house was in a slight valley, the driveway invisible from the road. Still, she felt a thread of disappointment that she couldn't see Emily or her bike.

Lyssa wished it could be just that easy—and she had known, deep down, that it wouldn't be.

The garden Lyssa used to tend so carefully hadn't been touched in the year since she'd been gone. Weeds sprang up higher than the saplings she'd planted three years before.

And the house she and Reginald had designed, their dream house, needed paint, a new window on the southeast corner, and patching on the roof. The house's dismal condition confirmed her worst suspicion: Reginald was off his medication again.

Her car slid into the valley, and the weeds thinned to reveal police cars parked in the driveway, one with its lights still revolving. The siren was off, but the light seemed to scream at her—blue and red and terrified.

Her chest hurt, and she realized she hadn't taken a breath since she saw the squads. She made herself breathe. There could be a hundred reasons for the police presence, all of them having to do with Reginald.

If he was off his medication, then he could be doing anything from terrifying the neighbors to lighting the bushes on fire. The police presence didn't mean that Emily had come here.

It didn't mean that Emily was hurt.

Lyssa stopped near the front door. She shoved the car in park as she shut off the ignition, and got out. As she ran through the tangle that had once been her garden, she heard sirens start up again, the whoo-whoo-whoo of an ambulance trying to get through the city's overcrowded streets.

It was almost impossible to hear sirens here, so near the lake. The sirens had to be really close.

The thought terrified her, and she blocked it out, running down the flagstone path she had laid herself the summer before Emily was born. The stones were broken, as if someone had gone after them with a hammer, and more than once, Lyssa tripped as she hurried forward.

Then the sirens shut off, mid-whoo. Her ears echoed. All she could hear was her own labored breathing. The grass smelled like dry hay and her roses, gamely blooming despite the neglect, gave off a heady scent.

She burst through the overgrown arbor onto the patio, and saw Emily's favorite beach towel—one her Grandmother Cassie bought for her at a coastal doll shop—rolled carelessly and flung aside.

Lyssa forgot to breathe. She grabbed the towel like it was a lifeline and hugged it to her chest. The towel was hard on the inside—Emily's book.

Police milled around the backyard, and several stood in a clump in the reeds near the water's edge. Two people sat on the dock, one of them slight, the other wearing blue, and Lyssa's heart flipped over.

The slight one had wrapped her arms around her legs, her knees pressing against her chest. The other person put a hand on the slight one's shoulder, and the slight one turned her head, making it clear she didn't want to be touched.

The movement was so Emily, so post-divorce Emily, that Lyssa felt her eyes burn.

Lyssa was running across the yard even before she realized she had given her body the command to move. Emily was all right—something here was wrong, but not with Emily. Emily, who shouldn't be here at all, in this dilapidated, once-loved house, with police poring all over the yard.

Just as Lyssa reached the dock, two police officers stepped in front of her, solid blocks of blue. She stumbled into them and they caught her, hands firm on her arms.

"Ma'am, what's your business here?" the officer to her right asked. He had a tasteful name badge above his left breast pocket. A single word—Mostert—had been etched into the gold.

"That's my daughter on the dock," she said.

"Did someone call you, ma'am?" This from the other officer.

Lyssa didn't even look at him. She was trying to peer over his shoulder. But she couldn't see past him. She couldn't see Emily.

She thought about screaming Emily's name, but realized that wouldn't get her through this blue wall.

"I'm Lyssa Buckingham," she said to Officer Mostert. He didn't seem as young as the other one. He had frown lines around his eyes. "I used to live here. I was married to Reginald Walters until this summer. That's our daughter on the dock."

The police officers exchanged a look that made Lyssa feel cold. Some kind of message went between them, some kind of warning. She didn't know what it was or what it meant, only that it terrified her.

"I want to see her!"

"Did she call you, ma'am?" Officer Mostert asked.

"No." Lyssa shook her right arm out of his grasp.

"Then how did you know where she was? Was she supposed to come here?"

"She's not supposed to see her father. He's dangerous. She knows better, but she's been missing him—"

"Dangerous?" the other officer asked.

Lyssa shook her arm from his grasp, and stepped back from both of them. Something had happened here, something she didn't understand.

Her face felt flushed from the heat. Sweat poured down her back, and she was tired. She hated this place. Once she had loved it. She remembered standing on this back lawn, as untended ten years ago as it was now, and thinking she could make this a beautiful home, having no idea the heartache she would feel in this place, how much of her it would destroy.

"My husband is mentally ill," Lyssa said, wishing suddenly for her attorney. No one believed anything bad of the Walters. No one understood that one of America's first families could have anything wrong with it. "He tried to kill our daughter, and threatened her several times."

"Yet she came back?" This from Mostert.

Lyssa made herself take a deep breath. She remembered all of this from before. The police had an advantage; they weren't emotionally involved in the situation. She had to be calm, remain calm, act calm or they wouldn't let her do what she wanted.

"Is there a reason you're not letting me see her?" Lyssa asked. The edge remained in her voice, but at least the panic was gone. Even though the panic lurked beneath, threatening to overpower her. Maybe the slight figure on the dock wasn't Emily at all. Maybe it was a neighbor child who had stumbled onto Emily's body, over there in the reeds.

"Do you have identification?" the other officer asked, and with that, Lyssa had had enough.

"I don't need it," Lyssa said, and shoved her way between them, pushing with all of her might.

To her surprise, the officers parted, letting her through. She walked to the dock, so that her movements did not seem threatening, and as she got closer, she was relieved to see that the small figure was indeed Emily.

Emily, with her short hair standing up in damp spikes. Emily, her wet clothes clinging to her straight childish form.

Her swimming suit must have been in that towel with the book.

Somehow Emily had made it all the way to the end of the dock and into the water without putting on her suit.

But the cabana was gone, the foundation still there. The concrete had char marks—a fire? That would be in keeping with Reginald's madness.

And no Reginald anywhere.

Lyssa felt the hair rise on the back of her neck. She was thinking of fire because the air had the faint odor of smoke, and with it, the distinctive smell of burnt hair. Beneath it was another, greasier odor, and even though she had never smelled it before, she knew what it was.

Burned flesh.

Her own skin crawled and she shivered despite the heat. She stepped onto the dock, the old wood sinking and creaking under her weight.

Emily didn't move, didn't even look up to see who was coming toward her. Next to her, the person in blue turned out to be a woman, a female cop who was either comforting her or interrogating her or both.

Lyssa felt a rush of anger, mixed with protectiveness. She had also inherited a healthy dose of her hippie mother's distrust of the police.

"Emily!" Lyssa called.

Her daughter's head rose, as if from a sound sleep, and then, when Emily saw her mother, she let out a little cry. Her arms fell to her sides, pushing her up from the dock, and she ran forward, her feet shuffling, as if she had almost no energy at all.

Lyssa hurried toward her. They met in the saggiest part of the dock, the wood bending beneath their combined weight. Emily stopped in front of her, as if she were afraid to hug her.

"Mommy?" Emily sounded like she had when she was really little and tired or very ill. Weak and defeated. Lyssa hadn't heard that voice from her in years.

"Come here, baby." Lyssa crouched and opened her arms.

Emily hesitated, showing a reserve she had never shown before.

"Hold me, Em," Lyssa said.

But her daughter shook her head. Her lower lip trembled and

tears floated in her eyes. Even though her cheeks were covered with dirt and sand from the lake, there were no tear tracks running down them.

Lyssa was the one who went forward, and put her arms around her daughter. Emily remained rigid, refusing to hug back, something she had never done, not even in the height of the divorce.

Lyssa crouched again, sliding her hands down her daughter's arms until she could see directly into Emily's eyes. The tears had receded unshed, but Emily's eyes were red. She also had shadows beneath them that Lyssa had never seen before.

"What happened, baby?" Lyssa asked.

"Daddy." That little voice again, trapped in some kind of pain. Emily's lower lip still trembled.

"What about him?"

Emily didn't answer. Instead, she swept an arm toward the reeds where all the police had gathered.

Lyssa's stomach clenched. What had he done this time? Called his daughter before he killed himself so that she would find the body? That fit with his psychosis. Reginald would do anything to destroy Emily's life.

"Are you Mrs. Walters?" The female police officer stood behind Emily. The wood buckled even more with the added weight. Lyssa wondered if this part of the dock would snap. But it seemed to have a lot of give. The wood was old and swollen from the humidity.

Still, Lyssa would have to move Emily off of there. Lyssa didn't want her daughter falling into the water again.

"Ma'am?" the police officer said. There was a sternness to her tone, a don't-fuck-with-me attitude that seemed inappropriate given the circumstances.

"My name is Lyssa Buckingham." Lyssa kept one hand on Emily's shoulder as she stood up. She wasn't going to relinquish any hold on her daughter. "I was married to Reginald Walters at one time."

"And this is your daughter?"

"She hasn't told you that?" Lyssa felt surprised.

"She hasn't said anything, ma'am, not until you arrived."

Lyssa drew Emily close. Emily wrapped her arms around Lyssa's waist.

"What happened here?" Lyssa asked.

"We don't exactly know," the officer said. She sounded formal, as if she were reciting the information in court. "I'd prefer not to discuss it here, if you don't mind."

The officer gave the top of Emily's head a pointed look. Emily had buried her face in Lyssa's waist. Lyssa ran a hand down Emily's hair, smoothing it.

"I'm going to take my daughter home," Lyssa said.

"Before you do, ma'am, we need to talk with you."

Lyssa gave the officer a cool glance. "About what?"

"We need your help, ma'am. It didn't feel right asking the girl."

The girl. As if Emily weren't even here.

Emily shivered and clung tighter.

"Help with what?" Lyssa asked.

"We'd like you to make an identification, ma'am."

An identification. The officer was trying not to be specific, apparently for Emily's sake. An identification of a body.

Although that made no sense if they had already asked Emily to help them. They wouldn't be trying to protect her.

Lyssa felt like she had walked into another world. "Let's get off this dock."

But Emily didn't move. Instead, Lyssa had to bend down and pick her up, and carry her to shore.

Emily's clothing was cool against Lyssa's skin, and her hair smelled of lake water. She seemed smaller than Lyssa remembered, as if she had shrunk one size down in the afternoon.

"Don't go, Mommy," Emily whispered in her ear. "Please. Don't go over there."

Lyssa looked at the officer. The woman had no compassion on her face. She was watching impassively, as if she were waiting for Lyssa to set Emily down and come help.

"I'd like to see what's over there," Lyssa lied. She had a hunch she already knew. But she also knew she wouldn't be satisfied until she went over there herself.

"No, Mommy. Please."

"Have you seen what's there, Emily?"

Emily nodded her head against Lyssa's shoulder.

"What is it?"

Emily's entire frame became rigid.

"Em?" Lyssa said, waiting for an answer.

"Can we go home?" Emily's voice was plaintive.

"You're Mrs. Walters?"

Lyssa was beginning to hate that question. This time, it came from a squat man wearing a cotton dress shirt with the sleeves rolled past his elbows, and a pair of black pants. His blond hair was badly cut, and he was sunburned in the bald spot on his crown.

"Not anymore," Lyssa said coolly.

"But you were married to Reginald Walters?"

For my sins, Lyssa thought. But she didn't say that. Instead, she said, "My daughter's obviously suffered some kind of trauma, Mr. —?"

"Detective Volker, ma'am, and I'm sorry for the trauma. But we have to keep moving on our investigation. Maybe Officer Dassen could hold your daughter for a moment?"

Emily clung tighter to Lyssa. Lyssa's arms and back were growing tired. She hadn't held her daughter like that in years.

"Em," Lyssa said, "let me take you to your towel and your book. I'll join you in just a minute, okay? You'll be able to see me the whole time."

Emily let Lyssa carry her as if she were still three. It was work carrying Emily up the lawn. Lyssa had done it countless times when Emily was little, but Emily wasn't that little any more.

When they reached the patio, Lyssa eased Emily down. Emily let go as if she hadn't wanted to be held in the first place. Then she grabbed her towel like it was a lifeline. She turned her back on Lyssa, making the point without speaking to it—she had asked her mother to stay away from those reeds, and Lyssa wasn't going to, so Emily wouldn't watch.

Lyssa ran her hand on her daughter's damp hair, then turned, and gasped. The detective was standing closer to her than she expected, probably to try to hear what Lyssa and Emily were saying.

Fortunately they had said nothing.

"What's going on, Detective?" Lyssa asked. The entire front of her shirt was wet. Emily had been soaked, which probably added a few pounds. Lyssa shook out the material, resisting the urge to squeeze it.

Volker glanced over his shoulder at Emily. Lyssa saw her through the corner of her eye. Emily had unrolled the towel, and tossed her suit on the grass. She was drying her face and hair, her book at her feet beside her.

"One of your neighbors—"

"I no longer live here, Detective," Lyssa said. "Reginald and I divorced in the spring."

Volker made an acknowledging grunt, nodding his head once, as if he had already known the information. Maybe he had. Maybe he was testing her in some way.

"Well," he said, as if they were having a comfortable conversation, "one of the neighbors called 9-1-1, said he heard a lot of screaming coming from the Walters place. Then another neighbor called, saying he saw a boat on fire near the Walters dock. They both stayed on the line—apparently they were from different parts of the neighborhood, because the screaming couldn't be heard on the second call. The dispatch got it on the first. The screaming was a man's."

A shiver ran down Lyssa's back.

"If you don't mind my asking," the detective said, his hands clasped behind his back, "what are you doing here, Mrs. Walters? No one called you. We weren't able to get a word out of your daughter, so we had no idea how to reach you."

Lyssa licked her lower lip. It was chapped and dry, odd for this weather. She must have been doing that a lot.

She glanced at the reeds. The other officers were still there. One of them was talking on his radio, and another was crouched near the waterline.

The detective walked halfway between the patio and the reeds. Lyssa did too.

From this position, she had to turn her head to see Emily. She did. Emily had finished drying off. She was sitting cross-legged on the flagstones, the book open in her lap. But she wasn't reading. She was staring at the house.

"When I got home from work," Lyssa said, "Emily was missing, and so was her bike. She'd been talking about swimming, and she'd never swam anywhere but here. I figured she had ridden to see her father."

"Does she do that often?"

Lyssa sighed. "No. Right now, he's not allowed to see her. My ex-husband is mentally ill, detective. He threatened Emily's life on more than one occasion."

"And she still wanted to come here?"

"She had no idea." Lyssa's voice broke, surprising her. She had thought she was under complete control. "I thought it was better to keep that from her. I mean, he's still her father, after all. She didn't need to know that her father focused his insanity on her. I want her to be a normal child."

The detective grunted again. Lyssa couldn't tell what that sound meant. Was it a disagreement? Or did it mean that Emily would have no chance at normal now?

"So you just drove over here?" the detective said.

"I figured if she wasn't here, then I'd panic." The words came out before Lyssa even thought them through.

The detective smiled slightly, and nodded. "I got two daughters myself. Just when I thought I had them figured out, they'd do something I wouldn't expect. And with my job, you think of the worst."

What was he doing? Trying to bond with her? Trying to be sympathetic? She didn't care about his life. She cared about that little girl on the flagstone, the one pretending to read while she longed for the childhood that had already escaped her.

"What happened here, Detective?" Lyssa asked.

"Wish to God I knew," he said. "All we know is that someone died, rather horribly, and your little girl is the only witness."

Even though Lyssa had expected something bad, she hadn't

expected the words "rather horribly." Her knees felt weak. "The boat fire?" she asked.

"There was no boat," Detective Volker said. "But there was a fire."

He put a hand on her arm. The gesture seemed comforting and demanding at the same time. He helped her forward, leading her to the reeds.

"Have you ever seen a dead body before, Mrs. Walters?"

Why hadn't she corrected him about her name? She had corrected Officer Mostert.

"No," she said. "Not outside of funeral homes and the *Discovery Channel*, anyway."

Volker nodded. "This isn't pleasant at the best of times. The first one, though, is always the worst."

The ground was dry and unfamiliar. There used to be a bit of a marsh here, water seeping around the shoes. But the summer drought had apparently taken care of that.

"Then why can't it wait until the body's been taken to a morgue and maybe cleaned up a little?" Lyssa asked.

"Because, ma'am, if the body isn't who we think it is, then our investigation proceeds differently."

"Who do you think it is?" Her heart was pounding. She slowed as they approached the other officers, even though Volker kept the pressure on her arm.

"We'd prefer you to tell us, ma'am," he said.

They thought it was Reginald. She had known that somehow. It was the logical thing. Or they wanted her to rule out Reginald. And if she ruled him out, then he would probably become some kind of suspect, especially after what she had said about Emily.

Her hand went to her throat. She looked at Emily again. Her daughter hadn't moved.

Suddenly all the pieces made sense. Of course. Reginald had set someone on fire, and Emily had tried to save him. That was why she was wet—she had tossed him in the lake, creating the burning boat image for the other neighbor.

But even as Lyssa thought of that, she knew it wasn't true. If there had been a fire anywhere near the shore or on the deck, there would be evidence of it, particularly considering how dry the grass was. And there wasn't.

"Mrs. Walters, please," the detective said. "Let's just get this over with."

She nodded, shook his hand off her arm, and walked to the reeds herself. Two of the police officers parted as she came, just enough to give her a view of the reeds.

They were flattened in the middle, and gone on the lake side. The other cops stayed in their positions, perhaps protecting the crime scene or just continuing their work. Lyssa couldn't see what they were focused on until she reached the first two officers' sides.

She saw the feet first. They looked surprisingly normal—untouched in any way. They were bare, the toes as long as fingers and the black hairs sprouting from the top of the arch were as familiar to her as her own.

The ankles seemed naked and vulnerable—Reginald was not a man who looked good in shorts. To Lyssa's surprise, her eyes filled and she didn't blink. She couldn't. She didn't want to cry for him.

That smell she had noticed when she first got near the dock was stronger here, only it had a damp quality to it, like wood from a fire that had just been doused. Only this smell wasn't wood smoke.

Her own stomach churned. She clasped her hands together and held them against her ribs, as if she were trying to control the nausea rolling inside her. She couldn't take her gaze from those feet, knowing that everything else she saw in these weeds would be infinitely worse.

No one spoke. Even the man crouching near the top of the reeds watched her. They all seemed to be waiting for her verdict, as if they had prepared this body especially for her.

She wanted to laugh at the ludicrous thought, but knew it wouldn't be appropriate. Any release of emotion at this time wouldn't be right, because once she let the emotion out, she wouldn't be able to rein it back in and she had to, for Emily. Lyssa had to be strong.

Lyssa swallowed the bile that rose in her throat and made herself look at the rest of the body.

She wished she hadn't. There was no torso, only a blackened

mess. The stench came from there, as if the fire had started inside him and burned its way out.

The pain must have been incredible. No one deserved that. Especially not someone she had once loved.

Someone Emily still loved.

Lyssa blinked, but her eyes were dry and sore. The stench was a palpable thing. She was slightly dizzy, and she knew if she stood here much longer, she would pass out.

Her gaze moved upward one last time. To his face.

It still looked like Reginald. Reginald, after a bad sunburn or too much time in the wind. Or maybe he had stood in front of an open oven too long.

His skin was red and cracked, his lips swollen, his eyes sunken into his face. They were open in a way he never kept them in life, making him look startled, even though the rest of his face had no expression at all.

His eyebrows, thick, bushy, and so much a part of his humor, were gone, burned away, like the cowlick in the center of his forehead. All of the hair around his face was gone, and she wondered briefly if he looked the same in the back.

But the fire had come outward. She knew that as if she had seen it happen.

She swallowed again, her Adam's apple bobbing dryly against her parched throat.

"It's Reginald," she said.

One of the men beside her put his arm around her shoulder and turned her around. She needed his help. Her feet weren't working right. He led her to a space on the grass where she and Reginald had once kept a horseshoe pit—now overgrown and weedy—and she sank onto it.

Her entire body was trembling. The screaming—that had been Reginald. The fire—that had been him too.

And Emily had been here, alone with him.

Emily, who was physically fine. Just a little wet.

The detective sat down beside Lyssa. His face was filled with compassion. "I'm sorry, ma'am," he said. "We just had to know if that was him or if he had somehow caused this."

"And then you'd go looking for him." Her voice didn't sound like her own, raspy, small.

"The neighbors said he'd been irrational lately."

Irrational. Such a small word for all the damage she saw around her. The cracked windows, the ruined flagstones, the destroyed path.

Irrational. Reginald had become so much more than irrational, and his famous family, so concerned with its own reputation, hadn't foreseen the problem.

Now they would have an even bigger PR mess than they realized.

Another shiver ran through her. Emily. Emily had been here alone and the tabloid press would swallow her whole.

Lyssa raised her head.

Emily was watching her, worry on her small face.

"Can you ask your daughter what happened?" Detective Volker said.

"I'm sure she tried to save him, Detective," Lyssa said.

"Her hands aren't charred," he said.

And that was when Lyssa knew. She would get no real sympathy from this man. Something terrible had happened to Reginald while Emily was here, and that made Emily at best a witness, at worst a suspect.

Lyssa stood, and walked over to her daughter, without saying another word to the detective.

Emily stood too, that expression still on her face. She hunched forward, as if she were protecting herself, but from what Lyssa did not know.

As Lyssa got close, Emily whispered, "I'm sorry, Mommy."

And Lyssa didn't have the needed moment to compose her face. Her daughter saw the full measure of her horror as the realization hit her.

The Buckingham powers worked away from Anchor Bay. Emily had come into her own, and Lyssa hadn't even noticed. Cassie had said that Emily would be more powerful than all of them, but Lyssa thought it a scare tactic, a way to make Lyssa run back to Cassie and Athena, who would turn Emily into another Buckingham witch.

Emily saw the look, and matched it, horror for horror. She turned away, bending down, grabbing her book, and stumbling blindly toward her towel. Her world was ending—her father gone, her mother disgusted by her—and Lyssa knew the feeling. She remembered it so incredibly well.

"Em, hon," she said.

But Emily wouldn't stop. She bent over, reached for the towel, and her fingers didn't grasp it.

Lyssa caught her, wrapped her arms around her and pulled her up. Lyssa's back protested again, but she didn't care. She turned Emily around.

"Em, honey, I'm sorry too. I love you. I love you more than anything."

But the words did nothing. Emily kept her head down, refusing to meet Lyssa's gaze.

Lyssa wanted to ask her what caused it, a release of power so strong that it burned a hole through the person nearest to Emily, but she didn't dare—not yet. Maybe not ever.

Lyssa held her daughter close, and knew they couldn't stay here. Lyssa had been wrong all these years. She would never get a normal life, and neither would her daughter.

They had to run to Anchor Bay so that her family could teach Emily how to be a Buckingham without ruining her life.

If it wasn't already too late.

PART II

THE PRODIGAL DAUGHTER RETURNS

NOVEMBER 2002

EIGHT

Highway 19, Mile Marker 3
Seavy County, Oregon

The rain was horizontal, pushed by the twenty-mile-an-hour winds. The gusts went as high as sixty, not out of the ordinary for the Oregon Coast in November, but damned uncomfortable all the same.

Gabriel tugged the hood of his rain slicker over his *Detroit Tigers* baseball cap. For once, the brim wasn't keeping the water off his face. His cheeks were numb with the cold and wet, and his nose felt like it was about to fall off.

He'd been out here since the rain got worse in the middle of the afternoon. The road half a mile west had become a lake too deep for even the most outrageous SUV to plow through. His town was becoming an island, and there wasn't much he could do about it.

His two deputies flanked him on either side of the road. One held the industrial strength flashlight which was making no difference at all in the darkness. The other was holding one of the county's few Stop/Slow signs—with the big red Stop side facing oncoming traffic.

Not that there was any. Everyone in the valley knew by now that this latest storm was washing away coastal roads. Highway 18 to the south, the only other route through the Van Duzer corridor, had already lost its outbound lane to a landslide. Highway 26, to the north, had been blocked by another slide for days. No one knew when that highway would open, given the extent of the damage.

Highway 101 had been closed all day south of Yachats due to high winds. So had Newport's Bay Bridge. Anchor Bay was shielded from some of the winds by the cliff faces on either side of the village, forming the bay, but both north and south of the village, the highway looked iffy.

Gabriel had seen it like that a handful of times before, and eventually, the road would fall away. The entire coastal highway system was built on sand, and in rains as bad as Oregon had seen this fall, sand simply crumbled away.

His radio squawked. He picked it up with his gloved fingers, fumbling to press the talk button.

In order to get good reception, he had to turn his face toward the rain. He sputtered, just like the radio had.

"What?"

"Oregon State Patrol finally made it to Valley Junction," Athena said. She sounded calm and collected, but of course, she would, considering she was inside the dry sheriff's office. "They expect to send a squad or two to the corridor entrance on 19 in the next half hour."

Gabriel wiped the water from his face. "That's what they've been saying for the past two hours."

"I know," Athena said. "But they'll make it this time. They had to close the road past Spirit Mountain Casino first. Apparently, Highway 18 is really bad."

"This isn't a lot better," Gabriel said. "I've been worried that we haven't seen any traffic for a while. Have you gotten any reports of problems between here and Joe's Tavern?"

Joe's Tavern was at the last intersection on the east side of the corridor before 19 became the only road. No little town had grown around Joe's, not like Valley Junction had grown in the nine years since Spirit Mountain Casino had opened its doors.

"Just talked to Joe," Athena said. "No one's turned around. Said he saw a few cars. Might be locals heading home to the mountains, might be a few tourists who couldn't buy a clue."

"Don't know why any tourist would be traveling in this weather," Gabriel mumbled. But then, he was the guy who didn't understand the tourists who poured over to the coast whenever big storms were forecast. Those folks complained more than anyone about the weather, and then they sat in their hotel rooms, watching the rains lash the windows and drinking hot toddies.

Of course, they also died in record numbers, trying to walk on the beach, standing in the look-outs when big waves came crashing by, or sitting on logs when the water picked them up and turned them into matchsticks.

"I'm pretty sure you're nearly done," Athena said. "Then I'd just set up some barriers and head home. Hell, I'd do that now if I were you."

Gabriel recognized her tone. "Did you want to go home, Athena?"

"I'm an old woman, Gabe. I've already been here for twelve hours."

She was old—seventy-something (he had never checked, mostly out of fear of Athena)—but she had more energy than all the rest of them combined.

"Well," he said, "I've been out here in the rain for six. You get to go when I do."

And then, like a coward, he shut the radio off.

He was probably going to pay for that. Athena pretty much got her own way around the sheriff's department. She'd worked as the dispatch longer than Gabriel had been alive. She had told him the story of his birth so many times that he had gotten sick of it. It had been a stormy night like this one, and at that time, Anchor Bay hadn't had its own hospital. His father needed an escort to get him to the nearest hospital, which was in Whale Rock.

In the end, the sheriff at the time had just driven the frightened family at high speeds across dangerous roads. Athena swore that was why Gabriel had come back from his wanderings. He was destined to be Seavy County's sheriff from that moment on.

Gabriel didn't believe in destiny, although he wasn't sure why. He seemed to believe in everything else. He just knew that, even on nights like this, he couldn't imagine being anywhere else.

So a few more cars had gone into the corridor. If they weren't going home to Pelican Creek or some of those mountain hideaways deep in the corridor, the ones that scared even him, then they'd get to Mile Marker 3 in 20 minutes, assuming good road conditions.

And that wasn't a good assumption on this night. He had another hour, maybe more, before he could go home, light a fire, and thaw himself out.

"News?" Zeke Chan, Gabriel's main deputy, yelled from his position near the squad.

Gabriel shook his head. The wind seemed to have come up, making the rain lash even harder.

They were standing in an open space on a bit of an incline. They had to be away from the trees, just in case one of the larger gusts knocked down a limb.

Gabriel was already worried enough about falling power lines. He kept trying to talk the power company into putting in underground cables, and they kept threatening to make the residents of Anchor Bay pay the costs.

Gabriel knew it would take someone dying from a downed cable, electrocuted out here in the middle of nowhere, before the power companies took some initiative themselves.

Zeke dashed across the road. The water was getting deep here too. The sheer volume of rain falling in the last few weeks guaranteed local flooding and landslides. The ground had been saturated at the beginning of October. This was the wettest fall that Gabriel remembered, and that included the famous fall of 1999. Usually, there were sun breaks and often days without rain, but not this time. When the weather turned in September, the rains came with a vengeance. It had felt like deepest darkest winter.

If this was fall, Gabriel didn't want to see what winter would be like.

Zeke reached him. The flashlight's beam showed the waves Zeke had made in the puddles with his boots.

Zeke's rain slicker was yellow, just like Gabriel's. They bought yellow after a police officer from Seavy Village was killed stopping traffic on a night like this. He had been wearing the regulation green.

Water dripped off the hood of Zeke's slicker. His heart-shaped face looked red and chapped. He'd been here even longer than Gabriel. Zeke was the first one to notice that the ditches on either side of the highway had converged to form Seavy County's newest lake.

"We haven't seen anybody for half an hour or more," Zeke said. "What say you we call this one? Set up a few barricades, let the motorists take their chances?"

Gabriel would have loved nothing better but that wasn't his mandate. Someone had to stay here until the highway patrol showed up. Once they arrived, they took control of the area, and decided how to protect the average citizen from the roadside hazard.

"The highway patrol's not going to get here tonight," Zeke said, "and I'll bet they're not going to make it through the corridor anyway. If the roads here are falling away, imagine that sinking section around Mile Post 25. It's got to be gone by now."

"I hope not," Gabriel said. "It's got a curve on either side. Only locals would know that it's even there, and they always drive too fast."

Zeke sighed. He apparently knew Gabriel well enough to understand that little statement as a refusal to leave.

"Well, at least one of us can go," Zeke said. "I'm sure there'll be another emergency elsewhere soon."

"Got a hot date?" Gabriel asked.

"With my shower," Zeke said, and laughed.

"Let's give it another half an hour," Gabriel said. "Athena tells me a few cars left Joe's Tavern awhile ago."

"Storm watchers?"

"Locals, I'm hoping."

Zeke shot him an exasperated look. They both knew that anyone driving through the corridor tonight was either a tourist or someone who couldn't get away from his job, even for one bad night.

The chance of those cars belonging to locals was pretty slim.

"Crap." Gabriel grabbed his radio and flicked it back on. He had meant to turn it on a few seconds after he spoke to Athena, so that when she called back in irritation, she couldn't reach him. But he'd left it off a good ten minutes now.

"What?" Zeke asked.

"Accidentally shut the radio off," Gabriel said.

Zeke grinned. "Accidentally my ass. Athena wanted to go home too, didn't she?"

Gabriel shrugged.

"You should let her. That precipice she calls a driveway has got to be nasty in storms like this."

Gabriel hadn't even thought of that. "She's a big girl. If she needs to stay in town, she will."

"If there's room at any of the inns."

"It's the first of November," Gabriel said. "The season was over long ago."

Although the tourist season had been changing lately, lasting longer and longer. With fewer people flying, and money tight, destination travel turned out to be somewhere close to home, like the coast, rather than Maui.

Not that Gabriel wanted to be in Maui. He wasn't fond of the islands.

"The first of November," Zeke said reflectively. "All Souls Day."

"All Saints Day." Gabriel adjusted the bill of his very wet cap. He never used to give the day after Halloween much attention until he went to France. There, in the Loire Valley, he had awakened on November first to the sound of church bells.

Church bells, and sunshine, and closed restaurants. He had to wander the streets until he found an open boulangerie, where he bought a croissant, took a bottle of water from his room, and went down to the center of town. There was one of France's more famous castles. He sat on the grounds, near the algae-covered moat, watching two teenage boys practice their juggling, with the bells still ringing, and felt like he had gone to heaven.

France was a long way from here.

"Gabe?" Zeke said. "Lost you somewhere."

"All Saints Day," Gabriel said. "Just remembering a trip I took."

"Yeah, like which one? You've taken more trips than anyone I know."

Gabriel nodded, but didn't share the memory. "I think you should check the east side of the highway. We've had two inches of rain since we've been out here, and I'm getting a bad feeling about this. I'm not sure we set up in the right place."

Zeke glanced over at Suzette Hackleberry, the other deputy. She was holding up the Stop/Slow sign. Usually she worked backup dispatch for Athena, but on nights like this, Gabriel needed more people on the road.

"Okay to leave her?" Zeke asked.

"She'll be all right for a little while," Gabriel said.

Zeke nodded. "If the road's bad up ahead, what do I do?"

"Radio the State Patrol, and have them shut down 19 through the corridor," Gabriel said.

He remembered that happening when he was a boy, but he doubted it had happened since. There would be a lot of fuss, particularly from locals who worked on the other side of the Coastal Mountain range. With 19, 26, and 20 closed, they would have only 18 to make it over the mountains—and that was if that highway didn't slide away either.

Water slithered down his back, somehow finding its way in from the front of his rain slicker. The chill made him even colder.

Zeke jogged off toward the trees and the darkness. The flashlight clutched in his right hand sent ripples of light along the soggy highway.

Gabriel watched him go for a moment. Maybe he would have to contact Athena, have her insist the state patrol guys showed up sooner rather than later, and talk them into driving the corridor.

Gabriel was a good driver, but he didn't have the equipment the state guys did. He would rather they take the risks on the saturated roads.

He couldn't see Zeke anymore. Just the flashlight, making its odd reflections in the road.

The light gave Gabriel the oddest sensation, an unease that made him as cold as the rain.

Something was coming from that direction, something important blowing in with the storm.

Then he tried to shake the feeling off. He wasn't Cassandra Buckingham. He didn't pretend to have precognitive powers.

But the feeling wouldn't shake.

Something was coming. Something that would change not only him and his little town, but everything.

Forever.

NINE

Highway 19, Van Duzer Corridor
Oregon Coastal Mountain Range

Rain slashed across the highway, pelting the car with thick, heavy drops. The clouds hid the moon. Trees, towering over the narrow two-lane highway, added to the blackness, their limbs waving and dancing in the wind.

The Bug's lights couldn't penetrate that kind of darkness. All Lyssa could see were two beams of light, filled with water, illuminating a black surface without lines.

The highway through the Coastal Mountain Range hadn't changed at all. It was still treacherous and isolating, things that had attracted her as a teenager, and frightened her now.

Her back and shoulders ached. She'd been sitting in the same position for hours now. Her eyes burned from trying to see through the inky blackness.

It had been a mistake to press forward. She should have stopped in Portland. But a hotel would have used the last of her cash, and her credit cards were maxed out. She had a very precious cashier's check in her wallet. Two thousand dollars, all the money she had left in the world.

She should have left the funds in her Madison bank account, and left that account open, but she hadn't wanted to. She had had enough trouble with the press these last few months. She didn't want them tracking her every move—and she didn't trust the bank's security systems enough to protect her.

Not that it would be hard to find her in Anchor Bay. She had grown up here, after all. But that wasn't something the Walters knew, nor was it something that had ever shown up in the cursory bios done of her when she married Reginald. And fortunately, Buckingham, while not the most common last name, wasn't that uncommon either.

Emily was asleep in the back seat, oblivious to this treacherous drive. She had always been good at shutting out the world, but she had gotten better at it these last few months.

Lyssa had hoped that this trip would interest Emily, that the sights of Western America, from the mountains to the raging rivers to the tacky tourist attractions like Wall Drug, would awaken some part of her, but Emily had barely seemed to notice. Most of the time she read her books or listened to her CD player, head bobbing to sounds that Lyssa couldn't hear.

There hadn't been a lot of mother-daughter bonding. There hadn't even been much mother-daughter talk. And Lyssa was beginning to get worried about that.

The road curved dangerously. Lyssa remembered this part of the highway. Suddenly the road hugged a cliff-face, and on the passenger side, nothing protected the car from the sixty-foot drop to the river below. Lyssa used to dream about this curve, because as a teenager she would slide around it much too fast, always regretting the speed as she fought for control of whatever car she had been driving.

But the road was different now. Someone had installed guard rails with little yellow reflectors which caught her headlights. The guardrails were dented—probably from teenagers who hadn't been as lucky going around this curve as she had—and one entire section had fallen away.

Lyssa slowed, remembering how hard it was to see anything

coming from the west even in broad daylight. The muscles in her back spasmed. She was clutching the wheel so tight that her arms were rigid.

She didn't want to come back here. She didn't want to see this little town with all of its memories and its oddities and its strange beliefs in itself. She had survived this place once; she wasn't sure she could do it again.

And she wasn't sure it was the best for Emily. Maybe Lyssa should have packed them both up and gone somewhere very far away, where people didn't care about the Walters, some place like England or Australia, some place where they spoke English and watched American TV, but only reluctantly.

She probably could have found money for that. Her grandmother, Athena, might have loaned it to her. The problem was that Lyssa wasn't sure how to survive in a foreign country, even one where the language was, in theory at least, the same.

And she still had to face all her legal troubles. Taking Emily out of the country would seem to most people like an admission of guilt. Leaving Madison seemed like one.

But Lyssa couldn't stay, for Emily's sake. Reginald's death had made the national news—a one-day curiosity about the loser Walters son, the one who hadn't joined the family business and didn't live like a multimillionaire, who had died under mysterious circumstances. After that, the national press had moved on to other stories, all them apparently more compelling than that of a mentally unbalanced man dying in his own backyard.

The regional press stayed on it, though, and it had become the nightly headlines on local newscasts from Minneapolis to Chicago. Lyssa often came home from the university to find reporters camped on her yard. She changed their phone number three times, only to have the unlisted numbers "discovered" by the press. She couldn't even have voice mail without someone hacking into it.

And there was nothing to do with Emily. Sophia had to quit when the press discovered that her visa had expired, and Inez couldn't handle the pressure. Emily had gone to the university's day care for one whole hour before the head of the day care found

Lyssa, complaining that Emily and her reporters were too disruptive.

So Lyssa kept Emily at her side, taking her from class to class, making the poor girl sit through office hours. Emily read more books than Lyssa realized existed, working her way through every mainstream children's classic that didn't have magic in it.

Emily had a newfound aversion to anything paranormal, including her formerly favorite television programs like *Charmed* and *Buffy the Vampire Slayer*. Emily wouldn't say why; she would only tell her mother, in a tone that brooked no disagreement, to shut the television off.

Then there was the investigation into Reginald's death. Lyssa finally had to have the attorney she had hired for her divorce help her find a good criminal defense attorney. The detective on the scene, Volker, who had seemed so understanding, now had an idea that either Lyssa or Emily had killed Reginald. The fire was of mysterious origin, and the coroner believed that Reginald's torso blew open, which started the fire. Somehow, the coroner said, he had swallowed something explosive, and it had killed him. Apparently no one believed in spontaneous human combustion anymore.

They would believe even less in what really happened. All Lyssa had been able to get out of her daughter was that Reginald had put Emily into the lake, fully clothed, and held her underwater. *He was playing, Mom*, Emily had said only once, and even she didn't sound all that convinced. But she wouldn't admit that he tried to drown her.

That night, Lyssa had stayed awake thinking about the circumstances. She knew, somehow, that her daughter had taken a power from inside herself and turned it against Reginald, making him let her go. But Lyssa wasn't sure what that power was or how it worked.

For that, she was going to see her grandmother. Athena was an authority on all things magical in the world.

Even if Lyssa and Emily went on to England or Australia or even Canada from here, they needed time in Anchor Bay. Lyssa needed to know what her daughter's powers were, and how to control them.

The rain seemed even heavier now, the drops pounding on the roof of the car like small fists. Lyssa had lowered her speed to twenty around the curves; it felt like she was crawling. But her visibility was down to only a few hundred yards. She needed to be able to stop.

At this rate, she would never get into town.

She rounded the last curve and hit the straight stretch that ran for four miles until it collided with U.S. Highway 101. Highway 101 covered the entire Oregon Coast, and was the main road in Anchor Bay.

The forest continued for a few more yards, but once she was out of the mountains, she was out of the trees. She didn't remember it that way; she remembered nearly two miles of forest before reaching town.

Hair rose on the back of her neck. Even here, things had changed.

As the Bug zoomed out of the trees, it passed a figure beside the road. Lyssa jerked in surprise. She hadn't seen the person at all, even though the figure was wearing a yellow rain slicker and carrying a flashlight.

The night was very dark. Very dark, and very dangerous.

She hoped she didn't get the person she passed even wetter.

For a brief moment, she toyed with stopping to see if the person was all right, then ruled it out. Stopping for solitary people wasn't a good idea, not even near small coastal towns, and it was a worse idea when she had her daughter and most of their possessions in the car.

Lyssa sighed. She had shipped all of their books, their summer clothing, and their linens the day before she left. UPS would deliver them after she arrived.

She hadn't called ahead to let her mother and grandmother know that she and Emily were coming, but if Cassie's talents ran true to form, Cassie and Athena already knew. If they didn't want Lyssa and Emily to show up, they would have called by now.

Athena had called the day after Reginald died, claiming she saw the story on CNN. She might have, but Lyssa knew that Cassie had put Athena up to it. Cassie had promised she wouldn't use her telepathic powers to spy on her daughter any longer, but Lyssa hadn't believed the promise.

And why should she, with all the times that Cassie had broken that very promise? Her mother was probably spying, even now.

Ahead, Lyssa saw lights from two cars parked across the highway. Other lights—the big lights used at construction sites—blared on either side of the road, revealing foundations and half-built walls of houses.

Lyssa slowed to a near-crawl. She wondered how she was going to get across the highway, with an accident in front of her. Maybe there were side roads now, near all the construction. She was surprised to see it. When she had moved away, the population of Anchor Bay was stable, and there was no point in building beach cottages this far away from the beach.

Her headlights caught two more yellow rain slickers, one near a car, and the other near the side of the road. The one near the side of the road seemed to be moving, and it took her a moment to see through the darkness that still shadowed everything.

The rain slicker beside the road was holding a construction worker's stop sign.

No one would be working in this weather. There had to be some kind of problem on the road ahead.

She slowed the Bug to a near-stop, then checked over her shoulder. Emily lay across the back seat, a book under her right arm, and her stuffed dog, Yeller, under her left.

Yeller had become her constant companion since her father died. He had given her the dog—an overstuffed cocker spaniel—the last summer he had been well. Emily hadn't treated it differently from any of her other stuffed animals then; the dog hadn't even had a name until August.

She started carting it around the night of her dad's death, and named it when she finished the weepy, *Old Yeller*, which Lyssa hadn't wanted her to read. But Emily had read it, then reread it, and then reread it again. Obviously the book spoke to her, and whenever Lyssa asked what Emily liked about it, Emily couldn't—or wouldn't —answer.

Lyssa finally eased to a complete stop. She could hear water slurping beneath her tires. Her headlight beams revealed water pouring over the road, the rain dotting it as if landing on a lake.

The man sloshed his way toward the driver's side of the car, and with a swirl of his hand, indicated that she roll down her window.

She did, letting in cold air and drops of rain.

He bent over. Beneath his slicker, he wore a baseball cap. She could see the Detroit Tigers logo just above the brim. His face was ruddy with the cold, and dotted with moisture.

"How was the road through the corridor, ma'am?" he asked, without so much as a hello. His voice was deep and official.

"Tricky," she said. She didn't want to add that she hadn't driven mountain roads in weather conditions like that in nearly fifteen years.

"But clear?"

"No branches on the highway, if that's what you mean," she said.

"And the road's still secure?"

Mountain roads fell away, something Midwesterners never believed. Once, when she was sixteen and crazy, she had driven through the corridor with a boyfriend. Fortunately, she had been at the wheel and something—maybe even a sending from her mother—had warned her that there was danger ahead.

She had stopped just in time to avoid a massive landslide that took the road with it.

"It was secure when I went over it," she said. She didn't like how this conversation was heading. It was nearly ten o'clock at night. She was exhausted, and she wasn't sure she could drive back to Portland.

He nodded and turned his head in profile, looking at the squad cars parked across the road. The wind blew hard, shaking the Bug, but the man in the slicker looked like the gust hadn't even bothered him.

He turned back to her, his face in shadow. She couldn't see his expression at all.

"I'm afraid I'm going to have to ask you to turn around, then, ma'am," he said.

Lyssa knew he would ask that. Rain blew in the window, spattering the side of her face. So close. She was so close, and like everything else, she couldn't seem to cross that final distance.

Emily moaned in the back and then stirred. "Mommy?"

Lyssa glanced over her shoulder. Emily's eyes were barely open. "Go back to sleep, hon. We're almost there."

Emily's eyes closed.

The man waited until Lyssa looked at him. Her left arm was getting wet from the rain blowing in the window.

"What's the problem?" she asked.

"All this rain we've had this fall," he said. "It's flooding everything. The ditches are overflowing, and the ground is saturated. We've had more than two inches today alone, and it's created a puddle on the other side of this barricade that's deep enough to drown in."

His words made her shudder. She didn't want to think about drowning. She hoped Emily hadn't heard him.

Lyssa looked through the windshield. The wipers were beating a pattern against the rain, but not holding it off. The water in front of her looked even deeper than it had a moment ago.

"I'm sorry, ma'am. I'm not an expert in this stuff. I'm just the lucky guy who happened to be on this side of the flood when they decided to close the road." His eyes were blue, and filled with compassion.

"Is Anchor Bay flooded?" she asked. That had happened once before—at least according to her grandmother. It had been right around the time Lyssa had been born.

"No, ma'am," the man said. "Just this part of the highway, at least so far as I know."

She made herself take a deep breath, to hold back the panic growing inside her. Sleeping roadside wasn't an option, no matter how tired she was. Trees could fall in winds like this, and staying on this open space wasn't wise either.

She might have only a short window to get back through the corridor, and even doing that was taking her life—and Emily's—into her hands. As dark as that road was, she might not be able to see if the road had fallen away while she had been down here.

Even if she did make it through the corridor, she'd still face a drive of more than an hour just to get to Portland's outskirts. And then there would be the problem of getting a hotel on a night like this. Most travelers booked in by now, and most of them heading toward the coast would have the west side of Portland full.

"I'm sorry, ma'am." The bill of his baseball cap dripped onto the side of the car.

He had no idea what he was asking her to do. Even if she did manage to drive back to Portland, there was no guarantee that the storm would let up before she ran out of cash.

Oregon Coast storms could end in an hour or last for days, with squall after squall coming through. There was no guarantee that she'd be stranded for only one night. She might be stuck for a week or more.

If she ran through the cash, she had her cashier's check, but that was in case her mother and grandmother wouldn't let Lyssa and Emily stay at Cliffside House. Lyssa needed a first and last month's rent, along with a security deposit. She hadn't even thought about the kind of work she would find in a village of 600 people. Obviously, it wouldn't be anything like what she was used to.

"How deep is the water?" she asked. "Maybe I can try to go through really slowly."

"I can't let you do that, ma'am." He leaned closer. She could see his face now. Something about the set of his mouth seemed familiar. "If the water hasn't washed away that part of the road yet, it will by morning."

Lyssa bit her lower lip, thinking. Maybe she could call her mother and ask her to wire some money to Salem or Portland. That might work. Cassie, one of the purest hippies who ever lived, did not believe in credit cards. She didn't believe in money either, but saw it as a necessary evil.

Cassie probably wouldn't even know how to wire money. And Lyssa's grandmother, Athena, tried to make it a policy to avoid getting between Cassie and Lyssa. Or at least, she used to.

Lyssa glanced around her, trying to remember landmarks.

"Ma'am, I'm sorry—"

"Does the Old Mountain Road still run along the ridgeline?" Lyssa asked.

The man looked startled. "How do you know about that?"

"I grew up here," she said, looking in her rearview mirror. She thought she had seen lights, but it must have been a reflection of the lights in front of her.

"I thought I knew everyone who grew up in Anchor Bay," the man said.

Lyssa felt her cheeks warm. The old embarrassment had come back and she hadn't even entered the village yet.

"I grew up in Cliffside House," she said in the same flat tone she had used as a teenager, daring people to make fun of her.

The man shoved his cap back, exposing his face to the rain. His jaw was square, his cheekbones high. His nose had been broken at least once, and he had very blue eyes.

"You're Lyssa Buckingham?"

She felt her flush grow deeper despite the growing chill in the car. Of course she was Lyssa Buckingham. No one else had ever left Cliffside House.

He didn't wait for her response. "I'm Gabriel Schelling. We went to school together."

It was her turn to be surprised. Gabriel Schelling had been the best-named person she had ever met. He had been thin, pale, and blond, his hair a mass of curls that made him seem almost ethereal. His eyes had been the color of the sky on a clear summer day, and his mouth—she had studied those lips, thin and mocking, wishing that she could convince them to kiss hers.

He looked nothing like this solid, broad-shouldered creature beside her car, a man who looked more at home in the dark and wet than he would with wings and a harp.

Except for that mouth. It still had that thin, almost feminine line. No wonder she had recognized it. She had thought of it enough as a teenager.

"Gabriel," she said, trying to smile and only partially succeeding. "Chemistry with Mr. Robertson, just before lunch."

Gabriel laughed. "The day he mixed the wrong ingredients—"

"—clearing the entire school." She laughed too. She hadn't thought of that in years.

His eyes lit up, making his entire face seem brighter, then he ran a hand over it, as if he were trying to get the water off. He pulled the cap and slicker back down, nodded once as if he were regaining his adult demeanor, and said, "Athena never said anything about you coming through tonight. I just spoke to her on the radio."

Athena was still working dispatch then, and Gabriel had to be working for the sheriff's office. Funny, Lyssa wouldn't have pegged him for that. He had seemed like a dreamer in school, someone who would live a literary lifestyle, who would spend his days around books and students, discussing Joyce and Wordsworth and the meaning of life.

"I always got the impression," he was saying, "that you weren't going to come back."

"Did my grandmother tell you that too?" Lyssa asked.

He shrugged. "Years ago now."

"You know that Grandmother can't see the future."

His smile faded completely. "She can be pretty accurate."

The "but" remained unspoken. Lyssa heard it anyway. She had heard it until she was eighteen years old.

But, people said, *if you really wanted accuracy, you should talk to Cassandra Buckingham.*

Lyssa shuddered.

"Sorry," Gabriel said. "You must be getting cold."

"I don't want Emily to get too wet." The door was already soaked. Lyssa put a finger on the armrest, wondering what she would do about the damp.

"Your daughter?"

Lyssa nodded, not willing to go into any more detail.

"I'm sure Athena and Cassie won't mind waiting a day or two to see her. There's a new hotel about twenty miles south of Joe's Tavern. You gotta turn at the intersection. They built the place a few years ago, when it became clear that folks got stranded on the way to Spirit Mountain."

Apparently people still didn't understand that western back roads were nothing like side roads in the east. Halfway to Spirit Mountain Casino would be right about the point where Intersection Road got very nasty.

Amazing that hotels could thrive out here in the middle of nowhere.

"It shouldn't be full," he said, "not at this time of year, no matter what the weather."

So maybe her assumption was wrong. Maybe the hotel wasn't thriving.

Lyssa bit her lower lip again, and stopped when she felt her teeth pull off a patch of skin. Going back to that hotel still meant a repeat of the nasty drive through the corridor, and then an equally nasty twenty miles of winding mountain road.

She moved her shoulders, hearing them crack. If she went back, she might as well drive to Portland. The extra hour would be worth the hassle. She wasn't used to this kind of driving anymore either.

Gabriel leaned closer, using his body to block the rain. "Don't try the Old Mountain Road, Lyssa. It's been in bad shape for years. You could get stuck up there and no one would find either of you for a long time."

She nodded. Bile rose in her throat—the taste of desperation. She was learning to recognize it after the summer.

But, she told herself, nothing could be as bad as that dismally hot afternoon by the lake, tramping through those reeds, and seeing Reginald.

She still saw him, every time she closed her eyes.

"All these new houses," she said, glancing at the construction, the dirt turning into a river of its own. "You'd think someone would have built another road in by now."

Gabriel studied her for a moment, then looked in the back seat, not so much at Emily as at all her toys. Lyssa didn't have to look to know what he saw: a box labeled *Emily's Things*, a pile of books behind the passenger seat, and every stuffed animal Emily owned lined up in the rear window.

The suitcases were in the trunk, along with boxes too precious to trust to the UPS system. She didn't want to think about everything she owned, everything she valued, traveling across the country in a succession of matching brown trucks.

Gabriel's expression became grave. Lyssa had a feeling he could tell, just from the evidence in her back seat, that Lyssa was moving back to Anchor Bay.

"Hang on," he said.

He stepped away from the car and pulled out a portable radio. Lyssa watched him surprised that he wasn't using a cell phone. Apparently old habits died hard here.

The radio squawked as he brought it up to his mouth. He turned his back to her, and she debated about whether or not to roll up the window.

In the end, she decided to. She didn't want to hear him talking to her grandmother, seeing what Athena's reaction to Lyssa's arrival would be.

Lyssa had a hunch that if her grandmother disapproved, Lyssa and Emily would have no choice. They would never be allowed in Anchor Bay.

But why wouldn't Athena approve?

Then Lyssa glanced in the back seat. Emily was huddled into even more of a ball, probably cold from the air that had blown in from the window.

If Cassie had had a vision, then Athena might not want them back. The predictions of Emily's power had been dire when she was a baby, so dire that even Cassie, who seemed to love the darker visions, wouldn't tell Lyssa everything.

Of course, Lyssa hadn't asked either.

Gabriel sloshed back over, still clutching the radio in his left hand. Lyssa felt her heart pound. She didn't want to talk to her grandmother, not like this, not with witnesses.

She'd had enough witnesses to her life these last few months.

"We're not hearing good things about the corridor," he said, as if he were trying to pretend that he'd spoken to someone other than Athena. Maybe he had. Maybe Athena had stopped working late. She was in her seventies now, after all.

"So I can't go back through?" Lyssa asked.

"I didn't say that." He stuck the radio into a pocket. "You still might have to risk it."

She closed her eyes. They ached with exhaustion.

"However," he said, "there is another route."

She opened her eyes. He was watching her closely.

"I'd have to take you on it," he said, "and we have to turn around if there's trouble."

Her heart twisted at the word "trouble." But she was willing to face a short difficult trip if it prevented the longer.

"Let's try it," she said, and hoped she was making the right choice.

TEN

Lyssa Buckingham. Gabriel tried not to look at her Volkswagen Beetle as he opened the back door of his squad car. He pulled the rain slicker over his head, bundled the plastic up, and tossed it in the back seat. The baseball cap went in after the slicker.

Then he hurriedly pulled open the driver's door, sliding behind the wheel before his uniform had a chance to get wet. He was acting like high school kid. His hands were shaking as if he were eighteen again, and the graduation ceremony was just ending.

He stuck his keys in the ignition, and turned the car on, setting the heat on tropical. He gave Lyssa a quick wave, then ran his hands through his mess of curls. He should have gotten his hair cut the day before, like he had planned to. At least then his hair would have been tame. Now he looked like an overage Jesus freak who was trying out for the main role in *Godspell*.

Not that it mattered. Lyssa Buckingham had left Anchor Bay decades ago, married, and had a little girl—a child big enough to fill the entire back seat of a car. She had looked fragile, that child, as if she were ill or under a great deal of stress.

Gabriel had made it a point not to follow Lyssa's life, especially after she married into the Walters family. He had no idea why she was returning to Anchor Bay now, on this night, when the weather was the worst he had seen in years.

He put the squad into reverse, carefully maneuvering it out of position. If he went too far, he'd get stuck in the ditch and he'd be of no use to anyone.

The route through the housing development wasn't finished yet, and only parts of it were paved. But Bay Hills was well named. It was on a hill, and the roads would be as clear as roads could be, if he could remember which ones were paved and which ones weren't. He should have warned Lyssa that he was going to go very slowly, that he would be feeling his way through the detour by Braille.

Lyssa. He turned the wheel, got onto the highway, and waited for her to turn around as well. She maneuvered that little Bug with confidence, and he was glad. She was going to need all of her driving skills to get through the housing development and across the driveway to Cliffside House.

Although he hadn't asked her if that was where she was going. Maybe she hadn't called ahead, which could be why Athena hadn't said anything.

Sometimes Cassandra Buckingham kept information from her mother—in fact, Cassandra kept information from everyone. Early in his tenure as sheriff, Gabriel had gone to her, asking if she would warn him when something awful was going to happen.

She had given him a bleak look and refused. When he asked why, she said, *After the first week, you would regret your request.*

He was never completely certain what she had meant by that—whether she thought she would visit him a lot, or whether her warnings would be too hard to understand.

It didn't matter. Every time he asked her, and he made a point of it once a quarter, she refused. And after that first time, she never offered an explanation.

Although Athena had once told him that Cassandra was flattered by Gabriel's attentions. *No one outside the family has ever shown that much faith in her abilities,* Athena had said.

It seems warranted, Gabriel said.

Athena had nodded. *My daughter has always been a frightening person,* she had said, and then changed the subject.

A frightening person and about as different from Lyssa as anyone could be.

He checked the rearview mirror. Lyssa was creeping along behind him, her headlights as low as she could make them and still see. As he approached the turn into Bay Hills, he realized that Zeke had never come back from his reconnoiter into the forest. Perhaps he had gone farther than Gabriel had wanted him to. And if the road was clear like Lyssa said it had been, then Zeke wouldn't have had any problem with water.

Still, Gabriel thumbed on the radio unit in the car.

"Dispatch." Athena sounded exhausted.

"I'm taking your granddaughter through Bay Hill," he said.

"Then pay attention to your driving," Athena said.

"I will after this. Get Suzette. Remind her that Zeke went to check on road conditions half a mile up."

"Can't you?"

"Not if you want me to pay attention to the drive."

"A half-mile up? You should have seen him," Athena said.

"Why do you think I want Suzette to check?"

"All right."

Athena started to cough and shut off the mike, to spare his ears. Gabriel almost signed off when she turned her unit back on.

"Big slide half a mile west of Joe's Tavern," she said. "ODOT has decided to close 19. We're alone out here, Gabe."

"That's news," he said. "I always thought we were."

"Lyssa was lucky to make it through. I doubt we'll see anyone else tonight."

"Or for days, if the slide is as big as you say." He shivered once, and glanced in the rearview. Lyssa was still behind him.

She had made it at the very last moment. If she had been a half an hour later, she wouldn't be here now, and he wouldn't be leading her up a dark hill, near rows of half-finished houses.

The houses looked like bombed skeletons in the dark. He'd seen bombed homes, dozens of them, in his travels. Some were old—World War II ruins that no one had bothered to clean up—and others were recent. He had been stunned at the levels of destruction he'd seen in the Middle East.

His thoughts were taking a dark turn this night, and he wasn't sure why. He still hadn't lost that uneasy feeling he'd had earlier, the feeling that something was coming, something big.

Had he been thinking about Lyssa?

"Since ODOT's shutting everything down," Athena said, "I'm going to contact Suzette, and then head home. She's obviously not coming in tonight for dispatch. You want me to turn this over to South County?"

"Looks like you'll have to," Gabriel said. "If I change my mind, I'll take dispatch tonight."

"And sleep through all the calls. Better to let South County take it," Athena said. "They're not getting the brunt of this storm."

"We can argue about it later," he said. The road was veering slightly left. "I've got to pay attention to the road. Thanks for staying late, Athena."

"Happy to do it," she said and signed off.

He followed the narrow lane past more skeletal houses. This side of the hill was easy; the roads were mostly in and had been paved for the construction equipment. It was the other side that had him worried.

Maybe it was foolhardy to take Lyssa through here. He had been planning to make the drive anyway—it was the only way he would get home—but he hadn't planned to lead anyone through this mess, especially someone as tired as Lyssa looked.

He hadn't recognized her at first. She had looked so exhausted through that car window, her hair hanging limply around her face, her eyes sunken into her skull. He had never seen her like that, not even in her early days at Seavy County Elementary, when she had been sad, like her daughter, and angrier than any other child he had ever met.

There had been lines around her mouth, sorrow lines, and a hollowness to her cheeks that hadn't seemed like Lyssa at all. But he would have known it was her instantly if he had first looked in the back seat.

Her daughter looked just like Lyssa had at that age, right down to the sad little mouth and sorrowful droop to her shoulders. Something had happened to the two of them, something he didn't know about.

The road crested at the top of Bay Hill. The developers had logged most of the trees, and now this area had a view of the ocean. There hadn't been anything Gabriel had been able to do about the deforestation, even though a number of people asked him to. The land was private, and in Oregon, private landowners could log even when the government could not.

He checked his rearview mirror. Lyssa had managed to keep pace with him. He was glad for that, because this was where the road got tricky.

From now on, it wasn't accurate to call this a road. He was going to take her on a series of unfinished blocks, and not a miniscule number of driveways, all of which were paved. He had mapped this route out at the beginning of the rainy season, knowing he would might need it this year. The weather forecasters had predicted a difficult winter—and they had been right.

He used his blinker before turning west and starting down the steep incline. The road was slick and mud-covered. His tires slid once, then caught. He had no idea what kind of steering system the Bug had, but he hoped it would be a good one.

He drove with one eye on the road, and the other on his rearview mirror. If Lyssa got into trouble, he wanted to see it the moment it happened.

Gabriel doubted he would have brought any other non-resident along this route. He remembered the Lyssa of their teen years. She had been hell behind the wheel of a car, trying things that had terrified him then, and made him smile now.

Lyssa had been the adventurous one, perhaps because she felt she had nothing to lose. He had always held back, at times even refusing to get into a car with her, despite his crush on her.

She had learned how to do things on these mountain roads that he had taken a special class to learn just a few years ago. They actually taught emergency driving at one of the police academies here. In Los Angeles, they would probably call what he learned stunt driving.

Lyssa had been born to it.

He turned south again, heading toward a finished Georgian that looked terribly out of the place. It had been the only house on this crest two years ago. Then the owner had died, the family—who apparently had never been here—sold the land and the house, and developers bought everything. Now the solid brick house would be the gatekeeper's cottage once this development became the gated community the developers had promised. The house, once a mansion on a hill, would be the smallest building in a series of cookie-cutter homes.

He turned west again, toward the ocean. He couldn't see it, not with the rain and the darkness and the wind, but he didn't need to. Its familiar salty odor filtered its way into the car.

What must Lyssa be thinking about all of this? And why was she coming back here? She had left the place so adamantly all those years ago.

He remembered it as if it had happened yesterday. The last time he had seen her had been graduation night, the night everything changed.

The graduation ceremony had been held in the old high school (which was now the middle school) on one of Anchor Bay's rare hot days. The wind had blown in from the east, bringing the hot temperatures off the Columbia River Gorge onto the coast. The temperature swelled to ninety degrees, and the high school gym, which doubled as the auditorium, had no air-conditioning.

Gabriel had sat near the last row, wearing a suit beneath that ridiculous graduation gown, clutching his diploma in its fake sheepskin case in his left hand, ridiculously proud that he had moved his red and gold tassel from one side of his flat cap to the other.

The band was playing "Pomp and Circumstance" badly because

all the good players were graduating, and so couldn't sit in on the performance, as the graduates filed out row by row. They hadn't cheered, they hadn't thrown their caps in the air, because Principal Barger had told them if there was misbehavior, none of them would get their diplomas, and they all waited patiently, in the growing heat, to get out into the first free summer of their lives.

Gabriel had known of a party to be held on Pelz Beach, just outside the village, and his stomach was in a knot because he had finally worked up enough courage to ask Lyssa Buckingham to join him. He figured they had the entire summer ahead of them, no matter what their future plans were, and he hoped to make that summer one neither of them would forget.

He watched her file out with the rest of the Bs. She looked beautiful, even in her cap and gown. Her black hair was up, her pale skin flushed, and her eyes sparkling. She seemed to be lit from within.

Gabriel waited, somewhat impatiently, for his row to be called. By the time he got through the double doors into the parking lot, Lyssa was standing stoically beside her mother while her grandmother took pictures.

Gabriel had thought he was in luck. He hurried over to them, ignoring his own parents who were shouting his name, and asked Lyssa if he could talk to her.

She looked at him as if she hadn't given him any thought since their chemistry lab sophomore year, then smiled and said sure. He led her to a row of parked cars before he told her, almost in a whisper, that there was a party at Pelz Beach.

Before he could ask her to join him at it, she interrupted, telling him that she couldn't go to any party. She had bought a car, she said, and it was packed with her belongings. She wasn't even going home that night. She was driving east and south, taking her time. She figured that by the time she got to Austin, she would know a large part of America.

She sounded so happy and excited. He had never seen this side of Lyssa.

Anchor Bay thinks it's the center of the universe, she had said to him that night, *and that's just wrong. If these people ever escaped this little dump, they'd know they don't matter at all. They'd see what the universe is really like.*

He had always known that his conversation with her on graduation night was the catalyst for his own travels. At first, part of him wanted to be as erudite as she was—a world traveler, someone with a lot of experiences, so that when Lyssa came home to visit her family, he could impress her with all that he'd done.

Only she never came home. Then she got married to a man from a famous family and had a child.

That had been years and two serious relationships ago for Gabriel. He had thought he was long past Lyssa Buckingham, but he should have known better. He had simply shoved her memory aside, trying not to think of her, even as he worked with her grandmother, and walked the same sidewalks he had walked when he had tried to hang out in the same crowd Lyssa had.

She had been so popular then, the kind of popular that some people were with no effort at all—and without knowing it. Lyssa put no premium on Anchor Bay. She had made it clear from the first moment Gabriel had met her that she wanted out.

He finally found the last turn that led out of the development. His tires bounced over ruts in the road, created out of mud by all the construction vehicles that had been driving in and out of this place for the past several months.

He waited at the exit for Lyssa and she bounced out much as he had, her back tires sliding slightly. Then, in case she didn't remember this part of Anchor Bay, he led her down a side street to Highway 101.

The highway was empty, as it often was in the winter at this time of night. The halogen street lamps made the rain glow yellow, and gave the highway's black surface golden highlights. All of the tourist shops were boarded up. Only the local strip bar, Mona's Oasis, was open, and it appeared to be doing its usual winter business—a handful of drunk local men playing pool. No cars were parked outside, which meant that the men had walked, which also meant that they wouldn't be Gabriel's problem later on.

He stopped the squad in the cable company parking lot, and

waited. Lyssa's Bug tooled down the hill, and stopped beside his. He rolled his window down.

She rolled down the passenger side window, and leaned toward him.

"You gonna be okay from here on out?" he asked. "The highway hasn't changed too much."

"Yeah," she said. She looked even more tired than she had.

Her daughter was sitting up in the back seat, fists rubbing her eyes. She didn't seem to have any interest in Gabriel at all.

"You going to your mom's?" he asked.

"Unfortunately." Lyssa's tone was dry, and in it, he heard the old Lyssa, the one who had told him that Anchor Bay was not the center of the universe.

"Remember that driveway is vicious on nights like this," he said, suddenly glad he wasn't going to accompany her to the house. He didn't need to get entangled in all the family drama between Lyssa, Cassie, and Athena. Especially now that Athena worked for him.

"I haven't forgotten," Lyssa said. She hesitated, as if she were going to say something else.

His breath caught, and he found himself wondering what hold she had on him. Was it memory or was it something more?

"Thanks," she said after that brief pause. "I would never have gotten through there if it weren't for you."

"It's no problem," he said.

"Maybe not for you," she said. "But I'm not sure I could have made it back through the corridor. It's been a long trip."

"Well," he said, feeling awkward, "I'm glad I could be of help."

Then he rolled his window back up before he could embarrass himself.

Lyssa smiled at him, and waggled her fingers, the kind of wave that grown-ups gave children. He wasn't even sure she was aware she had done that.

Then she backed the car out of the lot, and turned south on 101.

The daughter turned around then, her face pressed against the back window, surrounded by a legion of stuffed animals. He had been wrong to compare her to the childhood Lyssa. This girl's look was cold and empty.

A shiver ran down his back, and a memory tickled at the back of his brain, something his father used to say about Cliffside House and the women who lived there.

They hold the destiny of Anchor Bay in their hands.

ELEVEN

Cliffside House

The house was too big.

Cassandra stood in the entry hall—which Athena more accurately called the Great Hall—and wrung her hands. When she was a child, Cassie never knew what wringing hands were, but over the years, as she threaded her fingers together and twisted them, rubbing her thumbs against the side of her palm or her wrists, she realized she was wringing her hands as if they were a wash towel.

She had developed a lot of nervous ticks in the last three decades, but the hand-wringing bothered her the most.

She stopped, wiped her hands against her jeans, and then stuck her thumbs in her back pockets. Her feet were bare, and the stone beneath them was cold, but she didn't go get shoes. For one thing, her bedroom was too far away—three stories and half a wing from the entry—and for another, she wanted to seem casual when Lyssa arrived.

Lyssa, who should have been here by now. Cassie sensed her hours ago. Lyssa and Emily were exhausted, pushed beyond their limits, and heading here because it was the end of the Earth.

At least, that's what Emily thought. Then Cassie shut her grand-daughter out of her mind. People didn't like it when Cassie knew what they were thinking, and the last thing she wanted to do was alienate her granddaughter.

Grandmothers and granddaughters were supposed to have better relationships than mothers and daughters. Of course, considering the relationship that Cassie and Lyssa had, any relationship would be better.

Cassie looked at the black stone walls, glistening in bright over-head lights. Cliffside House was made of basalt, black lava rock that shined as if it had hardened wet.

The legend was that Cliffside House had risen from the cliff it was built on, in the middle of a thunderstorm, appearing like a castle in the fog. The legend first came from the local tribes that wandered up and down the coast. There were reports of Cliffside House as far back as 1800, before anyone had settled here, but Cassie always believed that what people saw was just the basis for the mansion that some crazy person had built.

Or she would like to believe it, if it weren't for one thing.

Cliffside House always changed.

The county had stopped trying to list how many rooms Cliffside House had or how many stories it rose from the side of the cliff face. On the 1920 tax records, the first that listed Cliffside House as Buck-ingham property, the house was recorded as two stories high with twelve rooms along with an indoor bath. By the 1940 records, the house had five stories and forty rooms, with five indoor baths.

Cassie had never found all five bathrooms, but she knew the house had six stories, at least when she was a child. Now the house went no higher than four. Her bedroom, in the south tower, was on the house's highest level.

That room had been hers since she was a child, and she could remember going out her bedroom door to the circular stone staircase, and going up a flight to her own grandmother's room, just above hers. When Grandma Iris died, Cassie no longer had a reason to go up there. One afternoon, when she missed her grandmother greatly, Cassandra started up the stairs, only to find that they ended around the corner from her room. A flat piece of black stone covered the top step like a lid on a jar.

Cassandra had placed a light in her window, then gone outside, and looked at the house from a distance. She saw her light at the top of the tower. Her grandmother's room was missing as if it had never been.

Cassie had lived through other strange things in this house. But the main part of the house remained the same. The Great Hall, kitchen, formal dining, and family room on the first level, a spectacular living room one level down, and a full basement below that. Then there were the first tier bedrooms on the level above the main level, and the branching staircases that led to the tower rooms.

Athena slept in the North Tower, and Cassie in the South. When she was little, Lyssa also slept in the South Tower, but Cassie knew Lyssa wouldn't want to be that close to her now.

Lyssa and Emily would have bedrooms on the first tier, the stately old rooms that Athena once used to impress guests.

Cassie had spent the last two weeks cleaning the rooms, refurnishing them from other parts of the house, and making an afghan for Emily. Cassie also spent a good part of her winter savings on new bedspreads, sheets, and towels for the bathroom that adjoined the two rooms.

Athena had no idea what Cassie was doing—they lived in the same house, but they rarely spent time together—and probably hadn't visited the south wing first-tier bedrooms since the last visitor nearly a year ago.

Cassie should have told Athena that Lyssa and Emily were coming, but she didn't know how. Athena would want to take over the preparations. She would have wanted to redesign the rooms, picking different ones than Cassie, of course. And she would have rehired that damn contractor to modernize a bathroom, just like he had modernized the kitchen.

Cassie hated the new kitchen. It no longer felt like part of the house. It looked like something out of *Architectural Digest* instead of the warm cozy place it had been during her first four decades of life.

Her hands were clasped together again, wringing, wringing. She pulled them apart. Her fingers ached. She glanced over her shoulder at the phone, sitting on an alcove that jutted from the stone wall.

No one had called her. So far everything had to be all right.

But the radio said the storm had gotten bad enough to wash away roads in the corridor. Anchor Bay was isolated—no way in and no way out. Maybe Lyssa and Emily were staying in Portland tonight.

But that didn't account for the feeling that they were just a few blocks away, the feeling Cassie had had for more than an hour now.

The front door opened, and she jumped. Athena walked in, holding a rain slicker over her head. The slicker was black, just like the night, and dripped all over the stone floor.

Athena looked at Cassie in surprise. "What are you still doing up?"

Usually Cassie went to her tower when she got home. She had a kitchenette in there, and she often made herself dinner. Then she'd watch television, read or knit until it was time for bed. Sometimes she'd go out on the widow's walk, especially on nights like this, and watch the waves.

Cassie shoved her hands in the back pockets of her jeans. The air blowing in the front door was cold; she could feel it through the heavy sweater she put on. Her toes had become little blocks of ice.

"I'm waiting," she said, and braced herself.

Athena put the slicker in the stone walk-in closet that was an original part of the room. Cassie made it a point not to use that closet. She had never found the back of it, and the entire thing gave her the creeps.

Athena, however, had no fears of anything in Cliffside House. She came out of the closet, rubbing her hands on her black pants. They were lint-free and still had a crease running down each leg, with no wrinkles in the back.

Somehow, Athena had perfected the art of looking regal, no matter how tired she was, no matter how hard she had worked, or how long she had been awake.

Cassie knew her mother had been up since dawn. They had collided in the kitchen. Cassie had decided to make a coffee cake, and needed the full stove. She had been unable to sleep, worrying about

Lyssa and Emily. She had known they were on the road somewhere, but at that point, she hadn't known where.

Athena had come downstairs fully dressed to make her own breakfast. Instead, she had a fresh piece of coffee cake, and a cup of coffee, complimenting Cassie on her cooking, something Athena rarely did.

Athena had looked as refreshed then as she did now. As far as Cassie was concerned, her mother hadn't aged a day since Cassie's earliest memories of her. Athena hadn't shrunk as she got older. She was still six feet tall, and slim, with her sharp aristocratic features making her look more handsome than beautiful.

The only thing about Athena that had changed in the past few decades was that she finally let her hair turn its natural silver. She still wore it in a chignon on top of her head, like the Gibson Girl she was too young to be, and when she dressed up, soft coils of it fell across her face. Usually, though, she pulled the knot back tightly, allowing her perfect bone structure to give her face extra authority.

Not that Athena needed it. She was always the most commanding presence in any room she entered.

Even in the large Great Hall, with the expensive bouquets of flowers that Cassie had scattered around the room, Athena dominated. She put her hands on her hips and studied Cassie.

"Waiting," Athena said, even though a good three minutes had passed since Cassie's comment. "Waiting for Lyssa, then?"

Cassie felt even colder than she had a moment ago. "Is she here?"

"Gabriel is driving her through Bay Hills so that she can get here. Highway 19 has been flooded all day. Don't you listen to the news?"

Cassie did, but she had no idea where Lyssa was on the road. She also expected her daughter, who had grown up here, to know the hazards of winter travel in the mountains.

"You should have warned her about the weather." Athena's tone was sharp. Her blue eyes flashed. She was obviously very angry, although she never raised her voice.

Cassie still felt like she was five years old when confronted with her mother's anger. "I never spoke to her."

That stopped Athena. "What?"

Cassie shrugged one shoulder, her hands still stuffed in her back pockets. "She never called. We only talked a few times after—you know, Reginald died."

Athena's dark eyebrows met over the bridge of her nose. "Good lord, Cassandra, she's your daughter, and she's in trouble. What were you thinking? You should have been there for her."

And so it began. Cassie's fingers curled, the denim material straining against her skin. Whatever she did wasn't good enough, not for Athena, and certainly not for Lyssa.

"She's the one who wanted no contact with me, Mother," Cassie said. "That last conversation, she made it clear she didn't have time for me."

"Then you should have spoken to the child. Lord knows, she's going to need some sympathy."

The child. Athena couldn't even be bothered to learn her great-granddaughter's name, or to remember it this late at night.

"Emily," Cassie said.

"Well, you should have spoken to her."

"I tried," Cassie said. "Lyssa wouldn't put her on the phone."

Athena made a sound of disgust. "Yet, you knew they were coming. I thought you promised Lyssa you weren't going to pry into her mental affairs."

Somehow Cassie managed to stretch the denim pockets enough to accommodate her fists. "I didn't pry."

"Then how did you know?"

Cassie could sense them—her daughter, her granddaughter, even her mother. Everyone she loved. She knew where they were and how they were every moment of every day.

That was, in the end, how she knew Daray was really and truly dead that horrible night thirty years ago.

She couldn't feel him anymore.

"You of all people shouldn't have to ask that question, Mom," Cassie said.

Athena harrumphed and stalked past Cassie. Athena's fashionable ankle boots left wet spots on the floor that Cassie had so carefully cleaned that afternoon.

"Well, if they're going to be here soon, we should have something warm for them," Athena said as she stepped into the kitchen.

Of course, Cassie had already taken care of that. The Mr. Coffee held a warming pot of decaf, and Cassie's favorite teapot sat in the middle of the new table, a tea cozy she had made when Lyssa was little keeping the ceramic warm. The teakettle kept water hot on the stove, just in case Emily wanted some hot chocolate, and cookies sat on the sideboard, laid out as if there was going to be a party.

Athena stopped and surveyed the entire thing. Cassie stopped behind her, surprised, as always, by the look of the kitchen. Its chrome and steel appliances made it seem colder than she liked. They did play nicely off the shiny black walls and the black and silver countertops. The teardrop-shaped lights which descended from the ceiling made the entire place look classy in a hot Los-Angeles-nightclub kinda way that Cassie despised.

"I see you're ahead of me here too," Athena said.

"Don't be mad, Mom," Cassie said, and wished she could take the sentence back. How many times had she said that in her life? "Lyssa's my daughter. She has the right to come back here."

Athena whirled, a gesture that always reminded Cassie of her mother's various powers—and how much more dramatic they were than Cassie's telepathy.

"You think I don't want Lysandra here?" Athena said. "I've missed her every day since her graduation. She belongs here, Cassandra, just like you do."

Funny way of showing it, Mother, Cassie thought. *You never once visited her, never went to her wedding, never met her daughter. Hard to believe you love Lyssa as much as the two of you claim.*

But Cassandra never said a word, and she never let those thoughts out, not once, because she knew how dangerous they were. Once known, they could never be taken back.

"I just wish you told me she was coming. We could have prepared a room, gotten everything just perfect, the way she likes it. It'll be good to have her in the house again. Lyssa always added an energy that we lacked."

"I got a room ready, Mom," Cassie said. "Two rooms. You forget Emily."

Athena's lips tightened. "I haven't forgotten."

"But you're not pleased about her."

"The child doesn't bode well for Anchor Bay. You've known that from the day you heard about the marriage. I distinctly recall you asking me how you should tell your daughter not to procreate with that Walters boy."

Cassie's cheeks heated. She had asked Athena that, but it hadn't been so much a premonition as selfish concern. In many ways, Cassie held the Walters family responsible for Daray's death, and she didn't want Lyssa to know that—especially not if there was a baby involved.

"It's all past, Mother," Cassie said. "Emily's here, and she's part of the family. She's a good girl. You'll see."

"A good girl who might have killed her father." Athena stepped deeper into the kitchen and stopped in front of the Mr. Coffee. "Caffeinated?"

"Not at this time of night," Cassie said.

"Then it's not coffee," Athena said and rummaged through the cupboards. Her fingers were the only things about her that looked old. They had age marks and swollen knuckles from an arthritis that Athena never complained about. But she continued to wear the diamond ring in an Art Deco setting, even though her finger sometimes swelled around it. "We have another machine, right?"

"Mom, you don't need—"

"I don't need my daughter telling me what I need." Athena sighed and rested her forehead against the cupboard doors. Cassie could barely reach those cupboards. She was shorter than her mother by nearly half a foot.

After a moment, Athena closed the cupboard without taking out the second, much older, Mr. Coffee. She grabbed a black mug from the cupholders on the far wall, and sank into her chair at the head of the table.

"I'm sorry, Cassie," she said tiredly. "It's been a hell of a day, and I'm taking it out on you."

"Was it the weather?" Cassie asked as she made her way to the cookies. She needed fortification if she was going to spend quality time with her mother.

Athena took the tea cozy off the pot, and poured the tea into her mug. The scent of peppermint filled the air. Athena wrinkled her nose —she had probably been hoping for something with caffeine—but she continued pouring anyway.

"The weather's been bad, and everyone is very stressed. When the roads fell away, I had a lot of upset people to contend with, but I've done that before. These kinds of emergencies happen on the coast."

Not that often, though, or Cassie would be more comfortable with them. Still, Athena had rarely left the coast in her seventy-five years, and she had worked for the sheriff's department for fifty of them. She probably saw more emergencies than Cassie could imagine.

"Then what?" Cassie asked.

Athena shrugged. She put the tea cozy back on the pot and pushed it into the center of the table.

"A feeling," she said. "I've been having a feeling."

Cassie took a large, soft chocolate chip. Usually she preferred peanut butter, but she wanted something with a touch of serotonin.

"Now you sound like me," Cassie said. "Feelings are my area."

She regretted the words almost as soon as she spoke them. She didn't want her mother to think she was feeling jealous or out of sorts.

But, as usual, Athena didn't seem to notice.

"I know it's odd," Athena said. "I even mentioned it in passing to Gabriel, and he said it was probably the weather. All this rain is putting everyone on edge."

Maybe, maybe not. One of the many things Cassie had learned about telepathy was that there were times when an entire group of people, psychic or not, shared the same feelings. Those times often meant something major was going to happen.

Cassie had ignored those signs once, and lost everything that was precious to her. She would never do that again.

"What kind of feeling?" she asked, trying to sound casual. She never discussed this stuff with Athena.

Athena gave her a sheepish look. "Like something's about to go wrong."

Cassandra sat in the chair next to Athena's. Cassie tore the cookie in half and offered part to her mother. Athena waved a hand and shook her head.

"Do you know what sort of something?" Cassie asked.

"No." Athena wrapped her hands around her mug. "It sounds funny, doesn't it, this vague feeling. Yours are always so specific."

"It's my gift," Cassie said, although she had never felt it was a gift. The word "gift" was her mother's, always used at a moment of great crisis, when Cassie was feeling particularly put upon or had suffered because she had told the wrong person something true.

Athena didn't catch the irony. "You're trusting my feeling?"

"I would be foolish not to," Cassie said. "You're the one who taught me that our gifts are simply extensions of the abilities normal people have."

Athena smiled down at her mug. "I may have exaggerated a little."

Exaggerated a lot, actually, especially in her own case. Athena had great abilities, mostly with the sea. She was a powerful swimmer who could practically live underwater, and she was strong, abnormally so.

Cassie had once seen her mother fight off a man twice her weight, and defeat him as easily as if he were a child. Cassie suspected her mother had a few other abilities—she seemed to make money with great ease—but she wasn't exactly sure what they were.

Secrets, especially about powers, had become a way of life in Cliffside House.

"Still," Cassie said. "I think everyone has a bit of telepathy, and a sense of the cosmos."

Hippy-dippy crap. Cassie heard the judgment as if Athena had spoken it. Her mother didn't look up from her mug, but she didn't have to. Cassie knew what her expression would be.

But Cassie wasn't sure if the thought was so strong it got through their magical barriers or if she had lived with Athena so long that she knew what the response would be.

"What's that 'something' that's going to go wrong, Mom?" Cassie asked.

The moment was passing, and Cassie knew it. If she didn't press now, Athena wouldn't tell her, and then Cassie might not have much-needed information.

"You think it's something to do with Lyssa, don't you?" Athena asked.

"No," Cassie said, and she sounded surprised because she was. She had no idea what her mother's something wrong was. "Do you?"

"No," Athena said. "Although I worried about it all the way home."

For the entire two-mile drive. Still, Cassie understood the sentiment. Lyssa and Emily were the new factors in town.

"What do you think it could be?" Cassie asked.

"I don't know," Athena said. "I just know the feeling is stronger when I look at the ocean."

Cassie started. She had had the same sense around the sea, but hers was more complex. It felt as if something buried had dug itself out, as if something that she thought was done had started again.

As if the book of her life, which was closed, had reopened.

Funny that she would think this was about her, and Athena had a more general sense.

"Have you talked to anyone about this?" Cassie asked.

"Good heavens, no." Athena looked up at her, and this time, Cassie saw the shadows beneath Athena's eyes. The day was taking its toll after all—or maybe the conversation was. "The town already thinks we're crazy."

"Yet they run to us every time something goes wrong."

Athena shook her head. "The old timers do. The younger folks are too sophisticated to believe that the Buckinghams can protect them."

"They just don't remember," Cassie said. She set the remains of the cookie on the table. Her stomach was suddenly queasy. "We've been lucky. There hasn't been a big emergency in thirty years."

"There've been a few," Athena said.

"South of here," Cassie said. "Whale Rock and Seavy Village. But not Anchor Bay."

"No." Athena spoke quietly. "There've been a few here too."

Cassie put her hands under the table. They wanted to become fists again. The anger was back—if indeed it had ever gone away.

"You didn't tell me," Cassie said.

"I figured you would know if you needed to."

Cassie made the fists. "We're blocked from each other, at your request."

"I never requested it, Cass," her mother said. "You intuited it."

"Correctly," Cassie said.

Her mother inclined her regal head forward.

"And because we're blocked," Cassie said, "I don't always get the same information you do. There's no way I could know if something was going on."

"You should be able to predict these things." Said so calmly as if nothing were wrong.

It took all of Cassie's strength to keep herself from slamming her fists on the ugly black table and leaving the room. This was worse than feeling sixteen. This was five decades of struggle, revived in a single conversation.

And it didn't help that they avoided this conversation as often as they could.

"You should know," Cassie said, putting a space between each word, "that while my telepathy is constant, my ability to predict the future is not. You may have named me after that horrible, unfortunate bitch in Greek mythology, but I am not her, and no amount of wishing makes it so."

"You're mixing your legends." Athena got up and poured the peppermint tea from her mug into the sink.

"I am not," Cassie said, even though she knew she shouldn't get sidetracked. "I know exactly what I'm talking about. Cassandra was cursed. She was given the ability to see the future, but no one would believe her when she told them what was going to happen. Well, I'm cursed too, but not with that particular 'gift.' People like that I can see the future. They just don't want me around. I make them nervous. I'm odd and too intuitive and I give them the sense, even when I'm trying not to, that I can read their minds."

Athena reached into the cupboard and took down the second Mr.

Coffee. "You know, some day you'll have to get past high school, Cassandra."

"I am past high school." Even though she still wanted to slam her fists onto the table like a teenager. "This is my life, Mother, and you refuse to recognize it."

"And you refuse to believe that I can't do anything about it." Athena rested her hands on the countertop and bowed her head. "I'm sorry, Cassandra. I'm tired. I'm going to bed."

Cassie wasn't sure what caused her mother's change of mood, but whatever it was, it hadn't affected Cassie. She snapped, "You're not going to wait to greet your granddaughter and great-granddaughter?"

Athena's shoulders hunched forward. For a moment, she actually looked her age.

"They don't need to see me in this condition," she said. "They'll understand. They didn't call ahead. For all they know, we went to sleep hours ago."

"Except that Gabriel talked to you and told you they were coming," Cassie said. And even if he hadn't, Lyssa would have expected them to be up. She knew what Cassie's abilities were, and she knew what their habits were. When Lyssa had been a child, at least, neither Cassie nor Athena went to bed before two a.m.

"Ah, yes." Athena raised her head and sighed. "I forgot."

That alarmed Cassie more than the change of mood had. It sounded true. Athena had forgotten. She never forgot anything.

"Are you ill, Mother?"

Athena turned. Her face was pale, her cheekbones sunken. The exhaustion had eaten away at her, and Cassie, in her anger, hadn't noticed how deeply.

"It's nearly over, Cass," Athena said.

"What is, Mother?"

Athena looked at the kitchen, at the darkness outside the stone-framed window over the sink, at the second Mr. Coffee lying in a heap on the counter.

"This," she said. "What you and I take for normal."

Cassie sat upright in her chair. It felt odd to have someone else reciting a prediction to her. Athena crossed the room, and placed her palm gently on Cassie's cheek. Her hand was cold and through the skin, her bones seemed brittle.

"You and I shouldn't fight anymore, baby girl," Athena slid her hand down Cassie's cheek and started to move away.

Cassie caught Athena's wrist. "You know something. What?"

"Nothing concrete," Athena said.

"But?"

"But I know the minute Lyssa and her child cross that threshold, the end has started, and, selfishly, I'm not ready for it." Athena slipped her hand out of Cassie's grasp and walked toward the door.

Cassie let her go. It wasn't so much Athena's words that had shaken her.

It was the tears, swimming in Athena's eyes.

TWELVE

Highway 101 South
The Village of Anchor Bay

The halogen lights arcing over the highway were one of the few new things in Anchor Bay. The extra lanes on either side, cut into a hill the town fathers had once vowed not to touch, were new, and of course, the names of the businesses were all different.

But the names of the businesses changed every summer—only the hardiest survived the winter season—so that wasn't different at all. Nothing else seemed different, not even the buildings. Except for the new construction outside of town, it looked like no one had invested a dime in Anchor Bay in more than twenty years.

Lyssa's body was shaking, but she wasn't sure if it was with exhaustion, anger, or fright. She had vowed she would never come back here. She even remembered shouting at her mother on the night of high school graduation: *Face it, Mother. You're a failure. Everyone who stays here is a failure. And I'm not going to be one. You'll never see me in this godforsaken town again.*

And yet, here she was, failure like the rest of them. Failed career —unable to be hired, since she had left her previous post due to personal problems, and a spectacularly failed marriage, even before her daughter killed her husband.

Not that Emily intended to kill Reginald. To this day, the girl didn't know what she had done.

The hill crested and turned toward the ocean. The businesses disappeared as the cliff appeared on the horizon. Even in the dark and rain, Lyssa could see its outline black against the night sky.

The cliffs on either side of Anchor Bay were what made the village memorable. They rose like pillars out of the sea. Made of black lava rock, they had no trees growing on them, no greenery except for the occasional lichen.

They were also tall and imposing, and they seemed isolated, even though they were not. The entire Oregon coastline had areas like it, places where the ground rose to terrifying heights, and the ocean boomed below.

The unique thing about Anchor Bay was that the cliffs formed a natural harbor, and inside that harbor was a beautiful six-mile-long stretch of beach that seemed like it had been transplanted from Hawaii. Because all Oregon beaches were public highways, protected by the state, no houses could be built on them.

Anchor Bay's beach, one of the best in a state with tremendous beaches, brought tourists in from all over. But many of them didn't stay. The cliffs concerned people—and then they saw Cliffside House, growing out of the south cliff like a castle born of the sea.

Lyssa leaned forward slightly. The car seemed cold, even though the heat was blasting. She wondered if Gabriel had noticed how nervous she was, and then she wondered why she cared.

She had had a crush on Gabriel Schelling when she was in high school, and he seemed nice enough now, but he was probably going home to a wife and two-point-five children who were nearly grown. She certainly couldn't imagine him ever leaving Anchor Bay, and discovering what the real world was like.

Fat lot of good discovering the real world had done her.

Emily was awake in the back seat, sitting up and clutching Yeller to her. She was looking out the ocean-side window, staring into the darkness as if she could see something.

Lyssa could smell the ocean. Its briny smell was familiar and devastating, one more thing she had run away from. She could also hear the ocean, as it pounded and slammed against the sand. But she couldn't see it. It blended with the night and the rain to form an inky darkness to her right.

She knew Emily could smell it and hear it too, but it probably frustrated Emily that she couldn't see it. She was—she used to be, at least—endlessly curious, and Emily had never seen the ocean. She grew up on lakes and rivers that didn't move, and land so flat the horizon looked like it was miles away rather than part of the sky.

"We're almost there," Lyssa said.

"Good," Emily said, and leaned back against her seat.

Lyssa didn't say any more and neither did Emily. Emily thought everything was fine—that casual trust that children had for parents. She didn't know that Lyssa had been horribly irresponsible on this trip, that Lyssa hadn't even called ahead to see if Athena and Cassie would welcome them into Cliffside House.

After the way Lyssa had treated her mother all these years, Lyssa wouldn't blame her for turning them out.

Fortunately, this was the off-season, and Lyssa had seen several vacancy signs on the beachside hotels they had passed. The trick was to discover whether or not she was welcome before the hotels shut their front desks down for the night.

She supposed she would know soon enough. Even if Cassie kept her promise and hadn't tapped into Lyssa's every thought, she probably knew that Lyssa and Emily were coming. If she didn't—if she had missed it somehow—well, then, Athena was bringing home the news because Gabriel had told her back there on the highway.

"Mommy?" Emily said.

"Yes, sweetie?"

"Daddy said this place was evil."

Damn Reginald and his illness. "Did he? When?"

Emily didn't answer. She just looked out the window.

"Does what he said worry you?" Lyssa asked.

But Emily was done. She had imparted the wisdom—if that was

what it had been; it seemed more like poison to Lyssa—that Reginald had given her, and felt that the problem was now her mother's.

The problem was that Lyssa would have agreed with Emily years ago. She felt that Anchor Bay was evil, not because of the magic that very clearly coexisted with people here, but because of its narrow, small-town single-mindedness.

She had had a brain, and she had been determined to use it. Her mother had applauded that much and her grandmother, usually her biggest supporter, had admonished her to bring her knowledge back to Anchor Bay.

Lyssa hadn't. In fact, she had fought with Athena the night she made that comment. And then Athena had never come to see her, not once, speaking to her by phone only rarely and barely acknowledging the high points of Lyssa's life, like her wedding and Emily's birth.

Did they even know about the divorce? Lyssa couldn't remember what she had told them. They knew about Reginald's death—the whole country knew about that—but they probably had no idea of all the things that preceded it.

That thought almost made her turn into the last row of beachside motels. She didn't want to rehash her history, and she certainly didn't want to justify it, not for the women who raised her, the women who didn't want her to leave Anchor Bay in the first place.

And then the road dipped and she saw it, towers rising off its corners like the art on a fantasy novel. Cliffside House's lights were visible in the rain, making it seem like a beacon against the hideous night.

It seemed to be missing a tower—she remembered three—but she knew that Cliffside House was never the same.

She hadn't explained that to Emily either. Maybe the problem wasn't her daughter. Maybe the problem was her.

But how to tell a child of ten that the world she grew up in wasn't the world she was facing now? Some differences had to be experienced to be understood.

The muscles in Lyssa's back tightened as the turnoff for the house loomed.

The cliff it was on, the Devil's Goblet, was actually part of a longer group of mountains that came all the way toward the beach at this section. The highway went over the lava rock here, and continued south. On the left side of the highway, the lava rock rose, black and foreboding. On the right, the ocean side, the cliff seemed far away.

That was because of the headland that led to it, a flat portion of rock too high for most (but not all) tides. On that rock, Lyssa's grandfather had carved a road to Cliffside House—or so the story went—even though she had no idea how he had done it. Once she had examined it, and thought the road too smooth to have been made by human hands and human machines.

But the water could have done that, running across the surface over all of the years.

The driveway, as everyone called the road, rose steadily, until it wound around the center of the cliff and led to a carved parking lot on the harbor side. That parking lot provided the only access to Cliffside House.

"Is that a castle?" Emily asked, but she didn't use the tone that Lyssa would have expected. Most children would have been excited and awed to go into a castle. Emily made it sound like the first day of school, a doctor's visit, and an hour in the principle's office combined.

"No, Em. That's where we're going." Lyssa made sure her voice sounded calm. She didn't want her daughter to pick up on her own nervousness.

"Is it a lighthouse?" Emily had seen more than her share of lighthouses in the Midwest. The Great Lakes were dotted with them, and Reginald loved to visit them, in healthier days.

"It's not a lighthouse either," Lyssa said. "It's Cliffside House. That's where I grew up."

"Is it a mansion?" Emily sounded interested in something for the first time in weeks.

"I don't know what you'd call it," Lyssa said. She couldn't remember ever having had those questions.

"But you lived there?"

Lyssa almost answered with *And you will too*, but stopped herself in time. She didn't know if Emily would live there, and Lyssa couldn't bear to disappoint her daughter. Not when Emily was so fragile.

"I did," Lyssa said. "And your grandmother Cassie and great-grandmother Athena live there now."

"Gramma Cassie lives there? She never said." Emily leaned even closer to the window.

"How many people did you tell when you lived in a Frank Lloyd Wright house?"

As soon as the question came out of Lyssa's mouth, she knew she had said the wrong thing.

Emily leaned back in the car seat, and her arms tightened around Yeller. "Nobody."

"See?" Lyssa said. "It's the same thing."

But they both knew it wasn't. Cliffside House had an aura. The Frank Lloyd Wright house had a reputation. And for all its oddities, Cliffside House had been comfortable. The Frank Lloyd Wright house never was. Both Lyssa and Emily had been happy to leave it.

Then the turn for the driveway appeared—not as suddenly as it used to, though. Someone had installed two lights that looked like gateposts. They were faint, but visible in the rain. There was a sign next to them that read "Private Drive," another that read "Enter at Own Risk," and a third that read, "Do Not Enter in a Plus Tide."

As if the people who would enter a private drive that had an "Enter at Own Risk" sign would know what a Plus Tide was. Lyssa shook her head. At least someone had tried.

She turned the car sharply and waited for the bump that she remembered, the moment she knew she had left the paved road and found herself on lava rock, but the bump never came. Her hands tightened on the wheel, and she sent a little prayer to whatever god would take it to protect her and Emily.

The lava rock was slippery in the best of times. Now it was wet and covered with a layer of water from the heavy rains. Her car had good traction, but it wasn't designed for something like this. It would take all of her driving skills to get to the house.

She had entered the driveway too fast, but she pulled her foot away from the brake anyway. The anti-lock brakes helped, but they wouldn't be a solution. The best thing to do was drive as if she knew what she was doing.

Confidence, a driving instructor had once told her, saved a driver's ass more than fear ever could.

"This a weird road, Mommy," Emily said.

"It's a driveway." Lyssa sounded more dismissive than she would have liked, but she couldn't pay attention to Emily at the moment. The blackness of the rock devoured the beams from her headlights, and no one had thought to put lights—or guardrails—on either side of the drive.

The ocean boomed and rose twenty feet below, threatening to send waves toward her. One wave would knock the car off the driveway and into the sea. If the Bug fell to the north side, the harbor might provide an escape. But if she fell to the south, there would be no surviving.

Lyssa felt a surge of anger rise. She had forgotten about this part of the drive, and it was stupid really, with all the modern conveniences. What were Athena and Cassie thinking? The house might be secure from large waves and tsunamis, but the driveway definitely was not.

She finally reached the curvy section, and realized it was just barely wide enough for her chubby little car. Still, she managed to get all the way up to the parking area without scratching either side of the Bug.

Lyssa parked near the main sidewalk, also lit now with two formal-looking light posts, and shut off the ignition. Then she rested her arms on top of the steering wheel and buried her face. Her heart was pounding heavily, and her breathing was short. She had sweated through her shirt.

She couldn't remember a more challenging night of driving, not even from her teenage years.

"Are you okay, Mommy?" Emily asked. It was the fear in her voice that gave Lyssa the energy to sit up.

"Tired, baby doll," Lyssa said. More than tired. Exhausted and shaky and scared. But the rest of it was a burden that Emily didn't need. "Want to see your grandma?"

Emily didn't answer, and Lyssa forced herself to turn around in her seat. Emily had brought her knees up to her chest, like they had been on that damn dock in July. Only then, she hadn't had Yeller clutched in her arms.

"What if she don't wanna see me?" Emily asked, her voice small.

"She will," Lyssa said, hoping she was right. Predicting Cassie's moods was always difficult.

"I'll wait," Emily said.

The car shook slightly with the wind.

"It's going to get cold in here," Lyssa said, "and I can't leave the ignition on. It's too dangerous. Come with me. I want to see my mother."

That almost sounded true. It sounded true enough, anyway, to get a solemn nod out of Emily. Apparently she understood the place where fear and desire crossed.

And why wouldn't she? Those two emotions, ultimately, warred inside her the day she had ridden her bike to Reginald's.

"Come on," Lyssa said, not wanting to lose her advantage. "Grab your coat."

"Are we gonna live here?" Emily asked.

The moment of truth. How was it that children always managed to find it?

"I don't know," Lyssa said. "Let's go find out, shall we?"

Emily gave her a grave look, then grabbed her raincoat. It was red with a little hood that made her look like a character from a children's novel. Emily had loved it when they bought it last year. All she had done since they arrived in Oregon was complain about it.

But she didn't complain now. Instead, she slipped on the coat, tugged Yeller underneath, and grabbed the door handle. "You coming, Mommy?"

Nope, Lyssa wished. *You go ahead. They'll want to see you. It's me that'll cause the problem.*

Instead she smiled wearily, grabbed her London Fog raincoat—which had come inconveniently without a hood—and her purse.

"We have to make a dash for it," she said.

They got out together, and Lyssa took Emily's hand. It was warm and comfortingly small. The rain had turned colder, feeling like hard little ice pellets pounding their faces.

"Let's go!" Lyssa said, and they ran toward the twin lights, and up the long curving sidewalk. Emily didn't even try to look at the landscaping that someone had finally managed to do successfully or even at the cliffside, not fifteen feet away.

She stared straight ahead, at the massive oak door and the arched entrance that did look like part of a medieval castle. All it needed was a moat, a drawbridge, and an iron gate to complete the illusion.

"The house missed me," Emily said as she jumped up the two steps leading to the entrance.

Lyssa put a hand on her daughter's back and held her in place. Any other parent would have taken that statement as fanciful and wrong—Emily had never been here before, so if the house had the ability to miss anyone, it couldn't have missed her—but Lyssa knew, with a certainty she rarely had, that Emily's statement was true.

The house had missed Emily.

And stranger still, the house had missed Lyssa too.

THIRTEEN

Highway 101
The Village of Anchor Bay

Gabriel sat in the parking lot, his car running, until Lyssa's car disappeared around the curve at the top of Leland Hill. He felt shell-shocked, but he wasn't sure if that was because of Lyssa's arrival, the long day he'd had, or the look Lyssa's daughter had given him as the car drove away.

Finally, he chalked it up to exhaustion, and reached for the radio. Athena had gone home, so he would have to patch himself through to Zeke.

As he did, Gabriel settled back in the squad car. The rain seemed lighter—or perhaps that was because he wasn't in it any longer. His pants legs were wet, but the rest of him was remarkably dry given the afternoon he'd had.

The empty road looked benign—the yellow light giving it an otherworldly cast—and it seemed like nothing had gone wrong this day. But Gabriel knew that when morning came, he'd have mess after mess to clean up, not just on the beach but at various homes and businesses.

The problems simply weren't visible at the moment.

It took a bit of work, but he finally got through to Zeke.

"Where are you?" Gabriel asked.

"Mile Marker Three," Zeke said. He almost seemed to be shouting. Behind him, Gabriel could hear the whistling wind. There didn't seem to be as much wind downtown, but that could be a false impression. The cable building was probably shielding his car from the worst of it.

"Problem?" Gabriel asked.

"I'm not sure."

Gabriel wished he could see Zeke's face. Sometimes Zeke had a very dry sense of humor, and it almost always sounded like this. But Zeke never joked about trouble.

Gabriel's hand tightened around the microphone. He shouldn't have left them alone out there.

He had let himself get sucked in by his old crush on Lyssa Buckingham, and hadn't followed guidelines that he had set up himself.

"Stop toying with me, Zeke," Gabriel said.

"Okay," Zeke said. "I found something in one of the ditches."

"What kind of something?"

"The kind that disturbs most people. I'll show it to you in the morning, if we can still get into town."

The conversation was frustrating Gabriel. They were talking in code, partly because they had to—too many people in town owned police band radios and listened to them for entertainment.

"It's something you can carry with you?" Gabriel asked, letting his confusion out.

"Yeah," Zeke said. "It's small, and it's a good thing we found it, not some tourist."

"Zeke—"

"Think, boss," Zeke said.

Gabriel sucked in a breath. "There was something in the forest after all."

"Frankly," Zeke said, "I think it floated up from the ocean, but Suzette assures me that's not possible."

"Nothing flows *from* the ocean," Suzette said, her voice still far away. "Jeez, Zeke, how long have you lived here?"

"Long enough to see some waves that would contradict your assumption," he snapped.

Gabriel changed his mind. He was glad he wasn't with them after all. "Is it alive?"

"Not anymore," Zeke said, and Gabriel frowned. He didn't want to ask if they'd killed anything, not over the radio anyway. Most of this conversation would have to wait until morning.

"If it's organic," Gabriel said, "you'll have to use proper storage techniques."

"My freezer won't cut it, right?" Zeke said, and again, Gabriel couldn't tell if he was joking.

"Fraid not," Gabriel said, knowing he couldn't explain freezer burns to Hamilton Denne. "You know the drill."

"I do," Zeke said, "and we can't keep this thing where we found it. There's no guarantee it'll be there in the morning. So we're taking custody of it."

"I could meet you at the office now," Gabriel said.

"Actually," Zeke said, "I think it would be better if we stayed on this side of the mess. From what I can see, this storm isn't getting any better, and Anchor Bay is going to be pretty isolated."

"How was the road through the development?" Suzette asked.

"Tricky," Gabriel said. "But I think it'll hold through the night if you want to come home."

"Thanks, sir," Suzette said, without giving him a definitive answer. It sounded like she was shaky, and whenever she got shaky, she didn't want to be alone.

Somehow, though, Gabriel couldn't imagine Zeke comforting her. He'd have to ask Athena about it. Athena kept up with all the gossip from all over the county, not just the office stuff. She would be able to tell Gabriel if his two deputies had moved to a less-than-professional relationship.

"I want to see this thing tomorrow," Gabriel said.

"Yeah," Zeke said. "It's pretty interesting."

"Any more cars since Lyssa's?" Gabriel asked.

"Nada. I'm sure the highway patrol's got this place shut down tight. We're setting up the highway barriers now so that no one local tries to drive through that pond at Mile Marker Two. Then we're done."

"Since this part of the county is isolating itself," Gabriel said. "I think we're going to have to share duties tonight."

"I figured as much. Does South County have our home phone numbers?"

"They'd better," Gabriel said, "because I'm not spending the night in the office."

Zeke chuckled, and signed off. Gabriel made a mental note to check when he got home, to make sure that the South County dispatch did have their home phone numbers, and to let the dispatch know that no one would be in the office for the night.

Gabriel put the car in drive and headed out of the parking lot. He wondered what Zeke had found that was small. There were all manner of creatures in this area, some that Gabriel was familiar with, and some he'd only heard about, and he couldn't remember any that were small.

That didn't mean there weren't any.

He paused at the driveway's exit, looking up and down the highway before turning onto it. He always felt a bit anal doing that when the highway was so obviously empty, but he'd been clipped more than once by people doing 100 mph down an empty 101.

It was always better to be cautious.

He turned right, going the opposite direction than Lyssa. He used to live near Cliffside House as a boy, but when he moved back to Anchor Cove, he'd stayed away from that neighborhood. His parents had already left, tiring of the storms and the strangeness, and retiring in Arizona with the sunbirds they used to claim they hated.

They still owned their house, however, and offered it to him. He couldn't imagine rambling around in that badly kept up ranch. When he went to the neighborhood, ostensibly to help his parents find some renters, his skin crawled. His entire youth returned—in fact, it never seemed to have left that place—and he didn't want to be anywhere near it.

But on the north side of town, he found an older neighborhood that he hadn't known existed. It was filled with Cape Cod cottages on crest leading up to the Devil's Candlestick—the north cliff—and some beautiful 1920s Arts and Crafts homes on the other side of the highway, all with ocean views.

Most of them were unaffordable on a sheriff's salary, but one, nearly ruined by its previous owners, was in his price range. During his off-hours, he fixed it up, room by room, and now he had a stunning house with the world's ugliest kitchen and bathroom —the two rooms he couldn't redo all by himself.

He headed there now, thinking of a fire in the fireplace, a something warm and soothing to drink, and a large meal, probably spaghetti, because he could put that together quickly. His stomach growled at the thought. He'd shut the curtains on the floor-to-ceiling windows overlooking the ocean, and pretend the storm wasn't happening, that it was just another day in his own little town.

The highway curved around the flattest portion of beach. There were no cars in the Anchor Harbor Wayside parking lot and, oddly enough, not even any gulls. Usually the gulls spent their entire winter in the wayside parking lot, as if they were having some kind of gull conference. They were there even during storms, their heads tucked into the wings like miniature optimists, believing that because they couldn't see the bad weather, it did not exist.

The lack of gulls bothered him more than anything else had that day—and it had been a fairly disturbing day. He slowed, wondering what had spooked them, when he saw something white over the guard rail.

He brought the car to a stop, hoping he wouldn't have to get out again, straining to see more of the whiteness. It looked like a sheet attached to the rail itself, or a bit of ground fog that had been trapped by some ocean current.

Only it was too windy and stormy for fog, and no sheet was that transparent.

His heart started to pound hard, and with it came annoyance. The last thing he wanted to do was get out of the car. He would see what he could from the car, and if no human being was in trouble, he would go home.

He turned the car into the parking lot. Water sprayed from his tires, and rain pounded his windshield so hard that for a moment, he couldn't see. The wind buffeted the vehicle, rocking it back and forth.

When he'd been in the cable company's parking lot, he thought the storm had died down, and when he'd been stopped a few moments ago on the highway, he hadn't noticed rain or wind this strong. Was he in some kind of pocket where the storm really powered through? Was that what had driven the gulls away?

He drove very slowly to the guard rail, stopped and turned out his headlights. The rain eased slightly, but his windshield wipers still had to work at top speed to keep the glass clean.

The sea glowed, as it so often did. It had a phosphorescence all its own, which high waves only amplified. The whitecaps came toward him now, foamy and powerful, slamming onto the beach below. The car shook with the water's power, and if the waves got any higher, he'd have to block off this parking lot too.

With his headlights on, all he could see were raindrops moving into and out of the light. He shut off the headlights, and the whiteness reappeared. It didn't look like a sheet up this close. It looked more like a person, clinging to the guardrail with one arm, and extending another to someone below.

Only Gabriel could see through the person-shaped whiteness. And, as he looked toward the ocean, he could see a trail of white heading into the deep.

The whiteness looked like a fog bank coming inward—except that someone who lived around fog as long as Gabriel had knew that fog didn't work this way. Not only was it too windy to sustain any fog at all, but fog did not come out of the ocean. It rode along the top of it like a milky part of the sea.

Whatever the whiteness was, it had more solidness than fog, and it was coming from underneath the waves.

Gabriel sighed and reached for his rain slicker. He was about to put it on when a wave slammed into his car, and pulled it forward with such force that the car plowed into the guardrail.

Gabriel cursed, and hung on, hoping the guardrail would hold. He was acting like a stupid tourist, forgetting the power of the ocean, particularly on stormy nights.

When the wave receded, Gabriel put the car in reverse and backed away from the guard rail. A wave like that usually brought its friends, and he didn't want to test his luck a second time.

As he drove, he saw the whiteness still clinging to the guardrail. Only its posture had changed. It still seemed to have a human shape, but the head wasn't looking toward the sea any longer.

It was looking at him.

A chill ran down his spine. He had never seen anything quite like that in all his years in Anchor Bay. The white thing wasn't a ghost— ghosts really did look like people, just as solid, just as colorful—but this thing did not. It only suggested a person, the way that the bleat of a dolphin suggested laughter.

Another white shape, and then another, joined the first along the guard rail. A wave swept over them, not as powerful as the one that had dragged him toward the sea, but powerful enough to throw a lot of water onto the pavement.

And still the white shapes didn't move. They appeared to be studying him, as if his behavior gave them answers to a question he didn't even understand.

No wonder the gulls were gone. These creatures—if that's what they were—were eerie. He'd seen a lot of what Denne called Fantasy-Life, and none of it had ever been this white, this transparent, and this spooky.

Gabriel reversed the squad all the way out of the parking lot onto the highway, watching not the road like the good driver he usually was nor even the rearview mirror, but the white shapes lining up like children denied access to a circus.

His back tires skidded on the watersoaked surface, and the car spun just enough to grab his attention. He shoved it into drive, then used one hand on the wheel to right the car in its proper lane.

The highway still glowed yellow and black, with no odd white shapes. But he couldn't resist one more glance as he headed home.

He could no longer see the white shapes, but the sea water

covered the entire parking lot, as if trying to reclaim that little bit of land and make it part of the harbor.

If he were a newcomer to Anchor Bay, he would have convinced himself that the whiteness he saw was just phosphorescence or weird-acting ground fog or maybe even some kind of mist on his windshield.

But he had grown here. He knew that he had seen something supernatural. And whatever he had seen, it was something he didn't much like.

FOURTEEN

Cliffside House

Lyssa and Emily stopped in front of the large oak door. Emily let her hood drop, and Lyssa shook her head, feeling the drops of water fly from her hair.

She wasn't going to look presentable, not on a night like this, maybe not ever—at least coming to this house. Nothing could make her presentable, not even a tailored suit complete with pearls.

She grabbed the door knocker with one hand. The knocker was shaped like an anchor and made of brass. It was as smooth and shiny as it had always been. Somehow years of exposure to the salt air hadn't touched it.

She pounded the knocker against the wood, listening to the solid thud echo through the house. She remembered that sound. Somehow it reached even the highest tower on the sea side, even though a shout from the main room never reached the first landing of the staircase.

Just one of the many inexplicable things about Cliffside House.

Emily sidled up against her, the plastic on her raincoat creaking as she moved. Lyssa brought her hand down and put her arm around

Emily. The bulge that was Yeller made Emily seem lumpy and unfamiliar, but Lyssa persevered.

Her breath was coming in short gasps, and she had a hunch that if she had been alone, she would have turned around, found a hotel room for the night, and slipped out of Anchor Bay without a word, letting Athena and Gabriel Schelling deal with Cassie.

Then the door opened, and Cassie stood there—thinner and shorter than Lyssa remembered. Cassie's long black hair, which went to her knees, was loose, and instantly caught in the wind, blowing inward like a model's hair in a makeup commercial.

Cassie and Lyssa stared at each other for what seemed like an eternity, but could only have been a fraction of a second because Emily started to move forward as the door opened.

"Grandma!" Emily shouted, launching herself at Cassie.

The look of joy on Cassie's face was unexpected and startling. Lyssa stood on the threshold as her mother crouched, opened her arms to Emily, and didn't even flinch when Emily's sopping raincoat soaked Cassie's clothes.

"Baby girl!" Cassie said, picking Emily up and twirling her around as if she were a toy.

The words surprised Lyssa. She had always thought "baby girl" was her endearment, something she hadn't picked up from home. She had always worked hard at keeping her mother out of her speech.

Emily had her legs wrapped around Cassie's middle, her face buried in her grandmother's neck. After a moment, Cassie stopped twirling and looked at Lyssa over Emily's shoulder.

"Come on in," Cassie said.

The warmth that had been in her tone for Emily wasn't there for Lyssa. Instead there was a coolness, a drawing back, maybe even a reluctance.

That made two of them, then. The house may have missed Lyssa, but Lyssa hadn't missed the house—or at least, she hadn't missed all the responsibilities that came with living here.

Lyssa stepped over the threshold and into the entry. It looked different. Cleaner, for one thing. The flagstone seemed newer, shinier, and the black walls almost sparkled. Someone had placed vases filled with flowers on all of the built-in ledges, and the vases added a touch of sophistication to the room.

The macramé plant hangers were gone as was the crocheted rug that always made Lyssa trip. In place of the plant hangers, someone had gone to the expense and effort of hanging those modern little martini glass lights. In such a large space, they looked like fairy lights.

Lyssa pushed the door closed, and felt one more surprise. The entry, always the coldest place in the house, was warm.

Cassie smiled at her. The smile was several wattages duller than the one she had just given Emily, but it was a sincere smile all the same.

"Welcome back," Cassie said.

Not *welcome home* or *good to see you*. Just *welcome back*. And, all in all, that phrase was more appropriate than the others. Now that she was standing here, Lyssa felt like she had never been gone.

"Thanks, Mom," she said.

Cassie's smile got a little wider. She set Emily down, then crouched and helped her take her raincoat off.

"I'm so happy to have you here," Cassie said, looking at Emily. "I've missed you so much."

Emily froze, as if the words hurt her. Cassie frowned, and stopped unbuttoning the coat.

"Did you really, Grandma?" Emily asked, using that sad small voice that seemed to belong more and more to her.

"Of course I did, baby doll. I miss you each and every day."

Lyssa could see the side of Emily's face. Her daughter's cheeks had flushed, and not just from the indoor warmth.

"You won't miss me anymore," Emily said. "Mommy says we're going to live here now."

That wasn't what Lyssa had said. She had said they were going to live in Anchor Bay. She had been very careful not to say any more than that.

"I was going to ask you, Mom," Lyssa said, "and Grandma too. I mean, I have enough money for a security deposit and everything. Emily and I can find an apartment. I figured that would be what you wanted."

Cassie looked up, but didn't break her crouch. Her face had fine lines on it that it hadn't had before. Otherwise, she looked the same— her narrow features and wide eyes gave her a waifish look, but her sharp little mouth tempered it.

"Buckinghams always live in Cliffside House," she said, and then finished taking off Emily's coat.

Lyssa's stomach ached. That wasn't the sentence she had hoped to hear. Even with all the problems she had with Cassie over the years, Lyssa had hoped for something more. One of those sentences from the movies, maybe, or from televised family show: *Nonsense, darling. We wouldn't dream of having you stay anywhere else.*

But she was a Buckingham, and apparently Buckinghams didn't live anywhere else. Nor did they show an inordinate amount of affection.

"Where's Grandma?" Lyssa asked.

"She was exhausted. She went to bed." Cassie put Emily's raincoat over her arm, then touched Yeller, whom Emily still held in a death grip. "Who's that?"

"Yeller," Emily said.

"As in *Old Yeller?*"

Emily nodded.

"I always liked that book," Cassie said. "Did you know there's a movie too?"

"A movie?" Emily looked up at Lyssa for confirmation.

Lyssa nodded, feeling a little lost. She had forgotten about the movie until now or she would have found it for her obsessed daughter.

"How come we never saw it?" Emily asked Lyssa.

"It's old," Cassie said, standing up. "I'm sure it's hard to find."

Lyssa felt her own cheeks warm. Her mother had just smoothed things over for her.

Then Cassie handed her Emily's coat. "Do you remember where the closet is?"

How could anyone forget that closet? It was large and endless, and always had a breeze.

Lyssa almost asked, *Are you still afraid of it, Mother?*, but that would really get things off to the wrong foot. Instead, she turned around and headed toward the back of the room.

Cassie took Emily into the kitchen, talking the entire way. Emily made small sounds in answer, but Lyssa couldn't hear all of them. She waited until the voices faded before leaning against the wall.

The black rock surface was as smooth as it was shiny. Lyssa pressed her hot cheek against it, reveling in the coolness. She had already reverted: she used to do this when she was a girl, especially when she needed comfort.

She had been right. No welcome for Lyssa, but a welcome for Emily. Which was probably good. Her daughter needed all the love and warmth she could get.

What Lyssa hadn't expected was Athena's absence. Gabriel had told her that Lyssa was coming. Was Athena angry that Lyssa hadn't called? That didn't sound like her grandmother, but then, Lyssa hadn't seen her in more than a decade. Sometimes age changed people. Maybe it had changed Athena.

Lyssa sighed. Change and Athena didn't seem to go together. Her grandmother had always seemed as solid as the cliff face. Wind couldn't move her; rain couldn't damage her; and even an ocean couldn't change her—not without taking decades of constant, incessant pounding.

Athena couldn't be tired. She was avoiding something. Probably her recalcitrant granddaughter.

Lyssa stood up and wiped her cheek, feeling a bit of rain that she had somehow missed before. She carried Emily's coat to the closet, and before reaching inside, took off her own.

Already she could feel the breeze. Once she had taken a flashlight and tried to find the back of the closet. Once she had gotten past the cloth coats her mother wore, and her grandmother's perfume-scented cloaks, she found a series of coats that didn't seem to belong to anyone.

Some of them were furs, untouched by time and damp, their pelts thick and warm and smelling of tobacco and rose-water. She found hats of all sizes and shapes, some with feathers and some with fake fruit, and some with tasteful nets that went over the eyes. First the hats were on a hat tree and then, farther back, there were hat boxes and coat boxes and gloves, and steamer trunks and more treasures than a person could imagine.

She had been deep inside the closet, opening a steamer trunk, when her mother had found her. Cassie had come into the closet in a blind panic, grabbed Lyssa's arm, and yanked her back to the entry. Then she had shaken her and told her never to go in the closet again.

Lyssa had been ten.

Oh, she had tried to go back. She had found the coats, and the furs, and the hat tree, but the steamer trunks seemed to have vanished, along with the hat boxes and all the other treasures. Each time, though, she seemed to find something different. A lace wedding dress, so small that she doubted even her tiny mother could fit into it. Shoes that required hooks to close them up, and once, a cache of jewelry, ropes of pearls hanging off a jewelry tree, earrings sitting in a bowl, and fans, dozens of fans, some yellowed with age.

She never told anyone about these discoveries and she never removed them from the closet. It almost felt that to do so would be a sacrilege. The closet gave up the clothes it could part with; anything else would be theft.

The breeze grew stronger as she stepped inside the darkness. The closet still had its familiar musky cigarette smell, as if someone had just come home from a smoky nightclub after a night of partying.

Lyssa reached up for a hanger, and overshot the bar—she was a lot taller than she had been when she used to spend a lot of time exploring this part of the house. She had to grope for a moment before she found an empty hanger, and then she put the little raincoat on it.

The moment felt like a monumental one—something of Emily's settling into the house. Lyssa ran her hand on the wet coat for a moment, feeling the familiar plastic, and apologizing ever so slightly to her daughter—not just for bringing her here, where the weird met the strange—but for bringing her into the world.

Like Lyssa, Emily could never be normal. And like Lyssa, Emily had once expected to be.

Only unlike Lyssa, for a short time, Emily had experienced the kind of life everyone else took for granted.

Lyssa didn't know if that was better or not.

She peeled off her own coat, and shivered slightly. The closet was as cold as the entry used to be. She groped for another hanger, found it, and was about to place her coat on it when someone whispered her name.

"Grandma?" she asked as she turned toward the sound. It came from the back of the closet.

"Lysandra." The voice was still whispering, but seemed to have more substance. "We're dying here."

And then her mouth filled with something thick and solid, and she couldn't get her breath.

She clutched her throat, gagging, and staggered out of the closet, her heart pounding. The light blinded her and the warmth seemed too heavy. She tripped on one of the flagstones and sprawled across the floor, dislodging whatever it was that had caught in her throat.

Nothing appeared on the ground in front of her. Whatever it was had vanished as if it had never been.

She coughed, taking in air as if she had been drowning. No one came to see if she was all right. No one probably even heard her fall.

She sat up, and brought her knees to her chest, wrapping her arms around them and rocking. She thought the house had missed her. She thought it was going to welcome her back.

The house had never hated her. It hadn't been her favorite place in the world, but it had been a refuge, and the closet—it had been her adventure, her secret place.

Lysandra.

The voice still echoed. She coughed again, and something flew from her throat. She caught it as it sprayed out of her, a little ball of black, solid as a handful of mud, but with a more rubbery texture.

Lysandra.

"What do you want?" Her voice sounded hoarse, as if she had been shouting.

We're dying.

"How does killing me solve that?" she asked.

Help us.

"Do what?" she asked.

But the voice didn't answer. And she knew as certainly as she knew this old house that whatever owned the voice was gone.

She coughed again, and realized how she was sitting.

Just like Emily had on the day Reginald had died. Lyssa had crawled into the same position, trying to take comfort from her own body, rocking to ease the pain and fear.

She rolled the ball between her fingers. She and her mother would have a little talk after Emily went to bed.

There might be an apartment in Lyssa's future after all. She wasn't going to stay here if the house had somehow become malevolent.

Maybe there wasn't a refuge anymore in this world for her. Maybe she was going to have to face whatever was out there with all the strength she had left.

FIFTEEN

Cliffside House

They let Emily fall asleep on the family room sofa, a cup of hot cocoa on the table in front of her. Cassie wrapped Emily in a quilt that she had made shortly after Lyssa left—something to do with her hands, she had thought then, but she realized now that the quilt hadn't achieved its real purpose until this night.

It looked warm and appropriate around her granddaughter, who seemed tiny and fragile and in a great deal of pain.

Clearly Lyssa knew that Emily had been traumatized by the events of the summer, but she probably didn't know how deeply. Like the rest of the Buckinghams, Emily was secretive and protective. She felt that her mother had gone through enough, and needed Emily's support more than Emily needed hers.

Poor thing. She hadn't even touched her cocoa before she faded into that twilight between sleep and wakefulness.

Lyssa looked shaken too, and she refused to go to the rooms that Cassie had painstakingly prepared. She wanted to talk first, maybe see if she was welcome, which hurt Cassie more than she wanted to admit.

Of course her daughter was welcome. Why wouldn't she be?

But Cassie didn't say that. She hadn't said much to Lyssa, sensing how deep the distance was between them. Besides, this Lyssa was a stranger to her. The short hair that looked like it had been cropped in fit of anger, the sunken eyes from too little sleep, the skin pulled tight over her face, didn't seem like Lyssa at all.

Lyssa had been freer than that, her hair flowing, her eyes sparkling, her skin reflecting her great good health. Stress and time had taken all of that away from her, and no one who looked at Lyssa now would think she was healthy. Just terribly unhappy.

The kitchen stopped Lyssa just like it stopped Cassie every time she entered it.

"Whoa," Lyssa had said after she took in the steel appliances, the modern table, the expensive cabinets. "I guess back-to-nature is passé."

Cassie's cheeks warmed. Lyssa thought she had remodeled the kitchen, going against all the things she had ever said about the environment and taking care of the creatures around her.

"Your grandmother did this." Cassie kept her voice low and tried not to sound judgmental.

"Without your approval, obviously."

Cassie shrugged. "It's her house."

Lyssa looked at her. The intelligence in those brown eyes was as sharp as ever. "I thought it was all of ours. That's what Gram used to say."

"I know what she used to say." Cassie took the cookies off the sideboard and set them on the table. "Ownership of Cliffside House is a dicey thing. I've even gone to the county to see the records, and was told that no one could find them. Later, the clerk called me and said not to worry about it. No one else did."

She hovered near the Mr. Coffee, her hands fluttering toward the mugs. "Decaf? Tea?"

"How about some bourbon?" Lyssa asked.

Cassie's breath caught. She hadn't expected that.

Then Lyssa smiled. It was the old smile, impish and warm. "Is it herbal tea?"

"Peppermint."

"And cookies." Lyssa sank into a chair at the far side of the table. "I have come home after all."

The word "home" warmed Cassie. She grabbed two mugs and brought them to the table, handing one to Lyssa. "You can stay, you know. There's no need for Emily to sleep on the couch."

Lyssa's smile faded. She took the mug with one hand, but kept the other under the table. She didn't even pour any tea.

"I was hoping you'd say that," Lyssa said, "and then something weird happened in the closet."

Her cheeks reddened slightly. It clearly embarrassed her to talk about the strange events of Cliffside House.

"Weird?" Cassie hadn't sat down yet. She pulled the cozy off the teapot, then poured. The steam carried with it the soothing odor of peppermint. She hoped it would ease some of Lyssa's stress.

"I think the house attacked me, Mom." The words rushed out of Lyssa. "I can't stay here if it's dangerous."

She glanced through the open door. Cassie followed her gaze. Emily was sleeping peacefully, one arm wrapped around that stuffed dog of hers. She looked content here. She looked like she belonged.

"Cliffside House isn't dangerous," Cassie said. "You know that."

"I knew that," Lyssa said. "Then it tried to choke me."

Cassie sat in the chair next to Lyssa. "It what?"

"It put something in my throat and I couldn't breathe. I had to force myself out of the closet before the stuff cleared. Didn't you hear me fall?"

Cassie shook her head, her heart sinking. Already, in Lyssa's mind, Cassie was failing her. But it was impossible to hear anything room-to-room in this house. Lyssa had to know that.

"Whatever was in my throat disappeared, but this I coughed out just before I came in here." Lyssa brought her other hand to the table top. Her hand was streaked with black. The lines looked familiar. Lyssa had that hand clenched into a fist, and she slowly opened it.

In her palm was a black ball. It was the size of a marble, and it left a stain against Lyssa's skin.

Cassie remembered holding hundreds of balls like that. Removing them, taking them one at a time, and trying to clean them off the beach.

She knew what the ball would feel like even before she touched it.

"A tarball," she breathed.

"What?" Lyssa asked.

Cassie brought her hand over Lyssa's, then paused. "Mind if I touch it?"

"Be my guest," Lyssa said.

Cassie took the ball. It was as rubbery as she expected and a little more gooey than she would have thought. It looked like it had solidified more than it had.

She brought it to her face, sniffed, and caught the faint chemical stench. Tears flooded her eyes, and she blinked them back.

"Mom?" Lyssa said.

"It's a tarball, honey. You find them at oil spills."

Lyssa looked at her as if she were crazy. There had been a number of oil spills up and down the Oregon Coast, and Cassie had worked all of them as a volunteer—even when Lyssa was little, never telling her where she was going, of course. But there had only been one in Seavy County. That had been in 1970, and it had nearly destroyed Anchor Bay.

"How do you know that, Mom?"

"I help with the cleanups sometimes." She handed the ball back to Lyssa, even though she wasn't sure what Lyssa would do with it. "You said you coughed this up?"

Lyssa nodded. Then she told Cassie what had happened in the closet, start to finish: the whisper, the choking, the request for help.

"Why would the house do something like that?" Cassie asked. "And to you of all people? It doesn't make any sense."

Lyssa flinched, and it took Cassie a moment to understand her daughter's reaction.

"I wasn't criticizing you, Lys," Cassie said. "It's just that you're—."

She paused. She had never told Lyssa about her father, more than what little she felt Lyssa should know, and she hadn't really talked with her about the Walters. It seemed odd to start now.

"—you're a Buckingham," Cassie finished lamely.

Lyssa frowned at her. "It scared me, Mom. Emily can't deal with more trauma right now, and the first thing that happens to me in this house is frightening. What if it goes for her?"

"It won't, honey," Cassie said.

"But it went for me."

"No." The voice came from behind them. Cassie looked up. Athena stood in the doorway, wearing a silver lamé robe that looked like something out of a 1940s movie. It brought out the highlights in her hair, which was down around her shoulders.

She looked both older and younger than usual—the hair accenting the soft papery lines of her skin and the robe accenting her strong, unbending frame.

Lyssa's eyes lit up at the sight of her grandmother, but Lyssa didn't move. Apparently, she was wondering about her welcome even with Athena.

"I thought you were tired, Mother," Cassie said.

"I couldn't sleep, not with my Lyssa here." Athena opened her hands, a less showy method of welcoming someone toward her than Cassie used. "Don't I get a hug, Lys?"

Lyssa got up, and for a moment, Cassie thought she might refuse. Then Lyssa walked over to Athena, and put both arms around her.

Lyssa closed her eyes, and Athena rocked her as if she were a child, murmuring endearments.

Cassie turned away. Her daughter hadn't hugged her, hadn't even made her feel like she had been missed. But then, that was the story of their relationship, wasn't it? The way they constantly avoided closeness, and the depth with which Cassie wanted it.

She washed her hands. Lyssa and Athena were still hugging, although not as close. They were speaking to each other softly, Athena offering words of comfort.

Cassie couldn't remember Athena ever doing that for her, not even as a little child. Cassie sighed, poured herself more tea, and took a cookie. It was small comfort.

"Would you like some tea, Grandma?" Lyssa said after a moment.

"It looks like I'm going to be awake for a while, so I don't have to drink that disgusting stuff." Athena walked over to the cupboards, her robe swishing as she moved. "I'm going to have something with caffeine."

Cassie didn't say anything. She finished her cookie and put a hand around her mug, letting the warmth flow through her palm.

It only took Athena a moment to prepare her coffee, and then plug in the machine. The smell of freshly roasted beans reached Cassie and her mouth watered, but she knew better than to have coffee this late at night.

"Now," Athena said as she took her favorite mug from the cupboard. "What's this nonsense I hear about Cliffside House attacking someone?"

Lyssa went through her story again, and when she got to the ball, Cassie pushed it toward Athena. Athena gave the tarball a passing glance, then raised her gaze to Cassie.

Cassie looked away.

"Cliffside House has never, in its entire history, attacked anyone," Athena said as she poured herself a cup of coffee. She waved the pot at Lyssa, asking if she wanted any silently. Lyssa shook her head. "What you've described to me is a request for help, and a demonstration of the problem."

"I gleaned some of that." Lyssa's tone was dry. "But it felt frightening. And why come to me? Why not go to you or Mother? I've only just come back to town."

Athena looked at Cassie again. Cassie took another cookie, broke it in half, and wished there was a fortune inside it. Something, anything, to take her away from this conversation.

"You belong here, Lys," Athena said. "You and your daughter."

Still she wouldn't say Emily's name, but Lyssa didn't seem to catch that.

"I know," Lyssa said. "Buckinghams should never leave Cliffside House."

"That's not what I said." Athena looked at Cassie a third time. "You carry a bit of the sea, Lys. You hear better than the rest of us."

"A bit of the sea? What's that, Gram?"

Cassie reached for the teapot, but her hand shook and she nearly knocked it over. "Sorry," she said.

Both Lyssa and Athena were watching her. But she didn't say anything. She wouldn't. She had promised herself long ago that Daray was hers, that she wouldn't share him with anyone, not for any reason. Lyssa was the gift that Daray had left her. He had known she was pregnant long before Cassie had and still, that day, he gone to the sea, knowing he would die.

"Mom?" There was actual concern in Lyssa's voice.

Cassie righted the teapot. She had only spilled a little bit. She grabbed a napkin, and started to wipe up, but Lyssa's hand caught hers.

"What's going on, Mom?"

Cassie swallowed. She silently cursed Athena, sitting across from them like the goddess she had been named for.

"You left," Cassie said, and instantly regretted pausing after that word. It made her sound like she had condemned Lyssa for doing something Cassie had always believed to be completely natural. "You left, and we never really got the chance to talk to you about Anchor Bay and Cliffside House."

"We always thought you'd come back," Athena said, and even though the comment was meant helpfully, it wasn't helpful.

Cassie balled up the soggy napkin, got up, and threw it into the trash.

"We thought you'd come back *sooner*," Cassie said as she returned to her chair. "Certainly, when Emily was born."

"She was the first Buckingham in six generations not born in the house," Athena said.

"Mother, please." Cassie was watching Lyssa. There was already a small frown on Lyssa's forehead. They were going to lose her again if they weren't careful.

Athena shrugged one shoulder. "I would have told this differently."

"You grew up here," Cassie said, a little desperately. "You know the house. You've seen it change, and you've seen the things that sometimes appear on the beach."

"I haven't forgotten the magic, Mother." Lyssa's tone was dry.

Cassie nodded. That was what she was checking. "Cliffside House is the link between the past and the present, between the real and the unreal."

Athena watched her, knowing as well as Cassie did, that Cassie was using the very words that Athena had used with Cassie when she imparted this secret decades ago.

"That's why the house changes," Cassie said, deviating from the script. "It wasn't built here. It was built there in ways we don't completely understand. But it lives here, as a crossroads. And we're guardians of that crossroads. We protect both sides of the link."

"You and Grandma?" Lyssa didn't sound skeptical, but she did sound confused.

"The Buckinghams," Cassie said. "You, me, your grandmother. And now Emily."

Lyssa blinked hard. She brought her mug of tea to her lips and then set it down again without drinking.

"I didn't bring Emily to this place to trap her here," Lyssa said.

"She doesn't belong anywhere else, child," Athena said.

"Mom," Cassie warned.

But Athena, typically, didn't listen to her. "That's why your husband got so ill. All those powers, untrained and unchanneled, mixing in his head. You're immune to the texture of magic, to the way it bends everything around it. You grew up here. But he had no defense."

Lyssa's eyes had filled with tears. "You're saying that Reginald's illness could have been prevented?"

"It was expected, Lys," Athena said.

"And you didn't tell me? You didn't warn me?"

It was Cassie's turn to wince. She knew what Athena was going to say.

"Mom," she said. "Don't."

But as Athena's gaze met Cassie's, her expression hardened.

"Sometimes, Lyssa," Athena said, "the men are irrelevant."

Cassie's breath caught. She remembered those words, that inflection. She had been standing on the beach, ankle-deep in the surf, and her mother, her damn mother, trying to comfort her, had said that men were irrelevant.

That Daray was irrelevant.

Has he already done his duty? Athena asked. *Are you pregnant?*

"Reginald was not irrelevant, Grandmother." Lyssa set her mug down. "I *loved* him. Losing him may have destroyed Emily. How can you say he's irrelevant?"

Athena looked down at her hands. Cassandra clutched her mug so tightly she could hear the ceramic crack.

But Lyssa wasn't done. "How could you," she said to Athena, "and you—" She turned to Cassie. "How could you both let me, let us, lose him like that. If we had known—"

"If you had known," Athena said, "you might not have married him."

"And you say that would have been better for him."

Cassie gripped her mug even tighter. This was what she feared from Lyssa's homecoming, this discord. It had always been Lyssa's hallmark.

"Yes," Athena said. "It would have been better for him."

Lyssa blinked hard, holding back tears.

"Mother," Cassie said. "That's enough."

It was too much, actually, and Cassie should have jumped in sooner.

Athena leaned toward Cassie. "She needs to know what is happening here. She needs to know—"

"Lys," Cassie said. "It's complicated. It's always complicated for us. And she's wrong. We all failed you. I failed you. I didn't want a Walters back in Anchor Bay…"

Her voice trailed off as she realized what she had said. Lyssa raised her head, and the tears seemed to vanish. Cassie felt her cheeks grow even warmer.

"Back?" Lyssa asked.

Athena touched Lyssa's arm. "Child, these old arguments are useless. We must stay focused on the present."

But Lyssa pulled away from her. "What do you mean, 'back'?"

Cassie sighed. Apparently it was time to tell her. It was past time, truly. Only Cassie's fear had held her back before.

She didn't want to lose her daughter—not that she had ever had her. And now that Athena had spoken up, the chances of losing Lyssa permanently were very, very real.

"Back," Cassie said. "His father was here, over thirty years ago."

PART III

DIGGING INTO THE PAST:

THE FIRST LAYER

SIXTEEN

January 1970
Anchor Harbor
Anchor Bay, Oregon

The storm had been predicted for three days and never showed, but when it arrived, it arrived fast. Winds over forty knots created thirty-foot seas, which turned the harbor at Anchor Bay into a death trap.

John Aluke, captain of the tugboat *Anchor One*, was halfway out of the harbor when the storm hit. He'd been through worse—most notably the Columbus Day Storm eight years before. He knew he could survive this storm, maybe even bring the ship that he was supposed to pilot into the harbor, but he also knew which risks were worth his while.

He radioed the *Walter Aggie* which, according to their last readings, was still twenty miles out, and warned them to come no closer to port. He told them to anchor offshore, and he would come for them as soon as the winds died down, perhaps as early as the morning.

He got no response. For by then, the *Aggie* was already in trouble.

Cliffside House
North Tower

Twenty-year-old Cassandra Buckingham woke out of a sound sleep convinced the cliff was going to fall into the sea. She had heard a large bang and felt a huge shudder run through the entire building.

She was amazed she had stayed in bed. When she woke, nothing seemed disturbed. Her lamp was still on low beside the bed, her hi-fi playing the same record over and over again, the last of the incense burning down.

She went to the window and peered out, but saw nothing. The storm had come. Rain lashed the glass and she could hear the wind howling ever so faintly.

For one brief moment, she pulled open the door to her widow's walk and stepped outside. The lava rock which made up the walk was slick with rain, and cold to her bare feet. The wind whipped her hair around her naked form, and the rain pelted her skin.

She held her hands up, asking the water to help her see, and for a brief instant, she saw the ship, sliding against the cliff face, the panicked sailors running around on the deck like crazy people.

Then she choked, her throat suddenly full of something so thick that she couldn't even swallow. She raised her hands to her neck, and touched something slimy.

She pulled her hands back. They were black and dripping, her skin losing its warmth as the substance coated her. She shivered, her body temperature dropping.

She was going to drown. She was going to freeze to death. She was going to—

Her hands were still in the air, and her eyes were closed. There was nothing in her throat, but inside her mouth, an awful taste remained, as if she had swallowed a cup of sour Vaseline.

She looked down at the rocks below. There was no ship. And there were no sailors scrambling across the deck. The ocean looked angry, the swells spilling over the tallest points at the edge of the Devil's Goblet.

A large gust nearly knocked her over. She clutched the stone barrier in front of her, catching herself, and then reached for the door. She had to pull herself back to her room.

She had left the door open, and the rain had created a giant, spreading wet spot in the shag carpet. The incense had gone out, either damped by the blowing rain or finally burned down.

The familiar scent was gone, replaced by the briny scent of the ocean, covered by the stench of rotten eggs.

Cliffside House
South Tower

Athena Buckingham woke to find a man standing at the foot of her bed. He was dripping wet and naked, holding a seal's pelt in his left hand.

"We don't have a lot of time," he said.

No one had ever invaded the towers before. She sat up, clutching her nightgown closed.

"What do you want?"

"There's no time, Athena," he said. "We're going to lose everything if you do not come with me."

She knew better than to turn on the light. He would be six feet tall, black-eyed and black-haired, and one of the most beautiful men she had ever seen. She could already tell that from his voice, deep and rich.

She had never seen him before, but she had seen his type, and she knew how dangerous they could be.

"We have to set up a barrier," he said, "and hope it holds. We don't have the power to do it alone."

He held out a hand, but she didn't take it. She threw the covers back, stuck her feet in her slippers, and pulled her hair back with a barrette.

"Do we need to hang up your pelt?" she asked.

"I'm going to need it. You'll have to trust me."

A lot to ask on the first meeting, but she had done crazier things.

For a brief moment, she wished her mother was alive—she always handled emergencies better than anyone—and then Athena let the man lead her out of her bedroom, down the stairs, to the levels below.

Cliffside House
The landing between the towers

Cassie had pulled on a pair of jeans and a University of Oregon sweatshirt without drying herself off. She had tucked her long hair inside the sweatshirt because she didn't have time to pull it back.

Her hair dripped cold water down her back, sending shivers through her as she ran down the circular staircase that led to the landing between the towers, flicking on lights as she went.

She had to get her mother. Something was going to go wrong. Something may have already gone wrong. Cassie didn't know, but it was her job to sound the warning, and she had to do it now.

The sour Vaseline taste grew stronger on her tongue and the stench of rotten eggs had grown worse. Her eyes watered from the smell. She couldn't tell if it was real or not, anymore than she could tell if the sounds she kept hearing—the groaning of metal on rock—were real either.

When she reached the landing, she nearly collided with her mother, who was running after a man. The man was tall and beautiful, with the liquid eyes of a seal. He held a pelt in his left hand and he was naked.

A selkie, who had sought her mother out.

Cassie felt a jolt of surprise, and stopped before she ran into both of them.

"Mother!"

"No time, Cass," her mother said, dashing across the landing to the door built into the wall. Her hand scraped at the black rock, trying to find the hidden release.

"Mother, something's wrong."

"I know, Cass."

"No," Cassie said. "You don't. There's a ship. I think it's going to hit the cliff."

Her mother looked at her, fear on her face. The selkie was touching the rock now, searching for the same opening.

"Can't you smell it?" Cassie asked. "The rotten eggs?"

"What kind of ship?" Athena asked, and for the first time in her life, Cassie heard fear in her mother's voice.

"We don't have time, Athena," The selkie said. "Tell the child to go."

"We need her," Athena said. "Her powers can augment mine."

Cassie looked from one to the other, feeling her heart pound. She had known that her mother did strange and magical things for Anchor Bay, but she had never known what they were.

"What do you want me to do?" she asked.

"Find the opening to the damn door for one thing," Athena said.

Cassie braced one hand on the wall, and let the house show her where the release was. It clicked open without her even having to touch it.

"I thought you said she wasn't as powerful as you are," the selkie said as he ducked inside the door.

Cassandra looked at her mother, who ignored her. She was holding the door open as if she expected it to close.

"I said her talents are different from mine." Athena nodded at Cassie. "Go. Follow him."

"Who is he?" she whispered.

"Whoever they sent this time. When there's an emergency, you don't have time to ask."

Cassie stepped into the darkness, wishing she had a flashlight. She could hear the selkie in front of her, his bare feet slapping against the stone steps.

A beam of light came on behind her. Athena had a flashlight. Her mother thought of everything.

"Hurry, Cassandra."

Cassie ran down the stairs, unable to see most of the way. These stairs were different from all the others in the house. They were shallower, sharper. She got the sense that if she fell, she would cut herself as she slipped down them.

"What are we doing?" she asked as she ran.

She could sense her mother behind her, pushing her forward, making her go faster than she normally would have.

"I have no idea," her mother said. "He said something about a barrier."

"What?"

"We'll know when we get there."

Athena seemed so accepting, as if nothing had changed at all, as if she did this every night.

Maybe she did. Cassie had no idea, and she wasn't about to ask. She was worried about the staircase. The walls had grown narrower, and they were covered with water.

She had never been in this part of the house before. It had the damp chill of the sea. She wished she could smell something besides the rotten eggs, so that she would know how close to the water she really was.

Then another scent enveloped her: smoke. Her eyes burned, and she gagged again, stopping, and clinging to the wall.

"Cassie?" Athena asked.

"Fire," Cassie gasped. She clutched the wall, unable to move. She couldn't see at all. Smoke surrounded her, and she couldn't tell if it was real or a vision.

"Here?"

That answered her. The smoke was part of a vision. But of when? Of now? And where?

"I don't know," Cassie said.

"Athena." The selkie's voice echoed from below.

"Go," Cassie said, moving her hand in the direction of the voice.

"But this might be important—"

"Go," Cassie said again. "I'll catch you if I can."

Even though she knew she wouldn't. Her eyes were tearing, and her lungs were filled with smoke. Something was wrong. Somewhere. Something awful.

"Child, what can I do for you?"

"*Go!*" How many times did she have to say it? Athena had been right. Cassie didn't have the same powers. Athena and the selkie would do fine on their own.

Even though Cassie was guessing. Her mind was working as sluggishly as her lungs.

She leaned her cheek on the wet stone and listened to her mother's slippers click their way down the steps. Athena's voice called out to the selkie, and he answered, his voice coming from very far away.

Cassie closed her eyes, and gradually the vision faded. The smoke disappeared and the thick feeling in her throat was gone. Her eyes still burned, and her face was streaked with tears.

She wouldn't be surprised if her skin was covered in soot. But she still didn't know what had happened.

Or what had caused the vision to fade.

She sank onto the steps. She would need a moment before she could go farther, to join her mother and the selkie on the rocks below.

She brought her knees up to her chest, wrapped her arms around them, and rocked, trying to find some comfort.

Only she had a feeling she'd never feel real comfort again.

Anchor Harbor

The wind had come up. Rather than gusting at forty knots, it was sustaining at forty-five. John Aluke had to fight to get the *Anchor One* close to port. Even then, he knew it would take all of his skills to bring the tugboat in safely.

His radio crackled and hissed. It had been doing that ever since he radioed the *Walter Aggie*. He had been contacting them repeatedly, trying to tell them to anchor as far out as they could. The storm was a serious one, and this part of the Oregon Coast had the worst shoreline for a vessel in a storm. There was no working lighthouse, and the rocks were treacherous, especially near the twin pillars of the bay.

They weren't named after the Devil for nothing. Aluke had seen too many pleasure boats hit the Goblet or the Candlestick and sink before anyone could get to them. Even though the *Walter Aggie* was not a pleasure boat—it was a tank vessel that wouldn't fare well in these choppy waters.

The waves revealed the pointed rocks below the surface. The volcanic uprising that had created the Candlestick and the Goblet had littered the entire area with jagged rocks and a basalt shelf that had ground up more than one boat.

It took special skills to be a tugboat pilot, but to be a tugboat pilot near Anchor Bay took the best of the best.

And even Aluke was calling it a night.

The radio spit once more, then a voice said, "*Anchor One*, this is the *Walter Aggie*. We are at the rendezvous point, but we can't see you. Over."

Aluke cursed. They hadn't gotten any of his messages. His hand kept one hand on the wheel as he lifted the microphone.

"*Walter Aggie*, this is *Anchor One*. Do not go to the rendezvous point. Return to deeper water. We cannot tow you into the harbor in these conditions. We will come to you when the storm abates. Over."

They didn't respond. Aluke continued guiding his tug toward port, wondering what it was that made his messages impossible for them to receive. The captain of the *Walter Aggie* should have been smart enough to know they couldn't dock in this kind of weather. He had the charts; he had to know how treacherous this area was.

Aluke tried again. "*Walter Aggie*, this is *Anchor One*. Do not go to the rendezvous point. Return—"

"*Anchor One! Anchor One!* We need assistance." This was a different voice, and it was very panicked. "Help us please! Help us!"

The hair rose on the back of Aluke's neck. He'd never heard anything like this. Even in the most dire emergency, radio operators remained calm.

But this clearly wasn't their radio operator.

"What's the trouble, *Walter Aggie*?"

The voice had disappeared. Aluke got nothing in return. He tried again, then again, the silence filling him with a panic he'd never felt before.

He'd never lost a ship. Were they in trouble because they had expected him? Or had they done something else?

There was no way he could help them. His tugboat was no match for this kind of sea. He kept steering inward, as he thumbed the microphone on, and contacted the Coast Guard, feeling handicapped.

He didn't know where the *Walter Aggie* was. He didn't know what had gone wrong.

All he knew was that whatever it was, it was very, very bad.

The Base of the Devil's Goblet

Athena stepped out of one of Cliffside House's many exits, finding herself on what the locals called the Base of the Devil's Goblet. Sea and time had worn the sharpness of the cliff away, bending it into a goblet shape, complete with stem.

Cliffside House grew out of the top of the goblet, but stairways and secret passages all through the house provided exits at various points on the cliff. This one brought her to the top of the base, an unprotected area at the best of times.

On this night, it was damn dangerous. The wind was so strong that she could lean into it without falling, and it seemed constant, which was unusual for the Oregon Coast. The rain was so much a part of the wind that it seemed like someone had turned on a cold shower, and leveled the showerhead sideways at her. She was drenched in an instant, and colder than she remembered being in her life.

The rock was flat here, and very slippery. Her slippers gave her no traction at all, and she kicked them off. As she did, a wave slammed into the cliff side, the water frothing toward her. It stole the slippers as if they were its heart's desire.

She wouldn't be able to stay up here very long. She had no idea whether the tide was coming in or going out—she had stopped paying attention to tide tables long ago—but her time on the base was limited.

Either a wave would drag her to sea or a gust—anything stronger than this current wind—would fling her over the side.

And then, no amount of power would save her.

She glanced once at the door behind her. It had vanished into the cliff side, just like it had been designed to do, even though she didn't remember closing it. She hoped Cassie would know that this was the place to come, this was the door she needed.

Maybe Athena shouldn't have left Cassie on the stairs. She had never seen her daughter like that, frightened, and in the throes of something more than she was.

Athena did not like how this night was shaping up.

The rain grew thicker, harder, and seemed to have chunks of ice in it. The temperature had fallen just in the time she had stood out here.

Her nightgown was plastered against her, her long hair glued to her face. Up ahead, the selkie stood, hands on his hips, waiting for her as if they were about to go on a picnic.

Behind him, she saw other figures. Men, women, she couldn't tell. Not all of them appeared to be human.

She clambered across the rocks, suddenly missing the chivalry of her own kind. All she needed was a hand extended, guiding, helping. But she had to make it on her own, the wind pushing her toward the restless sea.

A wave crested, sending spray across her face, mixing with the icy rain. She couldn't see what the problem was out there in that ocean, how she was needed, but she knew she was.

She was the lightning rod, the connection, the power source. The waiting group probably wasn't strong enough to prevent the problem on their own.

She climbed the last of the rocks, and suddenly there were hands helping her, grasping her upper arms, supporting her back. But instead of fingers, some of the hands had talons and others had scales instead of skin.

As she reached the very edge of the base, she saw some of the creatures waiting for her. It seemed like the entire population of the Refuge had gathered—fish women standing on the edge of the rocks, their faces turned toward the rain; real mer-creatures clutching the side of the cliff, hanging on despite the treacherous seas; selkies, some with their pelts and some without, but all in their human form; and more—creatures she had no name for, some so small she was afraid she would crush them with her bare feet.

The languages swirled around her like the wind, and the magic sent sparks into the air that felt like electricity, making her wonder about the danger of being electrocuted, here on the lonely lava rock, in the middle of a terrible storm.

"Athena!" The selkie who had brought her shouted her name. His voice, so deep and rich inside Cliffside House, seemed small here compared with the ocean's pounding and the wailing power of the wind. "We need you in the center of the circle."

A circle. She had never done one of these. Her mother had, and her grandmother before her, and they had never talked about them, only saying that they were the best and worst times of their guardianships.

Athena crossed the rocks and stood in the center of the creatures she had sworn to protect. They looked at her, not threatening her as they would other humans, and then they reached out—arms, appendages, tails, whatever worked—and touched the creature next to them, forming an unbreakable circle.

The wind howled around them, and the sea roared, and the rain became even fiercer.

Light surrounded her and the rain fell off her and she raised her arms. In the midst of the storm, the selkie reminded her, "Barrier, Athena, we need a barrier," but she wasn't sure if he spoke the words or sent them to her telepathically, like Cassie used to do when she was a child, before she had control of her powers.

Cassie should have been out here. This was a mind-magic, not a physical one. But something—someone—had crippled Cassie with a vision, and Athena had left her on the stairs.

The light grew brighter and in the center of it, she saw a ship, tilting in the waves. It was going to slam into the Candlestick. Athena set up the barrier, but too late. The ship already hit rocks. The barrier prevented it from tumbling into the harbor.

Something that looked like arterial blood poured out of the hull, but it was worse, much worse, and she realized she had put the barrier in the wrong place. She set up protections all around the harbor and deep into the ocean floor, not letting anything from this ship contaminate her world, her people, her refuge.

But the smell enveloped her, dank and oily and thick, and she heard screaming—human screaming—and she saw more blood pouring into the sea.

They were dying. Everyone was dying, and all she had done was put a Band-Aid on the wound.

SEVENTEEN

Cliffside House

"I don't understand, Mother," Lyssa said, sounding both tired and irritated. "What wound? What are you talking about?"

Cassie sank into her chair. Through the open kitchen door, she saw Emily, still wrapped up in the quilt, sound asleep. Emily would have understood. The child had a gift, a deep gift, that no one else seemed to notice.

"Oil," Athena said. "She's talking about oil. The *Walter Aggie* was an oil tanker. In the middle of the storm, it slammed into the Devil's Candlestick, swerved around it somehow and then ran aground in the bay."

Lyssa got up and poured herself some real coffee. Cassie poured the last of the peppermint tea. It was cold, but she didn't care.

Lyssa sat back down, and looked at her grandmother.

"You tried to prevent that?" Lyssa asked Athena.

She nodded. "We were too late to prevent the grounding. I think it was meant to happen, as a kind of test against the Refuge."

"Lyssa doesn't know about the Refuge, Mother." Cassie had been trying to get there, but the memories had overwhelmed her. That time lived in her mind much more than this one did. It wasn't just her past; it was her present as well.

"The Refuge?" Lyssa reached for a cookie.

Athena sighed. "It sounds so silly when you actually talk about it. But remember the end of the nineteenth century was the beginning of the conservation movement."

"I thought we were talking about 1970," Lyssa said.

"We're talking about the Refuge." Athena took a cookie as well. She held it up, examined it, and said to Cassie, "If we're going to be up all night talking, perhaps we should have a real meal."

"I just bake," Cassie said. "Real meals are your province."

"The Refuge," Lyssa prompted.

Athena ate the cookie and stood up. Cassie had seen her do this before. She hated talking about the true nature of the Buckinghams, of Cliffside House, of their history. But she was going to.

"In the 1880s, 1890s, my great-grandmother hated the direction the world was taking. This was the era of the robber barons, the first industrial age, and everything was considered ripe for the taking—trees, land, oil—"

"I'm an historian, Gram," Lyssa said. "I do know this stuff."

"You know the official American version," Athena said. "Not real version."

"But she does understand the context," Cassie said. The conversation had gotten away from her, but she wasn't going to lose it entirely.

Athena took a pan out of the rack beside the stove. She set it on the flat cooktop.

"Magic," she said as if she were giving a lecture in school, "exists all over nature. Not all creatures build and achieve like we do. Sometimes they believe other things are more important. My great-grandmother believed that when we tampered with the natural environment, we were destroying magic."

"A nineteenth-century environmentalist," Lyssa muttered.

Athena paused in her preparations to glare at Lyssa. Cassie tried to give her a cautionary look, but she wasn't sure Lyssa saw it.

After a moment, Athena went to the refrigerator and removed

eggs, bacon, ham, several vegetables, and cheese. As she set them on the counter, she said,

"Whatever you want to call her, my great-grandmother was adamant about this. But she was a Buckingham, and she knew if she tried to tell the officials or the heads of the various businesses or any man in power—"

"Why is it that Buckinghams are anti-male?" Lyssa asked, loudly enough to interrupt.

Maybe she hadn't changed from her teenage self.

"We're not," Cassie said. Then she looked at her mother, who had her back to them. "At least, not all of us."

"You're an historian," Athena said with some acidity. "You know how well women were treated in the nineteenth century."

"It was better in the West," Lyssa said.

Athena turned, gripping a wooden spoon like a sword. "Do you want to hear this or not?"

"Lys, please," Cassie said. She didn't want them driving again, and she couldn't let Emily go. She wouldn't. The child needed more help than Lyssa realized.

Lyssa paused, as if she were gathering herself, and then she shook her head. "I'm sorry, Gram. I'm exhausted. I was kind of hoping to come here, collapse on a bed, and not think about anything for a few weeks. Now I'm faced with some centuries'-old problem, not to mention the fact that my ex-husband's death might be due to my mistakes, and I don't know what I'm going to do to help Emily. So I'm not exactly primed for a history lesson."

"Well," Athena said, "you're going to listen anyway."

Cassie suppressed a smile. Her mother used to talk to her that way too, but she had never spoken to Lyssa like that.

"Can I help you cook?" Lyssa asked. "I'm good at omelets."

"Who said I was making omelets?" Athena grabbed a mixing bowl.

"I can do this, Mom," Cassie said, although she wasn't sure if she was offering to finish the story or to cook the middle-of-the-night meal.

Either way, Athena rejected the offer with the wave of her spoon.

"I was telling you about the Refuge," she said. "My great-grand-mother came to realize that she couldn't protect hundreds of places, but she had charge of Anchor Bay and, through connection, Seavy County. She convinced all sorts of species to come here, and because of who we are, she got mostly water creatures. She promised them protection, if they promised not to war upon each other, and she used her magic to help them create habitats all along this part of the coast."

"Even warm water spirits?" Lyssa asked, and Cassie let out a sigh of relief. Apparently, Lyssa was losing her objections to the story.

"No," Athena said. "She tried a few, but they couldn't survive off this coast. Still, you'd be surprised how many different kinds of creatures live here, and how important they are to the ecology of the area."

"I'm sure the State of Oregon would be surprised too," Lyssa said.

Cassie smiled. That comment didn't seem to bother Athena either. She was holding a mixing bowl under her right arm and cracking eggs into it with her left hand.

"The idea was to protect the FantasyLife, even the kinds that weren't exactly sentient, like the glowing water lilies you find in Dawson's Pond. It's created some problems over the years, particularly to the south. We lost a few men to the fish women, and we've had to renegotiate treaties over and over, but by and large it works. We pool our magic, and we guard off any threat to the entire county."

"But Mom said it didn't work that night." Lyssa grabbed another cookie. She seemed interested now.

Athena put the last broken eggshell back in the carton. Cassie got up, grabbed the carton, and took the shells out. She would keep them for her compost pile, which she had been using for years now to actually make a garden out of their little stretch of rock.

Athena grabbed a fork and started beating the eggs in the bowl. The fork made a scraping sound against the metal sides that grated on Cassie's nerves.

For a moment, she thought Athena wasn't going to answer Lyssa. Then Athena sighed.

"There were several problems that night, some of which your mother didn't mention."

Cassie stiffened. Not every detail from that night was Lyssa's business. Some of it wasn't even Athena's, which Cassie would remind her if she started to tell.

"But the big ones come from us. We Buckinghams don't have the same powers. Mine aren't cerebral, like your mother's. I have some mental abilities, but nothing like Cassie's."

Cassie felt her cheeks warm. She had never heard Athena talk about Cassie's powers in such a positive way.

"My powers are more aggressive. If we were under some kind of attack, I could have stopped it. I'm better than an entire army." Then Athena shrugged, holding up the dripping fork, and studying her hand. "Or, at least, I used to be."

"And then there's me," Lyssa said. "No powers at all."

"If that were true," Cassie said. "Then you wouldn't have had that vision tonight."

"You're saying my powers are like yours?"

"Not at all," Athena said. "You share a lot with your father."

"My father?" Lyssa sat up in surprise. "He had magic?"

"Of course."

Cassie's cheeks were even warmer. She gripped the side of the counter, her head down. "Mother, please."

"But," Athena said sharply, "he's apparently a topic for another night."

Cassie felt the muscles in her arms twitch, as the tension from her fingers ran all the way to her back. She wanted to curse her mother, but she wouldn't let herself. At some point, she would have to talk to Lyssa.

But on her terms, not her mother's.

Athena had no right to set things up like this. She had no right to interfere in everyone's lives.

"Why haven't you said anything about my father, Mom?" Lyssa asked.

The perennial question, which Cassie had dodged so many times that Lyssa finally stopped asking it.

"Because," Cassie said, opting for the truth, "it hurts too much to talk about him."

"Cassie's never gotten over him," Athena said. "I don't think she's ever tried."

Cassie closed her eyes. She never could see Daray as he had been in life; only in those last minutes, his body curled at her feet, after he had been released from the sea.

"Mom?" Lyssa asked. "Are you all right?"

Cassie shook herself, opened her eyes, and made herself smile as she turned around. "Your grandmother was telling you about that night, and how we failed."

The bite in her own voice startled her. Athena's gaze met Cassie's over Lyssa's head, and Cassie thought she saw admiration in it.

"Touché," Athena mouthed.

Cassie pretended she didn't see it. She sat down at the table, her back to her mother.

"Cassie got one of her first—and only, from what I understand—incapacitating visions," Athena said. "I believe something sent it to her. I think if Cassie had been able to join us that night, we would have diverted the ship. But the vision, as she told you, and my response to it, cost us precious minutes."

Cassie swirled the tea in her mug. "I don't think Mom's right about that. I never have. What I think is pretty simple. If you look at the history of the Buckinghams and the Refuge, you figure out that we can protect against things we know about. If we don't know about it, we're not guarded against it."

"You're saying you didn't know about oil leaks?" Lyssa asked.

"This wasn't a leak," Cassie said. "It was a disaster, one of the worst on the Oregon Coast. If it had been properly reported, it might have been considered one of the worst in North America."

"Properly reported?" Lyssa asked.

"Cassie's getting ahead of the story." Athena grabbed a knife and expertly chopped an onion in a matter of seconds.

"Lys," Cassie said, "the first big oil spill that got the attention of the world happened in 1967 off the Cornish coast in England. It was a horrible disaster, and not just for England, but for France and

Guernsey. It's not like now where people mobilize from all over the world and come to help with the cleanup. Thirty years ago, we were only guessing at what to do."

"And we had other things to think about besides the gulls and the clam beds," Athena said. "We had living, sentient beings we couldn't talk to anyone about, and they were being threatened, particularly the ones who spent most of their time on the ocean's surface."

"But we didn't know that that night," Cassie said. "That night, Mom and the leaders of the various communities used their powers to trap a lot of the oil here. The slick did not follow the currents the way others have, and the barriers that Mom set up did protect most everything under the water."

"So I don't understand," Lyssa said. "If you solved it, why is it even important to me being here now?"

Athena had chopped chives and green pepper, and was now working on a tomato. The thud-thud of her knife was comforting.

"That's what we're trying to figure out," she said.

"Mom said it was because I married a Walters." Lyssa pushed at the tarball with her fingers. It rolled around on the napkin, leaving a little black trail. "That's how this whole conversation got started. She never told me that she had known Reginald's dad."

Spoken as if she wasn't even in the room. Cassie got up and poured out her tea. Then she rinsed her mug, grabbed the caffeinated coffee pot as if it were a whiskey bottle, and poured.

"I'm assuming," Lyssa said, "that the *Walter Aggie* was a Walters Petroleum ship?"

"Yes," Athena said before Cassie could speak. Then she nodded toward Cassie, as if she wanted Cassie to finish it.

"Yes," Cassie repeated. "The *Walter Aggie* was a Walters Petroleum ship, and this was the first big Walters Petroleum disaster in years. Old Man Walters—your husband's grandfather—was grooming his son to take over the company, and this was his first chance to handle something that could destroy the company's reputation forever. Or at least, that was what he once told me...."

EIGHTEEN

January 1970
Anchor Harbor Wayside

Cassie stood at the beach access, a rake in her left hand. She wore borrowed rubber waders with her blue jeans tucked into them, and a ratty sweatshirt that she had once used for house painting. The rubber work gloves she wore belonged to a local contractor, and were too big for her hands. But the hardware store was sold out of work gloves, and no one had any extras in her size.

It was the middle of the morning two days after the disaster, and the sun was out. The sky was a cloudless blue, the kind of perfect that usually brought tourists to the beach, even in the middle of winter.

But no one thought there would be tourists in Anchor Bay ever again. The beach was coated in thick black sludge. Oil, as thick as mud, covered every surface and had turned the bay black.

No one was working in Anchor Bay these days. Everyone was on the beach, picking up solid bits of oil and seaweed, rescuing sea birds that looked like someone had coated them in tar, and using pressure hoses to wash the stuff nearest the highway into traps someone had built to catch the run-off.

The cinderblock restroom building had become a way station, where volunteers could change their clothes and wash some of the oil off their shoes. A group of local women had set up a coffee and snack station just outside the doors, so that the workers had something to eat when they took a break.

Athena had used her position in the sheriff's office to make calls to places that had suffered similar disasters, places like Santa Barbara, California, San Juan, Puerto Rico, and Lands End, England, to talk to the locals about the methods they used to clean their beaches.

Mostly, Athena had learned that it was long arduous work, that nothing would really get that inky black stuff off the sand quickly or easily. But a few people had mentioned using straw to soak up the oil, and then raking the straw into buckets, and that made sense to her.

She and Cassie tried it that very afternoon, and it had made it easier to collect the stuff. Now Cassie was leading a raking brigade, using younger people because the work was repetitive and incessant.

After the first day, Cassie's back and shoulders had ached so badly she thought she wasn't going to be able to move in the morning. But she had managed. Even though she wished her magic abilities—or her mother's—worked like Samantha's on *Bewitched*. A little twitch of the nose, and the entire mess would be gone.

Instead, it covered everything, and the stench was abysmal. The smell had invaded Cassie's nose during her vision, and hadn't left. The town stank of oil, and so did the sea.

The comforting briny smell was gone, and so was the sound. The pounding waves, which were so much a part of her life, had become muted, almost as if the oil was holding the sea in place.

Cassie knew that wasn't so. She could see the waves moving inward, and crashing on the other side of the bay. So far, the currents hadn't moved the oil slick south. Just the bay and the northern part of the harbor were affected.

But the local fisherman said that would change. They believed that the currents would take the slick and slime the entire coastline. They believed the disaster would ruin the fishing and clamming industry for the next year, maybe more, kill hundreds—maybe thousands—of sea birds, and destroy the seal and sea otter population.

And no one seemed to know what to do about it.

Cassie gripped the rake harder. The mayor, Ted Whitby, was dealing with the Coast Guard, trying to get someone to move the ruined ship away from the Devil's Candlestick. The ship was still leaking oil, and it was caught on one of the underground rocks, so no one knew exactly how much oil was seeping under the surface.

The sheriff, Robert Lowery, was trying to figure out a way to pursue criminal charges against the captain of the *Walter Aggie*. He wasn't having a lot of luck, at least so far. The only thing that worked in the sheriff's favor was the fact that the accident had happened in Oregon waters.

But the captain of the *Aggie* was blaming John Aluke, the tugboat pilot who had apparently not shown up for the rendezvous. Aluke, who had contacted the Coast Guard the moment he heard of the trouble, said that no one on the *Aggie* had responded to his radio messages. He claimed he had told the *Aggie* to anchor farther out, where it would be safe in a storm of that magnitude.

Cassie knew Aluke, and believed him. She also knew that he was in a great deal of trouble. He had told her privately that it seemed like his messages weren't getting through to the *Walter Aggie*, even though theirs reached him.

Like something blocked my signal, he said, as if there was some kind of master plan.

But she didn't know what that plan would be, and neither did anyone else. Athena kept saying that someone had sent Cassie an incorrect vision—the fire, which hadn't happened, and hadn't even been suggested—to distract her. With Cassie's mind power, the barrier Athena set up would have kept the *Aggie* off the rocks.

Athena was arguing some kind of conspiracy, but Cassie wasn't sure exactly who or what would want to destroy Anchor Bay. It seemed like great bad luck to her, with no intentional malice, although it would have been lovely to believe in malice.

But the accident benefited no one, not Anchor Bay, not the residents of the Refuge, and certainly not Walters Petroleum, which was sending one of its representatives to Anchor Bay that afternoon.

The substitute dispatch, doing Athena's job while she worked on the beach, had notified everyone that the Walters representative was arriving by helicopter.

Athena had cursed that, saying the downdraft from the helicopter blades would make everything worse. But no one listened to her. The Walters representative had made his choice. He wanted to get to Anchor Bay as quickly as possible, and that made helicopter the logical choice.

The helicopter would have to land on the highway near the beach access. It was the flattest area in Anchor Bay. Sheriff Lowery had to shut down the highway on either side, so that there would be room for the helicopter.

As he did, more and more volunteers left the beach, and Cassie got the uneasy sense that if this Walters representative handled his arrival wrong, he would be facing an angry mob. The accident had destroyed countless livelihoods, and no one in Anchor Bay made a more than a marginal living. Even the shops and restaurants would be affected once the initial surge of volunteers left. No tourists would come here; the tourism industry would die off, just like the fish and the oyster beds and the animals.

Anchor Bay could become a ghost town, because of the carelessness of one ship's captain.

Athena was even angrier than most people. She said that so far, few creatures in the Refuge were affected, but she was worried that the barrier wouldn't hold.

That would make the captain of the *Walter Aggie*, and the people from Walters Petroleum, guilty of mass murder—at least in her eyes. And there was little she could do to prevent it.

Cassie was here to guard her mother, as much as the bay. Which was ironic. Usually Athena guarded her. Athena was the prudent one, the one who believed the modern era mostly benefited the people who lived in it.

Cassie was the one who knew that corporations didn't have the little people in mind when they made their policies.

She heard the mechanical whoosh-whoosh of the helicopter in the distance. It was a familiar sound, and usually one that made her a bit nervous. The Coast Guard patrolled the beach with helicopters, going north in the morning and heading south in the afternoon. She could set her watch by them; 11:20 a.m. on the northern route and 2:20 on the southern.

Any other time, the whoosh-whoosh of helicopter blades combined with the roar of the engine meant trouble.

Everyone looked up, even the people still working on the beach. It was unusual to see a helicopter come from the valley. They usually came from the Coast Guard station in Newport. Helicopters flew north and south, not east and west. It disturbed the natural order of things.

Sunlight reflected off the helicopter's metal frame, blindingly bright. Most people turned away, but Cassie didn't, and neither did Athena. She stood rigidly beside Cassie, her mouth set in a thin line.

Cassie never really had a sense of all her mother's powers—she wasn't sure exactly what Athena was capable of—but she could feel them now, revving up like that helicopter's engine, preparing for some kind of battle.

Cassie put a gloved hand on her mother's arm. "Let the mayor handle this," she said.

"That fool has no idea what Anchor Bay is."

"Mother," Cassie said. "The representative from the oil company isn't going to want to deal with you."

"He isn't going to be able to avoid me," Athena said.

"It's not his fault," Cassie said.

Athena looked away from the helicopter to glare at Cassie. "You're the one who says anyone who even eats food made by a particular corporation is complicit in their crimes. When did you become a defender of the corporate mentality?"

Athena had a point. But Cassie couldn't express exactly what she was feeling. Something had gone wrong here, but it happened for a combination of reasons, things that no one entirely understood.

"All I meant was he's probably not the guy who can make changes. He's just here to make us all feel better, and not be angry at Walters Petroleum."

A small smile crossed Athena's face. "Now that sounds like my daughter."

"They've got minions, Mom," Cassie said, "and we've got the press. If you can talk Mayor Whitby and the sheriff into letting the Portland TV crews here instead of trying to hide this disaster, we can shame Walters Petroleum into sending people to help with the cleanup."

"They wouldn't know how to clean up," Athena said.

"As if we do," Cassie said, but her words were lost in the roar of the helicopter.

A wind rose around them, coming from above, like a downdraft, and the side, blowing in the wrong direction. Wind usually came from the ocean, not blowing toward it.

Cassie's rake moved in her hand, and she didn't look behind her, she didn't want to see what the wind was doing to the beach, the oil, the oil slick. At least, for a brief instant, the smell faded, replaced by the warm smell of a machine running at top capacity.

The helicopter was larger than she thought it would be. She'd seen the Guard's helicopter every day, but only flying past. She'd never seen it land.

This one lowered itself on the highway slowly. The blades were bigger—longer—than she expected and they made hideous noise that blocked everything else.

The welcome wind became overwhelming, and she wanted to run from it, move somewhere where it couldn't touch her. But she held her ground, feeling like she was about to defend her turf against some kind of interloper.

Athena straightened beside her. She looked like another person, her hair blowing behind her head, her skin taut.

The helicopter's blades didn't slow down as a door opened on the side, and some steps were lowered. Two men in suits climbed down, both of them holding briefcases.

Cassie ignored them, though. They weren't the Walters representative. They were his companions—minions, to use the word she had used earlier—people who were here only to serve the representative himself.

He came out the door slowly, as if it didn't bother him to have shut down an entire highway in the middle of a city, to have dozens, maybe hundreds of people, waiting for him to get out of their way.

He wore a light summer suit, cream colored, with a tailored jacket that went to his thighs. The pants were wider than she would have expected from a corporate executive, and his hair was longer—past his ears in the style of the early Beatles.

His face was lean and tanned. In his left hand, he held a cowboy hat that matched the suit. In his right, he had nothing except a class ring the size of a medal.

He wasn't what Cassie had expected. She had expected someone who looked like his assistants, dark suits, narrow ties, white shirts. She hadn't expected flamboyance or a touch of originality.

And she hadn't expected him to be so young.

As he came down the steps, his gaze met hers. Cassie had to use all her strength to keep from stepping backward at the power in the look. He found her attractive—very attractive. He smiled.

She did not smile back.

NINETEEN

Highway 101
The Village of Anchor Bay

Athena felt her breath catch.

They had sent a boy.

She didn't know whether to feel angry or relieved.

He certainly didn't look like he knew what he was doing. He made his way off the helicopter, clutching a cowboy hat. The boots he wore had heels that were higher than any she had ever owned, which told her that he was insecure.

The boots also had a design in the leather, fussy and pretty, rather like the suit, which looked like it belonged on the pages of some men's magazine rather than on a man who had come to inspect a harbor damaged by oil.

He ducked, running past the helicopter blades, and joining his people near Mayor Whitby. Then the boy waved his hat, and the helicopter rose as effortlessly as it landed, taking the annoying wind and sound with it.

Athena's ears ached, and for the first time since this all began, she actually felt tired. All the plans she'd had vanished with this boy's appearance.

She put a hand to her hair. It had fallen out of its customary bun. She didn't have time to repair it. Instead, she grabbed what remained of the clip and pins, and tucked them into her pocket, letting her hair fall about her face.

Cassie looked at her in surprise. She probably had never seen Athena in public with her hair down, but Athena wasn't going to miss a moment of this meeting.

She took Cassie's arm as if she were still a child, and led her to the group of men standing beside the highway.

Sheriff Lowery was in the road, directing his deputies and a few locals to remove the barricades. Cars waited on each end, some of their drivers standing outside an open door, watching the helicopter leave, a hand shielding their eyes.

As Athena got close, she heard the boy say, "My God. Is it all like this?"

He had finally turned to face the beach.

Athena looked too. She couldn't avoid it. On a perfect day like this, the beach should have been brown, the ocean gunmetal blue—grayer than the sky, but just as pretty—with the sun adding highlights to the waves.

Instead, it looked like the cliffs had melted onto the ground below. The shiny blackness of the lava rock seemed pale in comparison to the black blanket covering what had once been beautiful ground.

The locals who had watched the helicopter land had turned away, and were picking up oil-soaked seaweed a bit at a time. A group of women from the diner were holding a bird, which wasn't fighting them, and were trying to wipe the oil off its wings.

Athena's eyes teared, and she turned away.

Cassie had wrenched her arm from Athena's grasp and was staring at the boy. Her anger had risen; the placating words she had used with Athena now seemed like they had been spoken by another person.

No one had answered the boy. They had all turned to look, just like he had, as if the oil could vanish just because a helicopter landed and someone with some kind of authority had gotten out.

"No," Athena said as she strode toward him. "It isn't all like that. It's worse near the ship. It's still spewing oil."

"Spewing" wasn't exactly accurate. The ship was leaking, seeping oil like a wound that wouldn't heal.

The boy's eyes went to Cassie first, and Athena recognized the approval in them. Then he looked at her.

His eyes were a pale blue, made paler by his white eyelashes. His tanned skin made his eyes seem almost clear. There was something in them that made her realize he was older than she had initially thought, with some awareness, some intelligence that only came with experience, not with book-learning.

Maybe the company hadn't done the wrong thing sending this boy after all.

"I'm sorry, ma'am," the boy said. "I don't believe we've been properly introduced. I'm Sam Walters, but folks call me Spark."

Spark was not a name any adult man should claim as his own. However, judging from his last name, this young man came because he was part of the Walters family.

Athena extended her hand, to put herself on equal footing with him and the other men around her.

"Athena Buckingham," she said. "And this is my daughter, Cassandra."

Walters smiled. It was an impish smile, one that made it clear this was a man who liked women, alcohol, and a good time. "Someone in the Buckingham family had a love of the classics."

He didn't take her hand.

Athena had a choice. She could ignore his rudeness and his polite and seemingly innocuous way of dismissing what she had to say, or she could make an issue of it.

She decided for the issue.

"Do you always refuse to shake someone's hand when it's offered, Mr. Walters?"

His smile remained but the twinkle left his eyes. "Well, ma'am, where I come from, ladies don't shake like men do. Just ain't done. Specially when they're as pretty as the two of you."

Cassie started to object, but Athena moved in front of her, blocking her. She didn't need Cassie screwing this up, not now.

Mayor Whitby saw the interaction. He was a sensitive man, and he seemed more upset than Cassie had. Yet he was politic; he smiled at Walters, and said, "The Buckinghams have been in this town longer than anyone. I may be the official mayor, but it's Athena people go to when there's trouble."

Walters reassessed her, sizing her up as if she were a man. His gaze met hers again, and this time, she thought she saw something more in it, a coldness, a judgment, something that told her this boy was a person to watch.

"Beg pardon, ma'am," he said. "I'm not used to the way things are done in this part of the world."

"That's fine," Athena said, sticking out her hand. "Let's try again, shall we?"

This time, he took her hand, gently as if he were afraid he was going to break it. Still, he shook twice.

"It's a pleasure to meet you, ma'am. I'm sorry it's under these conditions."

"Me, too," Athena said.

"That's all?" Cassie hissed from behind her. "You're not going to say anymore?"

Athena turned slightly and smiled at her, a fake smile that intentionally did not meet her eyes.

"My daughter is going to get back to work. She's organizing the beach cleanup. I hope you'll excuse her."

Walters took Cassie's gloved hand and bent over it as if they were at a ball and he was going to kiss it. As he did, Athena noticed that his hair was already thinning on top.

Cassie grimaced as he touched her, but said nothing. When he was through, she took her hand from him as if he had stolen it, and marched back to the beach.

"I trust," Athena said as Walters watched Cassie walk away, "that you have some power, and you weren't just sent here to comfort the locals."

His gaze returned to hers, and this time, he let the surprise show on his lean face. Apparently, bluntness wasn't as common in Texas. Or maybe it wasn't as common among the women.

"Ma'am, my father owns Walters Petroleum. He sent me rather than some employee to show the good people of Anchor Bay that we are going to take care of this mess, and do it the best we can, given the circumstances."

"I hope you have a plan," Athena said, "because this is an ecological disaster of a type the Northwest has never seen."

"Not to mention," the mayor said hastily, "the economic impact. If we don't contain this spill, more than Anchor Bay will be affected. And we won't be able to keep the news quiet much longer. Walters will be in for some nasty publicity."

"We're aware of that," Walters said. "I'm a bit surprised the news hasn't gotten out yet."

"We're remote," Athena said, "and one of our main livelihoods is tourism. We'd like to have this under control before the vultures from Portland descend on us."

Walters nodded. "Well, we have a plan. We're thinking of using a detergent to emulsify and disperse the oil. I'm hoping that the ship is far enough out that we can burn her, and get rid of the oil in her hull that way. Both problems then'll be cleaned up, and we can concentrate on this here beach."

He winced as he looked at it. Clearly the smell was getting to him. That pleased Athena.

"What kind of detergent?" she asked.

He frowned at her. "We have experts to figure that out, ma'am."

"I only ask because when I spoke the folks in Lands' End, England, where the *Torrey Canyon* went down, they warned me about detergents. They said it was the detergents, not the oil, that killed off most of their seabirds. We have some amazing creatures here on the Oregon Coast, Mr. Walters. We wouldn't want your attempts at cleaning up to create worse problems."

His mouth was open ever so slightly as she spoke. Then he turned to Mayor Whitby.

"I've found," Walters said in a confidential tone, almost as if Athena weren't there, "that a negative attitude is counterproductive to solving serious problems. Perhaps we could have this discussion somewhere more private."

Mayor Whitby looked at Athena. He understood the rebuke as well as she did.

"Fine," she said. "I'll open the conference room in city hall. But every moment we delay, Mr. Walters, more oil leaks into our ocean. And we will keep track of the time wasted."

Walters' eyes narrowed even more. He obviously realized he couldn't get rid of Athena.

He had no smiles now. In fact, he looked like a man who rarely smiled.

"I'm sure you will keep track, ma'am," he said. "I'm quite sure you will."

TWENTY

Cliffside House

They thought she was asleep, but Emily heard every word the grown-ups in the kitchen were saying and, oddly enough, she understood what they were talking about.

Still, she couldn't open her eyes—or maybe she didn't want to, she wasn't sure. The smell of cocoa had faded as the cup Grandma Cassie poured her had grown cold. When the smell disappeared, though, another one rose around her. Like the lake, only better. There was something salty to this smell, and fishy too, and she knew, without anybody telling her, that she was smelling the ocean.

It felt like she had come home, and she'd never ever been here before.

The couch was the most comfortable couch she'd ever felt, and the quilt that Grandma Cassie had wrapped around her was warm and thick and heavy, just perfect for a rainy, stormy, windy night.

Even though she had trouble thinking of it that way. Because with her eyes closed, she could see that beach, all screwy with black stuff, and the blue sky and the pretty day, and the people in the funny clothes and the funny-looking cars, and the great big helicopter that looked like something out of the movies.

And she saw things that nobody talked about, like the little tiny women standing on the cliff sides, collecting the black filthy stuff in their skirts and pouring it into little stone buckets that little tiny men carried to the side of the road. None of the normal-sized people seemed to notice at all, and Grandma Cassie, who told most of the story, with the help of Great-Grandma Athena (at least Emily thought it was Great-Grandma—she couldn't open her eyes and see her) never mentioned this stuff at all.

There were real-sized people standing with the people on the beach, only these people all had really black hair that shined blue in the sunlight. And some of these people had pouches around their waist and inside the pouches, Emily knew without even looking, there was lots and lots of fur.

Then there was the really nice-looking man who was helping Grandma Cassie—only she didn't look like she did now. She had rounder cheeks and her eyes twinkled, even when she saw bad stuff, and there was something alive about her, something that had gone away when she got older. She was prettier, as if prettiness was something inside a person, not what was on her face.

She kept looking at the man, and he kept touching her hair, as if he couldn't believe she was there beside him, and then they'd rake up the black-soaked hay, so that other people could dump it in buckets.

Emily saw all that and she saw even more, like she had three pictures going on her mental TV set. There was the main story, which Grandma Cassie was trying to explain to Mom (and Mom didn't want to hear it. Emily could feel that too. Mom was feeling guilty, like all this was her fault, and she hadn't even been born yet), and then there was this other story kind of bleeding into that and even a third story bleeding into that.

Almost like two channels were trying to take away the program on the channel Emily was watching.

The other story was dark, like it was happening at night, and that man who had come in the helicopter, who had the same last name

Emily used to have and Daddy had, and who had Daddy's smile when Daddy was feeling good—

(And Emily hated it, hated it, when they said it was because she could do stuff that Daddy went crazy and wasn't Daddy anymore. Because it meant that when he tried to push her under the water, it was her fault because she got too close to him, and when her lungs hurt and she sent that hurt away—

(She squeezed her eyes tight, and made those thoughts go away. She would forget them, forget them, and think about all the stories going on around her because they were better than what happened to her. Everything was better than what happened to her.)

—that man, he was walking to a hotel room right on the beach, which Great-Grandma Athena made sure he got because she wanted him to smell the bad oil stuff, and he stood at the window and said, *It's like West Texas, only with water,* and Emily knew what it meant—the ocean that day was flat and went so far you could see the horizon, except he wasn't just talking about the looks, he had a sense of the creatures that Grandma Cassie and Great-Grandma Athena were trying to protect, and then that was it. Emily didn't get any more of that story. It kind of faded in and out, as if Mom had put on the parental controls and Emily couldn't find a way to shut them off.

Emily wanted to say something to her mom about this being true and important and Mom should listen and stop worrying about Grandma trying to manipulate everything, and stop thinking about threats to Emily and start thinking about bigger stuff, but Emily couldn't open her eyes.

So maybe she was asleep and the extra stuff was stuff she dreamed, and the voices were fading in and out, telling stories— because they were fading in and out, and she did get to see parts, but not other parts, and she knew, for instance, that Grandma Cassie was keeping stuff "close to her chest" because "it was hers" and nobody else's and not even Lyssa—Mommy—got to know about it. Because Grandma Cassie was afraid if she mentioned it, it would go away and not be real anymore, and it was all she had left, maybe it was all she ever had, except for Lyssa (Mommy) and sometimes Lyssa wasn't even enough to make up for it all.

That was the only thing Emily didn't like about this place was how sad everybody was and how many secrets everybody had. She wasn't sure how they could keep all the secrets, because the house wanted to tell her everything. It was talking to her, just like everybody else was, only all this talking didn't confuse her.

It felt right. It felt good. And if she could just wake up a little bit, she would tell Mommy that, and they would stay, and she would be able to crawl into that four-poster bed in the room upstairs that Grandma Cassie worked so hard at making perfect for her, the room Emily hadn't seen yet, except in her maybe-dreams.

Because she was going to need her rest. They all were. Because the black stuff had never really gone away. And it was coming back. Only it was worse.

Something was really mad about it. And something else was trying to change it, and everyone thought the Buckinghams could solve it, and not even Emily was sure of that.

Because, she was afraid, somehow it was going to rest on her, and she was only ten and her daddy was dead, and her mommy was sad, and she didn't have any friends at all.

She was all by herself and she didn't want to be. She wanted help and she didn't know how to get it. All she knew was she didn't want to leave.

But she also knew she never got what she wanted.

Not anymore.

TWENTY-ONE

Cliffside House

"Sam Walters hampered the cleanup efforts?" Lyssa shook her head. Her memories of Sam Walters, albeit few, were of a man who seemed fanatically devoted to his company, a man who would do anything to make certain no one ever spoke of Walters Petroleum in a harsh way.

Of course, he had been much older when she had met him—completely bald, whether through nature or vanity, she wasn't certain. He had a beautiful skull, perfectly shaped, and very smooth, and he kept it tanned like the rest of his skin. He had also still had those pale blue eyes with the pale lashes, making him look like an otherworldly creature, someone whose designer couldn't quite get him to look human.

"No, he didn't hamper them." Athena was sitting at the head of the table, eating daintily. She had made some kind of egg casserole—it wasn't a soufflé, and it wasn't an omelet, but the eggs held everything together, rather like huevos rancheros. "He couldn't hamper the cleanup efforts. This was the first major crisis his own father had put him in charge of, and if it went wrong, then Sam, no matter what his relationship to Old Man Walters was, would no longer work for the company."

Cassie sat beside Lyssa, picking through her food. Athena had put everything she could find into the egg dish, from bacon pieces to ham to onions, green pepper, and tomatoes. There was even salsa in there, and some spices that made this an evening meal, not a morning one.

It was all surprisingly tasty, and supremely fattening, and it was going to make Lyssa even more tired than she was.

"I don't remember Old Man Walters," Lyssa said. "I don't even remember anyone talking about him. I thought Reginald's father was the old man, and he had been in charge forever."

"Maybe by your husband's standards, he had been in charge forever." Athena didn't look at Lyssa as she said that, and she didn't have to. Lyssa caught the contempt in Athena's voice.

Maybe the reasons Athena had given for not visiting Wisconsin had been false. Maybe she could have left the coast unguarded. Maybe she had refused to come because Lyssa had been married to a Walters.

Lyssa stole a glance into the family room. Emily still slept comfortably beneath the quilt Cassie had wrapped around her. Even the smell of food hadn't woken Emily up.

Emily was a Walters too, no matter what her last name now was. She had the Walters genes, just like she had the Buckingham ones. She didn't look like a Walters—she favored the Buckinghams —but she was a member of that family, a family her own clearly hated.

Lyssa pushed at the eggs in front of her, uncertain why no one had told her any of this before. Cassie watched her closely as if worried about the revelations.

"I think his father died soon after," Cassie said, and it took Lyssa a moment to realize she was talking about Reginald's grandfather, Sam's father, whose first name Lyssa had never known.

"Soon after the accident?" Lyssa asked.

"Soon after Sam returned to Texas," Athena said, as if that were significant.

Lyssa pushed the tarball away from her plate. The little round black bit of oil bothered her more now than it did when she first coughed it up.

"None of this is making me feel any better," she said. "I'm not sure why this happened to me, and I'm still don't think Emily and I should stay in Cliffside House."

Both Athena and Cassie looked at her, identical stunned expressions on their faces.

"I'm not sure what you wanted me to get out of this story, except that you didn't tell me any of this. When I met Reginald at the University of Texas, and I told you I had fallen in love with him, neither of you told me that our two families had a history."

Lyssa's voice was rising. She was angrier than she had initially thought.

"I mean, when Sam Walters objected to me marrying Reginald, he said it was because of my family, and I asked Reginald what that meant, and he had no idea, except that his dad had objected to his girlfriends before, usually because they didn't come from 'the right set,' which, to Reginald, meant they didn't have money. So that's what we assumed. Not that Sam had met you, Mom, or that he'd found you attractive."

Lyssa shuddered. That detail bothered her more than she could say.

"I didn't find him attractive," Cassie said softly, as if that made everything better.

"So? You answer the small issue and not the big one. How come no one told me that I was getting in the middle of something that predated me? My daughter has paid for this in ways that I couldn't imagine. Her Walters grandparents have never met her. They never acknowledged her birth, and they're even fighting her inheritance from her father in court."

"Based on what?" Athena asked.

"Based on the fact that my husband wasn't sane when he died, and my daughter was with him at the time. Fortunately, they don't want the publicity, so every time my lawyer threatens to make this all public, they give in a little. We're going to win, so I'm told. We're not far from a settlement. But by then, I'll be completely in debt. I've already paid my lawyer everything I can, and now she's billing me monthly."

Lyssa's voice shook. She pushed her plate away, her eyes filling with tears. She wiped them away. She was tired and not in complete control of her emotions.

"And then you tell me this stupid story about some oil spill that may or may not have killed all the FantasyLife off the coast, and how the Walters are responsible, and you're telling me this so that Emily and I will stay here? How dumb do you think I am?"

Both Athena and Cassie were staring at Lyssa as if they couldn't believe what they were hearing.

"You hate the Walters too, Grandma," Lyssa said to Athena. "You've made that really clear. Do you want me to stay so that the house can get its revenge on Emily? Is she some kind of sacrifice to the creatures you've sworn to protect?"

Athena straightened her back, succeeding in making herself look both powerful and regal. "Maybe if you had let us finish the tale——"

"I've heard enough," Lyssa said.

"Then you'll have to understand that I don't sacrifice my family. Your girl is my great-granddaughter, and I would never harm her."

"Really?" Lyssa snapped. "How do you figure that? You're as neglectful as the Walters have been. You weren't even calling her by name when she first arrived. You've made sure you haven't said hello to her yet—not that that's any different from how you've treated her in the past. You've never met my Emily, Gram. Don't you think being treated as a pariah by both sides of the family harms a child? Hmm? Especially for something she can't change, something that's a part of her?"

Athena's cheeks had turned a livid red. Lyssa wasn't sure she had ever seen her grandmother blush before.

"You never brought her here," Cassie said softly.

Lyssa set her fork down. She was done eating. She was done, period. It was so typical of her family to blame her for their mistakes.

"Don't defend Grandma, Mother," Lyssa said. "You're a world-class hypocrite yourself. How many times did you come visit? How many times did you hold Emily and act like there was nothing wrong? How many——"

"I love Emily," Cassie said.

"You could have told us," Lyssa said. "You knew why her Walters grandparents rejected her, and you never said a word."

"Of course I didn't," Cassie said. "You never told your husband or your child about magic. How can I explain a problem that originates in magic, if they don't believe in it?"

Lyssa closed her eyes. She was so tired, and had wanted so badly for someone else to take care of things for a while. But that wasn't going to happen.

Now she had to get back into her little car, and drive around Anchor Bay, just to see if the small, family-owned hotels still had someone manning their front desks.

She should have gone to Portland after all.

She pushed her chair back. The legs scraped on the stone floor. She rubbed her eyes with two fingers, then looked around the room.

Both Athena and Cassie were watching her as if they were afraid of what she was going to do.

"I'm taking Emily away from here," Lyssa said. "I'm beginning to realize that she's not safe anywhere. I'll talk to you on the phone about training her, and helping her control her magical abilities. I'm sure I can do what I need. If not, Mother, you can fly out to wherever we end up and help her. Of course, you can't, Grandma, because you can't leave Anchor Bay without a Buckingham."

Lyssa put as much venom into those last two sentences as she could. She stood up, swayed a little, and headed toward the entry. She'd go to the car, get it ready for Emily, and carry her sleeping daughter out into the storm.

If they couldn't find a hotel, maybe Gabriel could put them up for the night, although Lyssa wasn't sure how she would explain her problem to him. Of course, he had lived in Anchor Bay his whole life. He knew about the Buckinghams, and the magic.

Everyone did.

"Mommy?"

Lyssa turned.

Emily was standing in the doorway, the quilt wrapped around her like a robe. Her short black hair was tousled, and her eyes, round and brown, looked even softer than usual.

"I want to stay," she said.

Beside Lyssa, Cassie caught her breath.

Lyssa shook her head. "It's not safe, honey."

"It's very safe, Mommy. This place, it loves you."

Lyssa felt her cheeks warm. "Honey, I—"

"Grandma and Great-grandma aren't saying everything. They think something bad is coming, and they think we'll be able to help. If we go away, things'll just get worse. The house didn't attack you, Mommy. It asked you for help. You told me you always gotta help when you get asked."

"The child's right," Athena said. "The voices you heard asked for help. They didn't threaten you at all."

"The child," Lyssa said with great emphasis, "is named Emily. I'd like you to give her the courtesy of using her name."

"Mommy," Emily said, "Great-grandma likes me. She's just scared of me."

Lyssa whirled and looked at Athena. Athena wasn't afraid of anyone or anything. At least, she never had been, not in Lyssa's memory.

Athena's blue eyes met Lyssa's, and Athena's lips turned up in a poor attempt at a smile. "The child—your Emily—is right again," she said. "I never thought I'd be a coward at this stage of my life."

"What are you afraid of?" Lyssa asked.

"Choices," Athena said. "Your daughter forces us all to face choices we may not want to face."

Lyssa looked from her grandmother to her mother. "What does that mean?"

Cassie swallowed and looked at her hands.

"Mother? Did you see something you're not telling me?"

Cassie shook her head.

"Mother?"

Cassie closed her eyes.

"Grandma, it's okay," Emily said. "She didn't tell you about

Grandpapa Walters because she wanted me to be born. She loves me, Mommy. I'm supposed to be here. Everybody needs me."

The words chilled Lyssa. Her daughter stated them so matter-of-factly, as if she had the same gift Cassie had.

"Is that true?" Lyssa asked Cassie.

Cassie nodded.

"You didn't say anything because my daughter, the Walters-Buckingham hybrid, was going to be useful someday?"

"It's not as crass as that," Cassie said. "She's a special child."

"Yes," Lyssa snapped. "She is. And I'm not going to let you people rob her of that."

"Mommy, please." Emily came farther into the kitchen, her quilt trailing after her. She looked like a little queen, giving orders to her subject. "Please."

Lyssa finally turned to her daughter. "How do you know all this stuff? You've never said things like this before."

Emily looked at Cassie, who nodded to her.

"Mother?" Lyssa said. "You know about this?"

"No," Cassie said. "I have ideas, but I don't know. What's changed, Emily?"

"The house," Emily said. "It shows me things."

"What things?" Lyssa asked.

Emily shrugged. "Pictures. Feelings. Stories. I like it, Mommy."

Lyssa sank into her chair. She hadn't wanted this either. "I don't like the sound of this," she said, mostly to herself.

"It's what Cliffside House does," Athena said. "It amplifies our powers, protects us, and helps us keep the bridge between the worlds safe. Emily is very important to that bridge."

"You're saying she's going to be telepathic, like Mom?"

"I don't know what her powers are," Athena said. "None of us do. You never let us develop them."

"Stay here," Cassie said. "We'll figure this out together. I promise."

"What do you know, Mom?" Lyssa asked. "What's going to happen that is so important that we have to stay here?"

Cassie looked at Athena again. Lyssa wasn't sure when the two of them had become so close. It seemed odd.

"I don't know anything," Cassie said. "Mom and I have had feelings, though. Something's changing, Lys."

"Because of me and Emily," Lyssa said.

Cassie shook her head. "Something else. And it's better if we're all together. Apart, bad things might happen."

"Like Daddy," Emily whispered.

Lyssa expected her mother to try to dismiss that. Instead, Cassie said very simply, "Or worse."

Lyssa wasn't sure how anything worse could happen to her daughter.

"I want to stay, Mommy," Emily said. "I feel like a person here."

"Like a person?" Lyssa asked.

"She belongs," Cassie said. "Maybe for the first time. Don't take that away from her."

"She's a special child, Lys, and you're in no position to take care of her alone." Athena was blunt, as always. "We can help with the lawsuits, and the care, and allow you some time to recover too. You've been worried about Emily, but you should look to yourself. I've never seen you so ragged."

"You haven't seen me for more than a decade," Lyssa said.

"Stay," Athena said. "The house will protect you, not harm you."

"It hurt me already," Lyssa said.

"It's just trying to show you something," Cassie said.

"Something about oil?" Lyssa looked at the tarball. She'd never forget how that felt. "Something about the Walters?"

"Or maybe something to do with the old spill," Athena said.

"Or maybe it's a message from someone else." Cassie's voice sounded small, far away.

"Like who? Who would send me a message like that?" Lyssa asked.

Athena looked at Cassie, as if she was waiting for Cassie to speak. But Cassie looked down, clearly not ready to answer.

"We don't know, honey," Athena said after a moment. "But whoever it is obviously needs us all."

PART IV

EXODUS

TWENTY-TWO

Seavy County Sheriff's Office
North County

The day dawned clear and cold. Gabriel Schelling was up early, surprised by the sun. It hadn't been in any of the forecasts, which predicted lingering storms through the following week.

Instead, the sun was so bright, the air so clear, that he could see for miles. The faint outline of oil tankers and cargo ships looked like tiny bricks on the horizon line.

The sky sparkled as if it had been washed clean. The ocean, however, was brown with mud, sand, and debris churned up by the storm. Logs, seaweed, and bits of garbage floated on the surface, as if the ocean were doing a self-cleansing that wasn't absolutely complete.

Gabriel had spent the first part of the morning driving around the village. Water still stood on the highway, gathering in the grooves, and along the sides of the road. Pine needles blanketed side streets, blown off in the severest winds. Tree branches were down, blocking road-ways and scarring lawns.

By the time he reached the edge of town, he discovered another surprise. Highway department crews were already working on the road. He suspected that other crews were working on the entrances to the corridor, and shoring up road damage in the mountains. He wouldn't be surprised if the entire coastal highway system was at least patched by nightfall.

The roadwork put him in a good mood, such a good mood that he didn't mind seeing the storm-made lake still covering Highway 19 at the north end of town. The lake would recede, given time. And if the weather held, maybe the saturated ground would be able to dry out, so that the next series of storms wouldn't devastate the area quite so badly.

He had hope, but he knew that this time of year, such hope could be futile.

Gabriel arrived at the sheriff's office at ten. The office was up a side street from the Anchor Bay post office. The post office had been built in the 1970s, but the sheriff's office was older than that. It dated from the 1920s, and had once been the only building in that part of town. Now it had grown rooms like fungus, and it no longer had real architectural structure—just additions that looked like accidents.

Still, he loved the place, and going into his job pleased him more than he liked to admit.

He parked in the lot next to Athena's truck, and an unfamiliar car. He paused as he looked at Athena's vehicle. He wondered how Lyssa's homecoming had gone, and then decided not to ask.

Two other cars were there, both squads. So neither Zeke nor Suzette was out patrolling. They were probably exhausted. He was surprised that he wasn't. Sometimes, having a four-person crew could really put a strain on the team, especially during emergencies, like yesterday's.

The entrance into the building was a glass door with *Sheriff's Office* etched at eye level. The door was, perhaps, the most dangerous entrance Gabriel had ever seen in an official building, and he reminded the county of that at budget time every year. But since the door had never been broken, not in the forty years it had served as the entrance to the North County Sheriff's Department, Seavy County officials didn't see the point in spending the funds.

They didn't seem to understand the value of prevention, and Gabriel didn't know how to explain it to them.

He stepped inside to a warm building that smelled of freshly brewed coffee. His department hadn't fallen for the Seattle frou-frou coffees yet. Whoever arrived first brewed good old-fashioned grocery store coffee, not from those pseudo-fancy beans the local Safeway stocked, but from the cans that had been around since Gabriel was a child. Judging from the acidic edge to this morning's scent, someone had brought in a can of Folgers.

Athena sat at her desk, clutching her coffee mug as if it were a lifeline. She looked worse than Gabriel had ever seen her—her skin so pale that he could see just how blue her veins were. She had shadows under her eyes, and the frown lines beside her mouth looked deeper than usual.

But she was impeccably groomed as ever. Her hair was pulled back in its customary bun, without a strand out of place. Her blouse —a cream color with just a hint of lace trim—looked like it had been laundered five seconds before. She wore a black ankle-length skirt that bloomed over her chair, and black ankle boots with just enough of a heel to add a touch of elegance.

She was always so put together that she made him feel like going home and getting dressed all over again, hoping that this time he would get it right.

When she saw him, she gave a weak version of her usual smile.

"Who'd believe there's sun today, eh, Gabriel?" she asked. She moved her mug aside, as if she hadn't really been clutching it like it was the only thing that kept her afloat. Athena's mood was always evident by which mug she chose from giant mug hanger he had put on the wall. This morning's was an old one with the characters from the old (and much missed) *Bloom County* cartoon strip—Bill the Cat looking like he'd stuck his paw in a light socket, and the words "Ack! Stress!" beside him.

Apparently Lyssa's homecoming had not gone well.

"When the rain stopped," Gabriel said, deciding that ignoring Athena's mood was the better part of valor, "it woke me up. I hadn't realized how used to it I had become."

Athena's smile grew into something real. "I would miss the storms if we didn't have them."

"Me, too," Gabriel said. "I'm just happy for the break."

He walked over to the coffeepot, which was full to the brim, and poured himself a mug. Unlike Athena, he didn't use the mugs to define his mood; he just grabbed whatever was closest. This one was yellow with a smiley face painted on it. The smiley face had a single fang showing, and a drop of blood falling to the bottom of the mug.

Perhaps it did mirror his mood after all.

He stirred in some non-dairy creamer, and frowned. There were no voices, not even the radio.

"Where is everyone?" he asked.

Athena started as if he had woke her up.

"Oh, sorry," she said. "Suzette and Zeke are in the back. You have a visitor."

Athena usually wasn't that mysterious.

"A visitor?" Gabriel asked.

"All the way from Whale Cove, and believe me, that's some distance on a day like today."

It was, too. Even though Whale Cove was only twenty miles south on 101, when 101 was down, the only way from one town to the other was through the Willamette Valley. That added at least 3 hours onto a twenty-minute trip.

"Who is it?" Gabriel asked.

"Hamilton Denne. He heard about Zeke's find last night."

Gabriel had forgotten all about Zeke's find. Gabriel carried his mug through the narrow, dimly lit hallway, to the room that served as a makeshift morgue, generally used only when a corpse had to remain in Anchor Bay until the medical examiner could arrive and take the corpse to Whale Cove.

The door was closed, but Gabriel could see through the single pane of glass. Denne was bent over the metal table, gloves on his hands, and white medical robe covering his clothing. Suzette lingered near the edge of the table. Zeke lounged against the wall, one booted foot crossed over his ankle. He toyed with a toothpick in his mouth, as if it were the most interesting thing in the world.

Gabriel opened the door, and nearly stepped backward from the smell of mud and wet fur. Those weren't the smells he had been expecting.

Denne didn't even look up. "Leave the coffee outside."

Gabriel leaned into the hallway, took a giant sip from his mug, and set the mug on the floor beside the door. Then he came in, letting the door close behind him.

"What've we got?" he asked.

"Come see for yourself." Denne was still bent over the table. Beneath his medical robe, he wore a pair of khaki pants and a pale blue dress shirt. An expensive brown sports jacket hung over a chair.

Zeke kept his gaze on the table itself, like a man who expected something to attack at any moment.

Gabriel stepped beside Denne, and looked down. At first, Gabriel thought Denne was examining a toy, a little girl's stuffed doll, and then he realized whatever it was had once been alive.

The creature looked vaguely female, although Gabriel couldn't tell what, exactly, made him think that. It had two arms and two legs, a torso with no definition at all—no breasts, no waist, no nipples—and a long neck that led to a very human face.

The face, however, was no bigger than the palm of Gabriel's hand. The eyes were closed, and the mouth slightly open, a bit of mud on the chin. The skin was grayish, and Gabriel couldn't tell if that was natural or not.

"What is it?" Gabriel asked.

"Water sprite, I think," Denne said. He pointed, very gingerly, at film that covered the top of the metal table. "See? Wings."

Gabriel saw no wings. What he was staring at looked more like fresh Saran Wrap.

"How do you know they're wings?" he asked.

Denne picked up the body, holding it two-fingered by the torso. The Saran Wrap on the back rose with it, folding out flat and clear as if something held it in place.

Denne used the edge of his finger to outline the structure of the wings. They were see-through, but if Gabriel looked very hard, he saw a hint of a rainbow, like looking at a bubble in sunlight.

"I've only read about these," Denne said, "and not in very reliable accounts. Apparently they move under the surface of the water like a beetle or like a dragonfly will float on top of it. The wings keep them in place, and hide them from predators that fly above them. I thought they were ocean-going only, but Zeke says he found this one on Highway 19."

"I did." Zeke said tersely. Sometimes Zeke and Denne rubbed each other the wrong way, particularly when they were left alone with each other.

"He did," Gabriel confirmed. "He found it up there just after I left."

Denne straightened. "What did you see?"

"It was face down in a mudhole," Zeke said. "My first guess was that it drowned."

"How did you notice it?" Denne asked. He had obviously waited until Gabriel arrived before talking to Zeke. Apparently Denne was aware that they didn't get along well either.

"My flashlight caught the wings. I thought it was an oil slick, and I learned a long time ago that tiny oil slicks in water near the highway could mean that a car had gone off the road."

Zeke had actually taught that one to Gabriel. Cars that bounced off the road often left a trail of fluids before vanishing into the under-brush. It always paid to follow those little fluid trails. Gabriel himself had found more than one unconscious tourist hidden by thick under-brush. Without Zeke's little trick, the tourists might have died.

"How did you know it was a creature and not a slick?" Denne asked.

"I saw the body," Zeke said. "I thought it was a doll, and I was worried. So I bent down, and pushed at it, and the whole damn thing moved—including what I thought was water."

"You knew then that it wasn't human?" Gabriel asked.

"And that it had been alive." Zeke grimaced. "I saw that face. I thought it had drowned too."

"It can't drown," Denne said. "These things live underwater."

"You think," Gabriel said.

Denne gave him a sideways look, with just a hint of amusement in the eyes. "I think. As I said, the things I've read about Water Sprites are unreliable. I'm going to have to take a real look at her."

"Like that breaks your heart," Zeke muttered.

"Actually it does," Denne said. "I'd like to keep her intact."

Gabriel winced. He didn't want to think about taking this little creature apart.

"You call it 'her,'" he said. "Is it female?"

"As I said," Denne said, "I'm going to have to take a closer look. She looks female to me."

"Looks like an it to me," Zeke said. "There aren't any defining characteristics. I mean, how do these things reproduce?"

"For all we know, they divide like worms," Denne said. "Or maybe they leave larvae somewhere and go through a pupa stage, like butterflies. Or they could spawn, like salmon, coming from eggs and—"

"In other words," Gabriel said, "you have no idea."

"And I'd like one." Denne could barely contain his excitement. "What I want to know first, though, is what killed her. To my knowledge, no one has ever found one of these so far away from the sea."

"But you just said we don't know anything." Zeke rolled the toothpick between his fingers. "For all we know, these sprites swim upstream to die."

"There's no stream there," Suzette said.

"I beg to differ," Zeke said. "There's a small creek that flows into the river. With all that rain, and the way all the creeks have swollen these last few weeks, it might be hard to distinguish the creeks from river water."

"Good point." Denne nodded at Zeke. "All of which we'll need to explore."

Gabriel bent over the little corpse. It was the source of the mud smell as well as a not-faint-enough odor of decay. Its eyes, which were open, had no whites, and looked inhuman. He wondered if they would look like that if that creature were alive.

This water sprite's mouth was partially open, and inside he could see hints of very pointed teeth—something he had not expected.

He straightened, and it seemed like everyone in the room had been watching him. It made him feel awkward. He was not used to being the center of attention.

"All right," he said, looking at Denne, "so what's the secret?"

"Secret?" Denne put a hand near the creature. The movement seemed proprietary to Gabriel, as if Gabriel had no right to be so close to the sprite.

"You drove a hundred miles out of your way to get here this morning," Gabriel said. "Now I know that for all your bluster, you trust us to handle a corpse here for a few days if you're too busy to collect it. So what's going on? What made you drive into the valley and back?"

"Aside from curiosity?" Denne said.

"Curiosity could wait a few days," Gabriel said.

"Spoken like a man with no interest in science." Denne's gloved finger lightly touched the sprite's torso. From Gabriel's perspective, the touch seemed to make no difference at all. The torso looked firm, unlike human skin, which would have changed slightly at a single touch.

"I wouldn't call this science," Zeke said. "This is pure fantasy."

"It's fantasy when it's made up," Denne said. "These creatures are quite real, and this year, I've gotten two corpses to prove it."

Gabriel frowned. "That's it, isn't it? The fact that you're actually gathering proof?"

"I didn't need proof," Denne said. "I'm not sure anyone who lives here does."

"But you want to become some big mucky muck who discovered the world's greatest collection of FantasyLife?" Zeke asked. "Like those guys who discovered lost tribes in the Andes?"

Denne shook his head. "I'm not sure, exactly. If I did that—if I went public with this little sprite and our fish woman—I would change Seavy County forever. Imagine all the tourists that would come."

Zeke played with that toothpick. "Not to mention the TV people and the magazine people and—"

Denne poked his fingertip in the sprite's mouth, moving her jaw. "I'm not equipped to write for scientific journals. I'm a practicing coroner, a doctor—even though my ex-wife never thought so—not a research scientist. I'd have to give these babies up to some research university."

"Where some other scientists would get the glory," Zeke said.

Gabriel wasn't sure if that was a problem for Denne. Denne had never been about glory. He was a man who enjoyed mystery and strangeness and the darker side of life. Denne not only found death fascinating, he found its causes just as interesting.

"It's not that." Denne moved his finger away from the creature's mouth and set his hand beside its head. "It's harder to articulate than that. It's that our proof is gone."

"Proof of what?" Zeke asked.

"Proof that what we know to be true actually is." Denne spread his hands apart in a gesture of helplessness. "We all know that there's strange things that happen here. We've experienced it, whether we like it or not."

Gabriel leaned against a counter, a realization coming to him as Denne spoke. Gabriel had come back to Anchor Bay because he liked the strangeness and the magic. Because, on some deep level, he needed it.

"It's like—I don't know," Denne said. He looked at Zeke, who shrugged. "It's like—believing in God. If you believe, you see evidence of God's existence all over the place, but you can't translate that evidence to other people. If they don't believe, they don't understand the evidence. But imagine if you could introduce them to incontrovertible proof—"

"Like taking them to some cloud and introducing them to a fatherly old guy with a beard and wings?" Zeke asked.

"Exactly," Denne said.

"If that's your view of God," Gabriel said, thinking of all the various views he had encountered in his travels.

"Which begs another question," Denne said. "If it's not your view of God, do you then accept the old man with a beard as God or as some old philosopher sitting on a cloud?'

"Why does it matter?" Zeke asked.

"Because," Gabriel said, "every country, every town for that matter, has legends and myths of its own. Some are rooted in history, and some have disappeared into time. Some are expected—like little ghost stories around a murder site—and some are so bizarre that you can't quite accept them."

Denne looked over at Gabriel, as if he couldn't believe Gabriel was getting into the philosophical part of the discussion. Gabriel wasn't sure he could believe it either. He tried to listen to conversations like this, not participate in them.

He said, "And if it turns out that all of Seavy County's legends and myths are true, then maybe all of India's are too, or those of the various African countries or the stories of the leprechauns in Ireland. And if those stories are true, and there are no more leprechauns, then what happened to them? How did they go away?"

Gabriel's voice shook a little, as he realized what he had been thinking. All the stories he had heard all over Europe. Elves and fairies and mermaids—pagan rituals gone awry, and Christians slaughtering non-believers. He shuddered. If all of those things were true, the bloody history of the world had just gotten a lot bloodier.

Zeke put the toothpick back in his mouth. "I still don't see how it matters. People aren't going to care if we call fish women mermaids or if God is some old man on a cloud or some benign being that can spread itself across the sky. We'll still go on and live our lives just the same as before."

"Really?" Denne asked. "We make accommodations to the other creatures in our lives all the time."

"Accommodations?" Zeke asked. "What do you mean?"

"Let's ignore the lengths people go to take care of their house pets and horses. Let's just talk about business. Like that fight a couple of summers ago in the Klamath basin over water rights. The farmers wanted to irrigate their land in a drought, and the state wanted to protect the salmon runs. Or the problems we're still having in the forests over logging rights versus old growth versus the rights of rare and nearly extinct species like the Spotted Owl. Seems to me, your father moved back to Anchor Bay, Zeke, when a lot of the logging jobs went to the tree farms in Georgia rather than staying in the forests of Oregon."

Zeke's eyes narrowed. Gabriel's stomach was jumping and he wished he still had his coffee.

"Still don't see how it matters," Zeke said.

"Like this," Gabriel said softly. "What if Hamilton tells the world about water sprites, and the world decides these creatures have value. Will we be able to continue running fishing boats in the harbor outside of Anchor Bay? What if the boats run over sprites? What if sprites are rare in highly fished areas? Do we protect fishing rights? Or do we save these little creatures?"

"It might be more complicated than even that," Denne said. "I gave you examples of things that are valued, but not sentient. What if we can prove these creatures—this little being right on this table—lives in a society with culture and a language and everything else? What if her brain is as powerful as ours? What if she just chooses to use it differently?"

"Differently?" Zeke asked.

"There are groups," Gabriel said, "that choose to live in primitive conditions. People sometimes chose not to live in a technologically advanced society, even though they have the knowledge and the ability."

"Like the Amish," Suzette said.

"For an American example, yes," Gabriel said. "Like the Amish."

Zeke sighed. He pushed away from the wall, rolling the toothpick over and over in his hands.

"Do you understand my point now?" Denne asked.

"Oh, I understand it," Zeke said. "But having brains and stuff hasn't stopped people from wiping out other cultures. It seems to be part of the human experience. We exterminate the things we don't like—only I guess, when it's something with a brain and a culture, we call it genocide, right?"

Denne's face had gone pale. "What are you saying?" he asked, his voice sounding shaky.

"I'm saying that you let people know these things exist," Zeke said, "and if these things have any of the mythical powers they're supposed to have from fairy tales and stuff, then I wouldn't expect tourists and CNN."

"You think we'd kill them?" Denne looked stunned.

"I think there's no doubt," Zeke said. "I don't think there's any kind of live and let live in that scenario."

"How can you be so sure?" Denne asked.

Gabriel swallowed hard. He looked at Zeke, who rolled his eyes, then grabbed his cap off a nearby table. It was obvious that Zeke was as close to done with this conversation as he could be.

"I'm pretty sure too," Gabriel said.

Denne whirled his head, and frowned at him. "How can you be sure?"

"Aside from basic human nature, which you should understand, Hamilton, given what you do," Gabriel said, "there's one thing you might not have considered."

"What's that?"

"These creatures must have existed elsewhere. That's how we got the stories about them."

"Yes," Denne said.

"But there are a lot more people in the world than there have ever been. We're encroaching on property no one has seen or used in a long time, and the elf sightings have not gone up. There aren't stories of tiny water sprites being found in someone's stream. No one talks about fish women."

Gabriel paused. Zeke was staring at the creature, an intense look on his face.

"So?" Denne asked.

"So," Gabriel said, "why not?"

Denne shrugged.

"We hear about little gray aliens and stupid criminals and dolphins and there's a program on the Travel Channel about haunted places all over the United States."

"I saw one about London," Zeke added.

Denne shook his head slightly.

Gabriel let out a sigh of exasperation. Sometimes Hamilton Denne was so in touch with the world, so in touch with the culture, and sometimes, he was absolutely clueless.

"If these fantastic creatures were as common as they once were—

as they would have had to have been to be part of folklore from every part of the world—then there should be shows on television devoted to them. Mermaid sightings, and centaurs mingling with horses, and the occasional werewolf baying at the moon."

Denne's eyes narrowed. He was watching Gabriel as if Gabriel were the enemy. But Gabriel didn't quit.

"We'd read articles about them in popular magazines, and the newspapers would occasionally cover some story about someone who thought they saw a group of gnomes crossing the road, but it turns out that all the person saw was a group of schoolchildren."

"They're part of the popular culture," Denne said.

"They *were* part of the popular culture," Gabriel said. "Shake-speare wrote about them—'low what fools these mortals be'—and the Brothers Grimm codified the stories in Germany a couple of centuries ago. But no one talks about them now, not that way, not really."

Denne ran a gloved hand through his hair, then winced, and looked at his palm, as if he couldn't believe he touched himself after touching the dead body.

"And you believe," he said slowly, "that this is because the magical creatures are what? gone? dead? in hiding? what?"

Gabriel sighed. "I think the genocide that Zeke was mentioning has already happened. I think that over the centuries, humans have wiped out most of the fantastic creatures."

"People kill what frightens them," Zeke said.

Denne shook his head. "So the leftovers came to Oregon? Get real, Gabe."

"I don't know why they're here," Gabriel said. "But if you look at other historical examples, like clusters with like, and often in out-of-the-way places. Until a century ago, the Oregon Coast was out of the way. What a great place for the water creatures to come to. They'd be alone and protected and safe."

"Until humans came to spoil that," Denne said.

Gabriel nodded.

"You think we're a danger to them," Denne said.

"I know we are," Gabriel said.

Denne stepped forward and touched the little body in front of him. "If that the case," he said, "then we have more of a problem than I thought."

"Why is that?" Zeke asked.

But Gabriel was nodding. He had finally brought Denne to the place that Gabriel had reached as Denne started with his theories.

"Because if this was their refuge, and they are smart creatures," Denne said, "they would be very, very cautious about their dead."

"That's why we haven't found any before this," Gabriel said.

Denne nodded. "These two have slipped through somehow."

"Or worse," Zeke said.

Denne and Gabriel both looked at him. Zeke put his cap on.

"They could be dying in bigger numbers now," he said.

"Or maybe," Denne said, "someone has finally found them."

"And is killing them off, leaving the bodies around as a warning?" Zeke asked.

"A warning to whom, though?" Gabriel asked. "If they were going to warn the FantasyLife, wouldn't they leave the bodies in the water?"

"They did," Denne said. "This one was in a creek, and the fish woman had been on the beach, in the tide. They were in the water, Gabe. And they were also out of it, close enough to us so that the secret got blown."

"Two birds with one stone," Zeke said.

"Not to put too fine a point on it," Denne said.

"Or maybe they're like the giant pandas," Zeke said. "Maybe they don't breed in the wild anymore, and they're just dying off. Maybe there's no one to care for the dead, and so the dead are washing up on the beach."

Denne looked frightened. "I've got a lot more work than I thought," he said.

The creature seemed so small there, so insignificant. And she wasn't.

Gabriel felt a small shiver run down his spine, as if fingers had lightly touched him there.

"And Gabe," Denne said, "maybe you should talk to Athena. She knows more about Anchor Bay than anyone."

"Why would Athena help?" Zeke asked.

"Because," Denne said, "maybe this is one of those things, like a locust year or something."

"You mean every fifty years the FantasyLife crawls onto the beach and dies?" Zeke asked.

"We've been discussing stranger things," Denne said.

Gabriel frowned. He didn't like how this was going. All he knew was that something had changed. And he doubted that the change was for the good.

TWENTY-THREE

Cliffside House

Lyssa sat in the window seat of her bedroom, her knees against her chest, and her arms wrapped them. She wore a flannel nightgown that she usually wore in the depth of a Wisconsin winter, and slippers that were lined with fleece.

She hadn't been able to get warm all night.

The room was big and drafty. It was square, with a shag carpet that should have been replaced long ago. The bed was king-sized, and someone had put thick blankets on it, just like Lyssa liked. The pillows were thick as well, and the mattress had a pillowtop, making it the most comfortable bed Lyssa had slept on in years.

But the chill remained. She couldn't get warm, no matter how hard she tried. And the boom of the surf had kept her awake, along with her fears, and the caffeine she'd sucked down much too late at night.

When she finally had fallen asleep, she hadn't slept well. She had gotten up twice to check on Emily. Emily had the room next to Lyssa's and it was a mirror image of Lyssa's, at least in layout. The furniture and design was different. Whoever had set that up clearly had had a child in mind.

The rooms were linked by a spectacular bathroom. It had three mini-rooms of its own—a shower and bath area, the sink and cabinets area, and a toilet, with its own private door. The bathroom had no carpeting. The floor was marble, and just as cold as the stone walls were.

Each time Lyssa got up, she forgot to put on her slippers, and that trek through the bathroom only chilled her more.

Emily slept like a baby through the rest of the night, her arms wrapped around Yeller, a slight smile on her face. Whatever had happened to Lyssa the night before in that closet had been worth it to see that smile, a real, contented look, something that Lyssa had not seen in nearly a year.

Her daughter was happy and Lyssa was not, and for the moment, that was all right with Lyssa. She would reassess the situation each day, and the moment she felt this place was bad for Emily, they would leave.

Lyssa just had to figure out how to afford it.

She shivered again. The chill stayed with her. Even when she woke up, not long ago, to find a tray at the side of her bed. Pastries covered the tray's surface, along with a glass of orange juice and a thermal mug filled with fresh coffee.

The orange juice was welcome, the pastries sinful, and the coffee delightful. But it hadn't warmed her up any more than anything else had.

Sitting in the window seat didn't help either, but she wasn't ready to go downstairs yet. She needed some time alone before she faced the day.

The window seat was carved into the stone wall, and even though someone had placed thick cushions on the base and the sides, a draft still came through the window itself.

The window was thick, and had no screen. If Lyssa opened it, she could stick her arm out over the beach below. When she sat back like this, she had a grand view of the Goblet and the ocean beyond.

If she sat forward, she could see the beach far below.

She couldn't believe she was here, not after all this time. The sunlight reflecting on the basalt giving everything an air of unreality. She had forgotten that sunlight could be so crisp.

In the Midwest, sunlight was only this crisp on cold winter days, often when the temperature was below zero. Then the entire world had a sharpness to it, edges upon edges, from the ice-covered sides of buildings to the stark points of the leafless tree limbs against a blue sky.

Here the sky seemed endless, like it probably had at the beginning of the world. The rocks looked softer than they really were, their edges worn away by water and time.

There was a deceptive beauty to this place, a beauty that made her trust it even less than she normally would have.

Or maybe she was just uneasy from the conversation the night before—and from that damn tarball. Her dreams had been filled with tarballs, floating in seawater. She was swimming beneath the surface, so far down that sunlight didn't reach, and she followed tarballs into the light, filtering through the water like a glimpse of heaven.

And the fear. Fear had run through her sleep like it had every night since Reginald died. Since before Reginald died. Since he went crazy—something caused, her mother and grandmother told her, by Emily's uncontrolled power.

Lyssa wasn't sure what kind of power that was. Lyssa never really had a lot of abilities, not like her mother who seemed connected to every part of the universe, and not like her grandmother whom, Lyssa learned, could sometimes summon the strength of ten men.

Lyssa had a subtler gift. She had the ability to charm, something that seemed unimportant when she lived here. Outside of Anchor Bay, though, she had learned that gift had its benefits. It made her a popular teacher, and got her through some of the difficult hurdles in college life. She had never had political problems within the university, not even after Reginald had gone crazy, and she attributed that to her ability—magical or not—to make other people feel comfortable.

Reginald's death hadn't changed that much. The dean had offered her the house permanently, and university support throughout any trials that might happen. Lyssa had resigned, not because she had to, but because she didn't want Emily to stay in Madison any longer.

Emily did not have the ability to charm. All the good press that Lyssa once got had no effect on Emily. People could smile at Lyssa and ignore Emily completely. And then, after Reginald's death, people failed to transfer that good feeling they got from Lyssa to her daughter.

Charm. What use could that have, here and now?

Lyssa sighed. She hadn't had time to make plans, to reassess her world, to figure out what was best for her and her child. All she had thought about, besides getting Emily out of Madison, was how to train her daughter's magic, knowing that it was more powerful than anything Lyssa had ever dealt with and not knowing the damage it had already done.

She would have to talk with Athena, find out how long the training would take. And then Lyssa would have to see if Emily could survive outside of Anchor Bay, in a world where most people did not have the ability to protect themselves with a single thought.

At least, that's what Lyssa guessed had happened. She still didn't exactly know. She figured Emily had thought of something to get her father's hands off her, to keep her from drowning. But what it was, and why Reginald had died so hideously, Lyssa still wasn't sure.

Something moved down on the beach. Lyssa frowned and leaned forward. There were people near the water's edge—two people, small figures bright against the sand. They appeared to be the only ones out there, and that made them slightly crazy.

The water was still churning from the storm. The waves were high and the ocean had a swollen look. A lot of debris was still washing ashore.

Lyssa bet the beach looked different this morning than it had days before. Storms like last night's brought in logs and garbage, as well as interesting treasures from other places.

Once, as a child participating in the beach cleanup, she had found a refrigerator. Another beach cleanup, she had found a diamond ring, glinting in the sand. Things that the ocean had stolen—large and small—and eventually returned, for no apparent reason at all.

The figures faced the water. Then one of the figures ran toward the beach grass, arms flailing.

Lyssa leaned forward. She squinted, and then realized she didn't have to.

Her mother was still standing beside the water, her long hair flowing around her like a scarf. She was watching the shoreline, watching Emily, who had run away from the surf like it was going to attack her.

Lyssa should have warned Cassie. Ever since Reginald's death, Emily hadn't liked water. She had been a fish before—impossible to get out of the lake, even out of the bath, and if they ever stayed at a hotel with a pool, she would remain in that pool until some official hotel employee came in and closed it down.

But on the trip out, Emily refused to climb in the pools, claiming she was too tired. She didn't even get out of the car to look at Lake Coeur du Lane—one of the prettiest lakes in the entire country, and she turned her head away from the Columbia River as Lyssa drove them down the gorge.

Water had gone from Emily's friend to her enemy, something which the shrink who had seen Emily after the death said was perfectly normal.

Over time, the shrink had said, *you'll have to get her used to water again. But it will take time. And she might never swim in lakes again. Don't push her. Let her choose when to make the plunge.*

Lyssa had disliked the pun then, and she disliked it even more now, since she hadn't been able to get it out of her head. She heard that as a warning as much as advice, and it seemed like the warning was a fair one.

Emily had bolted from the water's edge like someone possessed. Lyssa had seen it from a hundred feet up.

Cassie was gesturing, but Emily was not coming toward her. The waves rose behind Cassie as if they were beckoning too, but Emily huddled on the grass, her posture mimicking Lyssa's.

Lyssa sighed again, then swung her legs off the window seat. It was time to start her day. Her mother had promised to watch Emily so that Lyssa could take care of mundane things associated with the move—opening a bank account, getting Emily registered at school.

Looking for a job.

Lyssa grabbed another pastry before she walked to her suitcase. She wasn't ready to search for work yet. She wasn't ready to make any commitments to Anchor Bay.

But she would let Emily stay here for a while—provided the place wasn't as dangerous as it seemed last night.

Lyssa was going to remain vigilant. But she had to admit, it was nice to watch someone else deal with Emily for a day. Lyssa could get used to it.

She just wasn't sure she wanted to.

TWENTY-FOUR

The Beach

Emily sat in the beach grass, her arms wrapped around her legs, her face pressing against her knees. She could hear the ocean slap against the sand, the sound remarkably loud. The salty smell seemed familiar somehow, even though she had never been to an ocean before. The air had a tang of mist to it, and a chill that was built into everything, including the sand beneath her jeans.

Gulls cried above her, and mixed with their caws was Grandma Cassie's voice, calling to her, telling her it was all right.

But it wasn't all right. The water had reached for her, formed a hand and tried to touch her Nikes, and she didn't want anything to touch her. Not yet. Maybe not ever.

We'll go to the beach to start your lessons, Grandma Cassie had said, and Emily thought that would be a good idea, even though she wasn't sure what the lessons were.

She knew that someone had mentioned them the night before, but they had mentioned a lot of things in that long conversation, and she had listened to all of it with her eyes closed, so she still wasn't sure what she dreamed, what she made up, and what they actually said.

All she knew was that when the grownups did wake her up, they gave her some egg and cheese meal that had to be microwaved and was kinda gluey. Then they took her to this huge bedroom that was cold, but had this great bed and even neater window seat.

Emily wanted to sleep in the window seat—right there, with a view of the ocean and the clouds like she'd never seen them, and a bit of a moon peeking through—but Mommy wouldn't let her. In fact, Mommy seemed upset by the whole idea of Emily sleeping at the house at all. Mommy would have loved to go to a hotel, even though that would've been worse.

The house was perfect. Emily loved her room and the windows and the slightly damp smell that seemed to be everywhere. She liked the black walls, the way they felt so cool and smooth, and the fact that the house whispered to her—not in words, but in ways that made her calmer than she had been for a long time.

She couldn't remember the last time she felt like she was safe. Long before Daddy died. Even before she and Mommy moved out of the house. That house, which Emily had grown up in, didn't seem like her house anymore at all. It had a strange, scary feel, like it was going to explode at any minute.

And then she went back there, and everything did explode.

She wrapped her arms tighter around her legs. Grandma Cassie was trudging up the beach, like it was work for her to dig her feet in the sand.

Emily never really realized how skinny Grandma Cassie was. She was like a straight line, her hair gathering around her like a dress. Even when she tied it back, it still was the most obvious thing about her.

Daddy would have liked her hair. He liked long hair.

Emily's hair wasn't ever going to be long again.

"What happened, kiddo?" Grandma Cassie asked as she reached Emily.

Emily shrugged. "Nothing."

Grandma Cassie sat beside her. "Everything's different, huh? Strange city, strange house. Your whole world is different."

Different than what? Emily wanted to ask, but she knew better than to smart off to grownups. Her world had been different for a long time now. She could barely remember normal.

In fact, she was putting normal behind her. Because of normal, she had biked to Daddy's. Because of normal, Daddy was dead.

"Has your mom ever talked to you about your powers?" Grandma Cassie asked.

What happened, hon? Mom had asked over and over again. *Did you get a funny feeling when you were near Daddy? Did he do something that made you mad, maybe?*

"No," Emily said.

Grandma Cassie bit her lower lip and nodded, as if she had expected that.

"I already know you got powers," Emily said, "and can read minds and stuff. And you said Great-grandma has powers too. How come Mommy doesn't?"

"She has some," Grandma Cassie said. "She just hasn't shared them with anyone else."

Whatever that meant. Grandma Cassie liked saying things sideways. So did everybody else. Grownups always pretended to answer questions, but they usually didn't. They just said words, like words were an answer, and the words mostly didn't mean anything.

"Mommy says you know the future," Emily said.

"Sometimes," Grandma Cassie said.

Emily rested her chin on her knees. She stared at the beach grass. The blades came up through the sand, like they were trying to reach the sky and the sand was trying to stop them.

"Did you know my daddy was going to die?" Emily asked.

Grandma Cassie turned toward her, and Emily knew, somehow that Grandma Cassie wanted Emily to look at her. But Emily wasn't going to. She didn't want to look at anybody. She didn't want Grandma Cassie to read her mind and give her a fake answer.

She wanted the real answer.

"I knew your mom's marriage to your dad couldn't end well," Grandma Cassie said after a long silence.

"How come?" Emily asked. "Because you didn't like my daddy's daddy?"

Grandma Cassie picked a blade of beach grass and ran it between her fingers, like she was trying to smooth it out.

"It's an old cliché, honey, about oil and water."

Emily even knew that one. "So what?"

"Your mother is the water, honey. Your daddy came from oil."

"That's just where they lived when they were little. Daddy was a teacher, just like Mommy, before—you know. Before."

Emily didn't want to say anything about her father's death. She didn't like thinking about it, even though she thought about it all the time.

"When people come from backgrounds that different—"

"I don't care!" Emily was surprised to hear herself yelling. She didn't expect to yell, especially at her own grandma. She loved Grandma Cassie. She didn't want to be mad at her.

But she was. She was really, really mad. About everything.

"You knew that if they got married, my daddy would die." Emily had turned toward Grandma Cassie, and unlike most people when Emily got mad at them, Grandma Cassie didn't back away. "How come you didn't tell Mommy? How come you didn't stop it?"

Grandma Cassie reached toward Emily with the hand holding the beach grass. Grandma Cassie brushed some hair away from Emily's eyes, and the beach grass skimmed her skin. She caught the smell of green, and it smelled like Wisconsin, like what she used to think of as home.

But the old smell didn't make her feel much better. She didn't feel like yelling anymore, but she was shaking. She hadn't realized how upset she really was until now. Until right now on this beach, with Grandma Cassie next to her.

"I didn't stop it," Grandma Cassie said quietly, "because of you."

"Me?" Emily frowned. She didn't get that. "I wasn't even born yet."

"I know," Grandma Cassie said. "That was the problem. We needed you in the world, and the only way we could get you was if your mommy married your daddy."

"And then I killed him," Emily said. The words hung in the air, like words in a cartoon. She could almost see them, and they kept echoing, rolling over and over again with the surf.

She hadn't wanted to say that. She never really said it to anybody before, and Mommy would've been mad about it.

Your daddy was sick, Mommy said, *whatever happens, remember that. Your daddy was sick and because he was, you went through something awful. Because of him.*

"You killed him?" Grandma Cassie smoothed another strand of hair away from Emily's face. Grandma Cassie didn't sound shocked or mad. She just sounded like they were talking about normal stuff, like socks or classes at school. "You really think so?"

Emily couldn't answer that question. The words that had come out so easily a moment before wouldn't come now.

Instead, she nodded.

"Can I see?" Grandma Cassie asked.

"See?"

"What happened," Grandma Cassie said. "Will you let me see it?"

"How?" Emily asked.

"I'll show you." Grandma Cassie put both hands on Emily's face. The blade of beach grass got caught in the wind and fluttered away.

Grandma Cassie's hands were warm and dry. They smelled of grass and coffee. Emily wanted to lean her whole body against Grandma Cassie's, but she didn't. She didn't move at all.

"If you don't want to do this," Grandma Cassie said, "all you have to do is say stop."

Stop, Emily wanted to whisper. But she didn't. Instead, she closed her eyes.

"No, sweetie. We can't do this if your eyes are closed." Grandma Cassie sounded real calm, as if this was all normal for her. It was weird to think of this magic stuff as normal, weird to think all that had happened since July as stuff other people go through all the time.

Emily had to struggle to open her eyes. Grandma Cassie smiled at her.

"Ready?"

"Yes," Emily whispered. *Stop.*

But Grandma Cassie didn't stop. "Just think of the last time you saw your daddy."

Emily did, then tried to stop herself, but it didn't help. That feeling came back—maybe it never went away—that scared feeling, that feeling that everything had gotten even worse, that sinking feeling that happened the minute she understood that everybody who told her not to see Daddy, that Daddy was dangerous, everybody who said that was right, and Emily was the one who was wrong.

Then her memory slipped out her eyes—she felt it leave, like a gust of wind on her eyeballs, only the wind came from the inside— and then, on the grass, she saw herself and Daddy on the dock.

The dock and the lake and Daddy and her other self, they were all really tiny, smaller than Barbie, almost action-figure size. And she could hear everything, just like she was watching a tiny movie, only she couldn't feel it, not like she did when it replayed in her head.

She talked to him, and he talked to her, his voice sounding just like Daddy's, only tiny, like the sound turned down, and then he smiled that weird smile, and reached for her, and with one move, she was in the water.

And she wanted to close her eyes, but Grandma said she couldn't so she watched as Daddy's smile got weirder, as he leaned his whole body over the side of the dock, putting all his weight on her shoulders, and as she watched she remembered how that felt, how her hands were reaching for his arms, and how she fought, and how she knew she wasn't going to be able to hold her breath any longer, and how scared she was—

Then there was flames on Daddy's chest and he was slapping himself and screaming and screaming and screaming. She had heard the screaming underwater, but it was nothing like this. Even with the sound turned down, it was awful, and her eyes teared up, and the little people below her wavered, like they were underwater.

Daddy kept screaming and Emily couldn't take it anymore. She closed her eyes, and the tears fell down her cheeks. Grandma Cassie kissed her forehead, but Emily jerked away, and buried her face in her knees, trying to pretend that nothing was wrong.

But her breath hitched and she made little noises, no matter how hard she tried to keep quiet, and Grandma Cassie put her arms around her and said, "Let it out, Emily. Let it out."

Emily didn't know what that meant, but she did know she couldn't stop, and Grandma's arms felt good, and she was surprisingly soft for somebody so skinny, and she smelled like lotion and seawater and that made things all better.

Grandma Cassie wasn't mad at her and didn't push her away, and she saw the whole thing, even though she didn't know—she couldn't know—that it was the fire inside of Emily that Emily had pushed away, and that had started a fire inside of Daddy. And because he didn't have the magic that Buckinghams had, because he was oil, not water, he burned better.

That last thought wasn't hers.

Emily sat up, her breath still hitching, and looked at Grandma's face. It was filled with love.

"See?" Emily said, her voice husky. "I killed him."

"Emily," Grandma Cassie said, "he was trying to kill you."

"No!" Emily said. "No, he wasn't. He was my daddy. He loved me."

"He did love you," Grandma Cassie said, "when his mind worked right. But his mind had stopped working, honey. You did what you had to."

"I didn't have to kill him," Emily said.

"You had no other choice," Grandma Cassie said.

"What if the fire got his hands?"

"The same thing would have happened," Grandma Cassie said. "Besides, that would have taken control, and since you had no idea how magical you were, you had no control."

Emily wiped at her face. It was wrong. It wasn't fair. Her daddy loved her, and then this happened, and it was all her fault.

"A lot of things went wrong that afternoon," Grandma Cassie said. "Your daddy tried to hurt you."

Emily set her jaw, and stared at the spot in the beach grass where the little figures had been. The sand wasn't even stirred up.

"Then he put you in water. What he didn't know—or maybe some part of him did—was that water makes you stronger."

Emily frowned. Grandma Cassie put a hand on Emily's knee.

"Water amplifies your abilities, which is why you feel safest around water."

"I don't feel safe in the water," Emily said. "I hate water."

"Now," Grandma Cassie said. "After you'd been traumatized. But it wasn't the water's fault."

"It was my fault."

"No, honey," Grandma Cassie said. "Your daddy said some interesting things. The heat, the drought, and the dying lake. Was that lake really dying?"

Emily shrugged. "I don't know."

"You can tell, honey. The water should have receded so that you would see the lake bottom. There would be way too much algae, and everyone would be talking about how all the fish die."

Emily frowned, trying to remember. "They talked about the heat."

"But not the lake?"

"Nobody said stuff about the lake. And I never saw the bottom. It looked the same to me."

"It looked the same to me too, only smaller." Grandma Cassie smiled a little as she nodded toward the place where the image had been. "Then, after he said that, your daddy said you'd solve it together. Do you know what he meant?"

Emily shook her head really slow. She didn't remember anything her daddy said, except she had to, because she showed it to her grandma.

"Interesting," Grandma Cassie said like she was talking to herself. "I have some work to do."

"What kind of work?" Emily asked.

"Research," Grandma Cassie said.

Emily licked her lips. The breeze had come up and it was chilly, just like everything else.

"Grandma?" she asked.

Grandma Cassie took a moment to look at Emily, as if she were thinking about something else. "What, honey?"

"Did I make that picture of me and Daddy or did you?"

"We both did, sweetheart. We couldn't do that without each other."

"But could you do that with, like maybe, Mommy or that man who helped us get here last night?"

Grandma Cassie shook her head. "No," she said. "Our powers mesh, yours and mine. That's how we did that."

"How did you know they'd mesh?" Emily asked.

Grandma Cassie looked down, and Emily knew she was going to get a grownup answer, not a real answer.

"I just knew, honey," Grandma Cassie said. "I knew it all along."

TWENTY-FIVE

Anchor Bay Elementary School

Anchor Bay Elementary looked no different than it had when Lyssa was a child. It was two stories high, and a block long, made of some type of dark brick, and it looked forbidding. Even the hand-drawn pictures in the windows (which looked much like the hand-drawn pictures from the mid-1970s) didn't mitigate the school's gloomy appearance.

The school had been designed and built in the days when education was Good For You, like eating badly cooked peas or taking foul-tasting medicine. Even now, when school (and everything else in American life) was supposed to be fun, it looked like Anchor Bay Elementary hadn't gotten the message.

Lyssa's opinion changed somewhat when she went inside. The walls had been repainted from the institutional white that she remembered to bright primary colors. Each school room door had windows in them now, and through those windows, she could see brightly decorated classrooms, crammed with tiny desks and too many students, led by a teacher who seemed impossibly young.

Surely teachers had been older when she was a little girl. Even though she knew they hadn't been. Just like the desks hadn't been bigger, and the water fountains hadn't been higher.

Going back through these halls was like walking through a memory that someone had shrunk down to size.

Near all the water fountains, placed at child's eye level, were signs that Lyssa had never seen before. *Tsunami Evacuation Route*, the signs announced in big red letters, and Lyssa paused long enough to examine one.

Anchor Bay Elementary was on prime real estate across from the bay itself. The school had survived some serious storms in the 1960s and early 1970s, storms that had damaged windows and, in one case, nearly destroyed the building.

But when Lyssa attended, there hadn't been evacuation signs. She hadn't even known there was serious tsunami danger here. As she read, she learned that a fault line ran the length of the Oregon Coast, two miles off-shore. Should an earthquake hit that fault, residents who lived on the flats—or who happened to be in the elementary school—would have less than ten minutes to get to the highest ground.

The highest ground near Anchor Bay Elementary was a hill several blocks away, certainly not something that little children could reach easily or quickly.

She would talk to her grandmother about this when she got home, to see if it was a real threat or more CYA warnings from a school system that had to worry about an increasingly litigious group of parents.

The signs made her nervous, but nothing bothered her more than walking deeper inside the school, with all of its memories.

It didn't take her long to find the principal's office. No one had moved it. She had spent many days in that office, usually sitting on a bright orange plastic chair, kicking her saddle-shoe-clad feet.

She had been an angry child from the start, one Principal Gower had said she would never succeed at anything. He had died of a heart attack when she was in high school, so she couldn't go back and prove him wrong, although she often wanted to.

And now, it seemed, that his predictions might have been right.

Her cheeks were flushed, and that was partly due to the heat in the building. The elementary school Emily had attended in Madison had also seemed too warm, as if the schools were determined to keep the children comfortable even though they could no longer afford to educate them.

Initially, Lyssa had thought of home-schooling Emily. Home-schooling was legal in Oregon, and Lyssa was eminently qualified to teach her child, surpassing all the requirements mentioned on the Oregon Home Schooling website.

But that attack at Cliffside House had unnerved her more than she wanted to admit, and she decided that Emily needed outside contact. Outside contact was possible now that Cassie had started Emily's lessons. With luck, Emily would have at least minimal control of her powers by the time she started mingling with the other students.

The principal's office was no brighter or cheerier than it had been when Lyssa was a little girl. In fact, the only real difference that she could see was the computer on the secretary's desk. The secretary herself could have been the daughter of the draconian woman who guarded Lyssa: she had the same short hairstyle, the same John Lennon granny glasses, and even wore the same sort of shapeless knit dress that passed for fashion when Lyssa was a child.

Of course, that fashion had become fashionable again, which was part of the reason for Lyssa's flashback, but not all of it. Just the air in that high-ceilinged room, with its slow-moving ceiling fan, made her stomach tighten.

Registering Emily, though, wasn't hard. The secretary had smiled when she saw Lyssa and said, "You must be Athena's granddaughter. She called us this morning and said you'd be in."

The secretary had all the paperwork ready, the information typed into the proper sections—all obviously the work of Athena. All Lyssa had to do was sign, and promise that Emily would be at her seat in her new classroom promptly at nine a.m. on Monday morning.

The nine a.m. starting time amused Lyssa. She had forgotten how lax things were at the coast. Early morning meant eight a.m., because most shops opened at ten. Only the merchants kept regular hours.

Everyone else—from the fisherman to the hotel employees—worked various shifts, from before dawn to long past midnight.

Lyssa would have to get out of the rhythms of a city whose livelihood had three bases—government, corporations, and the university —and back into a blue collar world of split shifts and hand-to-mouth income.

Lyssa signed, promised, and found herself out the door before she even realized she was done. She took the back exit, which was closer to the parking lot, an exit she had forgotten existed. When she had come in, she had used the front, just like she had for six long years as a little girl.

The parking lot was nestled in a group of pines, old ones with thick knotted trunks and out of control branches. Dozens of cars parked near the trees—mostly teachers' vehicles, and the visitor parking was closer to the building itself.

From the parking lot, she had a great view of Anchor Harbor Wayside with its steel railing and modern rest area. The ocean still dominated the scene, however. It still had that bright blue unthreatening look, and it seemed deceptively calm.

But something made her shiver as she looked at it, and she couldn't forget the taste of that tarball in her mouth.

She walked to the Bug, unlocked it, and let herself inside. Then she leaned her head back and closed her eyes.

Part of her was tempted to just drive away—to leave Emily in the very competent hands of Athena and Cassie—and just keep driving until she reached Canada. From there, Lyssa could disappear into the wilderness, become someone new, someone who hadn't married badly, didn't have a screwed-up family history, and wasn't threatened by ghostly tarballs on her first day home in more than a decade.

That last made her smile and shake her head. No matter where she went, no matter what name she called herself by, she would still be a woman who married badly and had a screwed-up family history.

More importantly, she would still be a mother. Only she would be one who abandoned a child who was already traumatized, abandoned her to people who didn't know her well at all, people who believed things that, on good days, Lyssa liked to pretend never happened.

She had no idea how long she sat there, wishing she could run away. But even the daydream wasn't satisfying. She wouldn't be able to live with herself if she left, wouldn't be able to face any part of her life.

And she still had a lot of facing to do. Not only did she have to find a place for Emily in this tiny town, but she also had to find a place for herself. What did a professor do in a town that didn't have a college? The nearest college was in the valley, over the mountains and at least an hour away.

There was no guarantee she would get work there. Knowing how tight jobs were in Oregon, she probably wouldn't.

Not that she was suited to anything else. She hadn't waited tables since high school, and in her early years, she went to college on a hardship scholarship her mother had found. Once Lyssa married Reginald, his family money paid for her education.

She had a PhD courtesy of a family her own hated.

Lyssa sighed. She would probably end up like her mother, working in various retail shops and playing at tourist scams. Not that she had her mother's psychic ability or talent, but Lyssa could charm. At least she could make people feel like they had gotten their money's worth, even if they hadn't.

A flock of geese was passing nearby. Lyssa hadn't heard that combination of honking and gabbling since she had left the coast. Most of the places she had lived hadn't been quiet enough to hear birds on a regular basis, particularly those heading south for the winter.

Although it seemed a bit late to her for birds to go south, but what did she know? She knew about the military history of Prussia, but she didn't know anything really useful.

The bleating grew louder, as if the flock was flying east instead of south. Then something hit her car, rocking it.

She opened her eyes, and turned. Creatures, tiny and round, scrambled toward her on stubby little legs. Several were already climbing over her car.

But they didn't seem to be paying attention to her. She doubted they even saw her. They were running due east, as fast as their little legs could carry them.

And the line of them extended all the way to the ocean.

Her heart was pounding, hard. She'd never seen so many unknown creatures up close. There had to be twenty on her car alone, hurrying past, fear on their round faces.

They looked like miniature gnomes, with pudgy cheeks and sparkling eyes. Their hair was white and flowed behind them, and they appeared to be wearing clothing made of seaweed.

But they didn't have hands or feet. Instead, they had flat flipper-like substances with suckers on the end. They were using the suckers to pull themselves up the side of her car, and to keep balanced once they reached the domed back end.

They chattered as they ran, nonsense syllables, frightening in their variation. Sometimes they would stop to help another up or down, and they would keep running.

A few looked over their shoulders when they got to the top of the car, as if they expected something else to come after them.

Lyssa watched, her mouth open, afraid to move. She didn't dare back up for fear of squashing the little things. She didn't want to get out of the car either. Even though the creatures were tiny, there were hundreds of them, and if they had something against humans as so many of her grandmother's fantastic friends seemed to, she would be inviting them to hurt her.

No matter how small something was, in vast numbers, any kind of creature was dangerous.

So Lyssa slowly, quietly, locked the car doors and made sure the windows were rolled up tight. Then she remained motionless in the driver's seat, waiting for the stream of creatures from the ocean to end.

TWENTY-SIX

The Trawler Restaurant
Anchor Bay, Oregon

The woman standing in the restaurant doorway looked eerily familiar.

Cassie stiffened, but Emily didn't seem to notice. She had her face buried in the adult menu, the children's menu left carefully hanging off the end of the table, making it clear to anyone and everyone that she felt she didn't deserve cutely named peanut-butter-and-jelly sandwiches or tiny crab cakes, baked in the shape of a shell.

The woman was barely five feet tall, with hair as long as Cassie's, but so black that in the restaurant's fluorescent light, it looked blue. She was young—or at least, she seemed young—with flawless white skin, and wide, oval-shaped black eyes.

It was the way she held herself, as if her balance was slightly off, the vaguely flat-footed way she walked—what a former ballerina-friend of Cassie's once called "duck feet,"—and the rigid posture as if she monitored each and every one of her own movements, to make sure it blended in with everyone else's.

357

She looked around the restaurant, and Cassie kept very still, knowing that the woman was looking for her.

Cassie didn't want to be found, especially with Emily.

Cassie had brought Emily to the Trawler, an old family restaurant on the north side of the bay, because they weren't getting anywhere on the beach. Emily refused to go near the water and, after that little demonstration of how their powers worked together, did not want to practice any magic at all.

Emily said she was hungry, and wanted to go back to Cliffside House, but that dark and gloomy place was the last thing Emily needed on this sunny afternoon. Instead, Cassie brought her to the Trawler, hoping it would cheer her up.

The Trawler was a rarity—a tourist attraction with excellent food. But locals only went to the restaurant in the fall and winter, when the pace was leisurely and the portions generous.

Emily had chosen a bench in the back, with no view of the ocean at all. The waiter had teased her about that; people came to the Trawler for its magnificent view of the harbor and the open water beyond.

Emily sat with her back to the gift shop and what small view of the ocean was possible from this table. She had a perfect view of the kitchen and, until the waiter had arrived with their drinks and menus, had watched with great interest as the cooks made lunch for the only other couple in the place.

Still, she seemed to be enjoying herself. The restaurant was light and airy. It smelled of fried foods and fish, not an unwelcome scent after the morning on the beach.

Like most restaurants on the coast, the Trawler was decorated with a sea motif, but this one wasn't overpowering. Real Japanese floats, found over decades in the waters of the Pacific, hung from hand-knotted fishing nets attached to the ceiling.

The tables were plank wood, and instead of chairs, there were benches on either side. The center of the table held condiments and old-fashioned napkin holders, as well as a tiny pail complete with a tiny shovel, that could be purchased if the patrons wanted to go outside and dig in the sand.

Cassie had never seen anyone buy a bucket, but she had seen many a tourist stop in the small gift shop area near the cash register, and buy overpriced earrings, postcards, and seashell sculptures. She had never completely understood the attraction of junk, but then, she never had liked possessions much.

Emily was still studying her menu when the strange woman entered the restaurant. Cassie had long since given up on hers. She knew what she was going to order—she had since she had come in here. The Trawler had the freshest halibut in Anchor Bay, and they poached it lightly, making the fish seem like it had been cooked just enough to bake in the flavor. With their steamed broccoli and rice pilaf, a recipe that Cassie loved and couldn't get out of them, the Trawler had created a perfect fish meal.

The waiter was busy with the other couple, and didn't see the woman at the door. Emily didn't look up, and the cooks were laughing in the kitchen, obviously not paying attention to the front.

The woman waited for a moment, then looked around as if she were searching for someone. Cassie had never seen her before—she knew that much—but she also knew that the woman was searching for her.

The woman finally entered the main portion of the restaurant. She peered past the waiter, shrugged slightly, and then turned around to leave.

That was when she saw Cassie.

Cassie stiffened. Emily looked up from her menu, frowned at Cassie, then turned and followed her gaze.

The woman lifted her narrow eyebrows and a small smile played at her very red lips. She walked across the restaurant with purpose.

Cassie made her body relax. She didn't want to seem at a disadvantage, although she already was.

The smile continued to play on the woman's face as she walked. She wore a black suit, with a skirt that came down to the tops of her ankles. Little leather boots covered her feet, and in her right hand, she held a beaded purse that was better suited to evening wear.

It was her only mistake.

She stopped beside the table like a waiter would, and Cassie caught a faint musky scent. Emily must have too, for she squinched up her nose, and gave Cassie a pointed frown.

"Cassandra Buckingham?" the woman said. Even her accent sounded familiar. Her pronunciation was crisp and flawless, but the accents she placed on the syllables were wrong.

Most people emphasized the second syllable in Cassandra. This woman accented the last, as well as the "ing" in Buckingham. The difference was subtle, but noticeable, and marked the woman as a non-native English speaker.

"Yes," Cassie said.

The woman's smile had a softness to it that made her look like she was posing for a cheesecake shot. "I am Roseluna Delamer. Perhaps you have heard of me?"

"No," Cassie said.

Emily watched the exchange with interest. She set her menu on top of the child's menu, as if to hide it.

"Really?" Roseluna said. "I have heard of you."

She clutched her purse in front of her like a supplicant. Cassie wanted to tell her to go away, not to bother them, but she didn't know how to be that kind of rude in front of her granddaughter.

"Might I join you?" Roseluna asked after a moment.

"This is our special time," Cassie said, stopping herself from adding, *my granddaughter and me*. "We were hoping to be alone."

"It will only take a moment." Roseluna sat on Emily's bench, forcing Emily to scoot over.

Emily gave Cassie a confused look.

"We really don't have the moment," Cassie said.

"You need to have it," Roseluna said. "Besides, among my people, such things are courtesy. We are family, after all."

Cassie stiffened again. She couldn't help it. She wished she had the ability to control her movements like Athena did, but like so many things Athena did, this was something Cassie hadn't learned.

"You're a Buckingham?" Emily asked, and for the first time all day, her voice held awe. It was as if this exotic woman impressed her, as if being related to someone like that helped her own self-image.

The woman turned her soft smile on Emily. "Regretfully, no, child," she said. "Cassandra and I, we are related by marriage."

Cassie made a small gesture with her hands, hoping to stop Roseluna.

"Marriage?" Emily asked.

"Yes," Roseluna said. "I am sister to Daray, Cassandra's husband."

"You're married, Grandma?" Emily asked.

Cassie felt her cheeks flush, and her eyes fill. She blinked hard, willing the water back. "I was, once."

But her evasive answer didn't help. Roseluna knew from the moment Emily spoke, maybe even the moment she saw her.

"This is your grandchild?" She didn't want for an answer. "So she too is family."

Cassie sighed. "She's Daray's granddaughter."

It felt odd to say his name. Cassie tried not to speak it aloud. Her voice trembled as she did so, and she cleared her throat to cover the momentary loss of control.

Roseluna shifted on her bench, and leaned forward so that she was closer to Emily.

"Look at me, child."

Emily raised her head slightly. Roseluna took Emily's chin in the thumb and forefinger of her hand, turning Emily toward the light from the windows.

"It is in her eyes," Roseluna said. "She has the dark."

"She does," Cassie said. She had noticed it when Emily was a baby. The dark was the way that the iris bled into the whites, so that there was more darkness than light in Emily's eyes. Unlike Lyssa, in Emily's eyes, the darkness wasn't quite as pronounced. A person had to look at her closely to see the difference.

"Dark?" Emily asked, her voice tight because she was trying not to move her chin.

"It marks you as ours," Roseluna said, and then her hand moved up, into a caress of Emily's cheek, before falling away.

Emily touched her chin as if Roseluna had hurt her. "How're we related?"

"I am your..." Roseluna paused, as if searching for the word. "Your...great-aunt."

She looked at Cassie for confirmation. Cassie nodded, then blinked hard one more time. She didn't want to see this woman. She certainly didn't want to talk to her.

But neither Roseluna nor Emily noticed Cassie's distress. Emily was looking at Roseluna, and Roseluna laughed.

"Although I do not think of myself as old enough to be a great," she said.

She certainly didn't look old enough. She looked no more than thirty.

"How come you and Grandma don't know each other?" Emily asked. "Didn't you come to the wedding?"

Roseluna turned her head toward Cassie, not quite meeting her gaze. She clearly wanted Cassie to answer the question, but the answer was complicated.

"Your grandfather and I didn't have a big wedding," Cassie said.

"Like Mommy and Daddy," Emily said. "Nobody came to their wedding either."

She spoke so matter-of-factly, as if her parents were still alive and still happily married. Cassie felt her breath catch. Emily was giving her the answer.

"Sort of," Cassie said.

"You are how old?" Roseluna asked Emily.

"Ten," Emily said.

"This is in human years?"

"Huh?" Emily looked at Roseluna as if she had asked an insane question. From Emily's point of view, she had.

"Yes," Cassie said. "She knows no other way."

Roseluna's mouth tightened slightly, and she nodded, moving her head just once. At that moment, the waiter came over.

"Will there be three?" he asked.

"I should like some coffee," Roseluna said, "and the shrimp cocktail without the ridiculous sauce."

Apparently it would be three then. Cassie sighed, ordered, and waited while Emily ordered as well. Emily had opted for the fish and chips, which made Roseluna wrinkle her nose.

So they shared that gesture at least, although Cassie didn't point it out. She didn't want to see all the similarities between Roseluna and Emily, because that would make Cassie think about all the similarities between Roseluna and Daray. And thinking about Daray, at least like this, was more painful than she wanted to admit.

"You're not looking me up today because you're suddenly feeling like hanging out with family," Cassie said as soon as the waiter left. "What's up?"

Her fear was that Roseluna knew about Emily, about somehow word of Emily's power had reached Daray's family, and they too would want a piece of her.

Lyssa would hate that. Emily wouldn't understand it—at least not yet. Cassie needed time to prepare her, to ease her into her abilities, to let her know what was in trust to her, both here in the town of Anchor Bay, and in the ocean itself.

Roseluna took the plastic glass from the pile of 1970s amber glasses stacked in the middle of all the long tables. Then she grabbed the water pitcher, and poured. Her movements were languorous and graceful.

"I am an emissary," she said. "I have been sent to speak to you."

"From the family?" Cassie asked.

Roseluna shook her head. Her fingers, which were surprisingly stubby and thick, played with the lip of her glass.

"From my tribe. Daray made us promise that we would seek you out."

"What kind of help do you need?" Cassie asked.

Roseluna's fingers stopped moving. She raised her head slightly. "We do not need help."

"Then I don't understand," Cassie said.

"Daray bound us, our peoples, with a promise. We were to warn you when the time came."

Cassie's mouth was dry. Emily had frozen in position, her hands clutching the edge of the table as if it held her in place.

"Warn us about what?" Cassie asked.

"The end of our alliance," Roseluna said. "We have decided to defend ourselves."

Cassie shook her head. "Defend yourself against what?"

"The end of our people."

The waiter brought Roseluna's coffee, and her shrimp cocktail, which was just a cocktail glass with ice and shrimp hanging off the rim. She didn't touch it.

She didn't move until he left again.

"Your people? No one's planning anything against anyone," Cassie said. "I would know."

"It's not the planned events that are the problem," Roseluna said. "It is the unplanned ones."

"Has there been an accident?" Cassie asked.

Emily was staring at them, as if trying to understand.

"Not in the way you mean," Roseluna said.

Cassie hated the way she was dancing around the topic, and wondered if that was because of Emily or because Roseluna expected Cassie to understand.

But Cassie couldn't read Roseluna. She couldn't read any of the selkies unless they let her. It was as if, when they shed their pelts, they put on a different guise, one that protected them from her telepathy.

"I don't understand," Cassie said. "What are you warning us about?"

Roseluna sighed. "I am telling you to leave Anchor Bay," she said. "I am telling you it will be destroyed."

TWENTY-SEVEN

Seavy County Sheriff's Department
North County Office

They left Denne to his work with the water sprite. He wanted to look at it more closely before he took it back to Whale Cove. Maybe after an hour or so, he had said, the road south would be open again, and he wouldn't have to drive quite as far.

Gabriel would check on that for him as soon as Denne was ready to leave. But it would be at least an hour before Denne was done in his makeshift morgue, and Gabriel had a few things to do.

As he left the room, he grabbed the coffee he had set on the floor. The mug was cool to the touch and the coffee no longer steamed, but he didn't care. He drank it anyway, needing the caffeine more than the taste.

Then he went back into reception, poured himself another cup of coffee, and added more cream. The coffee steamed, but it didn't smell much better than the first cup.

Athena was thumbing through the morning paper, looking just as exhausted as she had when he arrived.

"Did you see what Hamilton has back there?" Gabriel asked.

Athena closed the paper. She looked up at him as if she hadn't realized he was there.

Something was wrong with her, something more than staying up all night to welcome Lyssa home. Athena seemed listless, and sad, as if a part of her had gone missing.

"I haven't taken a good look," Athena said.

"He thinks it's a water sprite," Gabriel said.

"It's the right size." Athena said that matter-of-factly, as if people were bringing dead water sprites into the office all the time.

"What can you tell me about them?" Gabriel asked.

"Not a lot," Athena said. "They avoid people as much as possible. I don't remember anyone ever seeing one before, let alone finding a dead one."

"Like the fish woman," Gabriel said.

A slight frown creased Athena's brow. "You know," she said slowly, "we should talk to some of the locals. I wonder if there aren't more."

"Locals?" Gabriel said, suddenly feeling lost.

"Bodies. Dead things from the sea." Athena picked up her coffee mug by the top, then grabbed the handle with her other hand. "The fish women, the water sprites, they aren't solitary creatures. They don't travel alone, not ever. In fact, the sprites are always in a flock or a pack or whatever you want to call it. You shouldn't have found one. You should have found a dozen."

"There might be more up there," Gabriel said. "Zeke didn't look. I'll check."

Athena nodded. "Let me call around to some of the fishermen, see if anyone has taken some trophies from the beach."

"You think they would have?" Gabriel asked.

"Hamilton isn't the only person who is fascinated by the Fantasy-Life in Seavy County. I'm sure if other people found souvenirs, they'd keep them." Athena rubbed her eyes with the thumb and forefinger of her right hand.

"You all right?" Gabriel asked against his better judgment. "Suzette could take dispatch if you need to go home."

Athena gave him a tired smile. "Sometimes my body reminds me how old I am. When I was your age, I could stay out all night and work harder than anyone else the next day."

Somehow, Gabriel didn't doubt that.

"I'll make the calls," Athena said, "and see if we're right."

"What do you think is going on?" he asked.

"I don't know," Athena said.

"Would you tell me if you did?"

She smiled at him. "If it concerned the sheriff's office."

"Well," he said. "It concerns the sheriff."

Her smile widened. Despite her age, despite her exhaustion, she was still one of the most beautiful women in Seavy County.

Then her expression became serious.

"It concerns me too," she said. "These are omens, Gabe."

"Of what?"

"Something big," she said. "Something very big."

"What does that mean?" he asked.

She shrugged. "I wish I knew."

"Have you asked Cassandra?"

Athena nodded. "She doesn't know either."

Gabriel sighed. He wondered if the water currents had changed or if something had happened within the ocean. A few years ago, there was a big fish die-off near Coos Bay because the ocean currents had become too warm—due to some El Niño effect or some La Niña effect or something else he didn't understand.

The year before that, whales beached themselves all along the coast, all the way down to San Francisco, and whale scientists—whatever that was—were at a loss to explain the "mass suicide."

As long as Gabriel had been in Seavy County, he'd seen strange things. And people often spoke of omens and portents, although each incident he'd encountered had seemed isolated, just like most of the crimes he ran across were isolated.

He had also heard about omens and portents in his travels through Europe, and never once had he come across anything that really seemed like it was foretold. That didn't stop him from believing that Cassandra Buckingham occasionally had the ability to see the future, but her abilities also seemed limited, an isolated incident.

He went back to his office, and put his feet on his desk, where he spent a good ten minutes on hold with the Oregon Department of Transportation. He'd already looked on the ODOT website for updates on the current road conditions, and found that the site hadn't been changed since five p.m. the night before—warning him that road conditions might get bad, that they were bad in a few areas, and advising him to stay home.

So he e-mailed down to South County where the Seavy County Website was maintained, and reminded them to keep their road updates current, since ODOT wasn't.

He sipped his third cup of coffee, ignoring the growling of his stomach, and listening to Lite Rock through the phone receiver, some innocuous combination of James Taylor, Gordon Lightfoot, and Olivia Newton John.

He found the music offensive—the music of his childhood, bringing all that baggage along with it.

While he waited, he scanned the web for news and weather updates, finding nothing. A few times, someone came on the line, asked him to hold a moment longer—they were trying to get information—and vanished before he could double-check that they were getting the correct information.

He hoped that the man who invented the "hold" button was in his own special circle of hell.

Then Gabriel's door opened. Denne came in, his mouth in a determined line, his blond hair slightly mussed. He brought with him the sharp, pungent scent of industrial strength soap, and Gabriel glanced at his hands.

Glove-free. Denne, for the moment at least, was done with the water sprite.

"You heading to Whale Cove?" Gabriel asked. "I think there's one lane open on 101 South."

Denne waved a hand dismissively. "I'll check before I go."

The tinny music had shifted to ABBA. Gabriel winced.

"I need to talk to you," Denne said. "Can you call whoever it is back?"

Gabriel shook his head. "And waste fifteen minutes of hold? You've got to be kidding."

Instead, he pressed the speakerphone button, and hung up the receiver. ABBA's close harmonies and bouncy rhythms infected the office.

"What the hell's that?" Denne asked, staring at the phone as he wanted to smash it. "A suicide hotline?"

"Our tax dollars at work," Gabriel said. "I've been trying to get an update on road conditions before I head out to 19."

"What're you going there for?"

"To see if there are more sprites, lying dead in the woods."

"It wouldn't surprise me," Denne said. "I think I figured out what she died of."

"Convinced it's a she, are you?" Gabriel asked.

"I still need to do some work, and it would be nice to have a sprite of the opposite gender, if there is such a thing."

"You're still operating on the worm theory of sprites?"

Denne smiled. "More like the butterfly theory, but none of it's for sure. However, what I do know is pretty astonishing in and of itself."

Gabriel put his feet on the floor and leaned forward. His chair squeaked in time to the music.

"Give," he said.

"Our little sprite has lungs and gills just like the fish women do. Which isn't a surprise, since Athena's been telling us for years that the FantasyLife is mostly amphibians. But, like that fish woman we found, this sprite died because her gills and her throat were clogged with oil."

Gabriel frowned. "You thought that the fish woman was an isolated incident. In fact, you were convinced of it."

"Well, it didn't seem like a lot of oil, nothing else died, and we had no oil spill. So I figured some pleasure boat was leaking a bit, or some yahoo tourist changed the oil in his car in a beachside parking lot, and the oil ran into the ocean." Denne ran his hands through his hair, something he had apparently been doing a lot this morning. "I know that these fish women come ashore often. We've both heard the stories about them."

"You more than me," Gabriel said.

Denne nodded. "I just figured she ran into something close to the shoreline. In fact, I even warned some of the local fisherman and clammers that there might be a small spill on one of the beaches."

"But you didn't let the Department of Environmental Quality know?"

Denne raised his eyebrows. "I'm supposed to call the state branch in where? Salem? and tell them I've found a creature that they have no idea exists in nature, and that she died because oil got into her gills, lungs, and throat, and she suffocated? Oh, yeah, and I'm not sure where she got into the oil, but they should search anyway."

"You would have to assume that it was in Anchor Harbor," Gabriel said, "since she was found on the beach here."

"I don't assume anything. I don't know how far our fish women travel. In fact, I don't know much of anything." Denne stood up. He moved restlessly around the room.

The music on the phone switched to Neil Sedaka. Gabriel did not find it to be an improvement.

"I thought the sprites were only surface dwellers, but I'm getting hints otherwise," Denne said. "I'd love to find out how that little body reacts to increasing pressure. Maybe these things can go deep. Maybe the wings have some other function. Maybe they're not wings at all."

Gabriel suppressed a sigh. He found all this interesting, but not quite like Denne did. Besides, Gabriel wanted ODOT to pick up their damn phone, and he wanted to find out how the road was. If he didn't get an answer soon, he'd just go up there, taking the back roads, even though he didn't want to do that again, and see if the storm-made lake had spread to the subdivision entrance.

"I keep thinking the torso is made of some kind of blubber or something. Maybe that's why it's so thick and unyielding. But I'd have to do tests, and even then I'm not sure what I'd find." Denne stopped, looked down at the phone, which was going on and on about lost high school romance, and shook his head. "They're never going to pick up."

"I'm beginning to agree," Gabriel said. "Look, Hamilton, as interesting as these creatures are, what I'm more concerned about is the oil. Can we find out where it's coming from?"

Denne sank back into his chair. "This probably isn't the same spill. From July to November is much too long a time."

"Actually, it's not if we don't know about it," Gabriel said.

"I've seen the satellite pictures of other oil spills. Those things are visible from miles up."

"The large ones," Gabriel said. "But what happens if we're just dealing with some garage that's decided to dump the oil it collects into the ocean or one of the creeks rather than go through all the regulations the government's heaped on them over the years?"

"No one'd be that dumb," Denne said.

Gabriel smiled. "We have a lot of anti-government types in the mountains. Everything runs into the ocean. If they're dumping oil rather than disposing of it properly, sooner or later it's going to end up in sea water—and in the same place."

"We just have to find the place." Denne leaned back in the chair and folded his hands over his stomach. "I wish we knew more about these creatures."

"Athena might. She said she didn't know much, but sometimes what she considers much and what we consider much are two different things."

Denne nodded. "There's Lucy Wexler down in Whale Cove. She follows some of this stuff too."

"I'm sure a lot of locals have expertise on these things," Gabriel said. "We just have to find them."

"Hello?" a tinny voice asked. It took Gabriel half a second to realize he had finally gotten through to ODOT.

He picked up the receiver and said hello. While he was gathering traffic information, Denne stood again, pacing. He picked up the photographs that Gabriel kept on top of the filing cabinets—one of Gabriel's favorite places in Greece, another in Rome, and one in London. Gabriel switched the photographs every month to remind himself of the places he'd been. Sometimes he didn't want to think about how he was isolating himself in a small community, even if the small community was as interesting as Seavy County.

The ODOT dispatch told him they had crews all over this part of the state. One lane was open on 101 going from Anchor Bay to

Whale Cove. Most of the trees across the highways in the corridor had been cleared. But Highway 19 was still closed on the valley side because a large chunk had fallen away.

"So you have no idea if the western end of 19 is all right," Gabriel said.

"Last we heard it was underwater," the woman said. "Considering how saturated the ground is, I wouldn't bet that water would disappear any time soon."

Gabriel sighed. Several other roads in the county were still closed, but Highway 101 around Anchor Bay was open again. In other words, his town was accessible, and even people from the valley could get here, if they wanted to take the long way like Denne had.

As Gabriel hung up, he said to Denne, "Looks like you can go directly home."

"Great," he said. "That'll help me figure out what's going on with our little specimen. Sure wish I had specialized in fish or marine creatures. I would be able to solve this a lot quicker."

"You could take it down to the Hatfield Marine Science Center in Newport," Gabriel said.

"And lose it to their scientists. No thanks." Denne stood again. "I've tried working with those people. They want control. And this is a Seavy County project."

It was a Hamilton Denne project, Gabriel thought, but didn't say. He stood too. "I'm going to head out with you. I'll let you know if I run into more of these. Maybe a herd of them or a school or whatever you want to call it got trapped in your oil slick."

Denne pulled the door open. "Zeke did say he was following a chemical rainbow to find this creature. Maybe I'm wrong about these creatures just being ocean-going."

He stepped into the hallway.

"You're not wrong." Athena's voice came from down the hall. Gabriel stepped out of his office. Athena stood at the bend in the hallway, as if she had been coming here. "They're just ocean-going. The river sprites are different—greener for one thing—and they aren't as delicate, if I remember right."

"We're going to have to check," Denne said. "I'm going to need to talk to you about all of this, Athena."

"I figured as much," she said.

Gabriel pulled his door closed. "You need me?"

"I'm thinking we might need a crew," Athena said. "There's something going on in the center of town."

"What kind of something?" Gabriel asked.

"I'm not sure exactly. We've been getting strange reports about things fleeing the sea."

Denne paused, and looked over his shoulder at Gabriel. "Rabbits before a wildfire."

"What?" Athena asked.

Gabriel ignored them. "Who called this in?"

"Two calls from the elementary school, one from that new hot dog stand that's illegally perched on the beach near the wayside, and one from some motorist who can't get across 101, says there's a whole stream of weird little animals running toward the school."

"The school?" Denne said.

"They're not getting inside," Athena said, "and they sound pretty harmless. It's just strange."

"There's been a lot of strange lately." Gabriel opened his door, grabbed his jacket, hat, and the keys for one of the squads. "Tell them I'll be right down there. Have Zeke meet me."

Athena nodded and headed down the hall.

"Give it one second to let me make sure our little specimen is on ice, and I'll come with you," Denne said.

"I don't need civilians," Gabriel said.

Denne got a faraway look in his eyes. "When it comes to Seavy County, I'm anything but a civilian."

TWENTY-EIGHT

Anchor Bay Elementary School

The car rocked with the weight of hundreds of creatures flinging themselves into it, on top of it, over it. Lyssa huddled in the driver's seat, wishing she still had a cell phone. Then someone would know she was in trouble.

Surely people saw these creatures. Surely the authorities—Athena, Gabriel, someone—knew what was going on.

Her car had become dark, despite the sunny day. The creatures blanketed it, always in motion, scrambling past. They weren't all the apple-faced humanoids that she had initially seen.

Some were frog-like, and left a trail of green slime across her windshield. Others had flippers that made flat prints in the green goo. Still others were large and ethereal, reminding her of drawings she had seen on posters of fairies, their entire beings suffused with light.

Only they weren't light. They were heavy enough to keep rocking the car.

Lyssa had turned herself toward the ocean, and when she could see out the passenger side window, all she saw was a stream of movement, almost as if the creatures themselves were a sea.

The noise was unbearable. Different levels of chatter, some with words, some with sounds—pongs and peeps and chirrups—as overpowering as the pounding on the metal sides of her car.

No one had come to help her. No one was doing anything. She felt almost like she was alone, as if, somehow, she had made this up and it was happening only to her.

Perhaps it was happening only to her. After all, no one saw that attack in the closet either, and she had nearly choked to death. Maybe her mother and grandmother were wrong. Maybe this was something else, something directed toward her.

Maybe she shouldn't have come back here at all.

Things kept launching themselves at the car. Some of them had human faces, albeit tiny, and she wondered at their intelligence. Humans would have gone around the vehicle, but these creatures didn't seem to be going around anything. Over, under, on top of—but not around, as if they were in a blind panic.

Some of their eyes looked that way—glazed, almost empty. That expression on a human would have indicated terror, but she wasn't sure what these things were. Certainly, they weren't anything she had had contact with before.

Something slammed into the roof of the car, denting it. Lyssa reached up, touched the dent, as another pounded into place. The dents were twice the size of a human hand, and shaped like a frog's leg.

Only the frog creatures she had seen didn't have the weight to create a dent like that. Not even if they had hit from a great height.

Lyssa sank down in her seat. If she started the car, would these creatures go around? Or were they so blindly panicked, so focused, that they would keep coming at her?

She had no idea. Humans sometimes got this focused, especially in terrifying circumstances—that was how people got trampled to death in fires.

Maybe the sounds she was hearing weren't conversation. Maybe they were screams of terror, warnings, and cries of panic.

Her own heart was pounding. She couldn't get out of the car if she wanted to.

She put the keys in the ignition, and swallowed hard. Her mouth was dry. She wiped her face with her hand, and then caressed the keys.

If she started the car, she might injure the creatures. So far, they hadn't hurt her. So far, they had done nothing.

In order to get out of here, she would have to back up, and the odds were that she would run over several of these creatures on the way.

She would probably kill a few.

Then what? She was a Buckingham, in the hometown of Buckinghams, sworn to protect magical creatures from the sea. What kind of revenge would the creatures have on her? What would they do if she killed some of them?

What if this was something that only she could see?

What if it was some kind of test?

She let her hand fall away from the ignition. Her stomach was churning.

The run of creatures had to end soon. After what Athena and Cassie had said last night—using the words "refuge"—there couldn't be a lot of creatures. It wasn't possible.

So this couldn't go on for days. Maybe only for a few hours.

If she didn't get home in the middle of the afternoon, people would miss her. Emily would wonder where Lyssa was. Cassie would go searching. Athena would know that Lyssa went to the elementary school.

Eventually, they would find her.

Or the teachers would come out and see her, maybe even the principal's secretary. If this was something only she could see, then she must be sitting in this car, cringing as if something were wrong.

Someone would see her and report to Cassie or Athena. Someone would let them know.

Of course, if this was only happening in Lyssa's head, then she could get out without causing any harm.

Maybe all she had to do was shatter the illusion.

She took a deep breath, then reached for the door handle with her left hand. Something large and black and slimy slammed into the passenger window. The underbelly—or whatever she was looking at —was covered with suckers, and they appeared to be oozing gray fluid.

Lyssa felt her stomach turn. She made herself look away.

Instead, she focused on the green goo slimed across her driver's window, at the little prints—some shaped like regular feet, some like frog's legs, and some like flippers—and tried to think of nothing.

Then her fingers wrapped around the cool handle, and she tugged.

The handle unlatched the door.

She let out a breath. For some reason, she hadn't expected the handle to work. But of course it would. The creatures hadn't gotten into the workings of the car; they only covered the exterior.

She pushed the door slightly, and something screamed. That was a sound she recognized, long, drawn-out, agonized. Then the scream was followed by a plop and a squishing sound.

The stench of rotted seaweed hit her, followed by dead fish, and brine. It was so overpowering that her eyes watered.

Lyssa grabbed the armrest on the side of the door, praying that nothing was between the door and the car's frame, and pulled the door shut, just as slowly as she had tried to open it.

This time, nothing screamed—and something, anything, would have if it had gotten caught in-between.

But the door eased closed, and clicked as it latched. The creatures didn't seem to notice that the door had moved.

Lyssa wondered what happened to the screamer, and then decided she didn't want to know. Her stomach was rolling over and over from the smell. She hadn't been this nauseated since she was pregnant.

The smell was trapped in there with her now. The smell, and the peeping, chirruping, and chirring sounds, along with the banging of bodies against the car frame.

The thing with the suckers had left gray ooze on the passenger side window, destroying the occasional view she got between the bodies.

If this was some vision something was giving her, then it was more realistic than the visions her mother got. Cassie always seemed to know when something was real and when it wasn't.

And if this all was real, then it meant that Lyssa couldn't back up without running over real, living, breathing creatures, creatures her grandmother was convinced were sentient.

Even starting the car was a risk. Not just because Lyssa might scare these creatures, but because some of them might be caught in the car's undercarriage or in the exhaust pipe or even, somehow, in the engine.

She was trapped here until someone found her. Trapped until this panicked run was over.

And she hoped that nothing was following these creatures. Not some kind of ogre or tsunami like it mentioned in the school.

Did creatures that survived in land and water always abandon the ocean before an earthquake? Some mammals and birds could tell when one was coming—sometimes days before. Maybe sea-faring creatures could too.

Maybe they were fleeing before something bad got them, something they knew about, something that drove them from their home waters.

Maybe she wouldn't survive after all. Maybe when they disappeared, maybe when the last one had clambered over her car and made for the hills, the ocean would have receded, and a wave the size of the Empire State Building would be heading her way.

She was making things up. She had no idea what was going on, and wouldn't until she was out of this mess.

And there was only one other thing she could do, one other thing she could try.

She was going to have to contact her mother.

There was no guarantee this would work. She had asked Cassie to block their mental link. But Lyssa was going to have to try.

She bowed her head and rubbed her nose. She felt like a little girl again, waiting for her mother to find her, waiting for her mother to save her.

That hadn't worked in the past.

Lyssa had no idea why she thought it would work now.

TWENTY-NINE

The Trawler Restaurant

"Who's going to destroy Anchor Bay?" Cassie asked, keeping her voice low. "You people? Nice try, Roseluna, but I know a bit about selkies. I spent a year with one, one who chose to be with me, and you don't have it in you to destroy a human city. And even if you did, you don't have the resources or the power. Most of your magic is long gone."

Emily frowned, as if she were trying to follow everything.

Roseluna took a single shrimp, held it between her thumb and forefinger, and then ate it, daintily, as if it were a great delicacy. She licked off her fingers before wiping them with a napkin.

"What you know of our tribe is old and out of date," Roseluna said. "You have lost touch with us, while we have worked on understanding all of you."

The waiter appeared with Cassie and Emily's meal. The halibut smelled heavenly, and as upset as she was, Cassie still wanted something to eat.

Emily smiled up at him as he set the plate in front of her, but it wasn't a sincere smile. Like an adult, she reminded him gently that she had ordered a root beer, and he apologized, promising to get it for her.

Cassie cut a piece of halibut with her fork. Roseluna took another shrimp between her fingers.

The waiter tucked his tray under his arm, and left, presumably off to get Emily's root beer.

"What do you mean, you've been working to understand us?" Cassie asked.

Roseluna ate the shrimp, then licked her fingers again, as if getting the taste of the shrimp off her fingers was as important as eating the shrimp itself.

"Did not Daray tell you?" Her voice had an edge of sarcasm to it, but the casual listener might not have picked it up, might have thought she asked an honest question. "I would have thought that he told you everything."

Cassie set her fork down. Emily had poured a pile of ketchup on one side of her plate and was busy dipping french fries into it. She didn't seem interested in the conversation, but Cassie couldn't tell for sure.

"We're not talking about Daray," Cassie said.

"Ah, but we should be. It is because of him that I am here, his request. You see, you are right. He did remember his past, and he did value it. And he valued his new family as well."

Roseluna looked at Emily as she said that, and Cassie felt a shiver run down her back. Emily continued to eat french fries, ignoring the deep-fried hunks of fish entirely.

"I don't want to talk about the past," Cassie said. "I want to talk about Anchor Bay. You threatened us."

"I warned you," Roseluna said. She reached for Emily's hair, and then stopped, as if realizing she didn't have permission to touch it. "Technically, that is all I have to do."

"But a warning means nothing if I don't know what the threat is," Cassie said.

"The threat is a simple one. Your mother promised that we would not have to move again, that our lives would be sacrosanct. You have broken that promise."

"I have?" Cassie asked.

"All of you," Roseluna said. "And I am convinced that you will continue to do so."

Cassie pushed her uneaten food away. The waiter came back with Emily's root beer. She took the glass from his hands as if it were a stiff drink that she couldn't live without.

The waiter left.

"Convinced how?" Cassie asked.

"I was sent, after Daray failed—"

"He did not fail." Cassie was breathing hard.

Roseluna raised her chin. "I was sent, and so were several others. Some came as children. We went to your schools, studied your language. After remedial education, since I had to start as an adult, I spent years in Oregon State University's marine biology program."

Cassie frowned. "I don't understand."

"Perhaps if you had some patience, you would." Roseluna paused, ate another shrimp in her unique style, and then licked her fingers.

Emily watched her, and then reached for a shrimp. Roseluna handed one to her. Emily ate it the same way, then grimaced, as if she didn't like the taste.

Instead of licking her fingers, she wiped them on a napkin.

"Your people understand many things," Roseluna said. "I learned a great deal. But there is no understanding of the subtleties of the water, no way to know how many creatures thrive below. Your so-called experts, the professors, seem to have no idea that there could be creatures they have never heard of, particularly in the deep."

"Most people don't believe in what they call the fantastic," Cassie said. "I can tell them their life story with uncanny accuracy, and they'll insist that I read about it somewhere, even if I encountered them at random. This shouldn't surprise you."

"It surprises me when people who claim open-mindedness lack it," Roseluna said. "Or it used to surprise me. In the past two decades, I have come to realize that your species likes to confirm its expectations of itself and its intelligence. It does not like to have those expectations challenged."

Emily used her fork to take a bite of fish. She chewed it, then chased it with more root beer. Her head was bowed, but this time, Cassie had a hunch she was listening.

"Many of us went to work at the Marine Science Center. Others of us went on deep-sea study trips. And some went inland for as long as they could tolerate the dryness, trying to learn about other aspects of your culture." Roseluna ate the last shrimp, then picked up her spoon, and started eating the ice. "After the crisis in July, we were all called home."

"July?" Cassie asked, trying hard not to look at Emily. How could they know what happened to her? It seemed like Roseluna hadn't even realized that Daray had a daughter, much less a granddaughter. Or had that just been Cassie's mistaken impression? Had they had someone watching Emily at all times?

"July," Roseluna said, setting her spoon in the cocktail glass. "We lost one of the *paestish*."

Cassie frowned. She got an image with the word, as if Roseluna was trying to tell her something, allowing her a peek, while blocking the rest of her thoughts.

Cassie saw a woman with straw-like blond hair, a face that was more fishlike than human, with suckers on the tips of her fingers, and scales instead of skin. Cassie had heard of women like that before. Gabriel Schelling called them fish women, and Hamilton Denne, who visited Athena too often for Cassie's taste always asking questions he did not deserve the answer to, called them mermaids.

No one ever used the word *paestish*, and Athena rarely mentioned them at all.

"You lost one?" Cassie said.

"We believe she died. There were reports of her body on your beach, but when we went for her, we did not find her. Later, I heard through some friends from OSU, that a strange creature had been found by Seavy County's coroner, and he wanted to have someone 'reliable' see it. I contacted him via e-mail, but he never responded to me."

Denne. Somehow Denne had gotten the corpse. Cassie would have to check into it. She wondered if her mother knew.

"The *paestish* had been prowling wrecks. They did that often, to find gifts, which they often brought to shore."

Cassie frowned. Roseluna was leaving something out, but Cassie didn't know what.

"These *paestish* were young, only recently allowed to fend for themselves, and no one told them about the *Walter Aggie*."

Cassie did not expect to hear that term again. She picked up her coffee cup. "The *Walter Aggie*? Why should that matter? It's ancient history."

"It's not history at all," Roseluna said. "I thought you knew about the ship. It is, after all, what killed Daray."

Cassie's hand started to shake so badly that she had to set her cup down. She blinked hard, then stood, starting away from the table.

"Grandma?"

The voice belonged to Emily. Emily, her granddaughter, sitting beside Daray's sister, in a restaurant overlooking the sea.

Thirty-four years later. A lifetime had passed.

Several lifetimes.

"Grandma?"

Cassie had to force herself back to the table. Her heart was beating hard, and her breath was coming rapidly. A headache was forming in her temples, and she hadn't even had a vision.

Although she was hearing knocking, like a hand pounding on a wooden door.

Roseluna's gaze was cool, as if she had only contempt for Cassie's strange interlude. But Emily looked panicked.

And it was the panic that put Cassie firmly back inside herself.

"I'm sorry, child," Cassie said, sounding more like Athena than she thought possible. "Old memories—"

"I know," Emily said with that matter-of-factness only children could achieve. "You do good with other people's memories, but not your own."

Cassie started. Roseluna smiled, ever so faintly, and took another spoonful of ice from her cocktail glass.

"What about the *Walter Aggie*?" Cassie asked, hoping her voice sounded calmer than she felt.

"You do know how your people handled it?"

"We wouldn't let Walters Petroleum burn the oil on the water, and we cleaned up the slick as best we could. Then the storm—" Cassie's voice broke.

"Not," Roseluna raised a hand, as if she didn't want to go into that either, "not the surface oil. The remaining oil, in the tanks."

Cassie swallowed. These last two days had brought her more memories than she had allowed in years.

"The Coast Guard and the Navy towed it about two hundred miles out to sea, and then they sank it, God, I can't remember, something like two thousand fathoms deep. It was supposed to be very cold down there. They promised us that the oil wouldn't leak."

Cassie's hand was still shaking. She reached for her water glass and nearly knocked it over. Emily grabbed it for her, steadied it, and held it until Cassie could take it.

She took a drink, more to calm herself than anything. It didn't really work.

"My mother and some of the other locals, they convinced the Coast Guard to keep checking the site. They did for years. They never saw an oil slick, except for a small one right after the ship sank."

Roseluna's cool look continued. Her eyes seemed even darker than they had before, as if the irises were swallowing up what little whites she had.

"The oil did not solidify as they expected," she said, "but it remained trapped in the tanks. Until the *paestish* found it. They went diving into the wreck, searching for treasures, and became coated. Two of them managed to find a colony of water nymphs, who helped them surface, kept their gills clean, and made them breathe."

Cassie didn't move.

"But," Roseluna said, "they never found the third. And she could not have survived on her own. That is why the reports of her on the beach made sense. She drowned, and somehow got caught in the current, making it to shore."

Cassie shook her head. "If she drowned in that deep water, she wouldn't have washed up."

"They were able to swim some distance. It took a while for the oil to affect them. The warmer the water got, the less viscous the oil became. It seeped through their scales, under the protections, into their gills."

Cassie bit her lower lip. "But it's their fault. They went into the wreck. I don't see why this is a crisis."

"Because the oil has continued to seep. We have lost our people, *paestish*, and *ailen* have been lost as well, and who knows how many others."

"There's been no report of a slick," Cassie said. "If they left something in that ship open, the oil should have come to the surface, and coated the entire coastline by now. July is a long time ago, surely long enough for someone to notice the problem."

Roseluna sat up straighter. "We noticed."

"I mean, someone in authority. Someone like the Coast Guard or people who handle that stuff. We try to monitor things like oil spills."

"Do you?" Roseluna's voice was cool. "Really?"

The shaky feeling left Cassie, replaced by anger. It went deeper than she expected.

"Yes," she said. "We do. There are whole organizations who monitor as best they can. We know things we didn't know thirty years ago. We know how to clean this stuff up. We know how to prevent it. We are doing our best."

"Then your best is not very good." Roseluna pushed her cocktail glass away. "Your own Coast Guard reports that there have been more than two-hundred-thirty thousand oil spills since 1973. I do not know how they compile their statistics, but I doubt that is worldwide, and I am sure it only counts those spills that were reported. The *Walter Aggie* was not reported, was it?"

"It was a different time," Cassie said tightly.

"I thought people knew." Emily looked up from her fish. "Otherwise, how did Grandpa Walters know to come here?"

"Grandpa Walters?" Roseluna raised her eyebrows. "Your family sleeps with these criminals?"

Cassie could feel the conversation slip away from her. "My daughter didn't know."

"Didn't know her father-in-law was a criminal or did not know about the *Walter Aggie*?"

"She didn't know any of it until last night," Cassie said, "and she still doesn't know all of it."

Roseluna raised her chin. "She does not know about Daray? She does not know how he died?"

Or how he lived. Cassie's heart twisted. She clenched her hand into a fist.

"My family has devoted itself to you people," Cassie said softly. "My mother and I, we have sacrificed everything. We've done all that we can to keep you alive. We've—I've—given up more than we should be asked to give up, and now it starts with my daughter. Last night, someone from your Refuge begged her for help, and she has no idea what to do. Now you come to me, and you tell me that all our sacrifices have been for nothing. Because you have an education—and an inadequate one at that—you believe you can destroy Anchor Bay. I don't see how the *Walter Aggie* and the tragedy with your friend gives you any license to take out an entire community."

"Because," Roseluna said, "nothing has changed."

"Nothing?" Cassie asked. "You want to know oil statistics? I can give you oil statistics. The number of serious spills has declined by more than two-thirds since 1970."

"While the number of minor spills remains the same," Roseluna said. "And those so-called minor spills account for most of the spills that occur. Nothing has been done to alter this. If anything, the crisis has grown worse. You people ignore everything. You do not change."

"I don't know why we're discussing this," Cassie said. "I don't understand why this has become important to you now."

"Because the *Walter Aggie* is a symptom of a larger problem," Roseluna said. "You call my education inadequate—"

"Of course it is," Cassie said. "You're throwing statistics at me like they matter. They don't. Even if we got rid of all of the oil usage in the world, there'd still be oil in the ocean. Oil occurs naturally and it seeps into the ocean from the floor below. We aren't the problem here."

"You are always the problem," Roseluna said. "It is not just oil.

That is a symptom. There are others, and they have gone on through time. Your Saint Patrick, for whom you wear green and drink hideous beer in March, he did not get rid of the snakes in Ireland. He got rid of the *c'au'de*. He slaughtered them and drove them into the sea, where they drowned. My people tried to save some, and heard the tales, but *c'au'de* were not able to survive in water, and whenever they returned to land, they were killed."

"That was centuries ago."

"And then there were the Arctic Wolf, murdered for their pelts. In this country, as recently as forty years ago. The Arctic Wolf, which your press confuses with the white wolf, has a native intelligence to rival your own, and the powers that kept the northern forests safe for wild creatures. When the last of the Arctic Wolf disappeared, the forests began to disappear, until there is little left."

Cassie spread her hands apart. "All of this happened somewhere else. We got rid of the oil here. If we had known about the *Walter Aggie* sooner, I'm sure so many of your people wouldn't have died. But we can't do anything about things we do not know about. And I don't understand why you have to punish Anchor Bay for helping you."

"We are not punishing," Roseluna said. "We are leaving. We have not been safe here, not as you predicted."

"You have too!" Cassie leaned forward. "We've taken care of you. We've—"

"Two dozen pelts stolen in Whale Cove three years ago, and our pups murdered. *Ailen* captured in fishing nets and stuck to walls with pins, as if they were not alive when found. The senseless slaughter of the *paestish* in Seavy Village in the mid-1990s. I could go on. We are not safe from your kind."

"Nor is our kind safe from yours," Cassie snapped. "We've overlooked how many murders? The *paestish*, as you call them, kill women who are married to men that interest them. Those creatures even brought down a ship in the 1930s, all because a young man they claimed for their own—a man who had no interest in them— was having an engagement party on it. And those are only the things I know about right now. My mother probably has a longer list."

"Your mother has been good to us," Roseluna said softly. "That is why we're warning your family."

"And not telling the rest of the town, which has tolerated you and made sacrifices for you, and told no one about you, even though it would have made for more tourists and maybe even made some of us rich?"

Emily had slid far down the bench, clutching her root beer. Her face was white, and Cassie could feel her distress.

The knocking precursor to her headache continued as well, like a drumbeat to her own anger.

"It is your job to warn those you believe worthy of saving," Roseluna said.

"Worthy of saving?" Cassie slapped a hand on the table. "Worthy of saving? What kind of bullshit is that?"

Emily winced.

"We think everyone is worthy of saving. That's why we stay here, why the Refuge is here. Even creatures we don't understand, we consider worthy of saving."

Roseluna stood. "The information is yours to do with what you will. I do not care how you will use it. This place no longer concerns me."

"How can you leave the Refuge?" Cassie asked.

"How could we stay so long? It drains us of our power, reduces us to caricatures of what we once were. Your people slaughtered ours because we were dangerous and frightening to you. We gave some of your people power, and you thanked us for it. Now you expect us to be grateful for a few nautical miles of ocean space."

Roseluna shook her head.

"We are not our parents' generation," she said softly. "We are recovering what was lost. We have realized that to live at the mercy of your enemies is no life at all."

"Enemies?" Cassie breathed.

"You have been warned," Roseluna said. "I have fulfilled my pact with my family and with yours. Except for one thing."

She turned to Emily, whose dark eyes mirrored Roseluna's.

"We had no idea you existed, child. We do not even know what others exist. You know the legend of the selkies, do you not? How we send our men to land to seduce human women?"

Cassie's cheeks heated. "Stop."

"We did so then to revive our lines. We had stopped until Daray—"

"Stop!" Cassie shouted.

Everyone in the restaurant turned toward her.

Roseluna ignored them. She kept her gaze on Emily, and Emily did not look away.

"You will be among the strongest of us, and your children, should you choose to have them with any of our people, will be even stronger. We need you to revitalize us."

Roseluna held out her hand to Emily. "Come with me. I will show you things you have never dreamed of."

Emily looked at the hand, then looked at Cassie. Cassie's entire body felt flushed. She was too far away to prevent it if Roseluna tried to snatch Emily but, Cassie supposed, she could call for help from the restaurant staff, who were all still watching.

"Is that why I killed Daddy?" Emily said, her voice small. "Because I'm evil, like them?"

Cassie's breath caught.

"We are not evil, child," Roseluna said, her hand still extended. "Merely different."

Emily slapped at Roseluna's hand. "Take it away," Emily said, her voice thick with unshed tears. "Take that stuff you gave me away. Make me a normal girl. I hate this. I want to go home and see my friends and be with my daddy like he was before I made him go crazy. Take it away. Let me go home. Please."

Roseluna brought her hand to her chest. She stared at Emily with something like compassion.

Cassie scrambled around the table, reaching her granddaughter's side. She put her arms around Emily, who melted into them, shaking but not crying.

"Get out of here," Cassie said.

But Roseluna didn't. Instead, she crouched and put a hand on Emily's back. Emily stiffened.

"We cannot take it away," Roseluna said. "We are part of you, and we can make you great if you but give us the chance. Come with me, child."

"No." Emily said into Cassie's shoulder.

"Child…"

Emily whirled. "I hate you! I hate all of you! Go away! Go away and wreck everything, I don't care. Because that's what you do. You ruin stuff, and you make my grandma want to cry. Just leave us alone. Leave me alone."

Her body was shaking, and she would have thrown herself at Roseluna if Cassie had let her. But Cassie held tightly, and felt, within herself, a power rising in Emily.

Cassie wrapped her mind around Emily's, holding her in place, in case she decided to use that power in this tiny restaurant. Emily didn't understand the consequences.

Cassie did.

Roseluna looked at her. "You can't restrain her forever," Roseluna said. "At some point, she will have to understand what she is."

"She told you to leave," Cassie said. "That's what you were planning to do anyway, so you might as well."

Roseluna opened her mouth and then closed it, as if she had changed her mind about what she was going to say. Instead, she nodded once, and walked out of the restaurant.

Emily leaned against Cassie. Tears dripped onto Cassie's arms.

"I'm not like her," Emily whispered. "They made me evil, didn't they?"

"They're not evil, honey," Cassie said. "They're just different."

"They're going to kill people," Emily said.

"No." Cassie pulled Emily closer, so that she could speak into her ear. "If they wanted to do that, they wouldn't have warned us. No one's going to die."

"I think you're wrong," Emily said, and her shaking started all over again. "I think you're really wrong."

THIRTY

Highway 101
The Village of Anchor Bay

A line of cars extended for five blocks on 101 heading south. When Gabriel saw it, he debated turning on his sirens and flashers, but decided that would make people even more nervous than they already were.

Instead, he turned east on NE 15th, behind the McDonald's, then went south on Quay until he reached the very center of town. In the illogic that dictated street signs in Oregon, the center street was not First Street or even Main Street, but McCool's, even though no one knew who McCool had been.

Athena was feeding some calls through the radio unit. It would spit and cough, then a small voice—usually androgynous—would complain about the weird creatures running across the road.

Denne leaned forward, as if he were trying to hear the radio better. He brought the scents of antiseptic, sweat, and very expensive cologne with him. He had offered to drive his own truck, but Athena had nixed that. She said there were already traffic problems on the highway; the last thing they needed was yet another vehicle.

Zeke followed at a safe distance. At first, it looked like he was going to turn on his siren and try to drive along the grass, but apparently he decided against it.

Which was a good thing, considering the grass disappeared into the sidewalks and the wayside farther down.

As Gabriel crested the hill, he saw the ocean sparkling out in the distance. Hard to believe the last time he had crested this hill, a little south of here, the winds had been so strong that the ocean frothed, and the night had been so dark he couldn't see the froth if he tried.

"Holy crap," Denne said.

He wasn't looking at the ocean. He was looking at the side of the road.

Gabriel glanced to his left, and saw the usual rundown houses, badly in need of paint after years in the salt air, a few overgrown rhododendron bushes, and too many For Sale signs that people had forgotten to take down when the summer tourist rush was over.

"What?" he asked.

"Next block over," Denne said.

Gabriel slowed down—he didn't want to hit anything while his own eyes were off the road—and looked at the driveway linking two fenced yards.

And then he saw it, the stream of creatures that everyone was talking about. It was so consistent that it looked like a dirt mound by the side of the road. Only when Gabriel squinted at it, really looking at each individual piece, did he realize that mound was moving—and it was composed of things of different shapes and sizes, some of which he would wager he had never seen before.

The stream was thick and wide, and even though he really couldn't get a good sense of perspective from here, he would wager that it covered the entire road.

Zeke slowed behind him, and leaned out the window, as if he were going to call to Gabriel. But Gabriel ignored him, moving forward, heading toward the bottom of the hill and the highway.

A different mess greeted him down there. Not only were the cars stopped southbound, but the drivers stood outside of their vehicles. A few people were talking, but most had left the driver's side doors open, the cars running, and had walked toward the first car, standing beside it and staring at the creatures as they made their way across the highway.

"God," Denne said. "They seem oblivious."

Gabriel couldn't tell if he was referring to the creatures or the drivers or both. Gabriel pulled his squad onto the highway and parked it across the empty northbound lane.

Zeke parked beside him.

Then Gabriel got out.

The wind was chillier than it had been that morning, and the air smelled of rotted fish. Usually he didn't mind that smell—it was part of the ocean's smorgasbord of scents—but this afternoon, it didn't seem like it was coming from the ocean.

It seemed like it was coming from the stream of creatures.

Denne walked down the highway, passed the parked cars, and headed toward the mass of people. Zeke stopped beside Gabriel.

"What the hell is this?" Zeke asked.

"Yet another challenge in a job full of them," Gabriel said dryly, and followed Denne toward the crowd.

The stream seemed to be going on forever. There didn't seem to be a break in it at all. As Gabriel reached Azalea Road, he saw that the creatures had made their way into the school parking lot.

No wonder people from the school had called the sheriff's department. The creatures weren't going around the parked cars. They were going over them and under them, covering them as completely as a stream of mud would. The only difference was that, so far, the creatures hadn't moved the cars out of their parked positions.

The sound was eerie. In addition to the usual surf banging against the shore, there was the thudding of a million feet—if feet was what to label the appendages on the creatures that were passing him.

None of the creatures looked at the humans. Instead, the creatures appeared to be running, almost like they were evacuating the ocean.

Gabriel turned to Zeke. "Call Athena. Tell her to put Suzette on dispatch and get down here."

"Okay." Zeke gave the stream one more look, and then headed back to the squads.

No one else spoke. Everyone just watched the exodus. One teenage boy had a camcorder out, and was filming the entire thing. Gabriel made a mental note to seize the disk when the time came. He might need the information.

Even if he didn't, the news departments and the so-called reality shows didn't need it.

Gabriel moved as close as he could to the stream without touching it. The creatures were all shapes, but not all sizes. None of them stretched higher than his knees. Unlike the water sprite that Zeke found the night before, none of them had wings. But he would wager all were amphibious.

Denne was crouching beside the stream, not touching, but clearly studying. He was too close for Gabriel's comfort, but Gabriel knew that he couldn't do anything about Denne. Denne had always done what he wanted. If someone told him to behave otherwise, he would nod, agree, and continue with what he was doing.

Gabriel didn't recognize any other faces. Most of these people seemed to be traveling through. Some locals had come out of the nearby shops, however, and stood in the doorways, arms crossed. It was a tribute to them and their entrepreneurial spirit that they didn't move too far away from their cash registers, in case one of the tourists decided to leave the stream and shop.

The hot dog vendor who had called them stood outside his illegal stand as well. No one was supposed to build on the beach, but that little shack had gone up overnight.

Gabriel hadn't cited him—hoping the village council would do so —but they hadn't so far. And now, after the guy had shown that he cared enough to do his civic duty, Gabriel wasn't sure he should cite him either.

The stream was getting wider, and the creatures that struggled across the road seemed to be moving slower. Was this the old, the handicapped, the impossibly young? Was this exodus just like all the human exodus of years past, dragging whatever they could to get out ahead of some disaster?

He had no way of knowing and no way to find out.

Gabriel sighed, and backed away from the stream just as Zeke reached his side.

"Athena's coming, although I don't think she wanted to." Zeke glanced at the stream, then looked away quickly, as if the sight burned his eyes. "What's wrong with her today anyway? It's like she's upset or something."

"I don't know," Gabriel said, and he truly didn't. He had his suspicions, but sometime during the day, he realized that even though he had known Athena most of his life, he really didn't know her at all. She had seemed the same, an immutable force, always there, always wise, and always strong.

Maybe it was just a shock to realize how mortal she was.

Zeke nodded toward the stream. "What are we going to do?"

"I don't know that either." Gabriel shoved his hands in his pockets. "Stay here."

He didn't wait for Zeke's answer. Gabriel walked toward the line of parked cars. As he approached, he heard the chatter of soft rock from one radio station, and the brassy sound of a big band from another. On a third, Dr. Dean Edell talked about gall bladder surgery, and on a fourth, one of the Whale Cove DJs was reading an ad for Mo's Restaurant.

Gabriel listened until the ad was done, knowing that the DJ would comment on the events in Anchor Bay if he knew about them. But after the ad, the DJ went into a discussion of the weather in his cheery voice, the one reserved for good days, when there wasn't life-threatening storms or accidental drownings by the sea.

Which meant that no one had reported this strange event to Whale Cove yet. Gabriel nodded to himself and pushed between the cars.

The heat from the exhausts rose around him, and the smell of gas overpowered the stench of dead fish, at least for a moment.

Then he left the lane, and walked up the curb toward the Anchor Harbor Wayside.

Oddly enough, no one had pulled out of traffic and parked in the wayside lot. Everyone seemed to think that the exodus would end soon—or soon enough that their cars wouldn't run out of gas. When Gabriel got back to his own car, he'd get the megaphone out and make an announcement, telling everyone to shut off their engines as this might take awhile.

Several gulls stood in the parking lot, their wings tucked against their sides. They all faced the stream as if it were an entertainment for their benefit. But they didn't approach it, like they would if they thought they could get food. Instead they watched, the way they watched a storm blow in, and seemed to be waiting.

Gabriel had to walk right into their midst if he was going to avoid the stream altogether. The stream covered the entire south side of the wayside, that part of the parking lot hidden under hundreds of bodies, moving forward.

This entire sight unnerved him more than he could say. He had truly never seen anything like it, and it did unnerve him.

He walked to the edge of the wayside where the metal rails separated the tourists from the beach, and peered over.

The stream continued along the beach, although oddly enough, the stream narrowed as it reached the wayside. The stream seemed to be coming from a block-long section of the ocean, and the creatures, without obvious direction, slimmed down so that they could walk on the wayside.

Gabriel knew that was important somehow, but he wasn't sure how. He'd learned long ago that when he ran into important things that he didn't understand, that he should let his subconscious work on them while his conscious worked on something else.

And what his conscious was working on was the extent of this stream. He had no idea how long this exodus had been going on, but he knew it had to be some time, for people to notice it and call it in to him, and for him to arrive.

He shielded his eyes with his hand, and squinted at the ocean. The stream looked like a blackness that went beneath the surface— and the blackness seemed even wider underwater than it did on the beach.

His squint became a frown. If there were that many more creatures—enough that they covered the bottom of the bay as they approached the shore—then this could go on for days.

Somehow, he was going to have to change that. Somehow he was going to have to get Anchor Bay back.

Gabriel leaned against the cold railing for a moment, and tried to envision the map of Anchor Bay in his mind. If these creatures were determined to go east, there was no way to reroute them around Highway 101.

Anchor Bay didn't have bridges over rivers, like Whale Cove and Lincoln City did, and no one had ever thought of building anything that covered the bay, like the famous bridge in Newport.

The highway was main road here, and there wasn't anything he could do about it. The creatures would have to go across it. He couldn't even make a makeshift bridge, not one strong enough to handle cars for a couple of days.

Gabriel leaned toward his left. Leland Hill rose, blocking the rest of 101 from his site. Then he tilted his head toward the hill.

At the base, years ago, the city engineers had built a concrete block that kept the hill's sand base from eroding too badly in storms. In order for that block to work, they had to route drainage systems through it.

Gabriel didn't think much of the system through the summer months—during the dryness it became little more than a series of pipes —but in the winter months, the pipes poured a steady stream of water onto the beach, so steady that it had carved a tiny canal into the sand.

If he could get the creatures routed toward Leland Hill, he might be able to get them to use the drainage pipes instead of the highway.

Of course, he had no idea how to do that, since this group didn't seem to want to go around anything. They just went over.

He turned, and found himself face to face with a broad-shoul-dered, red-haired man he'd never seen before. The man had pale freckled skin and light green eyes that looked like someone had taken tucks in the corners to eliminate bags. There was a smoothness to his cheeks that didn't suit the rest of his skin.

"I understand you're the person in charge here," the man said, with that kind of clipped authority people had when they were used to getting what they wanted.

Gabriel leaned against the railing. The metal was ice cold and rough against his back. "I don't think anyone is in charge here today."

"Look," the man said. "I've already spent too much damn time in this godforsaken place. I have a flight out of Portland at eight o'clock tonight, and I need to be on it."

"Matter of life and death?" Gabriel asked, trying not to sound as sarcastic as he felt.

"For me," the man said. "I have a meeting in Los Angeles that I don't dare miss. I built in two days for weather problems, but it seems that's what this state is all about."

This time, Gabriel looked pointedly at the stream of creatures. "This has nothing to do with the weather."

The man rolled his eyes. "You can believe whatever you want. I've been speaking to some of my people and they insist that there is some kind of weather-related problem from last night's storm that's causing this. They believe that if you just park a car in the center of that mess, you'll divert the mindless mass, and it'll go back to the sea."

For the first time, Gabriel noticed that the man was clutching a small black cell phone in his right hand. He had a beeper on his hip, and another electronic device in his shirt pocket, next to a pair of sunglasses, which he pointedly was not wearing.

That made Gabriel wonder if the man expected Gabriel to recognize him. Even if Gabriel had, he wouldn't have given the man the satisfaction of knowing it.

"Your people aren't here," Gabriel said with as much patience as he could muster. "They probably haven't seen the school parking lot. These creatures aren't going around anything. They're going over and under, but not around. I doubt I can change that."

At the word "creatures," the man glanced toward the exodus. For a moment, he seemed to understand that this was no ordinary event. Then his jaw tightened and he turned back to Gabriel.

"Look, it's imperative that I get out of here. Do you have an airstrip?"

"In Whale Cove," Gabriel said. "That's about twenty minutes south—"

"I know where it is, and that does me no good." The man shook his phone at Gabriel. "I stayed in that second-rate hotel until almost noon, when I finally got assurance that the highway south was open. I just got off the phone with my people, who have been in touch with the highway workers, and they tell me the roads north and east are still closed. You have to get these things off the highway. I have to get out of here."

"I would change my flight if I were you," Gabriel said.

The man's cheeks flooded a dark shade of red, but the skin near his lower eyelids did not, confirming Gabriel's notion that this man had had a lot of plastic surgery.

"I don't have that luxury," the man said.

"You don't have a choice." Gabriel skirted around him, and headed back to the highway. He could hear the man scurrying after him, demanding that he do something.

Gabriel would do something if the man wasn't careful. He'd have Zeke lock him up for threatening an officer of the law.

As Gabriel reached the mouth of the parking lot, Zeke was waiting for him. The man caught Gabriel's arm, and Gabriel looked down at the man's thick manicured, fingers.

Then Gabriel looked up at the man's face, slowly enough to intimidate anyone.

"I'd rethink that gesture if I were you," Gabriel said.

The man glared at him. "You need to do something."

"I am trying, but you're interfering. And the longer you bother me, the less time we have to get anything done."

"Look," the man said. "I'll pay you. I'll give you ten grand to cover any problems I cause, and then I'll just drive through this mess. If I run over a few of the critters, so what. That'll probably convince the others to go around. What do you think?"

Gabriel was actually tempted. It was an interesting plan, and if he didn't know how magical these creatures were, and how important they were to Anchor Bay, he would have taken the man up on his offer.

"What do I think?" Gabriel asked. "I think you have more money than sense."

He shook his arm out of the man's grasp and threaded through the parked cars to Denne. Gabriel looked out of the corner of his eye, and saw Zeke blocking the man from following. Zeke was gesturing as he did so, probably threatening the man with arrest.

The nice thing about Zeke was that he would follow through if he had to.

Denne was still in the same position that Gabriel had left him in. Denne was older than Gabriel by nearly a decade, but Gabriel didn't think his knees could handle a crouch for this long.

Denne didn't even seem to notice.

Gabriel crouched beside him and heard his own knees crack. The sound, which seemed like a gunshot to him, got the attention of a few of the bystanders, but not the creatures, and not Denne.

"What do you think this is?" Gabriel asked.

"It's not a natural migration," Denne said. "We'd have records. And we've been keeping records of this area for more than a hundred years, so this isn't a twenty-year locust cycle either."

"I could have told you that," Gabriel said, even though he couldn't have spoken with the same authority that Denne did. Gabriel hadn't learned all the ins and outs of the fantasy life of Seavy County. He left that for others to know, although he was beginning to think that was a bad decision.

"I can't tell you much more than that," Denne said. "I don't know what these creatures are. I've never seen them before. I don't even think I've seen pictures of them or drawings or read accounts of them."

Gabriel frowned. "I thought all of the things that lived offshore have shown up in one myth or another."

"I would have thought so too," Denne said, "but I don't pretend to know all of the world's folktales."

Gabriel looked at the stream. The creatures seemed lined up by height and speed. At the northern edge were black beings not much bigger than his thumb. They didn't have obvious heads, but they did have legs and feet, and they were moving forward with great determination.

The size progression moved up, some times with isolated creatures, and sometimes with an entire platoon of them. Some were frog-green, and others a deep ruby-red, and still others seemed to emit some sort of camouflaging gray goo.

But they were all different. It disturbed Gabriel that Denne didn't recognize any of them.

"I will say this. Judging from their smell, they don't come up from the depths very often."

"Things farther down smell worse?"

Denne shook his head. "It's just that someone would have commented if they saw things this tiny and this stinky. That's all. And if no one's mentioning them, and if they haven't shown up in fishing nets to be tossed over, then they probably come from somewhere deep."

"What does that mean to us?" Gabriel asked.

Denne shook his head. "Maybe nothing. Except that I'm pretty sure some of them don't have eyes—at least not as we know them. This sunlight has to be hard on all of them."

Gabriel sighed. "None of this is helping me, Hamilton. I have to get them off my road."

"You might just have to wait," Denne said.

"I've got some rich asshole from California who wants to drive over these things because he has to catch a plane. I'll wager that he's not the only stranded driver who's thought of that solution. I don't have the manpower guard this spot."

Denne nodded. Gabriel wasn't sure Denne even heard him.

"To make matters worse, we have kids in that school, and some of them have to go north to get home. Parents aren't going to like being separated from them." Gabriel looked across the stream.

More cars were stopped on the other side. There, no one had bothered to get out. They were watching from inside their vehicles, patiently waiting as if some ODOT employee was going to use a Stop/Slow sign to tell them when to drive forward.

"That's not your problem," Denne said.

"Like hell it isn't," Gabriel said. "I've got a situation here that could easily get out of hand. I need your historical- and folklore-filled brain to figure out what I can do to reroute these things."

"Where would you reroute them?" Denne asked. "You can't avoid 101."

"The storm drains."

"And keep them going east? Who knows what'll happen to them in the mountains or even on cross streets farther up."

"I can't worry about that at the moment," Gabriel said. "One problem at a time, Hamilton."

"I can't tell you how to control creatures I've never encountered before."

"Then get on the phone, call your friends in South County who've dealt with this stuff. Figure it out for me."

"What phone?" Denne asked.

Gabriel smiled and pointed at the guy with the red hair. "Borrow his. I'm sure he can afford the minutes."

Denne gave Gabriel a dirty look, then stood. Getting out of the crouch appeared to be difficult, which somehow pleased Gabriel.

Then Denne threaded his way through the idling cars toward the troublemaker still arguing with Zeke.

Gabriel braced himself with his hands before he tried to stand, and wished he hadn't. The pavement was covered with a thick slime. He looked down at his fingers. They were coated. The slime appeared to have many different ingredients, all of them different colors.

He stood quickly, his knees creaking in protest. Then he hurried back to his car to find something that to wipe his fingers with. Some non-magical creatures secreted acidic material. The last thing he wanted to do was wipe his fingers on his pants only to have them melt away.

Once he wiped his fingers, he grabbed the bullhorn. Then he sighed. The moment he told these people that the problem wouldn't be solved quickly was the moment the troubles really began.

But he didn't have a choice.

He braced himself, put the bullhorn to his lips, and hoped he wasn't making things worse.

THIRTY-ONE

Anchor Bay Elementary School

Lyssa slouched on the driver's seat. She could no longer see out of any of her car's windows. They were all covered with multicolored sludge. Most of it was opaque, allowing just a bit of light through—at least when the creatures weren't pounding over the glass.

The sludge wasn't running either, so it wasn't wet, at least not like water. Some of it glistened, like slug trails, and she wondered what it was doing to the glass.

The one thing she did know was that it was getting thicker. She could still see the feelers and the suckers and the tiny feet making prints in the sludge, but she couldn't see much more. And about fifteen minutes before, not even the bottoms of the suckers got through to the glass anymore.

She had a moment of panic shortly after the sludge blocked all her views. She toyed with turning on the windshield wipers, using wiper fluid to clear the window. But she had a hunch that would be as bad as driving over the creatures, and she was still feeling a modicum of responsibility for them.

She suspected as the day turned into evening turned into night that feeling of responsibility would disappear.

Her head ached, not just because she was tired, thirsty, and overwhelmed, but because she'd been trying to contact her mother. Whatever Cassie had done to block their link had worked; so far, there was no response at all.

Lyssa knew that there wouldn't be one, and this time, it would be her fault. She had insisted for so long that her mother not pry into her affairs that when she needed Cassie, she had no way to contact her.

Of course, this was one of the first times Lyssa had needed her mother in decades.

The car rocked and moved and creaked. No more dents forced their way into the roof, but the rear passenger window had cracked a while ago.

Lyssa desperately prayed that these things wouldn't break in. She wasn't sure if she could get away from them before they covered her.

Then something squealed outside, and some of the creatures on her windshield skittered, as if the sound had broken their stride. They caught themselves quickly enough, and kept moving, but Lyssa noticed, and for one brief moment, it made her heart rise.

Hey, folks—

The voice came through a bullhorn, accompanied by squeaks and small shrieks. The mechanized sound meant that it took a moment for Lyssa to identify the voice, but she had it by the time the voice identified itself.

I'm Gabriel Schelling, Sheriff of Seavy County. I'm sorry for the inconvenience, but we don't know what's going on either. Believe me when I tell you that this is not something we've ever encountered before.

Lyssa's breath was coming in short gasps. Gabriel was out there. Gabriel and a bunch of other people whom she couldn't see. She wondered how long they'd been outside, how long she thought she could see through the windows when she actually couldn't.

We're pretty certain some of these creatures on are the Endangered Species List, which does not give us the right to drive over them willy-nilly—

What unadulterated bullshit. Lyssa grinned. None of these creatures were on any list, except maybe Athena's. But good work on

Gabriel's part, apparently sidetracking a bunch of tourist traffic before it did the kind of damage that Lyssa was hesitant to do.

We're going to try to divert them, but as you can see from the school parking lot, these creatures don't seem to differentiate between road and obstacles. So it'll take us a bit of work to figure out what will divert them and how we can do it.

Long speech for someone with a megaphone. Lyssa would mention that to him when (if) she got a chance to speak to him. She would tell him that no one ever made friends by forcing them to listen to the tinny feedback from an electronic bullhorn.

I can't give you an ETA. I'm sorry. I can tell you that 101 North is still closed just outside of Anchor Bay, and 19 has been shut down on the valley side because there are problems in the corridor. In other words, those of you on the north side of the exodus stream are stuck in Anchor Bay for a while.

Lyssa swallowed, compulsively. They'd been outside long enough to call in Gabriel, and for him to gather enough of a crowd to speak to.

That meant no one knew she was inside this car. And how could they? It was covered with what Gabriel had just called an "exodus stream."

Those of you who would like to enjoy our hospitality for another day, I'd suggest you go back to the hotel you just left. As for the rest of you, shut off your ignitions, and walk down to one of the nearby restaurants to wait this out. We'll work as fast as we can.

Over the rocking and creaking of her own car, she could hear engines race, and doors slam. The outside sounds were faint. No wonder she hadn't noticed them before.

I know you have a lot of questions. We don't have any answers for you. Please let us do our jobs, and we'll get you out of here as fast as humanly possible. Thanks.

With that, the megaphone squealed a final time.

Now Lyssa could only hear the slap of feet and amphibious body parts against metal. Even the chittering that some of the creatures had done had stopped.

Gabriel was out there, and maybe Athena, and certainly those two deputies that had been working the night before.

People. People who could help her.

She sat back in her driver's seat, made a fist with her right hand, and then slammed her fist onto the horn. The sound, loud and powerful, startled her, and sent more creatures skittling off her window.

The horn wouldn't be enough. Someone would think her car malfunctioned. So she pounded SOS—three short, three long, three short—at least, she hoped that was SOS, and not the other way around. Not that it mattered. No one really knew the code any more. They just knew that longs and shorts in threes meant someone was in trouble.

The more she pounded, the more the creatures fell off her car. She no longer saw feelers and the suckers and the tiny little feet making prints in the sludge. Instead she heard some chittering and squealing sounds, followed by plops and squashes.

She frowned. Could her horn be causing them to avoid her? How would that be possible—and how could she check? She really didn't want to roll down the window.

But she kept pounding.

She thought she heard voices far away, but those voices could just be people discussing Gabriel's announcement. The thought discouraged her, so she kept pounding.

The chittering was fading, and so were the plops. The car wasn't rocking anymore either.

Tentatively, she reached for the door handle, and pushed open the driver's door. This time, nothing fell off. There were some squashed bodies on the pavement below her, but she wasn't sure if that was her fault or the fault of the stampede that had been running over her vehicle.

The stench of rotted fish and sewage and brine was so palpable that she could almost see it. Her eyes watered. She stopped pounding on the steering wheel, and leaned out of the car slowly.

The entire vehicle was covered in that sludge. No one looking at her Bug would be able to know that its original color had been blue. The sludge dripped off, falling on the squashed bodies, making tiny plopping sounds.

She didn't want to touch the stuff, and she didn't want to step on the ground for fear that some of those squashed creatures might still be alive.

She put one foot on the running board, and used the interior arm rest to balance herself, then rose out of the car.

The stream still continued from the ocean to the parking lot, but now the creatures were giving her car a wide berth. They were going around the rear of the car, as far from the horn as possible.

A dozen people were standing at the edge of the parking lot, staring at her. Another dozen or more were watching from the school windows.

Gabriel still clutched the megaphone. He jogged toward her, stopping when he encountered the creatures.

"Lyssa?" He sounded stunned.

She nodded.

"I gotta say this," she said with a relieved smile. "You guys sure know how to welcome a girl home."

THIRTY-TWO

The Trawler

What Grandma Cassie didn't understand was how empty Great-Aunt Roseluna was.

At first, Emily kinda liked that. Great-Aunt Roseluna was pretty and awful young to be the sister of Emily's grandpa, and she was smart too. There was a strongness to her that Emily never found before, and something else that it took Emily a while to figure out what it was.

During the whole meal, Emily'd been sitting with her eyes part closed, just trying to feel what Great-Aunt Roseluna was feeling. Emily could do that sometimes with some people—Mommy especially—but Emily never really thought of it like a gift, like Grandma Cassie did.

Only Grandma Cassie's mind had touched Emily's earlier, and when they did, Emily got a whole bunch of stuff she hadn't gotten before—words to describe things and ways of thinking about things and ways to understand stuff she always felt but never really talked about.

Like how she got a sense of the house, and how she knew Cliffside

House had welcomed her home. That she would've thought everybody could do until this morning.

Now she knew different.

She was still cuddled in Grandma Cassie's arms, and people from
all over the restaurant were staring at her—the couple at the nearby
table, that nice waiter, everybody in the kitchen. In fact, when
Grandma Cassie and Roseluna were fighting, everybody from the
kitchen came out at one point or another and looked, like it was their
business.

Emily wanted to tell them to go away, but she couldn't. She
couldn't do anything. She felt like such a baby.

Her face was still wet from tears. Crying surprised her. She hadn't
done it much at all since Daddy died, even though Mommy kept
telling her to. But something about this whole talk with Grandma
Cassie and then Roseluna broke something inside Emily, some worry
she'd been hiding from everybody, even herself.

She meant it when she asked Grandma Cassie if Emily had
turned evil. Because something about Roseluna felt evil. Felt wrong.

Grandma Cassie ran her hand over Emily's face, wiping away the
tears, and smoothing her hair.

"Doing better, baby?" she asked.

Emily didn't mind that Grandma Cassie had taken Mommy's way
of talking to her, calling her "baby" and stuff, because Grandma
Cassie said it with just as much affection as Mommy did. It made
Emily feel loved.

"She's really angry, Grandma," Emily said.

"Roseluna?"

Emily nodded. That much she was sure of. She could feel the
anger coming off Roseluna in waves. For a while, Emily'd even
enjoyed it because she'd been so angry since Daddy died, maybe even
before. Nobody told her the truth, even when Daddy was acting
weird, and everybody expected her to do what they wanted, even if it
meant giving up everything she'd ever known.

The more they didn't talk to her, the more she didn't understand.
And then it got worse. Because she didn't understand, she went to see
Daddy, and finally it all got to be clear—way too late.

At first, that was the kind of stuff she thought Roseluna was talking about. But something about Roseluna's eyes, the meanness in them, and the sadness in Grandma Cassie's eyes, made Emily change her mind.

There was a place in Grandma Cassie that hurt so bad, she didn't like to look at it. Emily understood that. She wished she could make her hurt place go away, but she couldn't. She kept looking at it and looking at it and looking at it, trying to understand it.

And no matter how much Mommy and Grandma Cassie and the weird lawyer-lady talked to her about it, Emily still didn't understand it. So she thought about it when she was awake and when she was asleep, and it got worse instead of better.

She thought maybe after the talk with Grandma Cassie this morning she might understand things—maybe they'd talk about it together or something—but then Roseluna showed up, and Emily watched her instead.

What worried Emily most was beneath that anger was something else. She called it emptiness, but that wasn't right. It was more like a not-caring. Like Roseluna didn't care who got hurt or if people she knew died. She didn't even really care about Grandma Cassie, but she cared about the promise her family had made to Grandpa, so she was here.

And even though Emily got a sense of everything else from Roseluna and from Grandma Cassie, she never really got a sense of Grandpa Daray. Roseluna saw him as a man who looked a lot like her, with longish black hair and pretty eyes. Grandma Cassie saw him sideways, as if she couldn't bear to look at him full-on, as if remembering him hurt as bad as him dying had.

Emily's body tensed.

"We should take you home," Grandma Cassie said.

Emily shook her head. "Grandma, when you get really mad, do you lie?"

Grandma Cassie frowned down at her. At that moment, the waiter came over. He was approaching slowly, as if he was afraid of the whole group.

"I'm sorry to bother you," he said. "I'm leaving the bill. I'm assuming the other lady isn't coming back?"

"I'll take care of hers," Grandma Cassie said.

"Is the little girl all right?" he asked Grandma, as if Emily couldn't speak for herself.

"She'll be fine," Grandma Cassie said. "It's been a long day. She just came in from the Midwest yesterday, and then she met an aunt she'd never seen before, and got all tangled up in the family drama. It's enough to tire anyone out."

The waiter smiled, apparently happy for the explanation. "Don't I know it?" he said. "Family dramas take way too much out of you."

His eyes met Emily's.

"You take care," he said. "Let the grownups worry about their own problems, and just deal with yourself."

She nodded, wishing she could.

He smiled at her, a secret smile, as if the two of them were alone, then he put two pieces of computer paper on the table, grabbed Roseluna's shrimp glass, and left.

Grandma Cassie watched him. She waited until he couldn't hear anything they said before asking, "What do you mean, do I lie?"

"When you get really mad," Emily said, wondering if she should go this direction, "do you say stuff that's not true just to make people mad?"

Grandma Cassie shook her head. "I want to, but I don't. Why?"

"Because most people do," Emily said, not sure if that was true. Surely it was true of most of her friends back in Wisconsin, but they were all ten like her. So maybe people grew out of it, like they grew out of their baby teeth or grew taller.

"Do you think Roseluna was lying?" Grandma Cassie adjusted Emily on her lap so that she could see her face better.

"Don't you know?" Emily asked. It bothered her that Grandma Cassie seemed to have no idea about anything with Roseluna.

"I can't read selkies," Grandma Cassie said. "That was always part of the attraction."

She was talking about the attraction to Grandpa. Emily didn't really understand it, but she didn't ask, either, figuring that was more grownup stuff.

"So you don't know what she was thinking or feeling or where she came from or nothing?" Emily asked.

"I know she is who she said she is," Grandma Cassie said. "I'm not sure about much else."

Grandma Cassie looked out the window at the ocean. Emily looked the same way. Water still creeped her out, but she had to admit the ocean was really pretty. The way the sun sparkled on it, how blue it was, the way it looked different from last night to now, and all the sounds it made.

Emily could fall in love with it.

She wondered if that was because she had selkie blood in her, whatever that meant. She had kind of a sense of selkies, but she didn't know a lot about them, and the way Grandma Cassie reacted, she wasn't sure she wanted to know more.

Grandma Cassie wasn't thinking about Emily or anything else, though. Grandma Cassie was sending her mind far away.

Emily felt it. She felt the way that Grandma Cassie's body was here, and her mind was swimming in the ocean, searching, searching, going into the deep dark places where there was no light.

There was lots of creatures, though, and they all seemed to be heading away from Grandma Cassie. Emily wanted to look at the creatures, but Grandma Cassie didn't seem to care.

She also didn't seem to notice that Emily was seeing through her eyes, traveling with her. She seemed focused on her journey, on the path ahead.

Emily'd never done anything like this, at least, not with her eyes open. She'd kinda done it the night before, but she hadn't been sure then what was real and what was not.

This time, she was. She knew that she was sitting on Grandma Cassie's lap in the restaurant. The bench was starting to make Emily's spine hurt because there was no back to lean on, and no cushions either. Grandma Cassie's legs had to hurt.

The couple had stopped watching them and everybody had gone into the kitchen and the waiter kept checking their water glasses as if he was afraid that without enough water, Emily would start crying all over again. And the sun was shining and the ocean was blue—

And a big part of Emily was under the waves, seeing other stuff, dark stuff, covered with green hangy stuff that Emily didn't know the name for. It wasn't algae, like in the Northern Wisconsin lakes that Mommy and Daddy used to take her to when they were all happy, because algae floated on top of the water, at least the kind Emily'd seen. But she knew she could be wrong, and she also knew that there was stuff in this part of the water she'd never seen before, like black fish with glowing eyes, and little minnow-like fish that seemed to circle all around her like they saw her.

She didn't feel scared of this water, because she couldn't feel it, even though she knew it was wet and cold and dark. She could only see through it, which she probably shouldn't have been able to do either, considering how black it all was.

It also helped that Grandma Cassie was right beside her, looking as intense as she did in the restaurant, heading someplace with a real purpose.

It took a few minutes to get there, going through water littered with junk. Emily didn't have words for most of it, stuff growing on rocks, the rocks themselves that didn't look like rocks, the weird animals climbing in and out of shell-like stuff.

Grandma Cassie kept going out and down until they were so far away from shore that Emily doubted people had ever been this deep in the water. She got no real sense of humans at all, although there were other things here, things Grandma Cassie and Roseluna and Great-Grandma Athena were familiar with.

Then Emily saw the bottom, all sandy and covered with more creatures, some of which she recognized, like big crabs that walked along the bottom as if there wasn't water there at all, and snake-like things, and even a shark.

Emily winced as the shark went by, but it didn't scare her, because most of her—almost all of her—was sitting on Grandma Cassie's lap in the restaurant. More people had come in, and they were going to their table near the window, laughing and talking as if nothing was wrong. They didn't even see Emily or Grandma.

Grandma Cassie finally stopped at this big lump of something on the bottom. It was covered with more of that green floaty stuff, and lots of sand had drifted onto the sides.

Emily actually had to lean on Grandma Cassie just a bit more to know what she was looking at. It was the *Walter Aggie*, the part they'd sunk, the part with all the oil in it that Roseluna was talking about.

The part that was leaking.

Emily held her breath, then remembered she didn't have to. The leaking oil wouldn't kill her. She was still outside, breathing air (thank God. She didn't want to think about how it felt to have no air. That had scared her too badly last July and if she remembered it too much, that burning feeling started in her chest and made her even more scared—this time of herself).

Maybe the water was black because it had so much oil in it. But the crab and the shark and the snake-like thing didn't seem to notice the oil. A couple of fish wove their way around one of the green-covered things, which, guessing from its shape, had to be a railing or something.

Emily wondered where the leak was, and the big emergency Roseluna was talking about, the big excuse for all the problems she was going to cause and the stuff she was going to do to Anchor Bay.

Grandma Cassie must have been wondering the same thing, because she leaned even farther forward in the restaurant and nearly banged heads with Emily. In fact, they would've banged if Emily hadn't moved away a little.

Grandma Cassie didn't seem to notice. Her mind was swimming faster, going onto the deck of the *Walter Aggie*, and then down into the hold—Emily knew all this stuff because Grandma Cassie was sharing now, whether she meant to or not. Maybe because she was so close.

Or maybe because she was so upset. Grandma Cassie was broadcasting upset without even opening her mouth. Emily wondered how the other people in the restaurant could keep laughing. The upset was so bad, it made Emily want to crawl off Grandma Cassie's lap.

But Emily didn't. She went with Grandma Cassie into the hold, and deep deep deep into the tanks where they stored the oil. The tank doors were closed, and they were made of reinforced steel. Grandma Cassie explored the edges of the steel, and all around the doors, and didn't find any leaking oil at all. Finally she slipped under the door, and slowed down even more because there was a lot of oil there, and it was cold (Emily could almost feel it) and it was thick, thick as ice.

Only Grandma Cassie didn't use the word thick. She was thinking "viscous." She was thinking "lies."

She pulled out of the tanks, and then went all the way around the hull, at least the parts she could see. There were no tarballs, no pieces of black stuff slowly floating their way to the surface.

There was no dead fish, and lots of algae, and nothing to show leaks. Nothing at all.

Grandma Cassie let out a sound like the cross between a moan and a growl. She touched the side of the ship with her mind and then everything vanished—the ship, the restaurant, the people, everything.

Emily panicked—she wanted to see! she needed to see!—and then something rose in front of her:

Three women swimming quickly toward the Walter Aggie, *giggling as they did, the sound registering more like gurgles than laughter. They had ugly feet and suckers on their hands, and scales instead of skin, but in the water, their straw-like hair looked kinda pretty, and they had something Mommy would call real grace, which made them look like dancers.*

Emily thought they looked like synchronized swim ladies from the Olympics with underwater cameras and everything, only they didn't move the same, and they weren't wearing stupid swimming caps. They swam right into the ship, and then they looked at each other.

One of them went into the tanks, and it took a minute before the others followed.

And then everything changed as the camera—Grandma Cassie?—pointed up. All around the ship were seals. Only seals didn't swim that deep. They were surface creatures.

"Selkies," Grandma Cassie said, and the whole picture disappeared.

The restaurant came back, and Emily let out a breath. She was breathing as hard as if she'd swum the whole thing herself.

"Selkies were down there," Grandma Cassie said.

"What does that mean?" Emily asked.

"I don't have the full ramifications of it yet." Grandma Cassie's voice was tight, like people's got when they got really mad. "But I'll figure it out. What I do know is that you're right, Em. Roseluna was lying—at least about the oil. I don't think she's lying about destroying Anchor Bay."

"But if she made up the oil stuff, why wouldn't she make up the other stuff?"

"I don't know exactly," Grandma Cassie said. "But I'm going to find out."

And then Emily got another flash, this one of burning. The tears formed in Emily's eyes—*Daddy?*—before she realized the smell was wrong.

It smelled like farts and matches just before they caught on fire. And then she realized she'd smelled something like that yesterday.

When she had that shared dream-memory with Grandma Cassie. Grandma Cassie, standing in the stairway at Cliffside House, unable to move because she saw fire everywhere.

"What does it mean?" Emily asked.

Grandma Cassie looked at her. "You sensed it too?"

Emily nodded. "The fire. You saw that a long time ago, right?"

Grandma Cassie tilted her face, wonder in her eyes. "You're a miracle, child."

"You saw it, right, Grandma?"

"I saw it," Grandma Cassie said. "And I thought we averted it when we convinced Spark Walters not to burn the *Walter Aggie*. I had no idea that it could be this far out in the future, that it could be something else, something not related to that night."

"I think it's got something to do with that night," Emily said, "or Great-aunt Roseluna—"

"Don't call her that," Grandma Cassie said. "Don't give her that kind of respect."

Emily took a deep breath, hating all the confusing stuff that grownups made her do.

"I think," Emily said again, "that she wouldn't have mentioned the boat. And the oil. And they wouldn't have gone to all the trouble to make us think the boat is leaking. They want something."

"Yeah," Grandma Cassie said. "They want an excuse."

THIRTY-THREE

Anchor Bay Elementary School

Gabriel tried to step into the parking lot, but the creatures wouldn't let him. He clutched the bullhorn in one hand, feeling the cold metal and plastic against his skin.

Why didn't the bullhorn disturb them? Why did Lyssa's horn?

She was still hanging out of her car, like a teenager on a drunken brawl. Her hair was mussed and her skin was blotchy, as if she'd been in there and panicked for hours.

She probably had. He had known about this for awhile, and it had never crossed his mind that any of the cars were occupied.

"What made them move?" One of the tourists, a man, had come up beside Gabriel. This guy was dressed in Northwest casual—khaki pants and a golf shirt, looking comfortable despite the chill.

"Just a minute," Gabriel said, not wanting these people to do anything on their own.

He leaned forward, and said to Lyssa, "I think it's safe for you to get down, so long as you wash off when you get inside the school."

Lyssa glanced at the goo on her car. She was leaning as far from the slime-covered metal as possible.

"Oh, I'm definitely doing that," she said. "It's getting across the trail that I'm worried about."

Denne reached Gabriel's side. Denne was holding a pile of slime in one hand.

"I don't think it's harmful," he said more to Gabriel than to Lyssa. "It's not burning me, and it doesn't smell toxic."

Gabriel's nose wrinkled involuntarily at the thought of sniffing that stuff. He didn't want to think about touching it.

"That doesn't seem very scientific to me," he said.

"Trust me," Denne said. "If she takes your advice and washes off, she'll be fine."

"Did you hear that?" Gabriel asked Lyssa. "You'll be fine. Just jump it as best you can."

Lyssa nodded, and then swung herself around the car door like a Hollywood stunt person. She landed at the very edge of the slime trail, splashing the goo up and out.

A few people who were standing near Gabriel made a unison sound of disgust. But Lyssa seemed buoyed by the fact that she was free.

He probably would have been too.

She waved at him.

"Thanks!" she shouted, and ran for the school's front door.

His heart was pounding. He didn't like the idea of Lyssa Buckingham trapped in her car, no matter how much she joked about it. She didn't deserve anything like that, especially on her first day in town.

"So," Denne said, shaking the goo off his hands. Gabriel stepped back so that none of the flying ooze would hit him, "we gonna take advantage of the lesson she just gave us or are we going to ignore it?"

Gabriel grinned and then looked at Denne. Denne didn't have a twinkle in his eye. Gabriel had thought that Denne was voting for tweaking the tourists, but he wasn't. He was serious.

"Why in God's name would we ignore it?" Gabriel asked.

"For the sake of science. Maybe we can figure out what some of these things are."

Gabriel nodded toward the tourists. None had left their posts, and only a few had taken his advice to turn off their ignitions. The kid with the camcorder was still recording the scene, only now his little lens was fixed on Gabriel.

Gabriel quickly turned away.

"That kid is recording things for posterity, and I see a few bodies around Lyssa's car. You'll get your chance," Gabriel said. "Now we just have to figure if all car horns divert these things or if it's just something in VW Bug's horn that works."

"Or," said an unfamiliar voice behind him, "perhaps it's the vibration on metal that they don't like."

Gabriel turned. A woman with streaked, blunt-cut brown hair stood behind him. She wore very careful makeup—not too much and not too little—that looked fresh. Her eyes were the brilliant blue granted by contact lenses and her nose was regulation WASP—straight, narrow, and petite.

A man behind her, scruffy and ill-tended, his jeans as sloppy as his hair, held a small news camera in his hands. Gabriel couldn't see the call letters, but he knew from the woman's precise prettiness that this had to be a Portland station.

She watched Gabriel's gaze shift from her to her cameraman and back to her again. Then she stuck out her manicured hand.

"Nicole Drapier, Oregon's Best News at 6." Somehow she managed to say that with a straight face. "And I understand you're Sheriff Schelling?"

Almost no one called him that, but he took it in stride. More in stride than he had taken the way she introduced herself. Oddly enough, though, the introduction had worked. He knew what station she was from because that was what it called its news—not Portland's Only Local News at Six—which would have been more accurate.

"Don't tell me," he said. "You were here on vacation and somehow got stuck in traffic."

Her smile was the prettiest part of her, and he could see how she would be able to wheedle stories out of unsuspecting people.

"I wouldn't try to fool someone like you, Sheriff. We drove in this morning, waiting until the road opened just south of here, and came to do a live remote on the road troubles." She looked down at the creatures heading toward the valley. "It looks like the troubles are a bit different this year."

That comment, with its touch of dry wit, endeared her to him instantly, and that worried him. He didn't want to like a reporter, especially one whose innocent little news story could change the nature of Seavy County forever.

Gabriel shrugged, trying to seem as calm about this as he could. "I think the storm last night disturbed them."

"C'mon, sheriff. Storms happen here all the time," she said.

"But not severe enough to close all the roads at once," he said. "Besides, have you looked at the surf? Lots of junk in it this morning. Something got stirred up."

Unfortunately, his comment didn't even get her to look toward the ocean.

"Mind if we do a brief on-camera?" she asked, already signaling her cameraman.

"Yes," Gabriel said. "I do."

It was his turn to signal. Zeke moved behind the cameraman, ready to stop the filming if he had to.

"It'll only take a minute," Drapier said.

"It's a minute I don't have." Gabriel pushed past her. "Now that we know what's going on, we just have to clear the road."

He headed into the highway, and the tourists gathered around him. The Los Angeles guy spoke first.

"I think we should all honk. Then these things'll run, and we'll be able to get across—"

"Actually," Gabriel said as he scanned the rows of backed-up cars, "we're going to try something else first."

"We are?" Denne's stage whisper was loud enough for everyone else to hear.

Gabriel nodded. "We need to get them back to the beach. I have an idea, but it'll take a bit of work."

"Work we can do," Denne said. "It's failure that we don't want. And, as you said, we don't want to lose any of these creatures."

"We won't," Gabriel said, but he wasn't so sure. Lyssa had given him part of the answer, that was true, but not all of it.

He knew that the creatures could be diverted by a car horn, but whether or not he could force those coming out of the sea toward the drainage pipes under Leland Hill was a whole other matter.

Oddly enough, the thing that bothered him the most was having this whole strange event and possible solution caught on camera. Normally he didn't mind the press, but this time he did.

Nicole Drapier's presence didn't feel like a coincidence, even though he wasn't sure why. But that niggly little voice in the back of his head—the one that Cassandra Buckingham said everyone had, and which dominated her mind—was telling him that none of this, not the creatures, not the reporter, not even the dead water sprite, was a coincidence.

And that disturbed him more than he could say.

THIRTY-FOUR

Highway 101
The Village of Anchor Bay

A long string of cars lined the southbound lane of Highway 101. No cars drove along the northbound lane. Cassie's stomach turned, and she wondered what she had missed.

Emily sat in the passenger's seat, staring out at the sea. Cassie had gotten the sense that Emily had been with her on the mental journey to see the *Walter Aggie*.

Some of Emily's powers unnerved her.

Emily seemed to have more abilities than all the Buckinghams combined—and she was untrained. The abilities could flare up at any moment, and take everybody by surprise.

Cassie had already been surprised twice that day, first by the miniature model of Emily's memory, and then by Emily's closeness during Cassie's mental journey.

Cassie crossed the highway and parked in the Sundance parking lot. Sundance was one of those nebulous coastal stores that seemed to have a lot of useless tchatchkes, glass sculptures that passed for art, and badly done watercolors of the seashore. Cassie never knew how those stores thrived, but they seemed to, for they were the only ones that never closed. All the others, with practical things like shampoo and toilet paper, couldn't seem to make it through a summer, let alone the long dark winters.

Hers was the only car in the lot, even though there were half a dozen stores on this block, and several restaurants. The string of cars were idling, as if they had hope that soon they'd get out of whatever was holding them in place.

If she hadn't driven across that part of town earlier, she would have thought that this was one of the areas that had flooded or fallen away. But she knew better. Something had happened while she and Emily were in the Trawler, and if it had cars idling this far up 101 on a late fall weekday, then it had to be serious enough to close down the highway for some time.

"What's going on, Grandma?" Emily asked.

"I don't know," Cassie said. "Let's find out."

She got out of the car as Emily let herself out of the passenger side. Cassie was a bit shaky—she hadn't eaten any of her lunch—and she was tired after the mental journey.

She was also a bit shell-shocked, not at all certain why Roseluna had picked her out or why she had come to Cassie with all those truthful-sounding lies. Cassie wanted to talk with her mother more than anything, but she didn't want to do it on the phone, and certainly not in front of other people.

Athena might have more than suspicions about what was going on. She might actually have reasons for what the selkies were doing.

Cassie had been thinking so hard about her mother that she wasn't surprised when she saw Athena cross the street, heading down the sidewalk toward the center of town. At first, Cassie thought she had imagined her—after all, Athena had insisted on working dispatch this morning, even though she hadn't gotten any sleep at all.

Emily's presence disturbed her, which was all Cassie could get out of Athena's emotions without feeling as if she were prying into her mother's thoughts. Emily and something else, the touch-end of a prophecy, or the feeling of a betrayal.

Or maybe Cassie only felt that way because Roseluna had obviously been preying on her memories to weave her lies. Daray might have made his family promise to protect Cassie, but she doubted it. Daray hadn't seen much, if any, of his family after he married Cassie.

At least, not until the day he died.

She shivered.

"You okay, Grandma?" Emily had reached her side.

Cassie nodded and extended her hand. Emily took it, instantly calming her. There was nothing like the simple trust of a child, even if the child herself was one of the most complex people Cassie had ever met.

They walked toward the center of town. A crowd of people was lined up in the middle of the street, and it took Cassie a moment to realize the crowd was lined up on both sides. Two different people, one a teenager, the other an adult male, were filming the ground with their camcorders.

A TV cameraman was standing at the edge of the Anchor Harbor Wayside, filming something on the beach. A woman stood beside him, struggling with her shoulder-length blondish hair in the wind.

Athena stopped just short of the wayside, took in the cameraman, and sighed visibly. Cassie frowned.

She kept a firm grasp on Emily's hand and crossed the highway. The air smelled of brine and fish and exhaust, a combination that made her empty stomach churn. She slipped between two SUVs and headed to the sidewalk on the beach side.

There she saw two sheriff's cars drive down the beach, a sight which shocked her. Even though the beaches were designated highways in Oregon, cars weren't allowed on them. The highway designation made the beaches public land, and prevented people from owning the sand. It was one of Oregon's many quirks, and something she loved about the place—something which made it very different from California or Florida where the beaches could be blocked off, and no one, save the very rich, could walk on them.

"What's going on?" Emily asked.

"I don't know," Cassie said. She stepped off the sidewalk and onto the beach grass, bringing Emily with her.

That was when she saw the wide streak of blackness making its way out of the ocean. For a moment, she thought it was oil, and her eyes filled. But she blinked hard, and the illusion vanished.

There were things in that black streak—creatures from sand pixies to gator-frogs, things she'd never seen on shore before. What were they doing? It looked like an exodus, but it felt too calm. It was almost like a march.

A protest march.

The anger she had felt at Roseluna flooded her, and Cassie had to beat it back. This was part of that plan that Roseluna had put into place. Shutting down the highway seemed like an outrageous display for the FantasyLife, which had always told the Buckinghams that magical creatures should be kept secret.

But Cassie was beginning to realize she was now in a completely different world, one she didn't entirely understand.

The sheriff's cars eased toward the stream. Cassie's queasy stomach got worse when she realized that the cars were going to drive over the creatures.

"You can't let them do that!" Emily shouted, and tugged her hand away from Cassie's. But Cassie had had a split second of warning, and she grabbed Emily's elbow, pulling her back.

"You're not going to be able to stop them," Cassie said.

Emily's scream had caught Athena's attention. Her shoulders slumped even further, then rose and fell in another sigh. She turned away from the beach and walked toward them, moving with purpose.

Cassie brought Emily close, holding her against her hips.

The cars had almost reached the stream. From Cassie's angle, she couldn't tell if the cars were driving on the stream yet or were just close.

Then the honking started.

It so startled Cassie that she jumped. Emily jumped too, and her little body tensed. She reached up and grabbed Cassie's hand, holding her in place.

The stream broke, as if in confusion, then reassembled itself. But, Cassie noted, the far edge of the stream had moved in an arc, away from the cars.

The cars continued forward very slowly, honking as they went. The stream moved just ahead of them, as if it didn't want to get anywhere near the noise.

Emily grabbed Cassie's arm so tightly that she was cutting off the circulation. Her breathing was ragged, and Cassie could feel an echo of something—pain—radiating from Emily.

"Does it hurt you, baby?' Cassie asked. "The sound?"

She wasn't sure how it could—Emily had grown up in a city. She was used to city noises. But Emily whirled, burying her face in Cassie's stomach.

Cassie put her hands over Emily's ears. The girl shuddered, and Cassie leaned into her, as if she could protect the child with her body.

"Here," Athena said as she approached. "Let me."

She ran her hands over Emily's ears, and Emily leaned back, looking up with gratitude.

"What did you do, Great-grandma?"

"Restored your human hearing, child. You can't go about as if you're a selkie." Athena's voice was not gentle. She had no calm when she spoke to Emily.

Cassie sent a thought to her mother, asking her to be kinder to her great-granddaughter, but Athena acted as if she hadn't heard.

The honking was still continuing on the beach. The cars were slowly moving forward. The tourists who had gotten out of the cars had moved to the railing on the wayside, watching the movement below.

The TV crew had moved to the side as well, the reporter talking as if she had a lot of interesting things to say. Cassie felt her skin crawl. News of this event might not shake up Portland, but eventually someone would pick it up—the *Enquirer*, the Sci-Fi Channel—someone, and Anchor Bay would never be the same.

Emily let go of Cassie, taking her hand once more. They started down the sidewalk, heading toward the crowd at the wayside—like lemmings, Cassie thought. But she didn't say so.

She was emotionally exhausted, unwilling to do much more fighting. At least that knocking in her head had quit. She finally had silence—inside, anyway.

426

Then the cars broke the stream in half. The creatures that they pushed away from the highway no longer arched, no longer hooked up with the last of the group that headed across 101. The break was still on the beach, but eventually it would reach the highway itself.

The tourists seemed to realize it too, and scrambled for their cars. The TV camera turned on them, the lights illuminating faces that seemed both eager and frightened.

Cassie wondered if the people looked much different from the creatures fleeing the ocean floor.

"Where're they trying to divert them to?" Cassie asked Athena.

"I don't know," Athena said. "I just got here. But I'm guessing that if they're not trying to turn them back to the ocean, they're heading toward the drainage pipes. That way the creatures can cross the highway without stopping traffic."

"Are they all the same kind of thing?" Emily asked. "Like Roseluna?"

Athena looked sharply at her, then raised her head, and stared at Cassie. "Roseluna?"

Cassie nodded. "She found us at the Trawler."

"No wonder Emily had selkie ears. She was triggered by that —woman."

The pause was just long enough to remind Cassie of old arguments. How inappropriate her relationship with Daray was; how Daray wasn't really human; how it had been a male selkie's role from time immemorial to impregnate a human female to add diversity to the selkie line.

"She probably was triggered," Cassie said. "I hadn't even thought of that."

And she should have. It showed how much Roseluna's visit disturbed her that she hadn't checked Emily to see what else had been triggered.

"What did she want?" Athena asked.

The honking was growing fainter, drowned out by the sounds of engines revving. No one stood outside the cars now. Only the TV reporter and her cameraman, catching the human response.

The last of the creatures were crossing the highway. A trail of silvery goo covered the asphalt. The goo glowed in the sun, the way a slug trail caught the light.

Cassie shivered. "She wanted to warn us."

Athena sighed. "Too late."

"Not about this," Cassie said. Then she told her mother the whole story, including the fact that the *Walter Aggie* wasn't leaking.

"You're sure of that?" Athena asked. "Because if it was, that would explain what happened to Lyssa last night."

"The tarball?" Cassie asked.

Emily was watching all of this as if it concerned her deeply. It probably did.

The cars were moving forward, and other cars, heading north, were crawling over the slime trail. No tires appeared to be melting, which was so far so good.

"The tarball and the attack," Athena said. "It was another warning."

"They asked her for help," Cassie said.

"Which bothered me right from the start." Athena put her hands on her hips, watching the cars go by. "Why go to Lyssa when she had newly arrived? Why not come to you or me, the ones pledged to take care of the Refuge?"

"Lyssa's a Buckingham," Cassie said. "Maybe they were just waiting for someone to go deep enough in that closet."

Athena shook her head. "I always make a point of going in there. It is a contact space."

Cassie always made a point of avoiding it for the same reason. The last thing she wanted—or needed—was contact.

"No." Athena turned and faced the ocean. She put her hands on her hips. "If what you believe is true—"

"It is, Great-grandma," Emily said. "I was there. I felt it too."

Athena nodded, to acknowledge that she'd heard Emily, but didn't respond directly.

"If it's true," Athena said again, "then they contacted Lyssa because she's part selkie. They wanted help with their plan, not with the fact that lives were being lost to oil."

"Lives?" Cassie said.

Athena glanced at the wayside. The only people left in it now were the reporter and the coroner, Hamilton Denne. He was ignoring the reporter, his hands on his hips, as he stared at the trail coming out of the ocean.

"Zeke found a dead water sprite last night. She had ingested too much oil. At least, that's what I understand." Athena frowned. "You know, with the two dead bodies, the conversation you had, and this, we would have thought that the *Walter Aggie* was leaking. We would have taken some kind of action, and it would have been wrong, but not in a way that would have harmed any of the Refuge. I still don't understand this."

"She kept mentioning Daray and the *Walter Aggie*," Cassie said, slowly.

"So you don't think this is about freedom, like she told you."

"Oh, I do," Cassie said. "But they could have left the Refuge in a non-dramatic fashion. So I think freedom is only one small part of this."

"What's the other part?" Athena asked.

"Oh, that's simple," Cassie said, looking out at the sea. It was strangely calm. The only problem was the black stream still pouring out of the water. "The other part is revenge."

"The *Walter Aggie* happened thirty years ago," Athena said. "They're bound to be over it."

Cassie shook her head. "Some of us will never get over it, Mom. No matter how hard we try."

PART V

DIGGING INTO THE PAST:

THE SECOND LAYER

THIRTY-FIVE

January 1970
Cliffside House
North Tower

He was there beside her, warm and naked in her bed. His arm stretched across her stomach, his legs tangled in her own. His pelt hung on the bedpost, which she teased him about, saying that she could keep him forever if she wanted to, just by hiding the pelt.

Daray used to smile at her, that winsome smile, one that lit his dark, dark eyes, and say, "You love me too much to do that."

And she did.

So when she woke, startled, out of a very sound sleep, he was holding her. She was convinced the house was going to fall into the sea, but it was a dream. It had to be a dream.

It couldn't be anything else, not with Daray's long hair mingling with her own, the musky smell of sex still in the air, the odor of incense failing to cover it all.

"White Rabbit" still played on the hi-fi, Grace Slick's voice imploring them all to go ask Alice. Daray loved the song, so fascinated by it that he insisted Cassie play it again and again, loving the magical content of it.

She tried to tell him it was a drug song, and he said it didn't matter. Psychedelic was psychedelic, man, no matter how you achieved it.

She thought, as she awoke, that his eyes glistened in the candle-light, but when she said his name, ever so softly, he didn't respond. His breathing was heavy and even, and she wondered how she had ever thought him awake.

She slipped out of bed, and went to the window, but didn't see anything. Then she went out on the widow's walk and saw the ship.

Daray didn't wake up that night, not with the storm, the winds, the terrible seas. He slept while Cassie ran blindly toward the stairs, when she met with her mother and Daray's father, and hurried, to try to save the Refuge, the people below.

Daray did nothing, even though his father had asked about him.

He didn't wake until dawn, then came stumbling through Cliffside House, finally finding Cassie, still sitting on the stairs, her heart pounding with a panic she didn't know how to shake.

His arms wrapped around her, and he rocked her, trying to soothe her. But she had seen something in his eyes, a sadness, an understand-ing, maybe even a fear.

Something she later tried to forget.

PART VI

THE DEVIL AND THE DEEP BLUE SEA

THIRTY-SIX

Highway 101
The Village of Anchor Bay

"Grandma?"

"Cassandra?"

The voices came from far away. For a moment, Cassie wondered what other people were doing in the staircase at Cliffside House. Her throat was raw from smoke. Her eyes burned, and Daray had his arms around her.

No matter how scared she was, she didn't want to leave.

"Cassandra, what are you doing?"

It was the fear in her mother's voice that brought her back. Athena wasn't afraid of anything. She was strong and tall and power-ful. Even when she had been running to the sea, she was in charge.

Cassie blinked, and the smoke-burning went away. Then she cleared her throat, and the greasy taste of oil, petroleum and fire, was gone.

"How did you do that?" Athena asked, her expression pale.

Emily didn't say anything. She still clutched Cassie's hand.

The honking continued, but only one car was doing it now. The

437

road was empty except for an occasional passing car and the slime trail.

And Lyssa had come out of the school, her walk so like Daray's that it broke Cassie's heart.

"Cassandra, are you all right?"

Cassie finally made herself look at Athena. Athena, who was three decades older, just as tall, just as strong, but somehow not as powerful.

"I'm fine, Mother," Cassie said, and even to her own ears, her voice sounded strange.

"What was that?" Athena asked.

"What was what?"

"The pictures." Emily squeezed her hand. "We made pictures again."

Cassie felt her cheeks heat. They had seen Daray? And her—that night when everything changed?

"The night the *Walter Aggie* went down," Athena said. "Your headlong rush down the stairs just played for us like a movie. I didn't know you could do that."

"I can't." This time, Cassie's voice sounded more like her own. "At least, not alone. That's me and Emily, together."

"You and Emily." Athena said that as if she were resigned. Then she crouched in front of Emily. "What kind of powers do you have, child?"

"Powers?" Emily's grip became so tight in Cassie's hand that the circulation cut off. "I don't have powers."

"The ability to make pictures. The selkie hearing. The—"

"Mother." Cassie's voice was sharp, a warning. She didn't want Athena to antagonize Emily—not because Cassie was afraid of Emily, but because Emily was, in her own way, as emotionally exhausted as Cassie was.

Athena gave Cassie that flat, measuring look, the one that she always used when she thought Cassie was being stupid. Athena opened her mouth, probably to ask more questions, when Cassie tugged Emily forward.

"C'mon, Em," Cassie said. "Let's go see your mom."

"Mom?" Emily looked away from Athena. "Mom's here?"

Cassie nodded. "Over by the school."

They walked around Athena, who glared at Cassie. Cassie ignored her. She didn't want to think about her mother or her mother's problems at the moment.

The coroner, Hamilton Denne, was striding up the sidewalk. His khaki pants were spattered with shiny goo from the creature stream, and his hair, which used to be his best feature, was ragged from neglect.

He didn't look like the same man he had been when he had been married to some Portland society woman. His features had softened, as if he were happier, but his clothing had deteriorated, as if he no longer took pride in his appearance.

"Cassandra," he said as if he were interviewing her. "What can you tell me about this?"

"About what?" she asked. Emily was gazing at the school, longingly. Lyssa hadn't seen them yet.

The reporter was still standing at the wayside, talking to Gabriel Schelling, who seemed distracted. And the honking continued on the beach.

"About this stream of FantasyLife. This exodus. Do you think they're acting like wildlife fleeing in front of a fire?"

Cassie put her free hand to her neck. The memory of the flame-vision returned as a taste, an acrid burning taste that scarred the back of her throat.

"No," she said.

"You don't think they're fleeing?"

"No, I can't tell you anything." She slipped past him, tugging Emily with her. Cassie was a bit amazed at herself. It was her day to be rude, apparently. Her day to tell people, as best she could, to leave her alone.

Emily had to run to keep up with her. Cassie slowed down as she approached the wayside. The cameraman was still filming, his hand at the front of his lens, obviously zooming in and out on the creature stream.

Behind her, Cassie heard Denne call to Athena, saying something about how he needed to talk with her.

"Mommy looks scared," Emily said.

Cassie looked across the street. Lyssa was standing near the slime trail, her head bent, her hands clasped behind her back. She didn't look so much scared as unnerved.

Then she looked up and her gaze met Cassie's. In it, Cassie saw blame. She felt herself flush, felt a memory rise—the knocking all throughout her conversation with Roseluna. Cassie had failed to recognize the sound.

It had been Lyssa. Lyssa, asking for help after all those years of silence.

Cassie stumbled into the road, Emily making a sound of surprise as she got dragged along. A car zoomed by, narrowly missing them, but Cassie didn't care. She ran to Lyssa, who stayed behind the slime trail, watching.

When Cassie reached Azalea Road, she paused. The parking lot was a disaster. It stank of dead fish, and the slime was everywhere.

Not just slime, but bodies too, flattened and emptied as if they had fallen from a great height.

All of the cars were covered in goo.

"That's our car!" Emily said, pointing. There was real loss in her voice.

Cassie squinted, followed Emily's finger, and finally saw the Bug. It was pearlish white and green with slime, and many of the bodies lay around it. Only the back end had any blue showing at all. The roof looked like it had caved in.

The driver's door was open, and no alarms tinged. The car seemed dead.

And it was obvious that Lyssa had been inside it. Lyssa, alone while those things crawled over her car. Lyssa, calling for help and unable to get it because their links had been shut off, and Cassie had been too dumb to realize that her only child needed her.

Cassie crossed the parking lot, and stayed on her edge of the slime trail. The stink rose from it, and she thought that an appropriate metaphor, given everything Roseluna had told her.

"I'm sorry," Cassie said. "I only just realized you were trying to reach me."

Lyssa's face flattened, as if she had cleared the emotion off of it. "It's all right," Lyssa said. "I managed."

Her voice was slightly hoarse, as if her throat was dry. Emily's hand slipped out of Cassie's and Emily stepped closer to the slime trail.

"Mommy?"

"It's okay," Lyssa said. "I think it's pretty safe to cross, but let me come to you."

Cassie watched her daughter pick her way across the goo. Until Roseluna's visit, Cassie hadn't realized just how much Lyssa looked like her father. She had Daray's dark coloring, right down to the tinge of her skin. Her eyes were slightly rounder than normal, and their irises were wider than most. Her pert nose came from the Buckinghams, but her mobile mouth was Daray's, just like Roseluna's was.

Lyssa moved like her father. She spoke with the same deliberation, and she had the same careless passion that he had, as well as an ability to impress people who needed impressing.

No wonder Cassie hadn't been able to handle her daughter in those early years. She still couldn't handle the memory of Daray, and she had seen him every day in her daughter's face.

Lyssa reached the dry pavement, her shoes covered. She held up a finger, silently asking Emily to wait, while Lyssa went to a small patch of grass and wiped the goo away.

"What is that stuff, Mommy?" Emily asked.

Lyssa shook her head. "Your grandma can probably tell you."

But Cassie had no idea. She sighed, feeling slightly dizzy from all the emotional highs and lows of the day. Lyssa was deliberately ignoring her, and Cassie didn't blame her.

She didn't blame her daughter at all.

Gabriel was watching Lyssa from across the street, worry and longing mixing on his face. Cassie had forgotten what a crush he had had on her daughter. She had forgotten a lot about Lyssa—or never really took notice, not on a deep level.

Cassie had done so much wrong. She was beginning to think she had done even more wrong than she had realized.

The reporter signaled her cameraman and started across the

street. Gabriel grabbed her arm, shaking his head, but the reporter just smiled at him. She slipped her arm from his grasp, and kept coming.

Cassie's stomach churned even more. The reporter was coming to see them.

"Do you know what's going on, Mother?" Lyssa asked.

"Yeah." Cassie sighed. "The FantasyLife has decided to leave the reservation."

"What?" Lyssa looked shocked. She had probably never heard her mother be politically incorrect before.

Cassie shook her head. She didn't know how to explain, not in the short period of time they had before the reporter got here.

"Everything's changed," Cassie said, "and I'm not really sure how to fix it. I'm not even sure if we should fix it."

And then the reporter stopped in front of Lyssa, pasted a smile on her too-pretty face, and thrust the microphone forward.

"So you're the woman who was stuck in the car," the reporter said.

That flat expression covered Lyssa's face once more. "No," Lyssa said. "I'm not."

Cassie felt shock run through her at the lie. Emily looked over at her grandmother, as if she was wondering if Cassie was going to correct Lyssa.

"But we saw you—"

"Did you?" Lyssa said. "I suppose you thought you saw a lot of things today."

"We have them on tape," the reporter said.

"Which I'm sure makes them all true." Then Lyssa took Emily's hand, and led her across the street, not looking back.

The reporter watched her for a moment, then turned to Cassie. "What's your relationship with that woman?"

"I wish I knew," Cassie said, and hurried toward her family on the ocean side of Highway 101.

THIRTY-SEVEN

Anchor Harbor Wayside

Gabriel wished he knew Lyssa better. She was walking across the highway, paralleling the slime, her daughter clutching her right hand. They had identical short black hair, as dark as Gabriel had ever seen, but Lyssa's was spiked from running her fingers through it. Her face was lined with exhaustion, and her clothes were spattered with goo.

She seemed remarkably calm, considering, and she had handled the reporter like a pro. He wished he had been as good. Nicole Drapier had finally cornered him after he had driven back up the beach, leaving Zeke to complete the honking. Drapier had asked Gabriel about his efforts to drive the creatures off the road.

He had said some garbage about the ways that improvisation was important on the coast, and the fact that a person had to prepare for anything. Then she had asked if he thought the creatures they saw were supernatural.

He had smiled at her, and said, of course not. If they were, they would have just disappeared. She had asked some sort of follow-up, a rephrasing of the same question, and he had given her his most condescending look.

The Oregon Coast is quite gothic, he had said. *People not familiar with it see beasties on the waves all the time.*

That response had angered her, and that was when she had left him. Now Nicole Drapier was standing in the school parking lot with her cameraman, looking confused, as if the story had gotten away from her again.

If only she would leave. The story was about to get bigger, and Gabriel didn't know how to keep it from her.

Lyssa reached the parking lot. She held Emily firmly, and Emily didn't seem to mind. Lyssa's gaze was on Gabriel, and his breath caught.

He had no idea how she had become more beautiful over the years. Even with the exhaustion in her eyes, and the slime goo on her clothing, she was still the most interesting woman he had ever seen.

He would have thought that he could have shaken her over the years, gotten her out of his system, replaced her with someone else. But he hadn't. Lyssa had gotten to him when he was young, in a way that no one else had been able to do since.

"You handled that well," he said as she stopped near him.

"What?" She looked over her shoulder as if she could see what he had meant.

"I meant the reporter," he said. "But you handled the car well too. I hadn't realized you were inside."

Her smile was tired but sincere. "That's all right. Looking at that car now, I can see why."

"It's wrecked, Mommy," Emily said.

The little girl had panic in her voice. Gabriel gave her a sharp look. It was clear that the car meant something to her, or that it had been important to the family somehow.

"I'm sure the insurance will cover it," Lyssa said in a voice that wasn't certain at all.

"At least you're here in Anchor Bay where you really don't need a car," Gabriel said.

Lyssa frowned at the highway.

"It's only seven miles long, and a few miles wide. You can walk everywhere if you have to." His explanation sounded lame, even to him.

"I suppose," she said. "I'm used to a city with public transportation."

After marrying into such a rich family, she was probably used to a lot of things that Gabriel couldn't provide. And now her memories of that time were about to get worse.

He had no idea if he should tell her about the call he had gotten from dispatch just before he got out of his car. Nicole Drapier had sidetracked him, and he had been partially glad for it.

The helicopter landing on the private landing strip outside of town created more problems for Gabriel than he wanted to think about. Mayor Asher avoided problems as best he could. He hadn't ever come down here, although Gabriel had had him paged.

He couldn't imagine how the mayor would deal with Samuel Walters, the head of Walters Petroleum.

Lyssa drifted past Gabriel, toward the beach. The honking still continued as Zeke kept corralling the creatures toward the drainage system under the hill. She seemed fascinated by the exodus stream pouring out of the ocean. Maybe now that she wasn't directly threatened by the creatures, they seemed interesting.

Her daughter stood beside her, still talking softly about the car. Gabriel sighed. He had no idea how to tell them that Samuel Walters was coming.

He had no idea why Walters was coming. The only thing that Gabriel could think of was that Walters had flown here to see his granddaughter.

But Gabriel didn't know why. He also didn't know how Walters knew Emily was here. Athena had been clear about the estrangement with that side of the family—an estrangement that had happened before Lyssa's husband had died so mysteriously.

Was Walters coming to apologize? If so, why had he flown in with so little fanfare, and why hadn't he contacted the Buckinghams?

The only reason Gabriel knew about this was because Walters had requested an emergency meeting with the local sheriff and the mayor.

Maybe he knew something about the oil that was choking the FantasyLife. But Gabriel couldn't think how.

Denne and Athena were walking toward Gabriel as well. They were deep in conversation, probably about the creatures and what to do about them.

Gabriel was even more hesitant to tell Athena that Walters was coming. She disapproved of the family so strongly that the topic of Lyssa's marriage always seemed to infuriate Athena, and her reaction hadn't gotten better over time.

Once Gabriel had made the mistake of asking Athena why she didn't go visit her great-granddaughter. Athena's eyes had flashed with an anger so deep that she frightened Gabriel.

Her last name is Walters, Athena said, and then left the room, effectively closing the conversation.

Her last name is Walters. He shivered, not sure what to do.

Cassandra Buckingham made her own way across the street, her gaze on her daughter and granddaughter. Cassandra seemed even tenser than usual. Her face was gaunt, and lined with fatigue.

When she saw Gabriel, though, she smiled. "Smart thinking, Sheriff," she said as she walked past him.

He assumed she was referring to the creature stream. He shook his head slightly. That had been as much luck as anything. Lyssa was the one who had found the solution, not him.

Cassandra joined Lyssa and Emily at the railing just as Denne and Athena reached Gabriel's side.

"It's working better than I thought," Denne said.

"It's just going on a lot longer than I expected," Gabriel said.

"There's a lot of magic in that ocean," Athena said.

Gabriel looked at her. She seemed sad, defeated, old. Something was leaving her as well. "You okay?"

She shook her head slightly. "I've been better."

"Athena seems to believe that the creatures are leaving of their own accord," Denne said. "That it has nothing to do with the oil."

Denne had just provided Gabriel with the opening he needed. This exodus had to do with the oil or Samuel Walters wouldn't be here.

Gabriel's gaze met Athena's. The powerful woman was still part of her. No matter how tired she was, she still had the ability to terrify him.

"If it has nothing to do with oil, then what is it about?" Gabriel said.

"I have no idea," Athena said. Then she looked across the street and visibly started. Gabriel followed her gaze.

A slender woman with black hair down to her mid-thighs stood beside Nicole Drapier. The woman looked familiar. At that moment, she turned toward the wayside, and Gabriel felt a pang of recognition.

She looked like Lyssa, an older, darker version of Lyssa.

"Who's that?" Gabriel asked.

Athena sighed. "No one," she said.

"It can't be no one," Denne said. "She looks just like your grand-daughter."

Athena shot him a glare so filled with anger that Denne took a step back.

"Her name is Roseluna," Athena said, her voice trembling with fury. "And she's the reason we're out here today."

"She is?" Gabriel couldn't hide his skepticism. "How is that possible?"

"She convinced them that life is better out here, that it's time to take back a world they once considered theirs." Athena had turned her attention back to the woman.

"What?" Gabriel asked. "The creatures? She convinced the creatures?"

Athena nodded.

"How could she do that?" Gabriel asked.

"I wish I knew," Athena said. "They were safe here. Now they're going to God knows where for heaven knows what reason."

"I think he means," Denne said quietly, "how could a human influence the FantasyLife?"

Athena whirled so fast that Denne took another step back. "You think she's human?"

"She looks human," Gabriel said.

447

Athena snorted. "Looks human. Of course she looks human. It's her secondary form."

"She's a selkie," Denne said, awe in his voice.

"Yep," Athena said. "A selkie with a modern education. God help us all."

She shook her head and walked toward her family, turning her back on the women across the street.

When Athena got out of hearing range, Denne said, "What do you think that was all about?"

"I don't know," Gabriel said. But he wasn't as intrigued by Athena's anger as he was by the woman across the street, and her resemblance to Lyssa. Lyssa, who had the same dark eyes, the same black-black hair. Lyssa, who had always seemed slightly otherworldly to him.

Perhaps the Buckingham magic had nothing to do with Cliffside House.

Gabriel shook his head. The mess he had walked into seemed even more tangled now than it had before.

"What's the matter?" Denne asked.

"I thought I understood this place," Gabriel said. "I'm beginning to realize that I was wrong."

THIRTY-EIGHT

Anchor Harbor Wayside

She felt him. She felt him as if he were right there beside her, as if she had just seen him fifteen minutes ago instead of thirty-four years ago.

Cassie shivered and moved away from her family. They hadn't acknowledged her anyway. Lyssa was watching the last sheriff's car corral the creatures still streaming out of the ocean. Athena was watching Emily. And Emily was staring out to sea as if she knew something no one else did.

Cassie walked toward the beach access. She wasn't going to go down there, but she didn't want her family to share in her memories again. The fact that her mother and her granddaughter had seen her memories of Daray upset her deeply.

She rubbed her arms as another shiver went through her. She made herself take a deep breath.

He had put his hands on her arms the afternoon he had arrived in his helicopter, rubbing them like she did now.

You look cold, darling, he said with that appalling Texas accent of his.

Cassie had stepped away, but he followed her. Daray was on the beach, raking up the straw, his shirt off, the muscles in his back rippling in the sun. He didn't see her standing near the wayside railing with Spark Walters.

I'm not cold, Cassie had said, trying to keep her distance. He looked a little less formidable than he had looked when he arrived. The wind off the ocean teased his hair, and somehow he had gotten oil on his cream-colored suit.

Cassie shivered again, forcing herself out of the memory. Spark Walters. She was sensing him because of last night, because of the memories that Lyssa had forced to the surface.

Cassie always associated Spark with the taste of oil and that horrible feeling in the center of her stomach, the feeling that didn't go away for years afterward. Her mother had called it a hard ball of grief, and told her that she had to diffuse it, but Cassie had been afraid to touch it, afraid that, if she really examined it, it would engulf her and she would never again be the same.

Lyssa shot her a worried glance, and before she had realized what she had even done, Cassie turned away.

Hiding her emotions from her daughter, even now. Cassie didn't want Lyssa to see how shaky she was, how even the memory of that period disturbed her more than she could say.

Still, the sense of Spark Walters grew, and it wasn't just the memory of the young man who had touched her inappropriately in the middle of an afternoon, or even of the man who had talked to her like an equal before she fled the group dinner, but of someone else, someone bigger, stronger, more powerful than that young man had been.

This feeling, this sense of Spark Walters, came from now.

Cassie backed away from the beach access. She turned toward the street, saw Gabriel Schelling head toward his vehicle, parked half on the sand and half on the pavement. Hamilton Denne was watching him, a frown on his face.

Then Denne glanced at Lyssa, and his expression seemed furtive, guilty. Cassie willed him to look at her and he did.

She was right about the guilt. He knew something, something he thought she should know, something he thought important. He knew—

Then he looked away, and she didn't fully get the sense of what it was that he knew. She could move closer, reach out with her own mind and touch his ever so gently—he might not even know. But she didn't. The years had taught her to respect other people's privacy, even at her own expense.

The hard ball of grief had settled in her stomach like a poorly digested meal. She ran her hand over it, like she used to do when she was pregnant with Lyssa, as if trying to confirm the truth of it. The feeling had been gone for so long, but now it was back.

Like the acrid taste of smoke in the back of her throat. Like the sense that Spark Walters was watching her, waiting, biding his time.

Cassie shivered again.

Then she looked across the street. That reporter, the one Lyssa had handled so thoroughly, was talking to Roseluna. Fortunately, the reporter's microphone was down.

But the conversation seemed like a pleasant one, an informative one, as if the women had known each other for a long time.

Was that how the reporter had gotten here in the first place? Had Roseluna told her something was going to happen, maybe bribed her with footage from the storm, and then promised something more?

Cassie clenched her fists.

Then Roseluna looked at her, and smiled.

The smile was so like Daray's—warm, open, pleasant—that Cassie's eyes teared. She blinked hard, not willing to wipe them, and praying that the tears wouldn't fall. She didn't want anyone to see her like that.

She didn't want anyone to know the depth of her feelings, even now.

As her vision cleared, she realized Roseluna was still watching her, smiling ever so slightly.

And Cassie knew, she knew with a great certainty, that Spark Walters was nearby, and that Roseluna had called him.

The telephone conversation came to Cassie as if Roseluna had revealed it—which she very well might have:

"Mr. Walters? I hope your secretary has told you that I'm with the Marine Biology Department of Oregon State University?"

Such a lie, but an effective one. Since Roseluna had gone to Oregon State, had spent most of her time in the Marine Biology Department, it would sound plausible.

"Yes, yes," Walters snapped. "She also told me this was an emergency."

"I know you're only talking to me because I'm from Anchor Bay—"

"I'm a busy man, young lady. Get to your point."

No Texas twang now. Or at least, the twang was hidden, pushed back, probably to make Spark Walters more acceptable in an increasingly international market place. He had become a player now. Athena had told Cassie that, before Cassie asked her to stop talking about him.

Cassie hadn't wanted to hear about Spark Walters once Emily was born. She didn't want any reminders of the fact that her blood and his had finally mixed and produced a child.

"My point is, Mr. Walters, that we're getting readings that show that the oil is leaking onto the ocean floor about two hundred miles off Anchor Bay. We've been checking the charts, and the oil's composition, sir. My colleagues aren't ready to jump to any conclusions yet, but—"

Cassie held her breath, as if the conversation she was eavesdropping on was happening in real time.

"—it's my job to check both modern shipping routes and historical accidents. According to our records, no oil tankers have gone down at that location, but it appears that some of the records are incomplete. As I talked to the old timers, I heard about a ship called the Walter Aggie, *which was owned by Walters Petroleum, and caused a massive, unreported spill on the Oregon Coast. One man I spoke to says that there was a cleanup by Walters Petroleum, as well as some reparations. He said the cleanup was led by you, sir, and that you successfully kept the news of this out of the local media, and somehow managed to keep records of the spill from filtering to the government agencies."*

"What do you want?"

"Actually, sir, I simply wanted to do you a favor. I've been to Anchor Bay. I was on one of the teams two years ago doing a random check of the Oregon beaches for oil residue after the New Carissa *spill—"*

The *New Carissa.* Cassie let out that breath. The *New Carissa* ran aground at Coos Bay in February of 1999. She had been part of that cleanup too, and it had been ugly. Even in the modern media era, sometimes information didn't get out. The ship's damage and the subsequent oil leaks made national news, but the damage to the local fish hatcheries and sea mammals and sea birds was so much greater than reported.

No one wanted to know that the oil they used to fuel their cars and their homes, to create the life that they all led, could destroy everything it touched.

"—and, well, sir, I was amazed. There isn't a drop of oil or oil residue on the Anchor Bay beaches. It's as if they're protected somehow, or that's how they were two years ago. I figure, if you can take care of this now, before my group does its report and word leaks to the media, then everything'll be all right."

"Why are you doing this? What do you really want?"

The suspicion in Spark's voice surprised Cassie. She would have thought he would have jumped on this chance.

"Honestly, sir, what I want is fairly simple. You clearly developed a cleanup method that works and continues working over decades. I understand why you haven't let that out—then you would have to admit your tankers and captains are fallible too. But I think the method should—dare we say—leak. I'd like to work with you, maybe learn the method, and write it up—without your name or your company's name—for the Journal—"

"No."

"Sir?"

But the buzz on the other end let Cassie know that Spark Walters had broken the connection.

He had ended the call, but he had come out here just the same.

Then she realized she was still looking at Roseluna, that they had been staring at each other for some time. Roseluna had sent her that phone conversation, which had happened…

…the day before.

The day before, and then someone—Roseluna?—had called him this morning about the exodus.

But the call had happened before the exodus even started.

Roseluna's smile increased. Cassie blinked, making herself turn away. Spark Walters was here, then, too, in time for the destruction of Anchor Bay.

Roseluna was going to bring him down too, along with everyone else.

I told you to get your family out of here. This time, Cassie heard Roseluna's voice in her head in real time, as plain as if they were standing side by side, conversing. *Do it soon.*

Cassie wrenched her gaze away from Roseluna's. The entire interaction—if that was what she wanted to call it—had shaken Cassie.

Everything was out of kilter and wrong.

And now, Spark Walters was going to walk right into the middle of it—just like he had done before.

PART VII

DIGGING INTO THE PAST:

THE THIRD LAYER

THIRTY-NINE

January 1970
Arno's Supper Club

Cassandra sat with her back to the grill, the flame the chefs used to impress the patrons and to sear the beef making her hotter than she wanted to be. Her mother had dragged her to this meal, because Athena thought that Spark Walters would want someone his own age to talk to.

Cassie hadn't wanted to come. Athena had had to beg. Even then, Cassie would have preferred to be on the beach, working under the glow of car lights, trying get rid of the oil that Walters company had spilled into her ocean.

Besides, Daray was there. He had said he would take care of everything. The selkies, he told her, had an idea about ways to clean up the oil, provided the Buckinghams promised that nothing like this would happen again.

Cassie had said they couldn't make that kind of promise. The world was getting more unpredictable, and there was no way to control humanity. But Athena had thought that they might be able to keep the Refuge protected.

She would work on it, she said. But first things first. She had to deal with Spark Walters.

Walters sat at the head of the table. He had changed into a darker suit with the same style jacket and even wider legs. He seemed to prefer bolo ties and cowboy boots, but he was civilized enough to check his hat at the door. He even gave the coat check girl a large tip, larger than Cassie had ever seen anyone hand out in a single moment.

He had done it to impress Cassie. He made that clear with the smile he gave her. He had offered her his arm as the maître d' led them into the dining room, but she pretended she hadn't seen it.

Her mother, on the other hand, wasn't pretending anything. "You may as well give it up," Athena said to Walters. "My daughter considers herself married."

"Considers?" He raised an eyebrow, seemingly amused.

"Well, she followed Daray's family customs, which are even more hippyish than hippie ceremonies."

Athena didn't even try to hide her contempt. Cassie felt her cheeks warm. She adjusted the shawl she wore over her granny dress, and wished she wasn't part of this conversation.

Walters smiled down at Cassie. "Barefoot on the beach?"

"Not quite," she said coolly, unwilling to tell him anything.

It would be impossible to explain the ceremony to an outsider anyway. Daray had given her custody of his pelt in front of his entire family. He had sworn loyalty and allegiance to her for as long as they both lived, and she had sworn to protect him in all ways whenever he walked on land, promising him at least two children—one to be raised in the customs of his people, and one to be raised in the customs of hers.

Athena objected to the entire ceremony, but she objected to the last part the most.

"I keep telling her that the ceremony is not binding until she steps before someone who can make it legal—a judge, a minister, hell, even a captain at sea, but she won't—"

"Mother," Cassie said. "Mr. Walters doesn't want to hear our family squabbles."

"On the contrary." Walters took her hand, wrapped it around his arm, and placed his own hand protectively over hers. "It's refreshing to hear someone else's problems for a change."

Arno's was nearly empty. During the fall and winter months, the supper club was only open on the weekends. Even then, it did a dismal business except over the Thanksgiving and Christmas holidays.

Arno's liked to say it stayed open for the locals, but most locals couldn't afford the place, no matter how much they wanted to come.

Athena had initially suggested the Trawler, which had cheaper food and meals that Cassie could eat. But Walters wanted the best in town, partly to impress Athena and partly to maintain his image— whatever that was.

Athena claimed she didn't care. She had gotten him to agree to a meal, without his minions or the mayor and sheriff, both of whom were irritating her with their conditions and willingness to listen to the rich boy.

They wouldn't do anything without her; they knew what kind of power she had. But they didn't like outsiders knowing that they answered to a woman.

No matter what Athena had envisioned, however, it wasn't happening. By the time her mother had had her Gibson, Spark had had his beer, and Cassie (who refused to drink) had eaten the entire relish tray, the conversation had gotten surly.

Athena wanted Spark to pay for the cleanup, the lost wages, and any other damage that might or might not occur in the future. Spark was willing to help with the cleanup provided there was no publicity, but he was not going to subsidize an entire village.

Their voices kept climbing, and even the chefs, hiding behind the steaks sizzling on the grill, shifted uncomfortably. Cassie's stomach growled, and her mind wandered—literally.

She searched for Daray.

He was on the beach, as he had promised he would be, only he wasn't cleaning up. He was standing in the shadows of the Devil's Goblet, Cliffside House rising above him in the darkness. In the distance, Cassie could see the lights of a dozen cars trained on the beach, along with some floodlights people had donated from their backyards.

The workers seemed small and dark, like ants working inside a lighted cage.

Cassie couldn't feel the wind, and she couldn't smell the oil, but she could see everything through Daray's eyes. He didn't seem to notice her, which was a first between them. He seemed too intent on the conversation with his father.

"I think it's dangerous," his father was saying. "Do you have any idea what would happen?"

"All I know is the history." Daray's deep voice warmed Cassie. She loved how it sounded from his perspective, even deeper than it was when she was listening from across the room, rumbling inside him like a cat's purr.

"History as told by whom?" his father asked.

"A number of people," Daray said. "They say the resulting storm will clean all foreign matter that we designate from the sea and its shore. We just need a place to dump it."

Cassie felt the hair on the back of her neck rise. She made herself focus, for a brief moment, on her mother and Spark. They were still arguing over the best way to clean the beaches, and Athena was accusing Spark of caring more about Walters Petroleum than about human beings.

Cassie shook her head slightly—what else could her mother expect?—and then let herself slip back into Daray's mind. This time, she went stealthily. She had a feeling—and she was uncertain whether it came from him or not—that he wouldn't feel free to have this conversation if she were listening.

"…I understand that no matter what the humans do, they'll leave some kind of residue. The entire area will be polluted, Father, maybe forever. We're not going to find another haven like this. I say we use our powers to guard our home—"

"It's not that simple, Daray." His father sighed, paced toward the waves breaking on the beach, and then walked back. "This storm you talk about is not created simply by dripping selkie blood into the ocean. If it were like that, we would create storms all the time just by nicking ourselves on a rock."

Daray crossed his arms. He was cold without his pelt, but he would not admit that to anyone. He had given it to Cassandra of his own free will.

"Then what?" he asked.

"The storm is created by the blood of a *dying* selkie. The selkie must bleed in the water and die before the storm will come up. And this is no ordinary storm, my son. It makes the storm that drowned the oil ship look like it was nothing."

Daray raised his head. "You've seen one of these storms."

"Yes." His father shuddered. "And I do not want to see one again."

"Not even to save the harbor, the beach?"

"There are other beaches, Daray."

"Not with these protections. Not with Cliffside House."

"You place too much faith in these women. They cannot—"

Cassie? Another voice sounded in her head. A male voice, one she did not recognize. *Cassie, are you with us?*

Cassie blinked and left Daray's mind. She came back to the table to see her mother and Spark Walters staring at her.

"I'm sorry," she said. "I was thinking about something else."

Spark's head was slightly tilted, as if he were studying her, as if he didn't believe her. She had probably misheard him. He hadn't been speaking in her mind. It had just seemed that way because her consciousness had been so far from the table.

"That must have been some daydream," Spark said. "You seem tense."

Cassie forced herself to smile. "You are fighting with my mother. That's enough to make anyone tense."

Spark smiled. It was a good ole boy smile, filled with impishness and the promise of fun. It was the kind of smile that made people smile back, even when they felt that they shouldn't.

"Your mother and I want the same thing," he said. "We want Anchor Bay returned to its normal form."

"I'd like it returned to its normal pristine condition," Cassie said. "But that's not going to happen."

"Why not?" Walters asked.

"Because I've been listening to my mother talk about the conversations she's had with people all over the world." Cassie looked at Athena, who was leaning back in her chair, her hands clasped on her lap. "They never fully recover. You don't get the fish back or the birds or the clamming season. You don't get any of it back, Mr. Walters—"

"Spark," he said.

"You don't get it back," Cassie said, ignoring his directive. "You might be able to restore some of it, but not even that, sometimes. The people in Perranporth, where the oil drifted after the *Torrey Canyon* disaster, they said they're still finding oil, deep beneath the sand. And that accident happened when? Three years ago? How can we live like that?"

Athena nodded slightly, and Cassie felt her anger turn toward her mother. This was why Athena had brought her—not for her youth and ability to flirt with Walters, but for her indignation. Athena could be upset, but she still had to negotiate with the man. Cassie didn't have to be diplomatic at all.

"We're going to do everything we can," Walters said.

"And it won't be enough," Cassie said. "Everything you can is coming too late. Your captain screwed up. He got too close to shore in the middle of a storm, and his ship wasn't built for that kind of punishment. We both know it. Admit liability, pay people for their lost wages, do what you can to clean up, and help us survive this. Don't make empty promises."

Spark Walters' smile had faded long ago. He had flung his arm over the back of his chair, in an attempt to look relaxed, but it wasn't working. He looked sad and more than a little trapped.

"So I'm the enemy," he said.

Cassie sighed. "It's not about you. It's about Anchor Bay, and all the places that this oil will eventually drift. Did you know the *Torrey Canyon*, which went aground in Cornwall, created three separate slicks, two of which made it all the way to France? We don't know where the currents will take this stuff. We've been lucky so far. The oil's been trapped in the bay. But that won't last, Mr. Walters. Other people are going to be affected. Your precious company's going to be affected."

He swallowed so hard that Cassie saw his Adam's apple move.

Athena leaned back even farther, keeping herself out of the conversation. She must have approved of what Cassie was doing.

The waiter finally arrived with their food. He set down a sizzling top sirloin in front of Walters, a petite filet in front of Athena, and an overcooked yellowish slab of halibut in front of Cassie. Her stomach turned, but she ignored it.

She did wait until the waiter had left before continuing.

She also lowered her voice. No sense in letting the entire restaurant in on the conversation.

"I keep telling myself," she said, "that maybe some good can come out of this. Maybe, if this spill gets the attention it deserves, this country'll start talking about alternative fuels and less environmentally dangerous ways of continuing our lifestyle. Or maybe—"

"Oil is natural," Walters said. "It's naturally formed. We extract it from wells, just like we do water. And we need it. We accomplish a lot of good things with oil. Not just petroleum, but plastics and—"

"Save it," Cassie said. "I don't really care. You may believe in this stuff, but I don't. All I see is how it's destroying my home and damaging my friends, and I keep trying to find a way that this could be turned around. I don't think it will. I think the word 'disaster' isn't big enough to cover what this spill will do to this area. You have no idea what kind of creatures live here, how unique this place is. You don't know—"

"The point is," Athena said quickly, apparently afraid Cassie was going to tell Walters about the Refuge, "that this isn't something that's going to go away."

Athena leaned forward and steepled her hands over her steak. No one had touched their food yet. No one seemed interested.

"Right now, you and I have a vested interest in keeping this spill quiet," Athena said. "Tourists won't come back here if they think Anchor Bay is destroyed forever. But I'm willing to risk that to make Walters Petroleum accountable. I know many reporters, Mr. Walters, and in these volatile times, they'd be more than willing to write a story with a slant my daughter would appreciate."

Cassie felt her cheeks heat up. She hadn't just been brought for her indignation. She'd been brought here as a representative of the

New Left side of her generation, the people protesting in the streets in other cities. The people who actually cared about the Earth, unlike Walters, who seemed to have taken up his father's banner—profit at all cost.

"Such a story would destroy you, Mr. Walters," Athena said.

"It won't help your tourism either." He leaned forward, grabbed his steak knife and deliberately sliced into the top sirloin.

"No," Athena said, "it won't. But it might save some lives, which are, after all, more important than industries and tourism dollars."

"Are they?" Walters took a bite of his steak. He spoke as he chewed. Cassie had to look away. "My father says that life is the most abundant renewable resource on this planet. And when you have a surplus of something, it really isn't worth very much, is it? Basic economics, after all."

"How can you say that?" Cassie asked.

"I didn't." Walters cut another piece of steak. "My father did."

Cassie felt herself grow cold.

"Don't lie and say you disagree," Walters said. "Not with a bit of cow sitting in front of you, Mrs. Buckingham, and that poor dead fish in front of you, Cassandra. Arguing with that point makes you both hypocrites."

Cassie pushed away from the table. "I'm sorry, Mother," she said. "But I can't stay here."

Athena nodded, as if Cassie had met her expectations and disappointed her at the same time. Walters cut another piece of steak, and before eating it, waved it at Cassie, smiling at her cheerfully.

He leaned back, his chair blocking her exit. "I can't decide if it's too bad that you're so pretty, or too bad that you're so naïve. Someday, you're going to find out how the world works, honey. And then you're going to realize that perfection is impossible. You just gotta do what you can."

"I know world's not perfect," Cassie said, sliding a nearby table sideways so that she could get past Walters' chair. "The *Walter Aggie* has taught me that."

FORTY

January 1970
Highway 101
The Village of Anchor Bay

Cassandra didn't go directly home. Instead, she walked out of Arno's, down Highway 101, toward the center of town. The January night was calm, with hardly a breath of wind. Perfect for working until all hours, no matter how she was dressed.

Above her, the stars winked. The night sky seemed even clearer than usual. The full moon cast enough light for her to see the high-way, even though half of the streetlights were out.

As she walked, she really looked at her town in a way that she hadn't looked at it in years. Most of the houses lining the highway were empty—second homes for the rich of Portland, people who thought they knew the coast, but really didn't.

The local businesses were dark and rundown from the effects of the salt air. Behind them stood the shacks that a number of locals had lived in for years, buildings that had somehow withstood the winds and the rains.

Most people in Anchor Bay had no money. They lived here

because they wanted to be near the sea and were willing to make sacrifices. They ran gift shops that got almost no customers in the winter, or they waited tables—again, making no money in the winter, or they mined the sea for its food, a marginal living at best. People who lived here year-round knew they wouldn't be rich, but they would enjoy the quality of life.

A quality of life that Spark Walters and his stupid company might have destroyed.

He had seemed so sincere, trying to show Cassie and Athena that he wanted the same things. And then he had said all that stuff about life being cheap, and tried to cover it by saying that was his father's philosophy.

Of course it was. His father ran one of the largest oil companies in America. The man couldn't care about living people. He couldn't, not and work with oil. Oil, which when burned became a pollutant. When used, its byproducts were dangerous, and horrible.

And that didn't consider what it came from. Hundreds of thousands of millions of years ago, oil had been living creatures. The prehistoric era had created a resource that was limited, that took forever to make, and was being used in the space of decades.

She sighed. She would have had that argument with Spark if she had stayed. But she knew better. He'd probably heard it before and had the corporate answer.

And he was already getting into the hypocrisy argument, which she knew she couldn't win. Because if she truly believed that oil and oil-based products were evil, she couldn't use any. And much as she appreciated the arguments of the back-to-the-earth hippies, she didn't want to live that way. She liked a warm house in the winter, and she liked traveling by car, and she liked plastic's smoothness beneath her fingertips.

She just wasn't sure oil was worth the price of Anchor Bay.

As she reached the wayside, she saw that a different set of cars were parked there, their headlights trained on the beach. The ocean's natural glow was gone, buried beneath blackness. Two dozen people were scattered along the coastline, raking the oil-covered straw and placing it in buckets. Still other people were gathered around the flatbed of a truck, parked illegally on the beach, working with some birds in the glare of a dozen flashlights.

Cassie stopped for a moment, and stared at her friends, who were working as hard, and cared as much, as she had. Spark had seemed sympathetic enough when he had arrived. He had looked at this scene on the beach, and his entire face had changed. He didn't even try to cover the shock that she had sensed from him.

He had been as upset by the damage as she had, and it wasn't just because of lost profits. It was also because he knew something beautiful was being destroyed.

All of his bravado and his quoting his worthless father couldn't disguise that.

Cassie made herself take a deep breath, and shake off all thoughts of Spark Walters. She had come down here in search of Daray. She hadn't done a mental search for him—she didn't want to get in the way of his conversation with his father, if that was still continuing—but she would if she had to.

She looked down at her dress, which was certainly not oil-cleaning clothing, and shrugged. If she had taken the car instead of walked, she could have stopped at Cliffside House to change before she had come down here. But she hadn't. And after that conversation with Spark, she felt uncomfortable even thinking of driving.

If she ruined these clothes, so be it. The dress wasn't that important anyway. She had made it one summer afternoon when she had had nothing else to do.

Cassie turned into the wayside. As she did, she noted several other cars scattered throughout the parking lot. Their lights were off. Maybe they were going to be used for light later, or maybe they were the cars that belonged to people working the cleanup.

Did those people think of the contradictions too? Or did they just focus on this one slick, this one mistake? Maybe they blamed it on the *Walter Aggie*'s captain, or maybe they blamed it on Walters Petroleum. Maybe they deliberately avoided the big picture so that it wouldn't interfere with their day-to-day work.

She moved through the parked cars to the ones giving up their battery power to provide light. A man leaned against one of the trucks, his right leg crossed over his left. He was sipping from a thermos of coffee, a half-unwrapped sandwich in his left hand. Over the stench of the oil, Cassie caught the smell of tuna fish.

Her stomach growled. Except for some radishes, carrots and celery, she hadn't had any dinner.

She stepped closer to the man. He turned toward her, half of his face catching the light from the cars.

"Cassandra Buckingham," he said.

"John Aluke," she said. "What're you doing down here?"

"I live here, same as everyone else." His voice was defensive, and she realized, in that moment, that he thought she believed he should have done more to prevent the *Walter Aggie* from going aground.

"I just meant I hadn't seen you down here before." She was digging herself in deeper. "Some folks help in other ways."

He nodded. "They never answered the radio."

"I know," she said. "My mother told me. You couldn't've piloted them into the harbor that night, even if you did get in touch with them. Anyone with half a brain knows that."

He looked out at the ocean, and she got a sense from him. He was willing to fight for his own honor, but deep down, he didn't believe it. Deep down, he thought that the loss of the *Walter Aggie* was his fault.

Cassie's stomach growled again, and Aluke turned back toward her.

"My wife made a lot of sandwiches," he said. "You want one?"

"Yes, thank you." She walked over to the truck as Aluke reached into the flatbed. He handed her a sandwich wrapped in wax paper. The sandwich smelled much better than that yellow halibut had at Arno's.

She would enjoy it more too.

"You're not dressed for working," Aluke said.

"I just ran away from the Walters Petroleum guy. He's out to dinner with Mother at Arno's."

"Made a pass at you, did he?" Aluke asked.

Cassie sighed. Some men would never believe that women would be involved in business discussions, particularly conservative men who made their living at sea.

"No, actually," Cassie said. "I just couldn't take his attitude anymore."

"Amen to that," Aluke said.

He sipped from the thermos cup. Cassie ate her sandwich so fast she barely tasted it.

"So," Aluke said after a moment, "you just come down here to look at the progress?"

Cassie shook her head. "I was looking for Daray. He was down here a little while ago."

Aluke gave a single nod, his face averted. He knew Daray was a selkie, and didn't like the fact that Cassie had bound herself to him. In fact, Aluke had tried to talk her out of the marriage, one afternoon at Covington's Market, saying creatures like selkies were attractive and interesting and had no feelings at all.

"I seen him," Aluke said, "talking to a whole bunch of his kind. They got something going, Cass."

Cassie crumpled the wax paper. On the beach, people were moving slowly, as if the darkness slowed them down.

"Maybe they've figured out a better way to clean this up," she said, remembering what little she had overheard of the conversation.

"I don't trust them like you do," Aluke said. "Those selkies— they're not like they seem, Cass."

"We've had this discussion," she said, turning the wax paper over and over in her fingers. "We can just agree to disagree."

"The thing is," Aluke said, "I'm a lot older than you. I seen what selkies can do. If they lost some magic, then I don't want to know what they were like before. When they work together, they can be pretty dang scary. If they're gonna try to get rid of this oil, they're gonna do it in a way that'll hurt us too."

Cassie looked at the round ball in her hand. "You got a place for garbage?" she asked.

He took the wax paper from her. "I know you don't want to believe me. I also know your mom's told you the same thing. If you find out something, you tell us, okay?"

Cassie bit her lower lip. She couldn't see Daray on the beach. She would recognize his form, his familiar movements, the way he tossed his long black hair over his shoulders.

He told her so many times that he liked humans, that he believed in them. He wouldn't suggest anything that would harm her or Anchor Bay.

"All right," she said, hoping her voice wouldn't betray her lie. "I'll tell you."

Aluke nodded. "I got some clothes in the truck. They're probably way too big, but they'll work better than that dress if you're heading to the beach. Otherwise, I can drive you to Cliffside House."

Athena had made noises about bringing Walters back to the house to impress him with it. *We show him the front area, serve him a nightcap, and send him on his way*, Athena said. *Maybe the house'll put the fear of God into him.*

Cassie had objected, but as usual, her mother hadn't listened. Cassie didn't want Walters to know about Cliffside House or its powers. She had a sense that he was looking for something to manipulate, some kind of advantage so that this wouldn't end badly for him, even though it looked like it was going to.

"Cass?" Aluke said.

"I don't really want to go home, thanks," she said. "But I will take the loan of the clothing, if you don't mind. Even though it'll get ruined, you know."

"That's what I brought 'em for," he said. "I figured other folks were going to need extra too."

She followed Aluke to the passenger side of the truck. He was a good man, and well-intentioned. She was sorry that she couldn't agree with him about the selkies. He had offered to tell her his stories, and she had made excuses every time.

Much as she trusted Aluke on most things, she didn't trust his opinion of the magical creatures taking refuge off Anchor Bay's shores. He hated most of them, spoke of wanting to crush the barnacle drivers that combed the bottom of his boat searching for food and of the afternoon he had caught the Fish of Many Wishes, only to refuse the wishes it offered.

Aluke had said he would have let it flop on the deck and suffocate, until he remembered that all protected creatures that lived in the water were amphibians—even the ones that looked like normal fish. He had wondered aloud about that—what did deep water creatures need with the ability to breathe air?—and no one had answered him.

It had been a speculation no one in Anchor Bay had wanted to make.

Cassie had heard variations on those conversations her whole life, and knew that the people who feared the FantasyLife in the protected harbor could not be trusted when it came to legends about the various creatures.

As well-intentioned as Aluke was, his attitude toward selkies and every other magical being in the sea was one of hatred. He would always see the dark side.

Aluke had a stack of clothing on the front seat, most of it suitable for the Salvation Army. Apparently, he had come here as prepared as he said he had. Cassie wondered what made him want to work in the dark, and then got the answer, filtered, directly from him.

He didn't want to see people looking at him, blaming him the way he blamed himself.

She wished she knew how to comfort him, but words were empty against such a strong belief. Maybe if he spent some time with Spark Walters, Aluke might change his mind about his own culpability.

Aluke handed her a flannel work shirt and a pair of Levi's that were stiff with mud. She took them gladly, along with the pair of gloves he handed to her.

"Thanks," she said. "I'll return them to you."

"Please don't," he said. "I brought them because they're not worth anything."

"Okay." She adjusted the clothes and put a hand on his arm. "I appreciate this."

"I know." He pushed the pile of clothing back and leaned on the seat, letting the interior light from the truck illuminate his face. It was a gentle face made harsh by years of exposure to salt water and the elements. "Do me a favor. When you see your boyfriend—"

"Husband," Cassie murmured.

Aluke didn't seem to notice.

"—tell him not to do anything rash. Tell him he's got you to think about. And tell him to make sure he knows all the implications before he listens to the rest of his group."

"Tribe," Cassie said.

This time, Aluke seemed to have heard. "Just tell him."

"I will," she said. That much she could promise. "Thanks again."

He closed the truck door. "Don't mention it."

Cassie started across the parking area. A cinderblock building with bathrooms on either side stood at the southern tip of the wayside. The coffee table that some local women had manned all day was still there, but no one sat behind it.

Cassie headed for the women's room, a two-stall that always smelled of disinfectant. Still, it would be the best place for her to change. She would just leave her clothes there, and pick them up when she was done.

The wind was starting to pick up. It was cold, and Cassie shivered. She'd never felt a wind with such bite to it, not in all her years in Anchor Bay.

Still, it was January, and she had seen pictures of snow on the beach. Her mother swore that Cassie had seen the snow, too, but she didn't remember—she had been much too young.

Snow, and ice, would probably be the worst thing right now. The oil would become viscous and even harder to get off the beach. Or maybe, if it was more sludgy, it would be easier.

Cassie let out a breath. She was out of her depth here, just like everyone else, and the only person who knew anything about oil probably wouldn't help any of them out.

The cinderblock restroom had a small wall that created a small hallway, a pathway into the ladies room. A dim bulb hung over the rusted steel door, revealing the filthy window and a pile of sand in the corner.

Cassie passed the faucet that children used in the summer to wash the sand off their feet. It seemed impossibly low to her, although she could remember using it more than once, whenever she had come to the beach by herself, when her mother hadn't allowed it.

Cassie pushed the door open. The interior smelled worse than she remembered. The smell of urine had overpowered the disinfectant long ago. The pungent stench of the oil had also gathered in here, making the bathroom a gathering place for foul odors.

The lights inside were dimmer than the one outside. A mirror, the silvering flaking off, hung over the sink. The concrete floor was wet, and smelled like it had never been dry. A single window was open several feet above Cassie's head. Through it, she could hear voices, the honking of a car horn, and the ocean.

Both stall doors were open, and Cassie took the one closest to the wall. She remembered seeing a hook in there that most women used for purses. She would use it for her dress.

The wind whistled through the window, and the voices grew louder—people were having an argument. She sighed. She had hoped that wouldn't happen, but she supposed it would be inevitable. Emotions were high right now; people were frightened. Eventually, that would find its way to the cleanup site, particularly at night, when the workers were tired.

She hung up the shirt and jeans, and reluctantly set the gloves on the back of the toilet. She hoped the slight dampness that seemed to cover everything wouldn't penetrate the gloves in the short time she would be in here.

Then she pulled her dress over her head, shivering in the cold and damp. The lights flickered, and the wind howled, and her shivering got worse.

A storm was blowing in, a rapidly moving storm. She wished she had listened to the weather predictions; then she would have been prepared for this. But she hadn't. And storms could come in quickly during the winter, particularly when the system had high winds.

She grabbed the flannel shirt and slipped it on. It smelled of cheap cigars, but it was warm. The shirt's ends went down to her knees, and she had to roll up the sleeves.

A gust of wind hit the building, and the lights flickered again. On the beach, she heard shouting—people warning each other to take cover.

Cassie had never heard that before. Coasties were a tough bunch; they usually didn't need warnings.

She slipped off her shoes, but kept standing on them so that her sock feet wouldn't touch the wet floor. Then she pulled on the jeans as fast as she could, losing her balance more than once and catching herself on the flimsy metal stall divider.

As she put her right shoe, a gust of wind hit the building so hard that the cinderblocks shuddered. The window rattled.

Cassie slipped on her other shoe. Then the rain started, pounding the ceiling as if rocks were falling from the sky. The window's rattling continued, and the rusted chain holding the window open vibrated dangerously.

The jeans were too long, but they fit loosely around her hips. She grabbed her shawl, rolled it up thin, and used it like a belt to hold the pants up. She had to pause to roll up the legs. The glass above her bounced as another gust hit.

Then the chain broke. The glass window fell next to Cassie and shattered. Instinctively, she closed her eyes. Glass shards pelted her, like tiny needles against the skin.

"Run!" a man outside yelled. "For God's sake! Run!"

And then the lights went out.

Cassie cursed, and felt for the door, finding her dress. It was still warm from her body, but the fabric was covered with more glass.

The wind was flowing in like a live thing, howling, knocking everything inside around as if the wind were trapped here with Cassie. She fumbled for the lock, found it, and unbolted it.

Except for the wind, there was only silence outside. She couldn't even hear the ocean—and that freaked her out. She hurried across the damp floor, her shoes splashing in water she hadn't even realized was there.

The moon was gone, and no light was filtering in. It was very dark. She could only guess where the exterior door was. She flailed for the exterior wall like a blind thing. Her knuckles scraped cinderblock, making her wince, but she kept her left hand on it, using it to navigate toward the door.

The silence had an eerie cast to it. She couldn't remember silence like this, ever. Even the wind seemed to have died down.

Then it hit the building with so much force that the walls shook.

She didn't know what it took to shake cinderblock. Her flannel shirt rose up as wind got underneath it, sending shivers through her.

She was breathing through her mouth, more rapidly than she had believed possible. Her heart was pounding, and she wasn't exactly sure why. She had lived through storms before—countless storms— and power outages and high winds. But something about this one felt wrong, unnatural.

Then she heard Daray's voice, as if it were coming from inside of him, as she had heard it just a few hours before: *They say the resulting storm will clean all foreign matter that we designate from the sea and its shore. We just need a place to dump it.*

"Oh, God," she whispered. His father had warned him against this. But maybe Daray had found a volunteer, someone who was willing to help him and the humans.

Someone willing to sacrifice himself to save Anchor Bay.

Daray wouldn't do it. He loved life too much. He and Cassie were together now, and they were going to have children and raise them to love the sea—

Still, she cast about in her mind for Daray, but she only got darkness. Her arm, the one supporting her weight against the wall, was shaking.

Maybe she was too frightened to find him. Maybe her powers didn't work in situations like this. Maybe something as simple as the storm was blocking her.

He was all right. He had to be. They were linked, heart and soul. She would know if something happened to him.

Wouldn't she?

The building shook again, and she thought she heard a scream from outside. Several screams. And then a roar—like a train engine, only worse. Like the helicopter, without the motor. A whup-whup-whupping sound that made her breathe even faster.

The ground rumbled, but this wasn't an earthquake. She would know an earthquake. It would feel different. It would feel like—

And then something slammed into the building. Water poured in through the open window, pushing the door open and shoving it against the wall. She heard the metal hit, felt the water, ice-cold around her ankles.

She screamed—not for help—but for Daray, and she wasn't even sure she opened her mouth to do it.

The water pushed at her from two different directions, and rose so fast that she had only a few seconds before she realized she'd better close her mouth and hold her breath.

She kept her hand on the cinderblock wall, but the water shoved her away. The entire bathroom filled, water pouring in from above and through the door.

She rose with it, trying to keep her head above water, until she crashed into the ceiling. The pain filtered through her, a sudden, unavoidable headache, but she didn't gasp aloud. Instead, she felt around in the icy water, hoping to find the top of the stalls.

If she found that, she could find the window and get out when the water receded, because it would recede. This had to be an awful wave, something that she had only heard about.

Not a tsunami. Those were caused by earthquakes and there had been no earthquake. But this was something else.

Something other.

...this is no ordinary storm, my son. It makes the storm that drowned the oil ship look like it was nothing...

Cassie found the metal top of the stall. It still held. But her oxygen was running out. Her lungs hurt, and she wanted to take a breath.

Daray! she screamed for him with her mind. *Daray, help me! Help me!*

But he didn't answer her. Maybe she had cast for him too late. Maybe he hadn't known the storm was coming either.

If he had had this idea, maybe other selkies had to.

She screamed for him one final time—*Daray!*—and then made herself focus on two things: holding her breath, and using the stalls to guide her toward the window.

The water's push didn't seem as strong now or maybe that was simply because she was submerged—the force of the water was going over her.

She flailed upwards with her right hand, keeping hold of the metal with her left—and her fingers broke through the water, their tips scraping the ceiling.

The water was receding, like she had hoped.

Instead of pushing herself forward, she just held on. Her lungs felt like they were going to burst. Stars flashed in front of her eyes.

Daray!

She kept her hand upward, felt the water go down to her wrist. Then she brought her hand down, and pushed herself up, like a kid trying to chin herself on monkey bars.

Her head burst through the water, slamming into the ceiling again, but she didn't care. She took a breath of icy air, and panted, glad for the oxygen, glad to be alive.

She was shivering—much too cold to make it long. The ocean was too cold for people without wetsuits.

Too cold and too powerful.

She frowned, thinking that the water felt like water, and realizing suddenly that that was odd. It should have been slightly thicker. She should have felt the oil on the surface, just like she had been feeling it for the past few days.

The wind continued to howl, but the water was draining. It had receded to her shoulders, and she didn't have to hold herself up any longer. She could tread water if she wanted to, but she didn't. She didn't want to tire herself. She had no idea if another wave would come.

She propelled herself, hand over hand, toward the window, and looked out. The moon had returned, which she hadn't expected, casting a thin light on the ocean before.

The ocean was phosphorescent again, the white, foaming surface of the waves glowing in the moonlight. The surf seemed outrageously high, and it came all the way to the base of the wayside. Water poured off the concrete parking lot as if it were part of a waterfall, draining into the sea.

The cars were gone, and so were the lights. She couldn't see the people either.

And to her right—movement. She looked, saw something she had never seen before, at least not outside of television news reports.

A funnel rising out of the water, black and dark and thick, whirling, whirling away from her. At first she thought it was a cloud, and then she realized it was the oil.

Oil, floating away, like it had a place to go.

A place to dump it.

"Daray," she whispered. But she didn't send. She didn't want him to feel her fear, not now, not when he might be behind this.

He probably thought she was safe at Arno's far from the beach, high enough to be protected.

The water poured out, suddenly, as if whatever was keeping it inside the building had moved. She flopped to the floor like a fish when the tide went out.

Her breath had been knocked out of her and she lay there for a moment, shivering in the cold.

But she hadn't been hurt. She was all right.

She got up, her clothes squishing as she moved, the additional material a weight that she hadn't expected. In vain, she reached behind the stall door, hoping against hope that her dress was still there, but of course it wasn't.

So she sloshed toward the door, which was still open, and stepped outside.

The wind was even stronger here, but it no longer howled. The train engine roar was gone, but there was still an underlying hum—the sound of the funnel, perhaps. She stepped around the concrete wall and stood in the rushing, ankle-deep water, somehow able to keep her balance.

The funnel still rose from the beach. Breezes caressed her, as if they were spun off from the greater wind that caused the funnel. She was alone in a parking lot that had been full not long before. She couldn't see anyone else. No other cars, no people.

Not even Aluke, whom she had somehow thought indestructible.

She looked behind her, saw the empty highway, and several shattered buildings. The cinderblock bathhouse and the elementary school were the only things inside of a mile still standing. Yet there was no debris in the water that ran toward the ocean.

The ground had been cleared of all human contact—all but hers.

Her throat was dry. She was shaking, but not so much with the cold. Had Daray known where she was? She had found his mind earlier without him noticing. Had he found hers as well, protected her as best as possible?

The funnel rose, its end looking like a little tail, wagging in the breeze. The wind gust the funnel created slammed her into the building, and then disappeared, like the last taunt of a bully.

Cassie remained against the cinderblock, staring up at the clear night sky. The wind was gone again, everything was calm. The water dripped off the edge of the wayside, but there was no longer an ankle-deep rush toward the ocean.

The waves were still angry, still high, but they weren't coming in as deep. The ocean was receding into itself, returning to normal, as if the last few days had never been.

Making it like the accident had never happened.

She blinked, colder than she had been in her life. She stepped forward, hoping she would find someone else alive, when the wind kicked once more.

Only this time, it came to her from the ocean, a powerful gust carrying something in it. The something whirled like a leaf trapped in a breeze.

And the gust let up, and the something dropped out of the sky, landing with a thud in front of her.

It was a body.

She crouched, her breathing shallow again, as if she knew before she actually saw. Her hands reached forward like they belonged to someone else, her body moved with them, and she saw—

Daray, eyes closed, face so pale that it didn't look like his anymore. His body was arched in an unusual position, his head turned awkwardly.

She touched his face. His skin was cold, too cold to be natural. His skin had always been warmer than hers—compensating, he said, for the lack of a pelt.

There was a shadow on his neck, a scarf, something that made it dark. She touched it—

—and cried out.

Her fingers had found jagged flesh, a bit of cartilage, maybe bone. And cold. Deep cold.

He was dead. And bloodless. Completely drained. His throat cut, his blood pouring into the sea.

The storm had come like his father had predicted. Come, worse than ever. And Daray hadn't listened to him.

Daray had saved Cassie's beach, her home, just like she had wanted. Only not like this.

Not like this.

Daray! Daray!

But there was emptiness where her husband should have been—a coldness where there had once been heat.

Noooo, she cried, and tumbled against him—against what was left of him, between the cinderblock, the concrete, and the water trickling back to the sea.

PART VIII

AND A LITTLE CHILD SHALL LEAD THEM

FORTY-ONE

Anchor Harbor Wayside

Grandma Cassie stood near the road, her back hunched, her mouth open. She held a strand of hair in her right hand, and twisted it like she couldn't even feel the pain.

Emily bit her lower lip. Mommy had a grip on her hand, a tight grip, and Emily knew she wasn't going to let go. Great-grandma Athena was talking to the weird man who thought dead things were cool, talking about old history and oil and the *Walter Aggie*.

Great-grandma Athena kept saying it didn't matter, and the weird man said it did, that the scientific evidence provided that it did, and Great-grandma Athena said that science didn't know everything, and the weird man was quoting something—*more things in your heaven and earth, Horatio*—or something like that. Emily didn't really pay attention.

She didn't really care. What she cared about was Grandma Cassie, and nobody else seemed to.

Grandma Cassie looked like she had been stabbed in the heart, and Emily couldn't tell why.

"Em?" her mother said.

"Look at Grandma," Emily said.

But Mommy looked at Great-grandma Athena, and Emily wanted to stop her, but she didn't know how, without taking her gaze off Grandma Cassie. And Emily felt like if she stopped looking at Grandma Cassie, Grandma Cassie would fall over into the road, and maybe even die.

"Your mom," Emily said.

Mommy was still looking at Great-grandma Athena though, and she started to say something, but Emily couldn't hear it, because there was a big rushing noise in her ears.

Child. Daray's granddaughter. Look at me.

Emily willed herself not to look. She kept staring at Grandma Cassie, who hadn't moved.

Look at me.

Now Emily recognized the voice. It belonged to her great-aunt, the selkie Roseluna that her Buckingham relatives hated, the woman who had tried to hurt her grandmother.

Emily let go of her mom's hand and put her fingers in her ears.

Silly child. I'm not in your ears.

Emily almost looked. But she didn't. Still, she could see sideways out of the corners of her eyes, see Roseluna standing next to the reporter lady that Mommy had yelled at.

Come with me, Emily. We need you. You'll save us all.

"Emily?" Mommy crouched in front of her, blocking Emily's view of Grandma Cassie, and put her hands on Emily's shoulders. "Emily, are you okay?"

Emily craned around her, trying to see Grandma Cassie, but she couldn't. For a minute, she thought Grandma Cassie had disappeared.

Emily, please. Come with us. All that magic they don't want you to use, all those things that are part of you, belong with us.

"Emily, what's wrong, honey?"

Great-grandma Athena stopped talking to the weird man, and they stepped in front of her too.

Emily shook herself away from Mommy, and started to run across the parking lot. Emily could see Grandma Cassie now, swaying like she was in a great wind.

"Grandma!" Emily screamed, but Grandma Cassie didn't seem to hear her.

Instead, Grandma Cassie toppled forward, hitting the concrete with a great smack. Emily ran faster, and now Mommy was beside her and Great-grandma Athena too, and all the other people were looking and talking and pointing and giving orders.

Except Roseluna, who was watching Emily.

Come with me. No one will notice. Not right now.

And Emily couldn't help it. She looked at Roseluna and felt a joy that she hadn't felt before, a sense of belonging, of knowing who and what she was—

Then she tripped against a parking block and fell forward, skinning her knees. The pain made tears come to her eyes, but that feeling left. It hadn't come from inside her anyway. It had come from Roseluna.

It's how you'll feel if you come with me.

Emily shook her head, and then Mommy took her arm, and said, "Baby, are you okay?" and Emily said no but Grandma's worse, and Mommy helped her up and they all ran to Grandma Cassie's side.

By the time they got there, Roseluna was gone.

But I'll send for you, she said as if she were getting very far away. *When the time is right, we'll be together. It's the only way.*

Emily wanted to tell her no, but she didn't know how. And Emily was afraid that if she couldn't say no, Roseluna would take her against her will, and she would go somewhere else, and be something else, like Great-grandma Athena thought she was, like everyone would know she was, if they found out she wasn't totally human.

But neither was Mommy, and Mommy didn't seem to hear it. She had a hold of Emily and was helping her up, and people were running to Grandma Cassie, and there was shouting about an ambulance, and that would make everything all right, right? Because it had to.

It had to.

Because Emily couldn't take anymore.

FORTY-TWO

Anchor Harbor Wayside

Lyssa helped her injured daughter over to Cassie. Emily's palms were scraped, even though she didn't seem to notice, and her knees were bleeding. She limped as she walked, her eyes searching the crowd across the street as if she had seen a ghost.

Lyssa's heart was pounding. Her mother lay in a crumpled heap on the curb, Gabriel beside her, his hand on her neck, checking her pulse. Lyssa's mouth went dry.

What if Cassie was dead? What if her heart, stressed by that too-thin frame, gave out? What would Lyssa do without her? She would have no one to push against, no one to worry about, no one to fear.

She reached Cassie's side as Athena did.

"She's alive," Gabriel said.

Athena let out a sharp breath, like a sigh of relief. Lyssa reached for her grandmother's hand, linking herself between her daughter and her grandmother, the circle of her family minus one.

"But I have no idea what caused this. I—"

Denne reached them, crouched beside Gabriel, and gave Cassie a quick examination. Lyssa watched him open her mother's eyes, run his fingers along her face and neck, check her head for lumps. He also counted her pulse.

Lyssa had forgotten that coroners were real doctors too. They just practiced on the dead rather than the living.

"I think we can move her," he said, his tone businesslike.

Lyssa stepped back, along with Athena and Emily. Denne and Gabriel picked up Cassie and lifted her into the parking lot. Gabriel cradled her head, as if she were his mother instead of Lyssa's.

Emily was watching, eyes wide. Lyssa wrapped an arm around her, wondering if her daughter was remembering that horrible day when Reginald died.

Lyssa hoped not. She didn't want all of Emily's thoughts of death to be connected to her father.

"What happened?" Denne asked Gabriel.

"Damned if I know," he said. "I just saw her crumple to the ground."

Athena's expression mirrored Emily's. Lyssa wouldn't have thought that they resembled each other, but something in their eyes, in the way they held their bodies, made it clear that they were related.

"She been having health problems, Athena?" Denne asked.

"She doesn't eat enough," Athena said. "But she never did."

"Yeah," Denne said. "I would call her anorectic. Amazing she's made it this long then. Prolonged starvation puts pressure on all the internal organs."

"She's not starving," Emily said. "She just fainted."

"It's all right, honey," Denne said. "I'll call an ambulance—"

"No!" Emily said. "She doesn't need one. She's all right."

Lyssa glanced at Athena, who shrugged.

"I don't think we should discount what she says." Athena spoke in a low tone.

Lyssa nodded, then put her hands on Emily's shoulder. "What do you know, baby?"

Gabriel's blue eyes took in everything. He was frowning as he watched Lyssa talk to Emily. Denne wasn't paying attention at all. He was still examining Cassie, but he had also taken a cell phone out of his pocket

"That lady," Emily said, and looked across the street. Lyssa followed her gaze. The reporter was still there with her cameraman, filming the whole scene.

"The reporter?"

"No, Great-aunt Roseluna."

Lyssa frowned. She didn't remember any Aunt Roseluna. She didn't remember any aunts at all.

But Athena crouched next to them. "What about her?"

Apparently Athena knew who she was.

"She was making Grandma mad. Then she got in her head, showed her some stuff, and stayed there." Emily shot a frightened glance at Athena. "She found it."

"Found what?" Lyssa asked.

"That place inside Grandma. The place that makes her so unhappy. The one where she doesn't want to live anymore."

Lyssa started. She never knew that there was such a place inside her mother, but it made sense. Cassie had never taken care of herself —rarely ate, often took risks that seemed silly to Lyssa, even to the young Lyssa who took quite a few unnecessary risks herself.

"She has a place like that?" Lyssa turned toward Athena.

Athena's patrician features were softened by compassion. "Lyssa, sweetheart. You're the only reason that she's still here. If she hadn't been pregnant with you when Daray died, she probably would have followed him."

"Followed him?" Lyssa repeated. "You mean she would have killed herself?"

Athena nodded, then put a hand on Cassie's long dark hair. "She was never the same after that."

"After he died?" Lyssa asked.

But Athena didn't answer.

"What exactly happened?" Lyssa asked her daughter. "What did that woman do to Mother?"

"Made her remember," Emily said. "I got parts, but I couldn't stop it. Grandma was too far away."

Emily's link to her grandmother was strong. Lyssa wasn't sure she liked that. She wasn't sure about anything that had happened since she returned to Anchor Bay.

"Why would she do that?" Lyssa asked, and the question wasn't just directed at Emily. She was asking everyone and no one.

"If what the little girl says is true," Denne said, "that woman— your aunt?—wanted to disable Cassie."

"I don't have an aunt," Lyssa said. "My mother was an only child."

"But your father wasn't," Athena said.

"Some selkie's been going after my mother?" Lyssa asked.

"She was across the street," Emily said. "She was at lunch."

"Mother had lunch with her?"

"It's a long story," Athena said, "and I don't think we have time to discuss it."

Gabriel glanced over his shoulder, as if he were expecting someone.

"You want to call the ambulance or should I?" Denne asked Gabriel.

Then Cassie's hand reached up and grabbed Denne's phone. "No ambulance."

"I'm sorry, Cassandra, but you could have a concussion at worst or something else. And if the little girl is right—"

"Emily," Cassie said. "My Emily."

Lyssa felt her breath catch. Her mother had never spoken about Lyssa like that. Not with such protectiveness, such love.

"And she is right," Cassie said. "I made a mistake."

"If someone got in your head, it's not your fault." Athena's tone was brusque. She knelt beside Cassie, so that Cassie could see her closely.

Lyssa couldn't remember ever seeing Athena look so vulnerable.

"It's my fault," Cassie said. "I let Roseluna there. She was telling me something I thought I wanted to know. I let down my guard, and she did this."

Cassie seemed to be getting stronger with each sentence.

"Did what?" Lyssa asked.

Cassie turned toward her, tears in her dark eyes. "Made me

489

remember the day your dad died. The day I realized everyone was right. You see, Lys, it was never about me or this great love I'd made up. Your father wasn't human, even though I wanted to pretend he was. He wasn't capable of loving me. He just used me, and when I wasn't important anymore, he took matters into his own hands, without consulting me. Without even saying goodbye."

Her voice broke.

"Cassie, it's past," Athena said.

"You've always said that." Cassie wiped at her face like a little child who didn't want anyone to know she was in pain. "And you've always been wrong. No one has gotten past that day. Not me, not the selkies, not even Anchor Bay."

"What day?" Gabriel asked Lyssa.

"The day of the great storm," she said.

"Right after the *Walter Aggie* went down." Denne sounded awestruck. "The day the storm cleaned the beaches."

"And destroyed most of Anchor Bay," Cassie said. "A lot of people died when that wave hit. John Aluke, Michael Sheehan, Andrea Thomesan. Friends."

"And my dad," Lyssa said.

Cassie shook her head. "He caused it."

Lyssa sank to the curb. This wasn't the story she had heard all her life. The story she had heard had been that her father—her marvelous, perfect, heroic father—had died while working on the oil cleanup on the beach. The storm had come in too fast for anyone to survive it. Her mother had lived through it only because she had been changing clothes in the rest area, and that building, one of the few left standing, protected her.

"Don't be silly," Lyssa heard herself say, using her mother's perfect detached tones, the tones she had grown up listening to. "No one can cause a storm."

"Selkies can," Athena said.

"I've seen it," Denne said, apparently not realizing this was a family conversation. "In Whale Cove, four years ago. A selkie staying at the Sand Castle Hotel decided—long story, short version—decided to get revenge on the hotel's owner for serious crimes his son had committed. The selkie slit her wrists and jumped off the balcony into the sea. The resulting storm destroyed all the homes along the D River as well as the Sand Castle—and the weird thing was, no other towns on the coast got hit by a storm that day. In fact, they were in sunshine."

"Like here," Lyssa said. She remembered that part of the story too. Everyone talked about the beautiful clear night that the rest of Oregon enjoyed—how clear the stars were, how bright the moon was —and yet the storm that hit Anchor Bay was so powerful that it created a tidal wave that leveled the entire downtown.

Denne nodded.

Cassie was sitting up, her chin on her knees. She was wiping her face with one hand, and with the other, she held on to Emily. Lyssa didn't remember when Emily had moved away from her to go to her grandmother, but the two of them seemed to be bonded in a way that Lyssa simply didn't understand.

"Why would this woman go after Mother?" Lyssa asked Denne.

He shrugged. "I don't know your family's history with the selkies."

"It's a long one," Athena said. "And not always pretty."

Emily put her arms around her grandmother and leaned against her thigh.

"But the question really isn't a matter of history," Athena said. "It's a matter for now."

"What does that mean?" Lyssa asked.

"A vision disabled Cassie only once before," Athena said, "and I've always wondered about it."

Cassie looked over her shoulder at her mother. "The night we could have stopped the *Walter Aggie* from going aground."

"Yes." Athena gave Cassie a small smile. Tentative, just the way that Lyssa was feeling.

Gabriel was watching closely, occasionally glancing at Denne. But Denne didn't seem to notice. He seemed completely involved in this conversation, as if discussing the past had some meaning to him.

"You think this—person—tapped into Mom's memories to disable her?" Lyssa asked.

"That's what Emily said." Athena looked at Emily, a frown on her face.

"That's what Dr. Denne said," Lyssa corrected. "Emily just discussed the place that selkie touched."

"To stop Grandma," Emily said, still leaning on Cassie's hip. "Grandma didn't like what they're going to do, so Roseluna wanted Grandma out of the way."

"What are they doing?" Lyssa asked.

"What Daray didn't manage the first time," Cassie said, her voice thick with unshed tears, "although he came close."

Lyssa shook her head. "I wasn't there, Mom."

"Destroying Anchor Bay, honey," Cassie said with sigh. "And all the Buckinghams with it."

FORTY-THREE

Anchor Harbor Wayside

Gabriel shoved his hands in his back pockets and turned away from the Buckinghams. Lyssa looked stricken, her eyes large on her narrow face. Emily merely seemed exhausted. Athena still crouched, a frown creasing her forehead, as if she were trying to put pieces together. And Cassie—Cassie seemed the same, fragile, broken, like a small bird that had never recovered from a damaging flight.

He wasn't sure he wanted to know this much about someone else's family, for any reason. And he wasn't sure what it meant to him.

He took a step down, onto the highway, saw that the slime trail had tracked a good fifteen feet in either direction, moved by tires as they crossed over the mound of goo. He was going to need to get someone to clean all that up, as well as deal with the mess that was forming around him.

If Emily's accusations were true—and after all the strange things Gabriel had seen, he had no reason to doubt her—then he was going to have to stop these selkies, and he wasn't sure how. State and county laws—human laws—didn't account for murder by magic. They certainly wouldn't accommodate attempted murder by magic, and he wasn't sure he would be able to prove conspiracy to commit murder either, not with a jury or even a judge who hadn't spent a long time in Seavy County.

Not that it mattered. Even if he could arrest these creatures, he wasn't sure his jail would hold them. Or if just being in the jail would stop them.

And that was the kicker. How did a man like him, a man who dealt with routine traffic stops, drug busts, and the occasional drowning, handle something this large, something so beyond him? He had no magical skills. He only had two weapons: his mind and his gun—and he had never fired his gun on the job, not once in all his years.

Nicole Drapier's cameraman was still filming. She was standing off to the side, her head tilted sideways, and Gabriel wondered if she was taping the Buckinghams' conversation with one of those parabolic microphones.

There was only one way to find out.

He started across the highway, only to be forced back by a horn sounding just a few feet away.

Gabriel turned, startled to see a stretch limo cross the goo line. He would have walked right in front of the vehicle, if it hadn't honked at him.

That wasn't like him. Usually he paid more attention.

Usually he had a lot less on his mind.

He stepped back beside the curb, and watched as the limo pulled into the wayside. Another limo followed directly behind it. They crossed the empty parking spaces until they reached his patrol car, still parked diagonally on the sand.

"Shit!" he whispered. He had forgotten all about the other player, the one arriving just a little while ago. Samuel Walters, Emily's grandfather.

It was old home week for the Buckinghams, and that couldn't be good.

Gabriel started toward the limos, but Athena stood and caught his arm in the same movement. She was surprisingly strong—not just for a woman her age, but for anyone. If the power in those fingers extended to the rest of her body, Athena could probably take him in a fight.

"What is this?" she asked.

"In the excitement, I forgot to tell you," he said.

The first limo's back door opened, and a woman dressed in a black business suit got out. She tugged her knee-length skirt down so that she didn't reveal any thigh as she stepped into the wind. She was short, curly-haired, and wore glasses. In her left hand, she held a briefcase.

The other limo was disgorging short people in black business suits as well. All of them were expensively dressed and seemed astonishingly out of place on the Oregon Coast.

"What is this?" Athena repeated.

Gabriel swallowed hard, not sure how to tell her after all this afternoon's revelations.

Then a man got out of the first limo. He was taller than the others, but heavy-set in the way of old football players who could handle a mean game of touch. He was completely bald, his perfectly shaped skull shining in the sunlight.

He wore a denim shirt and jeans, but on his fingers were gold rings with glittering jewels. The blue of his clothes accented the blueness of his eyes, but they were still pale, almost clear—making him seem otherworldly somehow.

Samuel Walters, who someone had told to come to the beach instead of the office.

Gabriel's stomach clenched. Next to him, Athena gasped. Cassie rose to her feet, followed by Lyssa.

"Son of a bitch," Athena whispered. "Son of a goddamn bitch."

But Lyssa stepped in front of her, grabbing her grandmother's arm and forcing her to hold on to Emily.

Lyssa's chin was raised, and she moved with an aggressiveness that Gabriel had never seen from her.

She pointed at Walters. "You have no right to be here. You never visited her, you never saw her, you never even sent her Christmas presents, for chrissakes. She's my daughter and you'll have nothing to do with her."

Walters grinned. His smile was wide, infectious, but it didn't reach his eyes.

"Well, hello to you too, Lysandra. It's been a very, very long time."

"Don't try to charm me," Lyssa said. "After everything you've done, after all you've been—"

"Everything I've done?" Walters leaned inside the limousine and grabbed a hat, a soft brown cowboy hat with tooled silver around the brim.

He set the hat on his head, making him look a lot younger. Even though he hadn't said a word since he reached for the hat, he still had everyone's attention.

"Missy." His voice was easygoing, taking each word as if he had an hour instead of a few minutes. "I'm not the one who married an innocent boy out of revenge and then got his own child to murder him."

Lyssa lunged for him, and Gabriel grabbed her around the waist, pulling her back.

"That's what he wants," Gabriel said. He'd seen enough men like Walters to know. Walters liked to bait. The problem was, a lot of what these people said was true. That was why the baiting worked.

"I loved Reginald," Lyssa said. Her entire body was tense, lean, muscular. If she twisted at all, Gabriel wouldn't be able to keep his hold on her.

"And that's why you divorced him." Walters took off the hat, brushed his hand over it as if he had encountered dust, and then replaced the hat on his head. "Now if you all'll excuse me, I didn't come here for some bizarre Buckingham family reunion."

Lyssa got even tenser. Gabriel held her close, trying to calm her as best he could without words.

Cassie stepped up beside Emily. Cassie seemed healthier than she had before she fell. Her face was tilted slightly, as if she were trying to reconcile the man before her with the one she remembered.

"Spark Walters," she said, her voice still husky from all the emotion she'd expressed earlier.

"Cassandra Buckingham?" A flush reached Walters' cheeks,

surprising Gabriel. He didn't think men like that blushed. "You look same as ever, darling. Still the most beautiful thing I've ever seen."

"You have no right to talk to her," Athena said.

Gabriel turned toward her. Her back was rigid, her chin up. She still held Emily's hand, but she looked like a mighty warrior who had rescued a child, instead of a great-grandmother trying to comfort one.

"I came for the mayor and the sheriff," Walters said. "I believe I have business with them, Athena. Unless you still run this town."

Emily held up her free hand, and Cassandra took it.

In that moment, there was a flare of white so bright it blinded Gabriel. He blinked and—

FORTY-FOUR

The Devil's Goblet

It was nighttime, full dark, and Gabriel was standing on the Devil's Goblet. The lava rock was slick with surf, booming below. The moon shone brightly above him, casting an eerie silver light that made the ocean, near the horizon line, glow.

The glow vanished near the shore. He wanted to turn, to see what was going on inside the bay, but he couldn't. He was standing in an open doorway, his hands braced on either side.

His perspective was off, as if he had shrunk a few inches. His hands didn't look like his either. They were long and slender and lined with age, female and familiar. He recognized the ring on the right hand—a diamond that glittered in an Art Deco setting. An unusual ring that only Athena wore.

Athena. He was Athena, looking out of Athena's eyes.

And as he realized this, his consciousness slipped back and he could smell petroleum in the air, mixed with the faint scent of cigarette smoke and alcohol coming from his—her—clothes.

She was wearing a dress and high heels, which made climbing on the rocks awkward. But she had lost track of Walters—it had been a mistake to bring him to Cliffside House. He had excused himself fifteen minutes ago, ostensibly searching for a restroom, and she hadn't seen him since.

Some sort of instinct brought Athena down the back steps between the two towers to the exit that led onto the base of the Devil's Goblet, where she had been the night of the storm.

As her eyes adjusted, she saw two men there, one sitting on the highest lava rock, arms clasped around his legs, the other climbing toward him.

The climbing man—tall, thin—was wearing a white suit that glowed in the moonlight. *Walters.* Athena took a step forward, then cursed, hating girl-shoes. She kicked them inside, and stepped on the cold rocks in her nylon-covered feet.

"The Buckingham ladies have been telling me about all the magic here," Walters said. "They think I'm some dumb buck who doesn't get what they're talking about, so they talk in code. But I know. I don't know what you are, but I know what you can do."

The man on the rock looked up, and Athena recognized his face. *Daray.* The moon caught the planes and hollows of it, making him look older than he was.

"You know nothing," Daray said.

"I know how magic's tied to the land. We got our own strange group of creatures in the Panhandle, and they give us our own special gifts. You can't just take oil from the land, you know. It ain't just blind luck and careful drilling. You got to find out, figure out, where the stuff is, and it ain't all geologists and rock formations. Some families got a gift for it, and along with that gift, they maybe get a few others."

His right hand was in the pocket of that suit. He was holding something—a knife?—and was turned slightly so that Daray couldn't see that hand.

Athena crawled over the rocks, her feet slipping.

"I was thinking," Walters said. "You gonna be able to get one of your people to bleed into the water?"

"What?"

Daray sounded as shocked as Athena felt.

"Because if you are, I know where that oil should go. We got another tanker down San Francisco way, empty, heading out to sea again soon. We just gather up that oil, send it to the ship—that ain't too far for you, is it?—and everything'll be just the same, like I promised that pretty Cassie Buckingham. No harm done."

"No harm?" Daray stood. He was taller and thinner than Walters, but he didn't look as solid. "What of the selkie who dies?"

"Small sacrifice, ain't it, to save what you all're calling a refuge?" Walters stood higher on the rock than Daray. He was braced better too.

Athena clambered toward them, her hands gripping sharp rock, her feet slipping on the wet. She wasn't going to reach them, and she was afraid if she shouted, she would only be a distraction.

"You'll get your refuge," Walters said, "I'll get to impress one of the prettiest girls I ever seen, and not a drop of oil'll be lost, except for the stuff in the Walter Aggie *herself. We'll sink that, so no press knows, and then the town is saved, there'll be tourists again, and everything'll be perfect, just like it was supposed to be."*

"You want to impress Cassie?" Daray sounded shocked. "Killing a selkie won't impress her, you idiot. She's my wife."

"So you're the one she's sort-of married to," Walters said. "I wondered when I saw her track you. Mind-sharing—rather intimate, don't you think? I mean, even for married people?"

"What're you talking about?"

"When you spoke to that old man, and he told you not to create a storm? She was with you. It was fascinating, really, but I thought she was just trolling for minds. I had an uncle who used to do that. Learned a lot of business things that way."

Athena reached the top of one of the stones, and balanced precariously on the peak. The two men were still in the same position. Daray didn't seem to realize he was at a disadvantage.

"So Cassie didn't tell you anything," Daray said.

"Not directly." From the sound of Walters' voice, Athena could tell he was smiling—that horrible infectious grin. "But I learned enough. Now. What do I gotta do to make sure that oil goes away?"

"We have to have a meeting of the council," Daray said. "It's complicated. We have a government just like you do."

"No," Walters said. "It ain't just like ours. It ain't anything near so powerful."

Then he took a step forward, grabbed Daray under the chin, and slipped his hand out of his pocket. It was all one fluid movement.

Athena didn't even get a chance to yell a warning.

Daray grabbed at him, trying to pull Walters over his shoulder, but he couldn't get a grip. Walters had his chin tight, pulling it upward so that it had to hurt.

Athena scrambled over the rocks, feeling them cut her legs, her feet, her hands. She didn't care. She was hurrying to Daray. She had to reach him before—

Walters took the knife and slashed it across Daray's throat. Blood spurted toward the ocean as if someone had opened a spigot.

"It's not just because you have a pretty wife," Walters said as he dragged Daray toward the sea. "It's also because you happened to be convenient."

Then Walters swung his entire body around and sent Daray over the edge of the Goblet, into the frothing seawater below.

Athena propelled herself toward Walters. She reached him while he was still bending over the edge, and shoved him as hard as she could.

He slipped off the edge, and bounced, screaming as he fell.

Athena didn't watch him land in the ocean. She turned her back and picked her way toward Cliffside House.

If he didn't fall into the ocean right away, he would when the storm hit. He would die horribly, more horribly than Daray had.

Athena half-wished she would too. Then she wouldn't have to tell her daughter that Daray had died, and she had failed to prevent it.

FORTY-FIVE

Anchor Harbor Wayside

The images winked out, vanishing like the picture in an old vacuum tube television set. For a moment, the world was black.

Cassie stood completely still, feeling little Emily's hand in her own. Emily, who was holding on to Cassie and Athena. That was how Cassie got lost in Athena's memories, in Athena's world.

Thirty-four years, and her mother hadn't said a word. Even after Spark Walters had somehow survived.

Even when Reginald Walters wanted to marry Daray's daughter.

Even then.

The darkness faded and gradually the wayside returned. The first thing Cassie saw was Spark Walters, standing in front of his limousine, looking like a caricature of his former self. Balding, big boots, big belt buckle, ten-gallon hat, and more jewelry on his fingers than Cassie had ever owned.

Rich beyond her imaginings. Married, with children, grandchildren, a life.

And she had been here, beside the beach, mourning Daray, and fearing—knowing—that all his words of love had been a lie.

They hadn't.

She's my wife.

He had meant everything he had ever said to her.

Walters looked wild-eyed at the minions beside him. They were looking a bit wild-eyed themselves.

Gabriel still held Lyssa against him. He said softly, "What the hell was that?"

And that was when Cassie knew—knew deep down—that everyone in the parking lot had seen this last vision. Athena and Walters's secret—the murder of Cassie's husband.

Athena looked paler than Cassie had ever seen her. Cassie couldn't even face her. Instead, Cassie dropped Emily's hand and started across the parking lot toward Walters.

"You fucking bigoted son of a bitch," Cassie said, "what did you want with me? You were already married."

Walters's pale eyes widened slightly, and Cassie sensed fear. But he smiled. God, how she hated that smile.

"Divorced, darling," he said. "See? You never did time to find out about me. Esme's my second wife. Looks a little like you—"

Cassie screamed and lunged for him, and this time, no one stood in her way. Walters held out a hand to stop her, but she slipped past it, shoving his chest as hard as she could.

She couldn't even budge him.

He grabbed her, held her close, just like Gabriel was holding Lyssa. He stank of cologne and cigars, his meaty body strong against her own.

She pounded him with her fists, and he grabbed them, holding them tight, pulling her as close to him as she could get. She looked up in his face, saw broken capillaries under the skin, the nose wider than it should have been, bloodshot eyes. So, life hadn't been kind to him after all. He had to anesthetize himself to make it through.

"Like what you see, Cassandra?" Walters asked quietly.

"How did you survive?" she asked. "How did you make it through that storm when it nearly killed me and Anchor Bay?"

"You know," he said, "back in Texas, we got ourselves ground pixies. Kinda like ground squirrels, only with brains. They got a little government too, and a society that sort of works for them. But they don't got any way of investigating things that happen to their clan. They just got rumor and innuendo and—"

"How did you survive after you murdered my husband?" she screamed, pushing herself at him.

"If you're gonna get all riled, Cassie, I'm not gonna tell you."

She whirled, pulling his left hand still holding her right fist down across her chest. Her other fist remained in the air, his hand clutching it. Then she leaned forward and bit his arm hard enough to draw blood.

"Stop it," he hissed. "Stop it."

He slid his arm down, then squeezed her left fist. His minions were watching from a distance, looking terrified. Gabriel had let go of Lyssa. He was coming close, as if he were going to get involved. So was Lyssa, and so, surprisingly, was Athena.

Emily stood behind them, her skin ashen, her little body shaking. Cassie had gotten words from her. Words that weren't her own.

Roseluna, begging Emily to help her.

"You're a tiny little thing," Walters said, "and I could break you like a twig, but I don't want to, Cassie. You and I, we could've been friends in other circumstances. And I learned from you. You were right that night. It's not acceptable to spill oil in our precious waters, because you can't clean it up. You can't make places what they were before. Unless you got some pull. Your husband, he gave me pull."

"I asked how you survived," Cassie said. "I already know how you murdered my husband."

"Well," Walters spoke in her ear like they were lovers, "I combined what I learned back home from the ground pixies, and what I saw when I followed your mind out of that restaurant that night. Your husband was talking to another selkie, and I figured after that conversation, they'd believe he offed himself to save the humans. Those selkies would never find out, and they could help me—help all of us, which they did."

"You called Daray's father to you?"

"I don't know who all came, but there was a bunch of them. They was already swimming to shore to do what they could, then they saw me. And I told them I knew where the oil could go. They made me promise to sink the ship, and never ever let anything like that happen again. I promised, Cass, and kept that promise. Till a few days ago, when the *Walter Aggie* started leaking all over again."

"The *Walter Aggie*'s not leaking," Cassie said. "They brought you here to kill you with the rest of us."

"What are you talking about, darling?"

"The selkies," she said, "they finally figured out what you did. And they want their revenge, Walters. On all of us. But mostly on you. The woman who called you, she's a selkie, educated on land. She knows all that stuff you thought they'd never know. And more."

Gabriel took another step toward them. "Let her go, Mr. Walters, and I'll make sure that nothing'll happen to either of you. I'm Gabriel Schelling. I'm the sheriff here. You were supposed to meet with me anyway."

"This ain't your fight, son," Walters said. "Back off."

Gabriel had given Cassie the moment she had needed. She finally had a plan.

"Let me go, Spark," she said, "and I'll show you that conversation I just had with Roseluna. You'll see it just like we saw the night on the Devil's Goblet. You'll see what they're trying to do."

"You did that?" Walters asked.

"Your granddaughter did it," Lyssa said, her mouth curled with distaste. "I had no clue that she got some of her powers from you. If you had just said something—"

"I already told you," Walters said, spitting as he spoke. Cassie could feel his hatred for her daughter as if it were a live thing. "I didn't want my son to marry you. I did everything I could to stop it."

"Maybe if you had explained—"

"Your grandmother could have explained," Walters said. "Obviously, she didn't either."

Lyssa looked at Athena, who bowed her head. Cassie was losing her moment. She could feel it. And this might be her only chance.

"It's too late for accusations. It's the selkies that are the problem. Spark, I can show you—"

"I thought only Emily could show me."

So he knew his granddaughter's name. Had he been keeping track of her? Probably. He struck Cassie as the kind of man who would keep track of everything that concerned him—even when he said he wasn't.

"Where do you think she learned how?" Cassie asked. "It's easier if I put a finger on each temple."

Athena's mouth opened, then closed, as if she thought the better of saying anything. Emily put her hands over her lips, a gesture that seemed involuntary.

Only Lyssa didn't move. Lyssa was watching Cassie as if she had never seen her before.

"That didn't happen with the previous vision," Walters said. "No one touched me."

"Because it was the three of us—Emily, me, and Mother. It was like a live broadcast. But this is just me. Unless you want Emily closer."

That last was a bluff. Cassie didn't want Emily any closer at all, and she had a hunch he didn't either.

"No," he said, and he loosened his grip on her, tentatively, as if he were afraid she was going to attack him again.

But her fists weren't the strongest thing about her. Cassie had never had real physical abilities, not like her mother. But it wasn't physical strength that mattered any more.

That was why the selkies were trying to neutralize her. They feared her mind, not her body.

She turned in Walters's arms, a parody of a lover's move. His face, its redness and fleshiness still shocking to her, seemed impassive. But his eyes were alive. They held a reservation and maybe even fear.

He wasn't the only one who could hide his emotions. She gave him a small smile, the one she gave tourists to calm them when she did her fake readings.

Then she put her index fingers on his temples. If she moved slightly, put her thumbs there, she could push...

But she didn't. Instead, she said, just as softly as she had smiled, "Ready?"

"This isn't some kind of weird revenge, is it?" he said. "Because if it is, then—"

"Selkies," she said. "We take care of them first. Then we figure out what to do about you."

A bit too much anger escaped through her voice, and he pulled back, but she caught him with both hands and held his head firmly.

He tried to yank away, and she held, but she wouldn't be able to work him.

Then Athena's hands covered her own, slipping past them to the back of his head so that Athena wasn't touching Cassie at all.

"Now, daughter," Athena said.

And Cassie closed her eyes, sending her consciousness into his brain, drilling a hole as she went, separating his powers—and he had a few, mostly parasitical, piggybacking on other people's—learned at his own father's knee. That ability, the secret to Walters Petroleum, the secret to their empire, their ability to use other people's powers as if they were Walters' own.

He reached for her in that moment, but she slipped past him, separating his thoughts from his abilities—at least that was what she hoped she was doing, mostly to protect herself.

Then she found the spot she was looking for. Scientists didn't know what this part of the brain did—the portion unused, they said —but it wasn't. It was a tiny area that kept the past and the present separate.

She poured her memories into that spot, the memory that had haunted her, the one that had made her collapse—the storm, finding Daray's body, the fear, the horrible, horrible fear that he had never loved her, that she wasn't worthy of love, that she had never been worthy of love—she sent those memories there, the emotions there, and then broke the barrier between past and present.

Walters would live with those feelings, as if they were happening now, as if they always happened.

The worst moment of her life, and now it was the worst moment of his, made personal, made into something he could feel—forever— unable to stop the pain, unable to block it, unable to do anything about that.

For the rest of his life, those feelings would be his reality. Just like they had been hers all the way up until now.

He stopped struggling against her. She backed out, feeling lighter.

Athena covered Cassie's hands with her own, and then eased her away from Walters. He stayed in the same position, his gaze on her, his eyes filling with tears.

"What did you do?" he asked. "What did you do?"

"Nothing," she said, lying, not for him, but for the people around them. "Once I got close, I found I couldn't do anything at all."

FORTY-SIX

Anchor Harbor Wayside

But her mother *had* done something. Spark Walters' eyes were different, more vulnerable, filled with some kind of pain.

Lyssa had never seen him like that before. He looked diminished somehow, as if he were being hollowed from the inside out.

He put a hand to his chest, then took a single step backwards toward the limousine. With his other hand, he felt the roof, then the seat, and slid back inside.

"Mr. Walters?" the woman with the suit asked. "Are you all right?"

"Fine," he said, his voice trembling. "Just fine. All I need is a minute."

Cassie slipped her arm around Athena. They walked toward Emily, going past Lyssa.

"What did I miss?" Gabriel asked.

"I don't know," Lyssa said. She truly didn't. She had never seen her mother do anything to harm anyone before. Her mother had never cared enough.

But the entire attack on Walters, and then the way her mother had talked him into letting her touch his mind, all of that had been new.

What was it Athena had said? Someone had tried to disable Cassie not once, but twice.

Which meant that Cassie had powers few knew about, and some feared.

"Don't you think it's odd," Lyssa said, "that Walters is here, and that Roseluna person tried to hurt Mother, and the exodus happened from the sea? All of it right now."

"Like something is going to happen," Gabriel said. "But what?"

"Before that storm in Whale Cove," Denne said, "the selkies made sure no humans were near the ocean. They destroyed fishing boats, left warnings—kept everyone they thought innocent away from the various crime scenes. The selkies knew what was coming, and they were making sure only the people who deserved to be hurt were."

Lyssa shoved her hands in the back pockets of her jeans. "But they didn't clear out the Refuge."

"No," Denne said.

"So this is going to be different," she said.

"They're also not warning any humans," Gabriel said. "So they must think we're guilty of something. But what?"

"The death of Lyssa's father?" Denne asked.

Lyssa shook her head. "If that was the case, then they might have attacked long ago. It's got to do with the oil, too."

"Athena said that your mother spoke to Roseluna at lunch," Denne said. "Maybe your family was warned."

Lyssa looked at her family. Cassie and Athena were huddled together in a way that she had never seen them before. They seemed close, which they had never been.

Emily was watching them, her little head upturned, a look of longing on her face. For the first time, Cassie was ignoring her grand-daughter—and that, too, made Lyssa uneasy.

Then she glanced around. Walters was still in his limousine, clutching the sides of the door as if they were all that held him upright. His assistants were clustered in a group, talking, seemingly uncertain about what to do. Only the female assistant stood by him, crouched in front of the door, talking to him, like a mother talking to a child.

Lyssa shuddered. She didn't want to know exactly what her mother had done.

Then Lyssa looked across the highway. The reporter was still there, talking with a few bystanders. Maybe the entire area had seen that broadcast from Athena's mind, not just the people in the wayside. Maybe the cameraman had even caught it on film.

Lyssa wasn't sure what that would mean for Walters or for his company—how could you prosecute a man based on visionary evidence?—but she really didn't care.

He had murdered her father, if that vision was to be believed. No wonder he had so adamantly opposed her marriage to Reginald. Had Reginald known? He had married Lyssa in part to spite his father, but had he really known how deep his father's involvement with the Buckinghams had been? After all, Reginald had been a few years old when Walters had traveled to Anchor Bay. Had Reginald known something was wrong when his father returned? Had he heard old stories?

Lyssa sighed. She would never know. Reginald was dead, and Walters would never tell her.

"Do you think they're going to cause another storm?" Gabriel asked Denne.

"The selkies? With the kind of sacrifice it requires?" Denne shook his head. "I have no idea. Killing yourself for a goal is antithetical to who we are. Maybe it's who they are."

"No, it's not," Lyssa said. "Human cultures have initiated suicide attacks for centuries. And the selkies don't need a suicide. Spark Walters over there proved that. Just kill an unwanted member of the tribe. That would be more than enough."

"But we have warning now. A storm like that wouldn't destroy Anchor Bay," Gabriel said.

"Probably should evacuate the school just in case," Denne said. "The last time all the destruction was down here. I would imagine that's where it would be again."

Lyssa frowned. All of this was well and good, but it still didn't answer the mystery of the exodus.

She crossed the parking lot toward her mother, daughter, and grandmother. Emily saw her first and ran toward her, slamming her body into Lyssa's, stopping her from going farther.

"What's going on, babe?" Lyssa asked, putting her hand in Emily's hair.

"Grandma doesn't want to talk to me," Emily said.

"I can imagine she doesn't want to talk to anyone right now," Lyssa said. She had seen that rage come out of her mother. It had been fierce. Lyssa just felt numb. She hadn't known her father, and she had just gone through two different theories of his death in the space of an hour.

"It's not like that," Emily said. "I don't think she likes me anymore."

Lyssa bent down and picked up Emily as if she were three again. Emily let her. Her daughter's too-thin body was shaking. She couldn't take more rejection, especially from the grandmother who, until fifteen minutes ago, had doted on her.

Emily was a lot heavier than a three-year-old. It took most of Lyssa's strength to carry her toward Cassie and Athena.

"Gabriel thinks the selkies are planning an attack of some kind," Lyssa said. "Some kind of storm."

Cassie gave Emily a wild look. "Ask your daughter."

Emily had her arm wrapped around the back of Lyssa's neck. Her other hand was braced on Lyssa's shoulder. "Great-aunt Roseluna said she was going to destroy Anchor Bay. At lunch. But Grandma heard it too."

"What's going on, Mother?" Lyssa asked. "If you knew about this attack, why aren't you doing anything about it?"

"Leave her alone, Lysandra," Athena said. "She's had a shock."

"So what we saw is what happened," Lyssa said. "You watched Spark Walters kill my father, and then you let me marry into the Walters family."

"It's not that simple," Athena said. "And I didn't just watch. I thought I had killed Walters myself."

"But you knew the next day, when he showed up again, that you hadn't."

"Actually, no," Athena said. "I didn't know until the village agreed to have the *Walter Aggie* towed out to sea and sunk, with the rest of her oil inside her. He was at the meeting. He actually tipped that goddamn cowboy hat at me. I talked to Sheriff Lowery, and told him that Spark had killed Daray, and Lowery told me that even if what I saw had happened, which it couldn't have since Spark was still alive, even if—Cassie had already reported Daray as a suicide, and since she was his wife, her word held."

Cassie gave Athena a sideways look.

"But you didn't do anything." Lyssa didn't know where her vehemence was coming from. She had thought she was numb.

"What could I do, Lys? The sheriff refused to arrest him. I couldn't kill him—supposedly we're a civilized society."

"So you let him go home to Texas—"

"Yes, and raise Reginald, and everything else that happened. I couldn't do anything else," Athena said.

"You could have told me. You could have told Mother."

"And have Cassie kill him? Lose her in the attempt? We had you to think about, Lysandra. Remember that."

"I do," Lyssa said. "You thought so much of me that you let me marry Reginald Walters."

"I couldn't have stopped you without hurting your mother." Athena sighed. "I figured Walters would stop you, but his opposition had the effect I was afraid mine would. It just made you two want each other more."

Lyssa blinked hard, feeling tears threaten. She didn't want to feel them. She didn't want to feel anything.

"Besides," Athena said, "you don't regret the marriage. It gave you Emily."

Lyssa glanced at her grandmother. Athena was looking with actual worry at Cassie, and Lyssa finally understood why. Cassie should have said that. She always defended Lyssa's marriage by citing Emily.

But she didn't now.

"What's going on, Mother?" Lyssa asked again.

"Ask your daughter," Cassie repeated.

"I did, and she doesn't have a clue. Tell us. What are you afraid of?"

Cassie looked at Emily. Cassie's expression was cold.

"I heard her, Roseluna, tell you to join them," Cassie said to Emily. "And you did, didn't you? That's why the vision came up. You did it to separate us, to make me hate Mother, to make me attack Spark. That's why, right?"

Emily tightened her grip on Lyssa. "Mommy?"

"It's okay," Lyssa said. She slid her daughter down to her legs, then pushed Emily behind her. This was what she had always expected, that she would have to defend her daughter against the world.

Even against her own family.

"My daughter isn't Machiavelli, Mother," Lyssa said. "She has no idea what you're talking about."

"Then let her answer," Cassie said.

"No," Lyssa said.

"You know what happened," Athena said. "We saw it earlier. The vision didn't spring up until you took Emily's hand. She was already holding mine, and I was remembering. That memory is one of my strongest, Cassandra, and it came again when I saw Spark Walters. There's no conspiracy here. Only truth, maybe for the first time between us."

"But Mother doesn't like the truth," Lyssa said. "She likes to pretend that everything is happy and pretty, even when she knows otherwise. I was never the perfect daughter, Mother, and you certainly weren't a perfect mom."

"Lys," Athena said. "Your mother was right about Daray, and I was wrong. He loved her. Even at the end, he was defending her."

Cassie's eyes filled with tears.

"But Mother didn't believe that when she was telling me about him. She thought he had abandoned her. She thought he had killed her friends and tried to kill her——"

"He was your father, Lyssa," Cassie said, her voice so low that Lyssa had to strain to hear it. "What was I supposed to do? Tell you how awful he was?"

"Maybe that would have been better," Lyssa said.

"But it would have been wrong," Athena said. She reached out, took the hands of her daughter and her granddaughter. "The selkies want us to fight each other. Think about it, Cassandra. They keep trying to immobilize you because you're our power source, our beacon. You make all of us stronger. But if you're weak, you weaken us."

Cassie's fingers were limp in Lyssa's.

"It's your power mixed with Emily's that makes visible visions. Your power mixed with mine would have given me superhuman strength. Your power alone is formidable. Imagine it in tandem with the rest of us," Athena said. "That's what the selkies fear. They know you, probably through Daray, who loved you. They are now rebelling against everything we've done for them, and they know you're the only one who can stop them."

Cassie looked at her mother, her lashes wet. Cassie looked like a little girl, like Emily had the day that Lyssa had told her she still loved her, no matter what happened to Reginald.

Lyssa reached behind her and took Emily's hand. "They want to separate you and Emily, Mom, because you two are strong together."

Emily clutched Lyssa's hand tight. "I didn't do nothing, Mom. I didn't like Great-aunt Roseluna. I don't know her family. I wouldn't help them hurt you."

"I know that, baby," Lyssa said. Then she raised her head toward Cassie. "And you know that too, Mom. You're just looking for someone to blame. You've been angry all these years at my father, and he didn't deserve it, and you're feeling guilty. But Grandma's right. What happened then is past. You can't change it. You can only make a difference for the future."

"And, if I understood you, Cassie," Athena said, "we don't have much of a future. Not if we don't take some actions now."

Cassie blinked hard. She looked down at Emily, then at Lyssa, and finally at her mother. "I don't know what kind of action to take," Cassie said.

"That's because we don't know exactly what they're planning,"

Lyssa said. "But you said Roseluna went inside your mind. I know you, Mom. You can do that too. Go inside hers. Find out."

"She'd be blocked," Cassie said.

"Would she?" Athena asked. "She thinks she destroyed you. Why use all that extra energy to block you out when she doesn't have to."

Cassie's gaze darted between Lyssa and Athena. The movement made her look nervous. It made her seem afraid.

"I can go with you, Grandma." Emily's voice was small, and it got even smaller with the next sentence. "If you want me to."

Cassie looked down at her, and this time, a single tear fell. She crouched, put her arms around Emily, and rocked them both back and forth.

"I'm sorry, child. I'm sorry I said all those things."

Emily put her arms around Cassie. "It's okay, Grandma. I say dumb things too when I'm mad."

Athena snorted and turned away. Lyssa smiled.

Cassie kissed the top of Emily's head, and then stood. "All right," she said. "Let's find out. But I don't want to do it here. Let's go home."

Lyssa looked at her mother. Cassie was still afraid, but willing to step by it. Her request to go to Cliffside House made sense. The house had its own magic. It would give that extra measure of protection.

"All right," Athena said. "But let's go quickly. I don't think we have a lot of time."

FORTY-SEVEN

Cliffside House

They went home in Great-grandma Athena's old car. Mommy's car looked hurt, like Emily had felt inside when Grandma Cassie was so mean. But Emily didn't say anything. She'd felt like Grandma Cassie felt the whole time they were in Great-grandma Athena's memory, and Emily'd never felt anything that bad, not even when Daddy died (even though it was close).

Great-aunt Roseluna wasn't far off thinking that she'd destroyed Grandma Cassie; Roseluna'd come awfully close. If Grandma Cassie had that much pain inside her all the time, she had to be awfully strong. Emily had no idea how she went from day-to-day.

Great-grandma's car might've been old, but she didn't drive it like little old ladies should've. In fact, there was nothing about Great-grandma that made Emily think about little old ladies. The way she'd pushed Grandpa Walters off that cliff—that made Emily actually feel better.

Sometimes there was stuff you had to do, just to survive, and no matter how many times you told people that, they didn't always understand.

But now, after seeing what Great-grandma did to try to save Anchor Bay, to try to get revenge for Grandpa Daray and for Grandma Cassie, Emily knew there was at least one other person who understood.

Maybe that was why Great-grandma always looked at her funny. Not just because she was a Walters (and now Emily understood why that bothered Great-grandma—it bothered Emily, and she didn't want to think about it), but because they were kinda the same. Tough people who took action they didn't always think about.

Mommy wasn't like that. Mommy thought about everything, and Grandma Cassie thought about stuff so much she could barely get out of bed without thinking about it first.

So when they got to Cliffside House, and Great-grandma Athena said they had to go into the closet that scared Grandma Cassie, Emily went right in. Because she knew that sometimes you just had to take action. You couldn't think about it.

Grandma Cassie was already thinking too much. Emily could tell. Grandma Cassie didn't want to do any of this. She was even rethinking what she'd done to Grandpa Walters, even though, from Emily's point of view, Grandma Cassie hadn't done much.

Great-grandma Athena might've done something worse. Great-grandma Athena might've killed him, if she had the chance. Mommy might've got the law to help her, because that's what she always did.

And Emily didn't know what she would've done. Something. Something to show Grandpa Walters you can't treat people like that. Even if they're not human people, but selkie people instead.

Cliffside House was cold. Nobody had turned up the heat in the morning. But sunlight poured in all the windows, making it seem like a much more friendly place than it'd been the night before. Then it'd seemed kinda spooky—in a good way—and now it seemed almost pretty.

Except in the closet, which, Emily had to admit, was a little too dark and damp and cavelike for her tastes.

The front part of the closet smelled like Great-grandma Athena's perfume—all heavy, syrupy, the only old-lady part about her. The front part even had a light that made the furs and the coats kinda shine. The light wasn't as strong as it could've been, and it was really yellow. Emily never seen a light that yellow before. Maybe the yellow was why the light got sucked into the black floors and black walls, leaving no shadow.

She thought the no-shadow part was the creepiest part of all. Not even the back of the closet compared for creepiness and the back of the closet didn't even seem to be there. It just kinda disappeared into darkness, but Emily could see farther than, say, Mommy could. Before the darkness got really black, the floor turned into laid rock, like the fake cobblestone stuff they had at one of the old houses in the Frank neighborhood in Madison. Emily could feel the floor slanting downward, and she thought at the base of it, she could hear the boom of the sea.

Great-grandma Athena made them all sit down on the floor. Mommy sat next to Emily, who sat by Grandma Cassie, who sat as close to the door as she could get. Great-grandma Athena sat between Grandma Cassie and Mommy, so that she was protecting everybody from anything that came up that slanted floor.

Emily felt better now, knowing that Great-grandma Athena was there.

"We don't have a lot of time," Great-grandma Athena said to Grandma Cassie. It was a sort of sideways way to push her to find out what was going on.

"It's okay, Grandma," Emily said. "I said I'd go with you."

"It'll be too dangerous," Grandma Cassie said. "If she knows we know—"

"Mother." Mommy was using her I-have-no-more-patience voice. "If we don't find out, we'll die. You might want to, but I sure as hell don't."

Great-grandma Athena rolled her eyes at Mommy, but Grandma Cassie just sighed.

Grandma Cassie held out her hand. She wasn't afraid of asking Emily for help, which actually made Emily feel good. Not even Mommy, who said she really trusted Emily, would ask Emily for help.

Emily took Grandma Cassie's hand. It was dry and cold, the skin even rougher than it had seemed before. Or maybe that was because Emily's hands got all scraped up when she fell on the parking lot.

Still, it didn't hurt to touch Grandma Cassie. The owies on her hand weren't so bad as they looked.

Grandma Cassie took another deep breath. "Ready?" she asked Emily.

Emily nodded. Her heart was pounding really hard. She wasn't sure exactly what Grandma Cassie was going to do, but she figured it was something like looking for that ship, that *Walter Aggie* ship they'd looked for before.

So Emily closed her eyes at the same time Grandma Cassie did, and then she pictured herself holding hands with Grandma Cassie as they walked through this tunnel. It was weird because the tunnel looked something like the closet, only lighter and cooler and it smelled more like the sea.

The walking changed to flying-floating when Grandma Cassie got the sense of Great-aunt Roseluna. Roseluna was far away, and Emily wasn't sure how she got there. Did the selkies have boats? That seemed weird, since they could live and swim underwater and everything.

But Emily didn't have much of a chance to think about it since Grandma Cassie shushed her and told her to be really really really quiet.

So Emily was, not even pretending to breathe or nothing, just hanging on and letting Grandma Cassie handle everything.

They kinda floated over the water. After a while, the sea looked all the same. Waves and stuff, but not big ones, and no ships. Just lots and lots of gray water in all directions.

Except over the place where the *Walter Aggie* was—and Emily wasn't sure how she and Grandma Cassie knew that was the *Walter Aggie's* spot. They just did.

Over that spot, ten selkies, their pelts on, stood on a barrier in the water, a barrier that Great-grandma Athena made to protect the sea and the Refuge. The selkies were holding knives in their hands, and they were looking in the water.

As Grandma Cassie got closer, she gasped—a sound so loud it

echoed over the water. Emily peered over her shoulder, saw even more selkies, floating in a big, big circle, treading water, and holding knives too.

"Oh, my God," Grandma Cassie said, only it wasn't really saying, it was more like thinking. "Emily, you have to go back. Can you find your way back?"

"No," Emily said. "I gotta stay with you. I promised."

Grandma Cassie shook her head—or shook her imaginary head —anyway, Emily felt the disagreement. And Grandma Cassie said, "You've got to tell my mother what we've seen here. Tell her I'm going to try to stop it."

"Stop what?" Emily asked.

"Em, honey," Grandma Cassie said. "You saw the storm that happened because Grandpa Daray died, right?"

"Yeah," Emily said, even though she didn't really get how it all worked. But she knew that now was not the time to ask.

"That's what happens when one selkie bleeds to death in the ocean. Imagine how bad the storm'll be if forty selkies bleed to death, all at the same time."

Emily couldn't imagine it, except maybe that the storm would be so big it would go over the mountains to Portland. Or maybe it would along the coast, north to Seattle and south to San Francisco, killing everything in its path.

Emily shivered, or maybe that was Grandma Cassie shivering with fear.

"You need me," Emily said.

"We need my mother," Grandma Cassie said. "She's the fighter. I'll see if I can hold this off until she gets here. Tell her. Please."

And then Emily got the sense that Grandma Cassie had some kind of plan, something to hold off the selkies at least till Emily talked to Great-grandma Athena.

"How do we find you again?" Emily asked, realizing that she might know how to get back but not how to return to the middle of the sea.

"Take my hand again," Grandma Cassie said. "I'll leave a pathway open for you. But hurry. I'm already tired."

Emily leaned over and kissed Grandma Cassie, and Grandma Cassie smiled at her, which warmed Emily right up and made her forget all the bad stuff that she'd felt earlier.

Then Emily slid along the path they'd already made and headed back to Cliffside House, hoping she would get there in time.

FORTY-EIGHT

Pacific Ocean
200 Miles off the Oregon Coast

The selkies didn't seem to notice her. Cassie hovered several feet away from their circle, uncertain what to do.

Roseluna wasn't too far from her, standing on the barrier, seemingly leading this group. Cassie could go deep into Roseluna's mind, as deep as Roseluna had gone into hers, and maybe Cassie could disable her like she had done Spark Walters, but Cassie wouldn't be able to do that to all forty of them.

The selkies had a lot of magic. Daray had taught her that. The magic had diminished with time, he said, but he had told her that almost two generations ago. Emily, his granddaughter, was very powerful. Perhaps other selkies had had other half-human children, replenishing the magic.

Cassie was outclassed, and she knew it. She did have the element of surprise, and she wasn't sure how to use it best.

But she did know that she couldn't wait very long. She had to act, and act soon, with or without her family.

The selkies all raised their knives above their heads. The blades glistened in the sunlight. Roseluna was speaking, but Cassie couldn't hear what she was saying. The ocean absorbed the sound, or maybe the barrier did.

Then the selkies looked down simultaneously. The water boiled beneath them.

Cassie moved a little closer, breathing shallowly, hoping no one would notice her. The boiling had gotten worse. Gossamer strings caught the light, filtering their way into the deep. Cassie followed one of them, and saw something that surprised her.

The selkies were raising the remains of the *Walter Aggie* off the bottom of the ocean.

Cassie rose up ahead of the ship, and floated on the surface again. What were they doing? Surely the storm was enough.

But even as she had that thought, she had the answer. When the storm was over, and the West Coast destroyed, the *Walter Aggie* would be found on the beach—a message to anyone who wanted to see it.

Roseluna had been clear: the selkies hated way the humans treated the oceans. And the *Walter Aggie* was symbolic of that, at least to the selkies.

Of course, all the humans who understood the symbolism would have died in the storm.

But that probably didn't matter to Roseluna. All that mattered was the fact that she had delivered the message, and somehow changed the destiny of her people.

Cassie glanced over her shoulder, through the pathway that she had left open. She needed help here. Her mother's strength, her granddaughter's courage—she needed it all.

Because she didn't know how to stop the selkies. Even if she managed it, she would still have to deal with the *Walter Aggie*. Freed from the bottom, it would drift to shore. Right now, its oil was warming, and as long as it would take the ship to sink back to the bottom, that would be a lot of time for the oil liquefy and spread.

Cassie would give her family a few more minutes. But if they didn't arrive soon, she would propel herself all the way into Roseluna's mind, and see if she could argue her side of this, maybe even take over Roseluna's mouth to convince the others that this wasn't the way to go.

It was a long shot but, Cassie knew, it was the only shot she had.

FORTY-NINE

The Pacific Ocean
200 Miles off the Oregon Coast

They saw it long before they got there, the giant back half of the *Walter Aggie* rising out of the ocean. It was black and covered with barnacles and moss, dripping into the sea. It rose up as if it were propelled from underneath, and yet somehow they knew that the selkies encircling it were making the difference.

Somehow, as they got closer to Cassie, they blended into one mind —Emily, Lyssa, Athena—they had the same thoughts and yet all of their own. No question, though that they were looking out the same pair of eyes, and those eyes seemed to belong to Cassie.

Even though Emily pulled them through the pathway that Cassie had created, the driver was Athena. She was already making plans, thinking of strategies, asking questions.

It took Emily and Lyssa a minute to realize that Cassie was with them, only reporting back in images, not in words. Athena would wonder where all the selkies were, and then an image would rise up— thirty in the water, and ten on the barrier that Athena had built with Daray's father's help all those years ago.

The only member of Daray's family in the selkie grouping was Roseluna. No mother, father, or other siblings. No one seemed to know if they had died or if they had gone to safety or if they didn't agree with the path that Roseluna was leading the selkies on.

All they could tell was that they were coming up on a troupe of forty selkies, armed with knives, an old ship that was coming apart, and an oil slick that would harm this part of the ocean even if the storm never hit.

All right, Athena sent to them. *Here's what we do: Emily, Cassie, Lyssa, disarm as many of those creatures as you can. I'm going for the barricade.*

No! Emily thought, and zoomed ahead of them. *Great-grandma, Grandma, make another barricade. Keep the selkies out of the water. Mommy, talk to them. You're half like them. Tell them this isn't right.*

Emily—Lyssa thought, then realized all of them had separated. The link that had made them see as one was broken.

Lyssa faltered in the passageway, her hand no longer holding Emily's. Emily had zoomed away from her, leaving her and Athena behind.

It's too soon for her to take over this family, Athena said.

It doesn't matter, Lyssa said. *She's already done it. And since we only have one shot at whatever we're going to do, I suggest we follow her instructions.*

Instructions from a child, Athena said. She shook her head, then floated through the passageway, leaving only her thoughts behind. *We're going to fail after all.*

FIFTY

The Pacific Ocean
200 Miles off the Oregon Coast

They didn't trust her. Not even Mommy trusted her, but not for the same reason. Mommy thought she was too little to know what she was doing. Great-Grandma Athena thought that she was reckless and stupid, and Grandma Cassie—Grandma Cassie was still worried that Emily was going to side with the selkies.

The whole thought made Emily's eyes burn. Her family didn't trust her, but they had to. They had to put up with her, had to do it her way because she wasn't leaving them any choice.

She got, from Grandma Cassie's mind, how awful all this was going to be, even if it was just the ship, the *Walter Aggie*, sliding back into the sea.

She hoped Great-grandma Athena was following the plan, because if she wasn't, then everything would get really bad. Emily couldn't think about that, though. She only had one chance, and Grandma Cassie had given her the idea the night before.

When Emily'd been asleep (sort of) on the couch, when she heard them remembering—if that's what you wanted to call it—all the stuff

528

that happened before Mommy was born. They said there was two ways to deal with the part of the ship still filled with oil. And they tried one.

Now Emily was going to try the other.

Only she didn't know if it was going to work. She made Daddy hurt—that fire, that day, had come from inside her, but she didn't know if she could just make fire happen. And she didn't know if she could do it when her body was in Cliffside House and her mind was floating here on the ocean.

But she was going to try.

She zoomed past Grandma Cassie, who was trying to signal her to stop. Emily ignored her. She didn't want to hear more talking and more arguments.

Emily went all the way to the selkies and past, zooming over Great-aunt Roseluna, who saw her and looked really scared. Emily liked the really-scared part. That meant Great-aunt Roseluna was going to take her seriously.

Nobody else was.

Then Emily stopped over the ship. It was a lot bigger than she thought it was going to be. It still hung over the water, held in place by thoughts from all the selkies.

They'd lied to Grandma Cassie. They had more powers than anyone knew about. But back then, they didn't have a lot of numbers. Not many selkies were still alive when they made their pact with the Buckinghams more than a century ago.

The selkies spent all this time replenishing their ranks, and because they weren't being hunted anymore and because nobody believed in them, and nobody knew they still existed, none of their people got killed off. There were lots and lots and lots of selkies, and if this group failed, another would try.

Emily froze in place. Those weren't her thoughts. That was Great-aunt Roseluna trying to stop her. Grandma didn't believe everything Great-aunt Roseluna sent, so why should Emily?

Emily put the thoughts out of her mind, and focused on the ship instead.

The ship, which looked even weirder out of the water than it had in the water. Then, when she had gone with Grandma Cassie, the ship had been all dark and spooky and weird colors because of the black water. Now it was kinda gray and kinda green and had stuff dripping off it and Emily could sense the black goo inside, and she knew in that moment, that sense of the oil, the useful oil, came from her daddy's family.

She made herself think about Daddy and his family because she hadn't very much. She hadn't thought about how one of her grandpas killed the other, and how Daddy tried to drown her—what had he known? He kept saying she'd be useful? Was he really crazy or was he trying to hurt her the way Grandpa Walters hurt Grandpa Daray?

Maybe with her magic coming, Daddy got afraid. Maybe he got really afraid.

Emily's chest hurt, and her stomach hurt, and she knew none of that was real, because her body was in Cliffside House. But she remembered how scared she was under that water and how her lungs burned and how her eyes were burning even now, because there were tears back there and she would be damned—to say what her mom sometimes said—she would be damned if she let those tears come out.

Instead, she closed her eyes, and pushed the burning out of her, and sent it into the black goo—the oil that everyone hated and everyone needed, and she sent as much burning in there as she had, even more than she had when Daddy died.

There was Daddy hurting her, and then his body, and then all those reporter people trying to talk to her, and the way that Mommy's eyes looked all sad, and Grandma Cassie loving her and then not trusting her, and that look in Grandpa Walters' eyes when he saw her, that look of hate, knowing she had killed his son, and that look of hate again when she saw the memory of him killing Grandpa Daray, and how it was all going to end and how nobody cared about anybody, and she pushed and she pushed and she pushed, until it felt like her head and her heart were going to explode, and then she heard it—the whoosh of something igniting.

She opened her eyes in time to see an orange flame inside the ship, glowing like a trapped sun, and then the ship blew up, tossing her end over end over end on top of the water, plumes of black, black smoke following her.

She skipped along the water's surface, then slammed into it, knocking the wind out of her till she remembered that the body she thought she was in was all made up.

Emily sat up on the water and saw the selkies floating above it, many of them on fire, a lot of them screaming, holding wounds, but their blood wasn't falling into the ocean. Great-grandma Athena had listened after all. And a bunch of the selkies were behind some kind of screen with Mommy. Mommy had talked to them and they had listened, and it was all going right, all of it—

Except she saw Great-aunt Roseluna, standing on the barrier Emily's grandmas had put over the sea. When Great-aunt Roseluna saw Emily, she grinned, took out her knife, and sliced open her arm.

Then she jumped as hard as she could toward the burning ship.

Nobody saw her. Nobody except Emily, and Emily had no more of herself to send. She couldn't make barriers like her grandmas could. She couldn't stop Great-aunt Roseluna.

Great-aunt Roseluna fell into the sea.

I won anyway, Great-aunt Roseluna thought loud enough for Emily to hear. *I won.*

FIFTY-ONE

The Pacific Ocean
200 Miles off the Oregon Coast

It took all that was left of Cassie's strength but, with her mother's help, she managed to gather all of the selkies onto one of the barriers and deliver them down coast to the Marine Science Center. The selkies were in their seal-form, and they were injured; the Center would help them, heal them, and send them on their way, without once knowing what their magical abilities were.

Cassie managed to deliver the barrier, let Athena knock on the Science Center's door, and keep the pathway open to the burning *Walter Aggie*.

Lyssa wasn't with them. She was staying behind to find Emily, Emily who had spun away with the blast when the *Walter Aggie* blew up.

Cassie wished she had known what Emily was going to do. She would have stopped her. By now, everyone would know that a ship had blown up out here, and in time, they might even figure out that it was the *Walter Aggie*. There would be a lot of explaining to do.

Or maybe not. Maybe the cover-up would be revealed, and

maybe there would be outrage at Walters Petroleum. It certainly was time.

Cassie floated slowly back down the passageway, and that was when she saw it, building like a funnel cloud in the middle of the sea.

The smoke poured off the *Walter Aggie*, and in front of it, a whirlpool swirling downward, then spiraling upward.

She knew without being told that it was a storm—a selkie-caused storm. She hurried toward the site.

Lyssa held on to Emily. Emily, who apparently was safe after all. She leaned against Lyssa, as if Lyssa gave her strength. who leaned against her.

It was Roseluna, Mother, Lyssa said or thought or let her know. Maybe the blocks separating them were completely gone. *She did it anyway. Can we stop her?*

Cassie looked at the swirling water, felt the wind rising, and knew that the storm was already building.

At that moment, Athena joined her. *We don't have the power*, Athena said. *We just have to ride it out.*

She was right. Emily was burned out—quite literally—and Cassie was exhausted. Athena still had some strength, but not enough to fight this, and Lyssa's talent was in her voice, her ties to the selkies, not in her mental abilities.

Cassie gathered them all to her, her family, the most precious people she had ever known, and carried them back through the pathway she had created.

They arrived in the closet at Cliffside House just as the wind came up, shaking the entire building. Cassie arrived inside her own body, then sank into a heap on the floor. The air smelled of rain, and she thought she heard thunder outside.

Emily collapsed beside her. Only Lyssa and Athena remained upright.

"Let's get them out of here," Athena said to Lyssa. "Let's move them somewhere safer in the house."

"Wait, Athena Buckingham!"

The male voice made Cassie lift her head. She felt hope in her heart for the first time in decades.

A man came through the darkness in the back of the closet. He was naked and tall and dripping wet, holding a pelt in his left hand.

For a moment, Cassie held her breath, thinking maybe Daray hadn't died after all. Then the man nodded, and Cassie recognized him. It was DaRu, Daray's father.

"Cassandra," he said, and bowed to her.

She nodded, but couldn't find any words. His voice was the same as Daray's, his build the same, even his face had similarities—this was probably what Daray would have looked like if he had lived this long.

"And you," DaRu said, turning toward Lyssa, "must be my grand-daughter."

Lyssa's eyes were wide at being confronted by a naked man who claimed to be her grandfather.

"I am DaRu," he said. "Forgive my intrusion, but we haven't a lot of time. It seems I always come to you in emergencies, Athena."

"This time it's an emergency your people caused," she said.

"I know," he said. "I need your strength. I can get Roseluna's body before it does more damage, but I need your help in doing so."

"Can we do it from here?" Athena asked.

"Yes," he said. "It'll take but a minute. But I cannot do it alone."

He extended his hands. In one of them, he kept the pelt. Athena looked at it, then at him.

"I'm so sorry," he said. He turned, bowed to Lyssa again, and handed her the pelt. "Pray keep this for me, Granddaughter. I'll have need of it in a moment."

Lyssa took it, and held it, her face upturned toward his. She looked even more like Daray than she had before, that angular face. The pelt in her hand made her seem otherworldly.

Emily crawled up beside her and put her head on Lyssa's lap. "Is this okay, Mommy?"

If Cassie hadn't known the child so well, she would have thought Emily was asking about resting against her mother. Instead, she was asking if it was all right for her great-grandmother to help her grandfather.

"If your great-grandmother says it is," Lyssa said. But her voice didn't sound very convinced.

Cassie used the last of her strength to touch DaRu's mind. He looked down at her with incredible patience.

"I would probably have done the same, Daughter," he said, giving her the title he had given her the day she married Daray. "Am I clear?"

"Yes," Cassie said. "He's fine."

DaRu smiled at her, then took Athena's hands. His head tilted back, his eyes showing white, and his mouth fell open. Athena closed her eyes, and held on to him, not moving.

Outside the wind whistled and rattled and howled. Rain slapped against the building.

And then—nothing. Silence. The rain stopped, and the wind died down as if it had never been.

Cassie sat up and leaned against the cold wall. Emily held on to Lyssa's knee. Lyssa clutched the pelt to her chest.

After a moment, Athena opened her eyes. DaRu lifted his head upright and closed his mouth. He bent over, kissed Athena's hands one at a time, and then let them go.

"I have to beg forgiveness," he said softly. "Our people's quarrels have spilled into your world, where they have no place."

Cassie blinked. "Roseluna?"

"My daughter was merely part of a faction that has felt that we have been powerless too long. They don't understand debt and mutual respect. They don't realize that Seavy County, the Refuge, and the Buckinghams saved not just our people, but hundreds of others." DaRu turned toward her, as formal as he had always been. "Please understand that we are forever grateful for your kindness."

"This could have been ugly," Athena said. "It came so close. If it wasn't for Emily—"

"Daray's granddaughter." DaRu smiled. "He would have been proud. Very proud."

Cassie swallowed hard. He would have been. Daray saw the blending of their two families as something that would make the world better.

She had forgotten that—or not allowed herself to remember it, not after the night of the storm.

Maybe he hadn't been so far wrong.

Then DaRu extended his hand to Lyssa. She handed his pelt, reluctantly, it seemed to Cassie.

"There's a lot I want to ask you," Lyssa said. "I know nothing about you or your family or—"

She glanced briefly at Cassie.

"—or my father."

DaRu nodded. "I would love to speak with you and your daughter. But not now. My people are in disarray, our Refuge is broken. I have much to do, and I am not sure I can heal it. I am sorry for that."

"My great-grandmother knew it was temporary," Athena said. "She would probably be surprised that the Refuge has lasted this long."

DaRu bowed again. "You are too kind, Athena. I shall return when I can. Until then, thank you once more for your help."

He slung his pelt over his arm, and headed back into the darkness. Cassie watched him go, feeling a longing follow him.

She would never get past Daray, never really move beyond him. But she felt stronger now, now that she knew what she had believed in —and thought lost—hadn't really been lost at all.

"What did you do?" Lyssa asked Athena.

"He took Roseluna's body out of the sea, and somehow managed to gather her blood. The storm stopped," Athena said. "All I did was provide the strength to let him do the magic."

"He asked you to do the same the night the *Walter Aggie* went down," Cassie said.

Athena nodded.

"You are not the first Buckingham to marry a selkie, Cassie," Athena said. "Our powers come from the selkie side. Most of our ancestry is human, but my great-grandmother's first love came from the sea. They did that on purpose, just like they designed Cliffside House as a gateway. It was part of the Refuge."

Cassie closed her eyes against her mother's words. If only she had known that years ago. But she hadn't, and she felt like she had been fighting a new fight all on her own.

"What happens to Cliffside House now?" Lyssa asked.

"It goes on," Athena said. "This isn't the first difficulty we've faced, nor will it be the last."

"But everyone'll know about the magic now." Emily said from her perch on Lyssa's leg. "Great-aunt Roseluna made sure of that."

Cassie opened her eyes. She looked at her mother, who seemed younger, stronger, than she had in years.

"Things have changed," Athena said. "But our family has lived through change before. I'm sure there'll be challenges. I'm sure we can handle them."

"If we stay together," Cassie said. She reached for Lyssa's hand. "We're so much stronger together than we are apart."

Lyssa looked at Cassie's fingers. For a moment, Cassie was afraid she wouldn't take them. Then Lyssa smiled.

"You know, Mom," she said, "two days ago, I wouldn't have believed that."

"And now?"

Lyssa took Cassie's hand. "Now I know you're right."

I value honest feedback, and would love to hear your opinion in a review, if you're so inclined, on your favorite book retailer's site.

Be the first to know!

Just sign up for the Kristine Kathryn Rusch newsletter, and keep up with the latest news, releases and so much more—even the occasional giveaway.

So, what are you waiting for? To sign up go to kristinekathrynrusch.com.

But wait! There's more. Sign up for the WMG Publishing newsletter, too, and get the latest news and releases from all of the WMG authors and lines, including Kristine Grayson, Kris Nelscott, Dean Wesley Smith, *Fiction River: An Original Anthology Magazine, Smith's Monthly,* and so much more.

To sign up go to wmgpublishing.com.

ABOUT THE AUTHOR

New York Times bestselling author Kristine Kathryn Rusch writes in almost every genre. Generally, she uses her real name (Rusch) for most of her writing. Under that name, she publishes bestselling science fiction and fantasy, award-winning mysteries, acclaimed mainstream fiction, controversial nonfiction, and the occasional romance. Her novels have made bestseller lists around the world and her short fiction has appeared in eighteen best of the year collections. She has won more than twenty-five awards for her fiction, including the Hugo, *Le Prix Imaginales*, the *Asimov's* Readers Choice award, and the *Ellery Queen Mystery Magazine* Readers Choice Award.

Publications from *The Chicago Tribune* to *Booklist* have included her Kris Nelscott mystery novels in their top-ten-best mystery novels of the year. The Nelscott books have received nominations for almost every award in the mystery field, including the best novel Edgar Award, and the Shamus Award.

She writes goofy romance novels as award-winner Kristine Grayson.

She also edits. Beginning with work at the innovative publishing company, Pulphouse, followed by her award-winning tenure at *The Magazine of Fantasy & Science Fiction*, she took fifteen years off before returning to editing with the original anthology series *Fiction River*, published by WMG Publishing. She acts as series editor with her husband, writer Dean Wesley Smith, and edits at least two anthologies in the series per year on her own.

To keep up with everything she does, go to kriswrites.com and sign up for her newsletter. To track her many pen names and series, see their individual websites (krisnelscott.com, kristinegrayson.com, retrievalartist.com, divingintothewreck.com).

www.ingramcontent.com/pod-product-compliance
Lightning Source LLC
Chambersburg PA
CBHW020456020726
47493CB00001B/52